D0388880
BROADVIEW LIBRARY
NO LONGER PROPERTY OF
SEATTLE PUBLIC LIBRARY

STAR
EATER

ALSO BY **KERSTIN HALL**

The Border Keeper

KERSTIN HALL

A TOM DOHERTY ASSOCIATES BOOK · NEW YORK

This is a work of fiction. All of the characters, organizations, and events portrayed in this novel are either products of the author's imagination or are used fictitiously.

STAR EATER

Edited by Ruoxi Chen

A Tordotcom Book
Published by Tom Doherty Associates
120 Broadway
New York, NY 10271

www.tor.com

The Library of Congress Cataloging-in-Publication Data is available upon request.

ISBN 978-1-250-62531-1 (hardcover)
ISBN 978-1-250-62532-8 (ebook)

First Edition: June 2021

Printed in the United States of America

0 9 8 7 6 5 4 3 2 1

for Sylvia Hall

DRAMATIS PERSONAE

COUNCIL OF REPRESENTATIVES

Saskia Asan, Reverend: Commander General of Enforcement
Dinea Bremm, Reverend: Chief Caretaker of Maternal Affairs
Yelina Celane, Reverend: Chief Archivist of the Department of Memories
Shaelean Cyde, Reverend: Head Custodian of the Moon House, former Chief Archivist of the Department of Memories
Olwen Kisme, Reverend: Former Head of the Department of Water and Sanitation
Jiana Morwin, Reverend: Head of the Department of Public Health
Deselle Somme, Reverend: Head of the Department of Food Management
Belia Verje, Reverend: Head of the Department of Water and Sanitation

HERALDS

Ilva Bosch, Herald: Senior nurse at the Department of Maternal Affairs
Rhyanon Hayder, Herald: Deputy Chief of Civil Obligations, Accountant at the Department of Civil Obligations, Jaylen Hayder's mother
Zenza Lenard, Herald: Senior Field Research Officer, supervisor to Elfreda
Netha Lien, Herald: Senior Enforcement officer
Vay Lusor, Herald: Leader of pilgrimage to the Moon Pillar
Kalis Nortem, Herald: Name attached to a bank account
Jesane Olberos, Herald: Notary in the Department of Judicial Affairs

ACOLYTES, OBLATES AND RELATIVES

Jaylen "Jay" Hayder: Rhyanon's daughter
Elfreda Raughn, Acolyte: Junior Field Research Officer at the Department of Food Management
Kirane Raughn, Martyr: Elfreda's mother, formerly Deputy Chief of Civil Obligations

Lenette Raughn, Martyr: Elfreda's grandmother, deceased
Fian Sebet, Acolyte: Participant in pilgrimage to the Moon Pillar
Rina Tahen, Acolyte: Administrator at the Department of Food Management
Megane Tersi, Acolyte: Accountant at the department of Civil Obligations, poet

CIVILIANS

Daje Carsel: Millie's boyfriend
Hanna: Millie's girlfriend
Osan Jerone: Rhyanon's driver
Declan Lars: Murderer
Faye Lenard: Zenza's wife
Lucian: Bartender at the Candle
Tenet Poll: Zenza's driver
Renson: Osan's friend
Lariel Sacor: Millie's alias
Finn Vidar: Elfreda's best friend
Kamillian "Millie" Vidar: Elfreda's counsellor, Finn's older sister

STAR
EATER

CHAPTER

ONE

THE SUN SKIMMED over yellowing leaves and filtered through the branches. Birds darted amongst the trees, passing from shafts of light into shadow, their feathers catching silver. Too hot, too close, the woods themselves seemed restless. Under our feet, the leaf litter crunched, and our white robes rustled as we wound along the path.

I was focussed on my breathing. In and out, in and out. Nice and slow and easy. Keep my mind on the immediate and tangible: the warm air brushing the nape of my neck, the loose, brittle earth under my shoes. Cicadas hissed, and I set my teeth. It had been seven days since I had last seen Finn, and I could feel the pressure building behind my eyes.

Concentrate, I told myself. *Leave no room for panic.*

In some respects, I had been lucky. The Moon Pillar pilgrimage was the shortest; only a day's journey from the city. Unfortunately, this trip had taken far longer than usual. Herald Vay Lusor had directed the cohort to stop at every settlement along the route; we were to bless the citizens, listen to their grievances, and collect any petitions or entreaties. Excessive? Probably. But with the drought dragging on, the Council had deemed our support for the farmers a top priority. If they turned on us, the city would starve.

That was all very well. I just had far more pressing personal concerns.

Before every Pillar pilgrimage, every errand that took me beyond the Fields, I arranged to see Finn. While the journey to the

Mud Pillar had cut it fine—six days there and back—the others had proved manageable. Not this time. Work had overwhelmed me, and then an Acolyte broke her wrist during a Renewal. I was suddenly called to serve as her substitute.

So here I was. Day seven, and in deep shit.

The trees thinned and the path grew wider, the dry undergrowth giving way to short, softer grass. We had arrived.

The Moon Pillar stood in the middle of the clearing, the massive granite column split down the centre by the roots of a long-dead beech tree. White and leafless, the branches threw jagged lines of shadow over the stone, and in the shade gleamed thousands of names. Every Sister throughout the history of Aytrium was memorialised here. When we died, the Order carved our names into the Pillars and filled in the letters with gold.

The cohort fanned out to ring the monument. I knelt and laid my forehead against the dark earth. Dirt anointed my face, blades of grass brushed my cheeks. I rested the pads of my thumbs against the base of my skull, pressing my other fingertips together to gesture submission.

Calm down. Just get through it.

Deep within my chest, my mother's power quickened. I stilled, letting the rhythm of my blood drown my other senses. The woods grew silent. Faintly, I could hear the slow breathing of my Sisters. Beneath that, quieter still, the sleepy heartbeat of Aytrium itself. Not a true pulse—it was only the echo of our ancestors' power. I drew out the store of lace nestled within my core, and coaxed the warm thread to twine with the Pillar's glacial current. Within seconds, my skin grew cold as the monument pulled lace from my veins.

On my first pilgrimage, I'd instinctively recoiled and severed the connection. The older members of my cohort had laughed at me.

The air around the Moon Pillar hummed as power drained into the ground. Deep vibrations rattled my teeth. Once my lace was spent, I sat back on my heels.

A six-legged goat stood tethered to the tree.

The animal had not been there when I started the rite. It bleated and tugged at the rope, straining to free itself. Its eye sockets were empty and lidless.

I did not allow myself to react. The goat tossed its head. Its fur was ink-black, except for the two white stripes running from its nose to its horns. Its nostrils flared.

Other members of the cohort began to sit up, their lace spent. Some gazed absently at the Pillar, while others watched the Sisters still occupied with the rite.

The goat struggled. Its legs moved awkwardly; a stray hoof drew blood from a rear shin. I sensed it too, the prickling dread. Beneath my knees, the earth trembled.

The last of the Sisters completed the rite. I stood, brushing dirt off my robes. I did not rush or speak. My face remained impassive. As usual, I allowed the others to lead the way, dropping to the rear of the cohort. The goat, now frenzied, scrabbled in the grass as the heavy footfalls grew ever louder, but I betrayed nothing, not a flicker of fear. I kept my gaze fixed on the ground and followed the Sisters ahead of me. I did not look back.

The goat screamed once in terror. Its hooves scrabbled against the earth and there was a sickening crunch, like bones crushed beneath the wheels of a cart.

The women ahead of me whispered to one another. Herald Lusor, at the head of the column, recited a ritual devotion to the Eater. Her voice rang sweet and clear.

"For your nourishment, for our nourishment, for the absolution of our mistakes, we give thanks. For your grace, for your sacrifice, for your wisdom, we give thanks. Let us lay our bodies beside yours, let us serve as we may."

Step by step, the pressure inside my skull eased. I relaxed my jaw. I was clear; we had moved outside of the vision's range. Not that I could see how I would ever make it back to the city like this.

Sunlight scattered through the branches overhead, warming

my face. The low conversation of the Sisters blended with birdsong and the rhythm of our footfalls.

"Have you heard from Ilva recently?"

"Wasn't she dating . . ."

"—she said nothing . . . I think so."

Breathe. Keep walking.

A year ago, almost to the day, I had awoken to find my dormitory room coated in a layer of ash. When I touched it, the powder had melted like frost. My first vision, just as I'd been formally inducted as an Acolyte.

The cohort reached the waypoint. A web of red scarves hung from the tree's branches. Beaded tassels and tiny copper chimes clinked in the breeze, and a rusted bell hung in the highest reaches of the canopy. Herald Lusor placed her palms flat on the smooth bark of the trunk. A pause, then the bell rang out, and a startled flock of sparrows took to the air.

As far as I was aware, anyone *could* enter the woods without announcing themselves, but the Pillar Houses' zero tolerance policy for trespassers was notorious. Once, on the way to the Salt Pillar, I had seen the bodies of intruders hanged along the roadside. Their bare chests were branded with the two overlapping triangles that marked them as heretics.

Over the trees, our signal was answered by a second bell from the Moon House.

Herald Lusor removed her hands from the trunk and turned to face us.

"Thank you for your efforts, everyone," she said. "After the delays this morning, I've decided that we should spend the night in Halowith. Are there any objections?"

My stomach sank. The other Sisters murmured approval, and I could say nothing, not without drawing attention to myself.

"Then it's decided," said Lusor. "Let's move."

The woods gave way to farmland; we crossed a stone bridge over a dry riverbed and emerged at the border of the orchards. Beyond the low timber fence, plum trees ran in parallel lines all the way to Fort Sirus. Workers tended to them with buckets, and a few waved to us. In the heat, their faces rippled like the surface of water. Pale pink blossoms lingered on the lower branches of the trees, dark fruit ripened higher up, and the barest whiff of fermentation carried on the breeze.

I could run, I thought, trudging down the road. My legs were leaden. *I could vanish during the night, make up some excuse once I reach the city. A plausible emergency.*

I almost collided with the Herald in front of me when she slowed. I looked up. The other members of the cohort were muttering to one another. Herald Lusor raised her hand.

The path ahead was deserted. The orchards were quiet. For a moment, I could detect nothing out of the ordinary.

Then I saw the man.

He crouched in the riverbed running alongside the road, facing away from us. It would have been easy to overlook him. Dust powdered his skin, hair, and clothes a uniform brown.

"Sir?" said Lusor.

Even as we approached, he remained stock-still, his arms wrapped over his head, neck curled toward his chest.

"Are you all right, sir?"

No response.

"Vay . . ." warned Herald Drishne, the cohort's second-in-command.

Thick drops of blood rolled down the man's arms where his skin had split open. I could see the lines of shallow red gouges through the ripped sleeves of his overalls. He had been scratching himself.

Lusor gestured, and we spread outwards to flank him.

"Please stand up," she said, without inflection. "I need you to identify yourself."

The man twitched. The motion undulated across the whole length of his spine. Then he was motionless again. His chest did not rise or fall; he could have been carved from the wood of the plum trees. Now that we stood closer to him, I could hear a furtive rasping sound, something between breathing and growling

Lusor nodded curtly to us. I slipped my hand into the pocket of my robes and found my emergency vial. I removed the stopper with my teeth and swallowed the sacrament inside. It slithered down my throat, cold and salty.

The rasping ceased.

Lusor made a swift slicing motion with her hand. We obeyed. Thirteen nets of lace flew through the air, snapping around the man's shoulders and pinning him to the spot.

He did not make a sound.

Sweat gleamed on Lusor's forehead. "Hold him."

We watched in absolute silence as she stepped into the gully and circled around the man.

"Sebet. Raughn."

I started.

"Drop your nets and come here."

Fine plumes of ochre dust rose around my feet. No one else spoke. Acolyte Fian Sebet and I were the youngest members of the cohort, and the least skilled in lacework.

Lusor never took her eyes off our prisoner. She lowered her voice so that only we could hear her. "Raughn, I saw your placement test scores. Your memory's good, right?"

"Yes," I said.

"I want you to make a report to the Moon House. Repeat exactly what I tell you to Reverend Shaelean Cyde, and request immediate assistance. Understood?"

"Understood."

She recited her report to me. When she finished, I nodded.

"Do you need to hear that again?" she asked.

"No, Herald."

"Good. Sebet, I want you to run to Halowith's chapter house and summon the Sisters on duty. They must help us to contain the Haunt until the retrieval cohort arrives."

"Understood," said Sebet.

The frozen man stared at me. His expression was unfathomable, his mouth worked soundlessly. Between the ceaseless movement of his lips, I could see two sets of teeth, the back row needle-sharp and pointed. Bubbles of bloody saliva drooled from his chin.

"Raughn?"

I snapped out of my daze. "Sorry."

"Try to stay focussed, okay?" said Lusor, not unkindly.

"Yes, Herald."

"Once reserves arrive from Halowith, I'll send a second runner after you."

I gestured compliance, weaving the tips of my fingers together and drawing them downwards.

Lusor dismissed me. "Go."

I clambered out of the gulley, and the cohort parted to let me through. Even as I hurried away from him, I could still see the Haunt's lips moving in my mind.

"Closer, closer, closer . . ." he repeated.

The sun had passed its meridian, but the heat blazed on, and it was scarcely any cooler beneath the beech trees. Perspiration trickled along the ridges of my spine. The Moon House was on the south side of the Pillar. Unless I circumvented the entire wood, the only route was back toward the vision. And I knew it was still there. The pressure in my skull was mounting again.

At the waypoint, I shut my eyes and drew on my lace, curling a thin thread of power through the tree's protective web. I found the hidden cord and pulled. Overhead, the bell clanged.

When I opened my eyes, a rose lay to the right of the path. Red, careless, a flower dropped from a lover's bouquet. The outer petals were marred by bruise-coloured marks.

I shook my head and took the left path, away from the Pillar.

The Moon House answered, their bell ringing in the distance. They must have been confused, but with luck they would ride out to meet me.

I came across a second rose, and then a third, tucked into the crook of old tree roots. A fourth, dangling from the branches. Their petals fluttered in the wind. Everywhere I looked, more appeared. Bruised, incongruous, a line of red dripped to the base of a fallen tree, where the petals pooled beneath the trunk. A slender black foreleg lay half submerged in the flowers. The rest of the goat was nowhere to be seen.

"Eater preserve me," I muttered.

The trees thickened, obscuring the sky, and the sound of my footfalls soaked into the dense vegetation. I had never been this deep in the woods before. Strange noises rose and fell, furtive creaks and chirrups, the sharp buzzing of unseen insects, the whirr of wings.

A blackwing hen burst from the undergrowth ahead of me. I jumped and swore. It flapped up into the canopy, squawking.

"Sorry," I said.

I came to a bend in the path and then, quite abruptly, the Moon House was spread out before me.

The complex rested against the rise of a steep hill, a semicircle of twelve dark brick buildings nestled in the shadows of the trees. A group of Sisters had assembled in the yard in front of the House stables. Oblates rushed to saddle Cats, and Reverend Cyde directed the preparations.

She saw me approach. A flicker of surprise crossed her face.

"Elfreda? What's going on?"

I reached the yard.

"Acolyte Elfreda Raughn, delivering a report from Pilgrim Guide Vay Lusor of cohort eight, identification code 2649B."

"Proceed," said Reverend Cyde.

I spoke loudly enough for everyone to hear. "Stage Three Haunt apprehended on the West Orchard Road, just past the bridge. Individual is largely unresponsive and contained by eleven Sisters. Reinforcement urgently required."

Reverend Cyde nodded and turned to address her subordinates. "Hina, Samas, ride ahead and provide support. Everyone else, prepare the retrieval cart."

My part done, I moved to leave. This was my chance. If I disappeared now, I could make it back to the city by nightfall. In the chaos, the Sisterhood would overlook the irregularity and—

"Elfreda," said Reverend Cyde.

"Yes, Reverend?"

"Wait in my office please."

My hopes crumbled.

"Yes, Reverend," I said.

CHAPTER

TWO

REVEREND CYDE'S ASSISTANT offered me tea.

The office was spacious and airy, with large windows overlooking the stables. Bookshelves dominated the right-hand side of the room. The vellum-bound volumes were arranged alphabetically and with meticulous care, more valuable books locked behind glass panels. Before taking her position at the Moon House, Shaelean Cyde had served as the Chief Archivist at the Department of Memories.

I sat in a plush blue armchair by the window and watched the tree line. The pressure in my head was faint now. The woods were still.

I took a sip of my tea. It tasted bitter.

The office was on the second floor of the main dormitory building. A longcase clock ticked in the passage outside, and old floorboards creaked from time to time. Through the window, I could see three Oblates locked in serious conversation. Most of the Moon House residents were accompanying the Haunt to the Edge, leaving the compound in the care of a skeleton guard.

Swift footsteps beyond the door, and then Reverend Cyde strode into the room. I half rose from my seat, but she signalled for me to dispense with formalities.

"You'll be pleased to hear that the situation has been contained," she said, taking a seat behind her desk. "No one was hurt."

Cyde was old for a Reverend, nearing sixty, with unlined brown skin and a no-nonsense haircut. On her shoulder, she wore a midnight blue badge and crescent moon pin to designate her rank. Head Custodian of the Moon House, one of the most powerful people outside of Ceyrun.

"I will need to file a report." She opened her drawer and drew out a clean sheet of paper. Her movements were brisk, effortlessly efficient. "I would like to hear your version of events."

I nodded. "Yes, Reverend."

"But first"—she folded her hands on the desk in front of her, fixing me with her stare—"are you all right?"

"Yes, Reverend."

"Please stop saying that."

"Ye—okay."

She gave me a hard look. "Are you sure?"

"Yes," I lied with greater conviction. "I'm fine. Thank you for your concern."

Cyde had been something like a mentor to my mother, back when the Reverend still lived in the city. I was surprised that she had recognised me in the yard; the last time we met, I had been fifteen. So much had changed since then that this reunion made me feel awkward.

"I'm glad to hear that." She wet the nib of her pen in her inkwell. "Right. This is mostly to corroborate what I already know, but can you describe the events leading up to your cohort's discovery of the Haunt?"

I nodded. "We completed the Pillar maintenance, and rang the bell at the waypoint. Pilgrim Guide Lusor proposed spending the night in Halowith."

"Why?"

"The pilgrimage took longer than anticipated. We would only have reached Ceyrun after dark."

She made a note. "The cohort was in agreement?"

With one notable exception. "Yes, we were tired. We left the woods via the north-east bridge, and encountered the Haunt shortly after that."

"Did any civilians see you?"

"A few farmers saw us on the road, but I don't think they

witnessed our capture of the Haunt. At least, that was the situation when Herald Lusor sent me here."

"How did Herald Lusor react to the Haunt?"

I frowned. "She was calm, under the circumstances."

"Did anyone in the cohort behave unexpectedly?"

"Not that I recall. We were surprised."

"I would imagine so." She did not look up from the page, still writing. "So there was no one whose reaction to the Haunt struck you as out of the ordinary?"

"No, Reverend."

She finished her sentence and set down her pen. "That should do, unless there's anything else you want to add?"

I thought for a moment, gazing down at the floor. I gathered my nerve.

"Reverend, do you need someone to deliver that report?"

"Hm?"

"I would be happy to courier it to Ceyrun."

"How generous of you." Cyde leaned back in her chair, folding her hands in her lap. Her dark eyes gleamed. "Elfreda, it strikes me that you are *very* eager to return to the city."

"Uh . . ."

"Any particular reason?"

"The Council should be made aware of the situation as soon as possible."

Cyde raised an eyebrow fractionally. She was far too sharp for my liking, but then, she had been a Councilwoman prior to her retirement.

"That's it?" she asked.

I decided that a measure of truth might help my case. "It's my mother's anniversary tomorrow. I had hoped to be there."

Her face clouded.

"Oh. Of course," she said.

"I realise it might seem sentimental, but—"

"No." She shook her head. "No, I understand. It's been a year already, hasn't it?"

I nodded.

Cyde stood up. She walked over to the window, eyes sweeping the woods, hands clasped behind her back.

"You won't be able to cover the distance on foot," she said. "Not before sunset. You would need a Cat."

She caught my expression and her lips curved upwards in amusement.

"I have a precondition," she said.

"Yes, Rev . . . Yes?"

"Make that two conditions. Firstly, 'Shaelean' is fine; I've known you since you were six. Secondly, I want you to consider applying for reassignment."

"Reassignment?"

"To the Moon House."

I blinked.

"I don't need an answer now," she said, "but I want you to think about it."

Positions at the Pillar Houses were highly sought after; House staff were exempt from Renewal duty for months at a time, received a much higher stipend, and enjoyed better lodging. Most Acolytes would not dream of applying in their first five years. The fact that Cyde had implicitly offered a post to *me* bordered on the scandalous.

"Thank you," I said, disoriented. "I . . . I will consider it."

"You would like working here. Consider it my favour to your mother." She released her hands from behind her back. "I'll finish up my report; you may head down to the stables in the meantime."

I gestured respect and stood. She returned to her desk.

The lacquered walls of the passage outside the Reverend's office flickered with the shadows of incipient visions; brief impressions of dark shapes that twitched and rolled like flames in the wind. I shut the door behind me and pressed the palms of my hands to my eyes. My head pounded; colours bloomed under my eyelids.

"Shit," I muttered.

I walked unsteadily toward the stairs. The floor was covered in soft woven rugs, the walls lined with old portraits of prior Custodians. Their painted faces bulged; their bodies melted and reformed within their gilt frames. The oil paint glistened as if newly wet. Behind me, the clock struck fifteen, and its gong reverberated through the walls of the Moon House. I felt the sound within my bones.

It was better outside. The sun touched the highest branches of the trees and stained the buildings orange. I passed the locked entrance to the House's underground Martyrium, dry grass crunching under my boots. The air remained blistering, oven-hot and thick. With luck, the humidity heralded a storm.

A Cat handler reclined in the shade of the stables. Sweat shone on her forehead and beaded her upper lip.

"I am to courier a report for Reverend Cyde," I said.

She straightened, eyes narrowed. "Now?"

"She'll be down in a minute."

The handler, who I guessed was an Oblate despite her plain clothes, got up and dusted off the back of her trousers. I understood her suspicion. The use of the Cats was generally restricted to Heralds and Reverends, or Acolytes who worked in communication. I clearly did not fit into any of those categories.

"You've ridden one before?" she asked.

I shook my head.

"I'll saddle Claws, then. He's the easiest to control."

The stable was largely empty; most of the Cats were with the retrieval cohort. Three animals remained; the handler approached the smallest.

Haqules, to use their proper name, were intimidating. They were as lithe as their smaller feline cousins, with eyes that saw as well in the dark as in daylight and excellent hearing. Adults stood shoulder height to humans, and a fully grown Cat's head was as large as my entire torso. Their fur was coarse and variegated, their canines capable of puncturing iron. Although few other animals could slow a Haunt, prides of Cats tore them to pieces.

When interacting with their human handlers, however, they had the personality of puppies.

"Heel, Claws," called the handler.

The Moon House housed eight Cats, seven for service and one reserved for Reverend Cyde's personal use. Claws was evidently the runt of the litter. He bounded over to the handler, forked tail swaying.

"Good boy!" She stood on tiptoe and scratched behind his massive, bat-like ears. He shivered with pleasure. The handler cast me another doubtful look.

"He's very quick," she said.

"I'll manage."

I kept out of the way while the handler fit a leather harness to Claws's back. One of the other Cats wandered over to investigate, sniffing my clothes. I patted her, a little uncertain. She sneezed, arched her back, and ambled off into the cooler shadows of the stable.

Reverend Cyde's boots crunched on the grass outside and she appeared in the entrance. She handed a wax-sealed letter to me.

"Deliver this to the Council as soon as you reach Ceyrun," she said.

"Yes, Reverend."

She smiled. "I despair."

"Kneel, boy," said the handler.

Claws crouched. I slung my leg over his side. His fur smelled of grass and prickled against my exposed skin. I hugged him around the neck, feeling his muscles shift beneath me.

"You can just sit tight. He'll head to the city on his own." The handler adjusted the leg straps of Claws's harness until they squeezed my calves. "You want to stop, tell him. He's smart."

She tapped his rump, and he rose. I swayed dangerously as his body tilted.

"Have a safe trip," said Cyde.

The handler unclipped the Cat's restraint from the collar around his neck.

"City, Claws," she ordered.

The sensation was like falling. Half a ton of muscle and fur surged through the stable door and out into the yard.

If not for the harness, I would have lost my balance within the first thirty seconds. I clung to the Cat's neck, helpless as a ragdoll, as we streaked into the woods. Each bound hurtled us over rocks and shrubs and fallen trees; wind whipped my face and roared in my ears. Claws strayed from the path, finding his own route, but he moved with absolute surety, silent and precise and lightning-quick.

I didn't care about the discomfort; I was finally heading in the right direction. The pressure clouding my mind evaporated and I laughed with delight.

We slowed once we reached Orchard Road. The workers had left the farms, and we loped along the path alone. Claws panted and I shifted in the harness, trying to find a more natural seat. The road ended at a T-junction; one way leading to Halowith, the other toward the main road and the city. Without any instruction from me, Claws turned left and started up the steep hill.

I squinted at the sky. There was at least an hour left until nightfall. If we continued at our current pace, we would reach the gates in time.

We crested the slope, and the capital province of Aytrium spread out before us. The basin of Malas Lake stretched from the base of the hill into the far distance. The water levels had withered over the last two hot seasons, and the banks were wide and bone-pale. Iron pipes snaked from the centre of the lake to the small villages dotting the northern shoreline. The great waterwheels stood still and dry.

Beyond lay the Fields, yellow with millet and corn, and then the city. Ceyrun's pale gold walls rose a hundred feet from the valley floor, shielding the lower quarters of the city from view. From this distance, I could see the oldest trees of the Central Gardens, the taller houses of the Minor Quadrants, and Martyrium Hill. Glass and polished stone reflected the sunset, and shadows thickened at the base of the eastern wall.

Claws skidded down the flinty road, struggling for purchase. I lurched forward, and only the harness prevented me from flying over the top of his head. He mewed when I pulled his fur too hard.

"Sorry," I said, and patted the side of his neck. His ears flicked.

The road ran alongside the edge of the lake. I wiped sweat off my face. It was a few degrees cooler here, and the faint breeze carried the smell of mud. Jewelled dragonflies flitted through the air. Amberwings. They were breeding in larger numbers this year.

The path ahead bubbled.

Claws slowed, and his hackles rose.

"It's okay," I whispered.

He growled. I didn't think that he could sense the vision, but he knew that I was disturbed.

"Keep going," I told him. "Go on."

He took a few uncertain steps forward. I continued to murmur encouragingly. The ground beneath his paws reddened, dark blood seeping out of the dirt. The smell of smoke and jasmine caught in my throat, chokingly sweet.

"They are coming, they are coming, they are coming, they are coming, they are coming . . ." The voice swelled from the earth below us: female, rasping, a relentless stream of fear. As I watched, the ground bulged with strange protrusions, fat red seedlings sprouting and unfurling in the sunlight. They squirmed beneath Claws's paws and burst like pustules. I flinched and pulled my feet up higher. *"They are coming, they are coming."*

The protrusions grew taller. They wound around Claws's legs like river weeds.

"They are here."

A scream filled the air, and I clasped my hands to my ears. The sound was inhuman and agonised; it stretched on and on, so loud that I thought my eardrums would rupture. The protrusions reached my ankles, and their touch seared my skin. I kicked them away.

With a wet, tearing noise like meat pulled apart, the vision ended. The protrusions crumpled to dust.

I breathed hard. Claws shied sideways, shaking his head and whining. His claws extended and scratched lines in the dirt.

"It's all right," I said. "Hey. It's all right, boy. I didn't mean to scare you."

I tried to stroke his head, but he snapped at me. I withdrew my fingers. The fur along the ridge of his spine stood straight up.

"Why don't you let me down, okay?" I said gently. "It's not far now."

He whined again, but bent his knees. I loosened the harness straps, and slid off him.

"That's better, isn't it?"

I steadied myself against his flank, and Claws shivered. My ankle stung where the vision had touched me. Not serious. I stroked the Cat in jerky, mechanical motions. Had to keep my composure.

Millet grew on both sides of the road; we had almost reached the city walls. Up ahead, I could hear workers singing the day-end song. The evening was humid. Crickets rasped from the grain, and flies buzzed circles around us.

I took another deep breath. When I started walking, Claws followed me.

The singing grew louder as we approached the silos. Although harvest time was still a month away, the Fields bustled with temporary labourers. The Department of Food Management was collaborating with Water and Sanitation to introduce a new irrigation system, drilling boreholes below the Fields. It was proving more complex—and expensive—than anticipated. At around ten feet deep, the drills in the northern-most Fields had hit a hard bed of granite. The excavation team had assured us that they would break through the rock, but not before the end of the week.

I attracted a few curious looks and deferential gestures as I approached the city. I must have appeared important, with a Cat walking behind me. I returned the greetings.

Sing the storm clouds, sing them in,
There will be food on our tables,
There will be food in our stores,
The Eater's grace upon us.

The day-end song was familiar and mindless. My mother had told me that the lyrics were altered seventy years ago. I'm not sure how she knew of the original, but she liked to collect odd information like that. In my head, I recited the older version.

Call your children, call them in,
There will be blood in the fields,
There will be blood on our hands,
It will not be ours.

I circled around the side of the silo and leaned against the wall. Claws yawned and stretched. He lay down, flapping his ears to fan himself. The workers were returning their tools to the equipment store; they talked loudly and occasionally laughed. I scanned their faces.

"Hey."

I turned.

All the visions threatening to emerge from the shadows of the silos bled away. The tension inside my chest eased.

"Good evening, Finn."

"'Good evening,' El. Feeling formal today?"

Finn was tall and wiry, with messy shoulder-length hair and a wide smile. He carried himself with a disarming confidence, propping a dusty pitchfork across his shoulders as he walked over to me.

"Sorry." I shook my head. "I'm all over the place."

"Don't apologize. What's with the Cat?"

Claws eyed Finn suspiciously and yawned again, cracking his jaw. His long teeth gleamed.

"That would be Claws. Reverend Cyde of the Moon House had a report for the Council." I lifted my bag. "I volunteered to deliver it."

Finn checked if anyone was close enough to overhear us, and lowered his voice.

"Are you okay?" he asked.

"Now? Yes."

"Good, because I was worried out of my mind." He glanced toward the queue of workers clocking in with the shift supervisor. "Can I walk you to the Council Building?"

"Sure, if you want to."

"I do." He smiled. "Let me just sign off on this shift."

With my visions banished, I allowed myself to relax a little. Finn had been my best friend since I was seven, and was one of the few people I trusted completely. In his company, I felt stable, secure in myself, which seemed key to suppressing the visions. I watched as he joined the queue of workers, cracking a joke that caused the people around him to groan. These days, he was doing well. I was glad to see him happy, even if it left me feeling a little lonely.

The breeze shivered across the pale gold fields, brushing the shadows of the city wall. I rubbed my arms. Hopefully, delivering the report would not take too long.

Finn returned, stretching his arms overhead.

"I've discovered that I am not cut out for farming," he said with a grimace. "Or hard labour, generally."

"You look tired."

"Thank you for noticing. I feel ready to drop dead."

"So dramatic."

Finn made a show of pretending to faint, leaning against the silo wall for support. Claws growled.

"Don't upset my Cat," I said, although I could not help smiling. "Can you drag yourself to the city please?"

"So . . . far . . ."

"Enjoy sleeping in the Fields, then."

"That sounds pretty appealing right about now." He straightened. "But I've got a shift at the Candle tonight, so unfortunately it's not an option."

"Oh. You don't need to walk halfway across the city if . . ."

He waved off my suggestion. "I want to. Don't worry, I'm just whining. Let's go."

Claws rose reluctantly. Ahead of us, the city walls stretched tall and shining, and we followed the path that led to Ceyrun.

CHAPTER THREE

THE COUNCIL BUILDING was situated in the Minor East Quadrant, the wealthiest sector of the city. It stood four storeys high, overlooking the college grounds and the Department of Memories. The old building projected an air of stately grandeur, with its yellow stone walls and fine latticework, its mythic friezes, its jutting balconies and sloping gullwing roof. The oldest wing of the building was home to the Conclave of Representatives, and dated back to the Great Fire of the Ash Disciple rebellion almost four hundred years ago.

I seldom had reason to visit the Council Building. In fact, I had not seen the interior since my induction as an Acolyte last year.

"I'm not sure how long I'll be." I gazed up at the carved pillars. Sisters were leaving the building, work concluded for the day. "If the Council is in session, it could be a while."

"I'll take that as a hint," said Finn. "Want to drop by the Candle afterwards?"

"It's been a long day."

"I thought you might say that." A strange expression passed over his face. "El, I've been thinking . . ."

He trailed off.

"What is it?"

"Probably nothing. Forget it."

"Are you sure?"

"Yeah." He smiled. "Yeah, I'm sure. Listen, are you free tomorrow? Millie has plans."

"What kind of plans?"

"It's Daje's birthday. I'm supposed to convince you to attend. So, you know, please come."

I laughed. "Convincing."

"I try. So?"

"I don't know, would Daje really want me there? We aren't exactly close."

Finn shook his head. "It's fine, it's just a casual thing in the Gardens. I get the impression it's more for Millie's benefit anyway."

"Still . . ."

"He won't mind."

I thought for a moment. Sisters were granted a day off after any pilgrimage, and although I wanted to see my mother, that wouldn't take more than an hour.

"All right," I said, still a little uncertain. "If you're sure it's okay."

Finn grinned. "Great. Meet me at the graveyard at third bell?"

"Fourth?"

"Sure." He leaned forward quickly and kissed me on the cheek. "See you then."

He was walking away from me before I could think of anything to say. My cheek burned, and I felt, suddenly, as if the eyes of the whole city were upon me.

I hurried up the steps. *Reckless idiot.*

Cool, dry air wafted out into the evening; the walls of the building were thick, and chambers within always cold. At the entrance, the Acolyte on guard gestured welcome to me.

"Is the Council still in session?" I asked.

She nodded. "I believe so, but they should finish shortly. Do you need help finding them?"

"I think I'll manage, but thank you."

My footfalls echoed on the tiles. The foyer was vast and dim; red carpeted stairs bordered the chamber, and a great brass chandelier hung from the ceiling. Marble busts of prior Councilwomen sat in recessed alcoves. Their eyes seemed faintly accusatory to me. A statue of the Star Eater stood on a raised pedestal in the centre of the room. The old woman had a stern expression, but her hands reached outwards, ready to embrace penitents. Small offerings covered her bare feet.

I paused to pay respect, then headed up the right-hand staircase to the third floor. The workday was done, so the Council must be running late. Probably struggling to reach consensus on the water crisis.

Oil paintings crowded the walls of the eastern wing corridors. The old floorboards groaned as I made my way toward the Council chambers. I had never been to this part of the building before, and could not quite shake the sense that I was trespassing. The murky glass of the windows only let in thin, watery light, and the smell of lantern oil and varnish was cloying.

I followed the sound of voices. As I got closer, I could catch snatches of an argument.

". . . won't *be* anything left to preserve if they tear down the walls!"

Someone spoke with a mollifying tone. I did not catch their words.

"I don't think you understand the severity of the situation." That was Reverend Deselle Somme, Head of Food Management. She spoke slowly and clearly, and her deep voice carried well. "If we don't implement measures now, we are setting ourselves up for full-scale civilian revolt."

An Acolyte stood outside the doors to the Conclave. She wore a heavy yellow uniform, with tasselled shoulders and a tricorn hat. When she caught my eye, she grimaced. Outside the door, the Reverends' every word was audible.

"It's high time that the radicals were served a reminder of who rules this city. We can handle the situation."

"Who is 'we,' Jiana?" A new voice, icy and authoritative. "Because I'm fairly certain you mean 'Enforcement can handle the situation,' and that means *I* will have to handle the situation."

"They've been at it for an hour," the Acolyte whispered to me. "If you have a message, I can pass it on for you. This could last all night."

I winced. "Unfortunately, it's urgent."

The Acolyte nodded sympathetically. "In that case, rather you than me."

At least I was back in the city. If I could handle the visions, then surely I could face the Council. I raised my hand and knocked on the varnished wooden door.

"Your convenience is not a priority."

"This is not about convenience. You know what will upset the civilians? The cancellation of a festival they've been preparing for since last *year.*"

The uniformed Acolyte gave me an embarrassed smile.

"They probably won't hear you," she whispered. "You'll have to intrude."

Better to get it over with. I steeled myself, and pushed open the door.

The Conclave of Representatives chamber fell quiet. The room was much larger than I had anticipated, with the thirteen representatives seated in a ring behind individual stone podiums. A huge map of the island was painted on the floor, the names of towns and rivers etched in gold. Three of the Reverends were on their feet, their argument stalled by my appearance. The other ten remained seated beneath the coloured banners of their departments.

I stepped inside and gestured respect and regret. My throat felt bone-dry.

"What is the meaning of this?" Reverend Jiana Morwin of the Department of Public Health fixed me with a cold stare. Her skin was flushed with anger.

"Please forgive my intrusion," I rasped. I cleared my throat. "I have an emergency missive from Reverend Shaelean Cyde of the Moon House."

"Whatever it is, I hardly think it justifies disrupting session."

I swallowed. Although I knew who all the Councilwomen

were, I had only ever spoken to Reverend Somme, who was the head of my department. The thirteen most powerful individuals on Aytrium, and I had barged into the middle of their meeting.

"Come now, Jiana," said Reverend Yelina Celane, the Chief Archivist of the Department of Memories. Her robes bore the green quill insignia of her department, and she appeared quite at ease. She smiled at me. "No need to be rude. Your name, Acolyte?"

"Elfreda Raughn, Honoured Councilwoman." I drew Cyde's report out of my bag and hesitated, unsure who I should present it to. To my relief, Reverend Somme held out her hand.

"Very good," said Reverend Celane. "Thank you for your service, Acolyte Raughn. You may go now."

"One moment."

Reverend Saskia Asan was the youngest member of the Council and its most recent addition. She served as the Commander General of the Department of Enforcement, the Sisterhood's military force. Rumour suggested that she was one of the most talented lace-weavers of the last century, and, despite her coarse demeanour, one of the smartest women in the Sisterhood.

"You aren't a House member," she said. "Unless you're wearing someone else's robes."

"I was part of the Moon Pillar pilgrimage and available to deliver Reverend Cyde's report."

"Please speak louder."

"The House members were occupied," I said, raising my voice. Other members of the Council whispered to one another. Sweat rolled down my back.

"Huh." Reverend Asan folded her arms and slouched on her chair. "Irregular."

Reverend Somme finished reading Cyde's letter. Her gaze flicked toward Reverend Asan, and she set down the paper.

"Thank you, Elfreda, that will be all," she said.

I bowed. The whispering grew louder. I backed out of the room and closed the heavy door behind me. My hands shook.

"What was all that about?" asked the Acolyte.

"I'm not authorised to say." Although, given her position, she would no doubt find out shortly. One of the perks of her job, I imagined. I could hear the murmur of Reverend Somme's voice as she read Cyde's report to the Conclave, too low to understand. The Acolyte frowned at me.

"Enjoy your evening," I said.

The truth would leak to the rest of the Order soon enough anyway. I doubted that the Reverends could keep the Haunt a secret, not after so many Sisters were involved in its capture and disposal. I hurried back down the corridor. The news would be all over the dormitories by tomorrow.

By the time I reached the entrance to the building, evening had fallen. An Oblate was lighting the votive candles at the base of the Star Eater's statue, murmuring a devotional as she moved from one taper to the next. Tiny white moths fluttered around the open flames. The tiles below were already dotted with the singed wings of the dead.

CHAPTER FOUR

During the night, a bank of thick cloud rose from below Aytrium and shrouded the city in white. Outside my window, the dark streets glistened with moisture. It was early. The lanterns had not yet been extinguished, and their coloured lights floated like phantoms in the mist.

I rolled out of bed and dressed in civilian clothes. The cool floorboards squeaked under my bare feet; in the neighbouring room, an Acolyte grumbled in her sleep. My quarters were on the third floor of the dormitories—a small bedroom and a private bathroom, filled with second-hand furniture and a few keepsakes I had saved from my mother's house.

I scraped my wild hair back into a bun. The crack which bisected my bathroom mirror split my reflection in two. I had reported the problem to maintenance soon after moving in, but no one had acknowledged my request for a replacement.

The air outside was cold. I breathed in, clearing my head, and set off toward Pearl Boulevard.

The mist dampened the sounds of the city. In the distance, I could hear the ringing of the second bell. The Acolyte dormitories were situated at the end of Reverence Street, in the Minor East Quadrant. Although I had only been a full Sister for a year, I already knew all the shortcuts to reach the Martyrium. I sidled down a narrow alley between a butchery and a chemist's shop. Refuse had been left out the previous day, and the air was thick with the smell of spoiling offal. The refuse collectors would arrive before the fourth bell, pick up the scraps and transport them to the worm farms or the swineries outside the city.

A black smear near the base of the butchery wall caught my eye. Someone had scrawled *let Aytrium fall* across the bricks in charcoal. I paused, then hurried on.

On Pearl Boulevard, everyday noises grew louder: squeaking wagon wheels, boots clicking on cobbles, muted conversation. Figures loomed out of the mist and then faded away.

Rubbing my arms to ward off the chill, I began the steep climb up to Martyrium Hill. Caged fowl squawked and vendors greeted one another. A baby wailed. The Hill constituted the highest level of Ceyrun, rising above the Minor Quadrants, and served as the spiritual heart of the Sisterhood.

Pearl Boulevard ended and I reached the stairs, which were slick with dew. It was still early; I felt a faint shiver as I passed through the lacework net looping the crown of the Hill. Beyond the dawn streets, the world grew quieter once more, and I climbed through the mists alone. A single black bird wheeled through the sky, dipping in and out of sight. My breath emerged from my mouth in pale gusts.

Just for a moment, I considered deliberately slipping on the slick stone steps.

Ahead of me, the domed roof of the Martyrium drew slowly into focus. Although the building shone pearl and ivory in sunlight, today it appeared ashen grey against the fog.

On the plaza before the Martyrium, a huge bronze statue of the Star Eater held her arms up to the heavens. Mother to us all, righteous fire of our people, the first weaver. In the late afternoon, the old woman would grasp the sun, but for now she held nothing at all. I lowered my head in deference as I passed her.

Two junior Acolytes were on duty, standing sentry beside the stained-glass doors of the Martyrium. They gestured acknowledgement when I approached. I raised my arm to reveal the Sisterhood tattoo on my wrist.

"You're here early, Acolyte," said the taller woman. "I thought the weather would keep everyone away until at least the third bell."

"Eater's grace upon you," I said, ducking my head. "I only returned to the city last night, but wanted to attend to my duties as soon as I could."

The two of them exchanged a look.

"Were you part of the Moon Pillar pilgrimage?" asked the second Acolyte.

Rumours spreading already. "I was."

"We heard . . ." She glanced at her companion again. "Um . . ."

"May I go inside?"

"Oh, of course," she said, crestfallen, and pushed the doors open. "Who will you be visiting?"

"Martyr Kirane Raughn."

The taller Acolyte made a note in her record book, and motioned for me to enter. "May her dreaming be lit by the Star."

"May the Star shine brightly on us all," I replied.

Inside, it was cold and still. Flowering vines grew over the entrances to hundreds of alcoves, and skylights cut shafts of pale luminescence through the roof. The marble walls shone bright silver, as if with interior light, and the alcove entrances formed a glittering honeycomb above my head.

I followed the spiralling stairs as they curved up the side of the dome. The air was laced with the fragrance of herbs and incense, but there was a faint whiff of ammonium and iron beneath it all. The smell had always bothered me. On some level, the whole place bothered me, but I could not wholeheartedly hate the Martyrium either. It was too beautiful for that, and too entangled in my understanding of myself.

Outside my mother's alcove stood a ceramic basin full of water. I washed my hands carefully, taking my time. A scalpel rested on the rim of the basin. Once I was done cleaning, I picked it up.

My mother lay beneath a richly embroidered shroud, her bed pressed up against the far wall of the chamber. The candle beside the door fluttered as I passed. Her face was relaxed; it had an ease that I never saw before her martyrdom.

"Happy anniversary, Mom," I muttered.

Her chest rose and fell, in and out, in and out. I drew a stool over to the bed and sat down. For a while, I just watched her.

"I saw Reverend Cyde yesterday," I said. "She's doing well. She recognised me, which I didn't expect."

I straightened the corner of her shroud where it was skewed, aligning it to the edge of the pallet.

"I think that she tried to offer me a job at the Moon House. Which was . . ." I lapsed into silence. I could hear the chirping of birds outside. "I'd have to leave the city, and I don't know if I can. Even though the Moon House was very beautiful. And I liked Reverend Cyde."

And I would have to perform fewer Renewals. I fingered the edge of the scalpel, running my thumb over the blade.

"She said it was a favour to you, and I'm still thinking about it. But I can't ask Finn to leave Ceyrun for my sake; that wouldn't be fair to him. And without him or Millie, I'm not sure I could manage the visions, so—"

The scalpel nicked my thumb, and I cursed under my breath. A thin line of red welled up just below my nail. It stung.

"I'm seeing him again later this morning," I said, sucking the cut. "Millie's plan. Maybe I'll discuss it with him then."

My mother's face was unchanging.

I sighed and drew back the shroud. Her legs were a mass of scars, neat cauterized grooves chipped into her calves. I knew exactly which scar was the first. Right above her ankle bone, the white indentation bright against her deep brown skin. Even then, I had been precise.

My hand was steady. I cut a neat rectangle into her calf, less than an inch in length, and drew out the hot flesh. My mother did not even twitch. Her expression remained as serene as ever. Blood ran from the wound, but I used the last lace in my body to tie the skin back together. The binding would dissolve in a few hours, but the Martyrium staff would cauterise the cut long before then.

I put the bloody sliver into my mouth and swallowed it without chewing.

"I'll see you soon," I said softly. "Sleep well."

There was no need to take a spare vial for emergencies; I would not have to leave the city again this week. I walked over to the basin and dropped the scalpel inside. The nurses sterilized the blades every night, replaced the water, and ensured that our mothers were clean, tidy, and fed. I washed my hands and made my way down the stairs.

"May the Eater watch over you," intoned the Acolytes at the door.

Most of the fog had cleared and the day was brighter. The third bell rang as I reached the bottom of the hill, by which time Ceyrun had roused.

Street vendors lit their stoves, tossing diced peppers, onions, and fruit into spitting skillets. People moved briskly, but many paused before the *Resounder* offices to buy a copy of the broadsheet. The *Resounder* would have long gone out of print if it relied entirely on factual reporting, but people didn't seem to care much about that. A young woman whistled while she swept the pavement; carriages rattled over the streets.

Pearl Boulevard bisected the city, drawing a straight line from Martyrium Hill to the South Gate, interrupted only by the city's Central Gardens. Tall bridges spanned the road, providing safer walkways to pedestrians and allowing keen-eyed Enforcers to monitor the thoroughfare from above. I made my way down the boulevard until I reached the first intersection, and then turned right onto Weaver Road, and from there onto Rose Crescent.

The Minor West Quadrant was home to the merchant class districts, full of bright storefronts, small galleries, and shady cafés. The pretty little canals that ran between the buildings had run dry, but the fountains still held water.

The entrance to the graveyard was on Rush Street, but most people jumped the low wall at the end of Rose. I was no exception, although I did first check that no one was watching.

Since Finn's sixteenth birthday, the graveyard had served as our usual meeting place. The gentle slope was overgrown with crooked trees and soft sweet grasses. He waited in the shadow of the city wall.

Without acknowledging one another and in perfect unison, we spat onto the grave marker.

"You're early," he said.

"So are you."

"Couldn't sleep."

"I thought you were exhausted. Didn't you have a shift last night?"

He shrugged. I noticed that he was holding a copy of the *Resounder*. I gestured to it.

"You must have planned a long wait, if you brought reading material," I said.

"Were you attacked by a Haunt yesterday?"

I spluttered. "What?"

He raised the newspaper so that I could read the headline. The bold black text at the top of the page read "Pillar Under Attack!" followed by the subheading *Rogue Haunt on the Loose, Sisterhood in Shock!*

"We weren't attacked," I said, snatching the newspaper from him and scanning the article. "We just found the man mumbling to himself in the orchards."

"That sounds worrying."

"It wasn't dangerous." I kept reading. This was bad; the Reverends were going to be livid that the news got out to the public. "My full cohort was present, and he was only in the second phase of the transformation."

"The article says fourth."

"You shouldn't believe everything you read."

Finn raked his fingers though his hair, a nervous habit. "El, be serious. Why didn't you tell me?"

I sighed and handed the newspaper back to him. "Because it wasn't that important. No one got hurt."

"But what if there are more Haunts?"

"Then the Sisterhood will handle them."

"How?"

"There are protocols," I said, brushing aside the issue. "And this was a freak incident. There's no need for concern."

"You don't know that. If there was one infection, then—"

"The man could have contracted the sickness via airborne exposure."

"He was a farmer!" Finn threw up his hands. "He would be the *least* exposed to the Sisterhood."

"Some men are more susceptible than others."

"You don't really believe that it was airborne," he said, seeing right through my evasion. "So, a renegade?"

I hesitated, then shrugged. "Maybe, but I hope not."

"You'll be careful, though?"

"Only if you stop hassling me about it."

"El . . ."

"Fine, yes, I'll be careful," I grumbled. "I guess the whole city is talking about this by now."

"Just about."

"Great." Mass hysteria on top of everything else. I scuffed my shoes against the grass. "Look, there will be an inquiry. If one of us, well, *strayed,* the Sisterhood will hunt her down."

Finn sighed. His gaze travelled past me, up toward Martyrium Hill, and I knew what he was thinking. He gave a small shrug.

"Well, I hope she's good at hiding," he said.

"Me too, I suppose." The taste of my mother's blood lingered in the back of my mouth. "Although I shouldn't say things like that. Where's Millie?"

"She told me she'd meet us on Hyacinth. Want to get moving?"

I nodded. Finn cast a sidelong glance at the headstone, then stuck his hands in his pockets and walked toward the gates. I followed him.

CHAPTER FIVE

BY THE TIME the fifth bell tolled, the sun had banished the last of the morning mist. Thin, bright clouds rolled across the sky.

We waited for Millie on the corner of Rose and Hyacinth. Oak trees lined the streets in the Morkith District of Minor West, and the ground was littered with acorns and crushed leaves. Horse-drawn cabs rattled past. A squirrel hopped from branch to branch, and a fat house cat followed its movements from the windowsill of a grocer, tail twitching.

I pulled blades of grass from the pavement and arranged them into circles on my knees, while Finn leaned against the tree and read through the *Resounder*. As he had anticipated, Millie was late.

"A man has gone missing in the Berai province. Enforcement requests anyone with information to come forward," he said, tracing a finger across the text. "Food prices are expected to rise . . . Oh, that's interesting. The Council is planning to hold a symposium on the subject of the drought. They're calling for contributions from the public."

"Huh. Where is it?"

"The Tivaria Community Hall. 'Sources say that the dry spell is heating up existing conflicts within the Council. Reverend Deselle Somme of Food Management continues to push for greater rationing and water pressure reduction, but she has been met with fierce resistance from the Department of Memories and the Department of Public Health, who are against Somme's austerity policies. Enforcement has reputedly thrown its weight behind Food Management, although it remains to be seen how the other nine Council members cast their votes. With Moon Tide approaching, some experts predict that the Sisterhood may call a halt to the festivities.'"

"So we should," I said sourly.

"It's that bad?"

"I am not authorised to give an official statement."

He chewed on his lip. "It'll cause a riot if they cancel Moon Tide."

"Oh, they know. That's why the Reverends are arguing. Allegedly. According to some sources."

"Which side is winning?"

"Hard to say." I gazed up at the sky. "But if they take too long, the weather will make the decisions for them."

"It could still rain."

"It could. But counting on it is . . ."

"Stupid?" he proposed.

"Ill-advised." I sighed and brushed the grass off my legs. "Listen, I wanted to talk to you about something."

Finn lowered the newspaper. "Sounds ominous."

"Not really. Yesterday, I had a conversation with Reverend Cyde of the Moon House."

"You mentioned her last night, and the name was familiar."

"She used to be friends with my mother."

"Ah, that must be why." He looked past my shoulder. "Hold that thought; Millie's here."

I turned and saw her stepping down from a cab at the end of Hyacinth. She flashed me a quick smile. In one arm, she held a bunch of colourful flowers.

"We can talk about it later," I said.

Millie paid the driver and strolled over to us. The fabric of her long sundress fluttered in the breeze.

"Hi, gorgeous." She selected a single blue chrysanthemum from her bouquet and handed it to me. "You are looking especially lovely today."

Millie had darker hair than her brother, but the same blue eyes. Her skin was liberally dusted with nut-brown freckles, concentrated across her nose and cheeks. Today she had twined a constellation of tiny white flowers into her loose plait.

"You appear to have a dandruff problem," said Finn.

She smacked him over the head with her free hand.

"It looks beautiful," I said.

"Why, *thank* you. They took a while but, you know, I have to look my best for you."

"Was that why you left us waiting for an hour?"

Millie ignored her brother. She offered me a hand and pulled me to my feet. "How was the Haunt hunt?"

"What Haunt?"

"Yes, very convincing. Daje and Hanna should be in the Gardens already. Maybe you can save the details for them?"

"You know I won't tell you anything about the incident, right?"

"She says now." Millie looped her arm through mine. Her skin was sun-warmed, and she was wearing perfume, something light and feminine and sweet. "Sounds like a challenge."

The Central Gardens were only a few blocks away. They formed a belt of lush greenery between the eastern and western sides of the city. Huge stepped terraces jutted up from the Major Quadrants, and a maze of stairs, ladders, and bridges connected the different levels. At the base of the Gardens were the city greenhouses, row upon row of glass rectangles packed with ripening vegetation. Food Management had plans to build more to decrease the Sisterhood's dependence on the farms. It was one of Reverend Somme's more ambitious projects, and an ongoing headache for me.

". . . want to see the Moult perform. I hear they've planned an act for Moon Tide." Millie had been talking for some time.

"Are they the illusionists?" I asked.

"Yeah. Daje saw one of their performances a few months ago." She squeezed my arm. "You seem distracted. Something on your mind?"

"Sorry. I was thinking about Sisterhood problems."

"Ah." She smiled. "Should have known."

We reached the Iron Gate, the main entrance to the Gardens in Minor West. A few people milled around the shaded path and an Enforcer leaned against the fence, an expression of extreme boredom plastered across her face. A labourer read a book in the sunshine.

"Over here."

Hanna waved from a little way up the path. She was a short woman with a heart-shaped face and multiple piercings. Although the two of us feigned friendliness for Millie's sake, our relationship was civil at best. The coolness between us was probably my fault.

"You took a while, sunshine. I was getting bored." Hanna kissed Millie's cheek and nodded to me in greeting.

"Hello," I said, perhaps a shade too cheerfully.

The Gardens were busy, with civilians making the best of the cooler weather. Children played tag along the walkways, and the elderly practised stretching exercises beneath broad trellises. A trio of Sisters from the Department of Water and Sanitation sat on a bench in the shade, engrossed in conversation. I had heard that the department was in a state of turmoil ahead of Reverend Kisme's martyrdom. Reverend Belia Verje was set to replace her next month, and rumours suggested that the new Head intended to reshuffle the entire Department.

Hanna led us across the dry lawns to a smaller path through the trees. She had linked arms with Millie, and the two of them were discussing people I did not know. I fell back to give them space.

Finn caught my eye.

"Something the matter?" he asked quietly.

I was silent for a while, thinking. Millie laughed at something Hanna said, and shoved her playfully. It was difficult to put words to my feelings.

"Some days, I want to . . ." I shook my head. "It doesn't matter."

"But you seem sad," he murmured.

"I'm not. Just caught up in my own head."

Deeper in the Gardens, a man broke out in song. Finn glanced backwards.

"El," he stopped and cleared his throat. "Look, if you and Millie wanted to, uh . . . This isn't the most comfortable topic for me. But if you feel . . ."

"Please stop."

"Got it. Gladly."

I laughed, and my melancholy retreated. Finn looked over his shoulder a second time. His eyes narrowed.

"Why do you keep doing that?" I asked.

He did not answer me immediately, but at the bend in the path, he paused.

"I think someone is following us," he said.

"What?"

"It could be my imagination." He nodded toward the stairs leading to the lower levels of the Gardens. "Check once we reach the steps."

"It's probably just someone heading the same way. Why would anyone follow us?"

"I don't know."

For some reason, I felt certain that Finn was lying to me. More than anything else, that made me uneasy. I had lace to spare, so there was little danger, especially in such a public place. And yet he was clearly nervous.

"A friend of yours?" I asked lightly.

He flinched. "No."

Interesting. I filed away his reaction for later consideration. At the top of the stairs, I bent to retie the laces of my shoe and glanced back down the path.

It was the same man I had seen reading a book at the Iron Gate. He strolled toward us, hands buried in his pockets. There wasn't anything particularly remarkable about him; he had medium brown skin and deep-set eyes, five or so years older than me. Easy to overlook in a crowd, indistinguishable from hundreds of other men in the city. Our eyes met.

To my surprise, he grinned and tipped his hat. I quickly turned away, as if he had caught me doing something wrong, and the man walked past the stairs and toward the Winter Gardens.

"That was weird." Finn shrugged. "Sorry. I guess I was wrong."

I wasn't so sure. There had been a kind of camaraderie in the stranger's grin, like we shared a secret, or played a hidden game. *I know you see me,* he seemed to say, *but what are you going to do about it?*

I straightened. "Can you tell Millie that I'll catch up with her?"

"What are you planning to do?"

"I'm not sure. I just want to see where he's going. Like you said, it's probably nothing."

"Yeah, well . . ." Finn's frown deepened.

"What's with you today?"

"Nothing."

"Uh-huh." I elbowed him. "Then stop worrying me. I won't be long."

"Who's worrying who?" He rolled his eyes, although his nonchalance felt forced. It gave me pause; he seemed strangely vulnerable, almost afraid, and I could not understand why. But I didn't want to lose sight of the stranger either, so I shook my head and hurried down the path. I would talk to Finn later.

The man had disappeared around the corner. I walked faster. This was likely a waste of time and, of course, I didn't know what I would actually do if I caught up to him. Demand an explanation? An explanation for what? I climbed the broad flight of stairs to the upper eastern sector of the Gardens, taking them two steps at a time. No law prohibited smiling.

An Enforcer greeted me at the archway to the Winter Gardens. I nodded to her. Beyond the arch, wooden walkways snaked between the evergreen trees. Luck chimes clinked in the breeze.

The Winter Gardens were the one sector that stayed green all year round, which made it amongst the most popular areas in the Gardens. As a child I had climbed these trees with Finn while my mother met with her friends on the benches below. We had invented all kinds of fantasies back then, about what we would become when we grew up. Stupid childhood dreams.

The man was waiting, standing in the shade at the first fork in the path. When he saw me coming, he smirked and beckoned.

That caught me off-guard, and was irritating enough to overcome my natural reticence. I advanced toward him.

"Excuse me," I said. "I'm not sure . . ."

"Corpse eater," he called.

I stopped in my tracks. A nearby woman's head whipped around.

"Uh . . ." I wet my lips. "Sir, I think . . ."

"You are a corpse eater." He pronounced the words carefully, as if speaking to a child. He was still smiling. "Isn't that right, Acolyte Elfreda Raughn?"

He's mad, I thought, reeling. To so casually blaspheme against the Sisterhood was insane. *And how does he know who I am?*

The handful of people in the vicinity were all staring at us.

"Did you hear me? I can say it louder," he said.

"I heard you."

Although my words were soft, a shiver rippled through the onlookers. The Winter Gardens had become very quiet.

"So?"

What was this? With so many witnesses, I knew I needed to respond. His behaviour verged on the treasonous. Actually, it probably *was* treasonous. And yet he clearly wanted me to react, which meant that this had to be some kind of trap. Absurd. My anger, always close to the surface, spilled over.

"I don't know who you are," I said, still without raising my voice, "but you seem to be under the impression that I give a damn about your opinions."

"Oh, but you do, corpse eater."

"Don't test me."

"Or what?" He knew that he had gotten under my skin. "Gonna send me to the Renewal Wards?"

It was a push too far. I drew on my lace and slammed a rope into his torso, intending to throw him off his feet.

Instead, my power hit an invisible wall and rebounded.

I took a step backwards.

He laughed. "What's wrong?"

I tried again; wound the lace tighter and stronger this time. Again, it snapped away from him like a repulsed magnet. The civilians whispered. To them, it looked like I was doing nothing at all. A horrible feeling of helplessness welled up from the pit of my stomach.

"Anything to say?"

I took a step toward him.

"Don't test me," he mocked, and snapped his fingers.

An invisible rope caught me around the shoulders. I jerked to a halt. My anger and shock made it difficult to weave lace; it turned slick and slipped away from me. As I fumbled to sever the first rope, another took its place.

I was outmatched.

"How are you doing that?" I growled.

The man feigned a look of innocence. One of the civilians edged closer to him, apparently with the intention of tackling him from behind. She came to an abrupt stop.

"Please stay back," I said to the onlookers. *Where is Enforcement?*

"Very noble of you." The man walked toward me.

I smiled thinly. "You must realise that the Sisterhood will not tolerate this. There's no way you can evade us."

He patted me on the head as he passed.

"Want to bet?" he whispered.

Outrage rendered me speechless. I drew on my power and hacked at the rope until it disintegrated. How dare he? The power binding me fell away. The civilian woman stumbled as I freed her.

"Please do not leave the area!" I shouted to the onlookers, as I turned on heel. "You may be required to serve as witnesses!"

The man was already at the arch. Eater, he was fast. I ran after him, my feet pounding on the walkway. The Enforcer shouted in surprise, her body stiffening as if paralysed. This made no sense; only Sisters could use lace, and yet those had definitely been lacework bindings. I balled my fists. Humiliated. He had treated me like a child in front of civilians.

Through the arch, and past the Enforcer. The man was halfway down the stairs.

Even though the distance was too great, I threw a lacework rope at him. The binding fell short, but clipped his ankle. He staggered sideways and knocked into the balustrade. For a moment, I thought that he might fall over the edge. There was a twenty-foot drop to the level below, enough to break his neck. My stomach lurched. Then he caught himself and stumbled on down the stairs.

"Stop right there, Acolyte!"

The Enforcer had worked her way free from the binding and caught up to me.

"Let him go," she panted. "I've triggered the alarm. Enforcement will apprehend him at the gates."

"But . . ." The man had reached the base of the stairs.

"We don't know what he's capable of, Acolyte."

Another person to identify me without my robes, I thought, as the man vanished into the lower Gardens. For the first time it struck me that the woman did not resemble an Enforcer. Although she wore the sharp-cut maroon uniform of their order, she had black lace-ups instead of work boots, and the brief run had left her out of breath. A suspicion formed in my mind.

"Understood," I said. I gestured regret with my hands. "I'm sorry for getting in your way."

The woman shook her head. "No need to apologize; there wasn't anything I could have done anyway."

She's lying, I thought. There was something slightly false about her expression, too much emphasis behind her words.

"You'll have to make a witness statement at the Detainment Offices. Ask for Herald Rhyanon Hayder." The woman sighed heavily. "I must reassure the civilians. Please excuse me."

Rhyanon Hayder did not work in the Detainment Office; she was Deputy Chief of Civil Obligations. But I nodded anyway.

"Eater's grace upon you," I said.

I watched the Enforcer walk toward the Winter Gardens. The man was long gone now, and I stood alone at the top of the stairs. A breeze rustled through the trees.

I wasn't sure why she had tried to deceive me. But it looked an awful lot like both she and Herald Hayder were impersonating Enforcement staff. That interested me.

I turned right and headed toward Minor West and the Detainment Offices. Time to find some answers.

CHAPTER SIX

THE NAME 'DETAINMENT Offices' was misleading. Few criminals were ever housed within the triple-storey complex. Depending on the severity of their offenses, felons were either sent to the mines, the Cosun province jail, or the Renewal Wards. Although the Detainment Offices did have a limited number of holding cells in the basement, it primarily served as the Enforcement Department's administrative headquarters.

I sat on a chair in the first-floor corridor, waiting for an appointment with Herald Hayder, which—disconcertingly—was to take place in one of the building's interrogation rooms.

The Enforcer who had sent me here was a senior Acolyte. I had filed a preliminary report with her, sketching the outlines of the incident. To my surprise, she took down the details without comment. She scarcely batted an eyelid when I asked to speak to Herald Hayder.

"She'll return shortly. You can wait outside room fifteen."

I followed her directions, and sat where I was told. Doubts had crept into my mind. In the years prior to her martyrdom, my mother had spoken of Herald Rhyanon Hayder more than once. They had been colleagues at Civil Obligations. When I was a child, Rhyanon had hosted a daughter-naming celebration, and I brought a gift for her newborn. Jene? Joane? That might have been the name. My memory of the day nagged at me; something unusual had happened, but I couldn't recall the specifics.

Then again, this woman could simply have transferred to Enforcement. I grimaced. I had no grounds for making wild assumptions, and yet . . .

Down the corridor, the stairs creaked. I looked up.

Herald Hayder was unassuming. She had a slightly frayed, frazzled appearance, and her skin was milky and flushed at the cheeks. When she walked, she hunched her shoulders forward, the posture of someone who worked at a desk all day. But for all that her appearance was forgettable, she was also definitely the same woman from my childhood memories. And, I noted with interest, she was not wearing an Enforcer's badge.

I stood and gestured respect.

"Yes?" Her gaze flicked to me. "Can I help you?"

"Are you Herald Hayder?"

"That's me. You are?"

I introduced myself and explained that I had been sent to provide a witness statement. The Herald had sharp eyes, a deep reddish brown colour like cedar bark. I had assumed she was in her forties; up close she appeared a little younger.

"I'd better ask you a few questions, then," she said.

The interrogation room was sparse and undecorated, the walls a dull beige. A large table dominated the space, with a writing pad and an inkblot at one corner. If not for the cuffs on the chairs and the mirrored panel set into the left wall, it could have been an ordinary meeting room.

Rhyanon closed the door behind her and sat down. She gestured to the other chair, and I took it. She stared at me, and I stared right back.

Eventually, she smiled.

"So, an instance of civil disobedience?" she said. "Strange, that this man would target a Sister who wasn't wearing robes. Please tell me everything that you can remember."

I recounted the situation, but carefully excluded my interactions with the Enforcer. The man's appearance, his insults, and the witnesses, I described in methodical and precise detail. Rhyanon did not take notes. Through it all, she was silent.

"That's enough," she said at last. She propped her elbows up on the table and rested her chin on her hands. *Weak neck muscles,* I thought. "Do you normally attract this level of trouble?"

"I'm not sure I understand, Herald."

"Hm. And this stranger . . . now, what was it that you said? He *repelled* your lace. Any idea how a man might suddenly be capable of using the Eater's power?"

"With respect, I can only tell you what I experienced."

"You must realise that this all sounds rather unlikely."

Another long silence.

"If you have no further questions, Herald, I can see myself out," I said, with all the politeness I could muster. I stood up.

She leaned back in her chair, examining her nails. "So let's say that everything you've told me is true. How *would* a man be capable of using the Eater's power?"

"He wouldn't."

"And yet . . ."

"Someone else could use it on his behalf."

Rhyanon's eyes widened in mock surprise. "Oh? Please explain, Acolyte."

"I'll be happy to, as soon as you tell me why the Deputy Chief of Civil Obligations is posing as a member of the Enforcement Department."

This time I did surprise her. She blinked, and her smile slipped. Then she laughed.

"Hah! I hadn't counted on you recognising me. Bit of a miscalculation there."

I said nothing.

"Oh, sit down." She waved at the chair. "And stop scowling."

"You set this up."

"Yes, of course I did."

"Why?"

"I wanted to test a few things. And I needed a private conversation with you."

"You could have asked for one."

"Well, I also needed collateral."

"Excuse me?"

Rhyanon looked pointedly at my chair. I hesitated, then sat.

"I'll sketch you a picture," she said. "A troubled Acolyte with a history of instability attacks a civilian in the Gardens. When questioned about the incident, she raves that the man wielded lace against her. Then her story changes. Suddenly there is a grand conspiracy at play. She starts talking about secret meetings with Heralds from other Departments. Heralds who possess irrefutable alibis."

I kept my voice even. "There were witnesses in the Gardens."

"Were there? When called upon to give testimony, they all present a rather different and consistent account of what happened. They say that the man did nothing to provoke you."

Her smugness was infuriating.

"So sad," she continued, "when a promising young Acolyte is martyred for—"

"What do you want?"

She grinned. Her teeth were straight and white. "I have a proposition for you. If you say no, I want you to forget this meeting took place. In return for your discretion, your preliminary incident report will get lost in the Enforcement filing cabinets."

"I would prefer it burned."

"Then how could I be sure of your ongoing silence? I'm sure you understand."

I nodded stiffly.

"Good," she said. "In that case, what are you doing tomorrow evening?"

"Herald, if you wanted a date . . ."

"Funny, but no. I need you to attend Reverend Olwen Kisme's party."

That caught me off-guard. "I'm not invited."

"I can get you onto the guest list." Her eyes glinted. "While you're there, I want you to take a look at some papers in Kisme's office. Nothing too delicate, but I need a bank account number."

Alarm bells were going off in my head. "Why?"

"Because I want to check the transactions listed against it."

"And you couldn't do this yourself?"

"Well, no. I would be a reasonably high-profile guest. You are more, um, obscure."

I rubbed my forehead. "You set this up so you could ask me to break into a Reverend's office?"

"Actually, I set this up with the hopes of forming a long-term arrangement. But for now, yes. That will do."

She smiled genially, and I found myself smiling back. Then I recognised the faint numbing sensation that had been seeping outwards from my temples since the start of the meeting.

Rhyanon was compulsing me. To do so to a citizen was taboo; to compulse a fellow Sister was unthinkable.

"You're mad," I said.

The pressure behind the compulse increased, demanding that I stay. With a thread of my lace, I severed the bond. Rhyanon felt it give way and frowned.

"I'm done here." I rose.

"I chose you for a reason," she spoke calmly, as if I hadn't said anything. "You have an excellent memory and a keen eye for detail. Your hot-headedness, however, might be a problem."

"You have the wrong woman."

"I can get you out of Renewal duty."

I thought that I had misheard her, but no, she had said those words, and now she observed me to gauge my reaction. Sly, calculating, like a snake watching a mouse through the grass.

I gripped the back of the chair, my mouth dry. "Excuse me?"

"Not the Renewal you're scheduled to perform tomorrow. But subsequently, it's a possibility."

She can't be serious. "How did you know—"

"That you're expected at the Wards in the morning?" She shook her head. "That would be telling. Suffice to say I know a lot about you, Elfreda. Your placement test results, for example, and the way you scored exactly seventy-five percent every year.

That your counsellor happens to be a childhood acquaintance, and she muddies the official records to allow you to skip sessions. Kamillian Vidar, I believe."

I stiffened.

"Relax," she said. "I'm not here to harm you. All I'm offering is an opportunity."

"What you're offering amounts to treason."

"I'm well aware of that. Are you saying no?"

She had me there. I hesitated a moment too long, and she continued.

"Think about it, then. A cab will be waiting on Reverence Street in the evening. Eighteenth bell. If you decide to attend the party, the driver will provide further details." She got up. "The choice is yours to make."

I didn't perform the gestures for respect due to her station. "I'll consider it."

She inclined her head in acknowledgement. "I'm glad to hear that. If you'll excuse me, I have a preliminary report to misplace."

Was it a trick? I wondered as she left the room. Some kind of cruel and extravagant test of my loyalty to the Order? And, if so, had I already failed?

The sun had travelled halfway across the sky when I emerged from the Detainment Offices. Rhyanon's words repeated in my mind.

I can get you out of Renewal duty.

So casual, so self-assured. If nothing else, the woman was bold. Difficult, then, to reconcile this smirking stranger with my memories of her daughter's naming ceremony.

The details surrounding the event still remained a little hazy in my mind. I had been young, perhaps eleven, and while I had not fully understood the situation at the time, I had been aware that everyone at the gathering was deeply uncomfortable. The guests spoke too loudly, and the conversation moved in circles. Rhyanon sat in the corner beside the cradle. She cried over her sleeping infant.

I remembered handing her the doll I had brought.

"What's wrong?" I had asked.

"Hush, Ellie," my mother scolded, but Rhyanon smiled and shook her head.

"It's fine, Kirane," she said. "I should pull myself together, shouldn't I? It's just . . . twenty-five is earlier than I expected."

My mother muttered something. We left soon after that, but not before Rhyanon slipped me a packet of caramel sweets. I felt too uneasy to enjoy them.

"What did she mean, twenty-five is earlier than she expected?" I had asked.

"It's her age."

"How can her age be earlier than she expected?"

"You'll understand when you're older," said my mother.

And I did. The older we are when we have children, the longer we live. Unless we're unlucky. My mother was unlucky.

I headed for the Gardens. Finn and Millie would be worried; I needed to apologize. I needed to invent an explanation for my disappearance. And then I needed to go home and think.

Although I already knew, deep down, that my mind was made up.

C H A P T E R

SEVEN

When the sun pierced the moth-eaten fabric of my curtains, I kept my eyes closed.

Acolytes in the neighbouring rooms opened doors and windows, and blurred voices seeped through the walls. Water gurgled up from the boiler in the basement. I had slept badly. My sheets tangled around me like vines.

Renewal duty. Again.

I sat up. Goose bumps prickled across my bare arms; the corners of my window panes were washed white with mist. Outside, the sky was overcast. A good thing. Less evaporation on cloudy days, a higher chance of rain. But I could not bring myself to care.

I dressed. No robes today, they would not be needed. I made my bed, and set a jar of salve and flask of water on my sideboard. Every movement took a conscious effort. One small action, then another. I squared my shoulders and left the dormitories.

The world outside had developed a raw, over-saturated quality. On the street, voices rang loud and crass. Colours smouldered. Even the air tasted sour, contaminated by the press of thousands of other people. I came to a stop halfway across the bridge spanning Pearl Boulevard. My skin burned, but the sweat running down my back was ice-cold.

First, I could hear Millie saying, *remember to breathe.*

In and out. I counted each exhalation and imagined myself alone in some vast, empty place, with only the sky surrounding me. I let the city fade.

Allow yourself to experience the fear. Denying the panic won't make it stop. You can't reason with feeling.

By slow degrees, the heart-thumping nausea began to recede.

But remember that feelings will pass eventually. The fear is real, very real and very frightening, but it's also only a reaction. The feeling itself won't harm you.

I watched the people pass below the bridge. Children, free from school for the rest day, laughed and shoved one another. A toddler sat on his father's shoulders. He stared up at me with enormous dark eyes.

I carried on. Left to join Weaver Road, then onto Calamite, then Steel.

The Renewal Wards pressed up against the eastern wall, overlooking the old execution grounds. Enforcers stood on either side of the front door.

One more time, I told myself. *One last time, and then Rhyanon said she would get me out of this.*

The Wards differed from the surrounding buildings. Thick walls, few windows, metal barbs around the frames and along the gutters. The plaster was chipped and stained with long streaks of dark mould.

I raised my wrist to show the Enforcers my tattoo. The women gestured for me to enter the building. None of us spoke or smiled, and I appreciated that. There was no expectation of social nicety here.

The foyer smelled of camomile and soap. The door on the left led to the cells; the one on the right to the purification chambers. A mosaic of the night sky covered the wall behind the front desk.

The Masked Sister on duty looked up when I approached.

"Elfreda Raughn," I said.

The woman's eyes glinted through the thin slits in her mask. She nodded, and noted down my name. Like all Masked Sisters, she wore gloves, a floor-length dress, and a head wrap that concealed her skin and hair. Everything was bone-white, from the mask to her shoes.

She indicated that I should continue. No matter the circumstances, she would not speak.

"This is the name given to me upon my birth, by my mother, Kirane, so named by her mother, Lenette." My voice was smooth as the surface of water. "This is the name I now forget, this is the affectation I lay aside."

The Sister drew a circle with her hands, absolving me of vanity. Shorn of my name, I followed her through the right door, into the first purification chamber.

The floor sloped to accommodate the pool in the centre of the room. Steam drifted up from the water. I took off my clothes and shivered. Sprigs of herbs hung from hooks in the ceiling. Their fragrance mingled with the warm steam, dizzying and humid and hard to breathe.

I lowered myself into the pool. The edges were rough as sandpaper and bit into my hands and the soles of my feet. I slid down until the hot water reached my chin.

"This is the body given to me by Kirane, so given by her mother, Lenette. This body is a vessel, this flesh is an oath. I give it freely."

The words were familiar on my tongue. Oblates rehearsed the verses for years before their induction, each syllable and vocal intonation practised until the words ceased to have meaning. I submerged my head and counted to thirty. From the doorway, the Masked Sister observed me. When I rose from the water, dripping, she drew the second circle to acknowledge my emptiness. I was of history, not blood.

We walked to the second chamber. The air prickled against my skin. Cooler here. The room was windowless and quiet; oil gleamed in shallow ceramic bowls on a stone table. Water from the pool gathered at my feet.

"To the Star Eater is this flesh committed. By the Star Eater is this flesh consecrated." I placed a drop of oil on my lips, throat, sternum. "All is as she wills."

The Masked Sister lifted a candle from the table and traced the flame down my chest. I did not flinch. It passed too quickly to burn me; I only felt the heat.

The Sister doused the candle between her fingertips and set it down. Then she bowed, gesturing reverence with splayed fingers. Until the completion of the rite, I would be equal in status to the Star Eater herself. And, from this point on, I was forbidden to speak.

Covered lanterns lit the Chamber of Renewal, casting soft, rosy shadows across the walls. The bed had new sheets and stood in the middle of the room like a threat. Another door on the left, and a silver bell beside it, which the Masked Sister rang. She took up her position behind the headboard, and I lay down. My breathing sounded loud in my ears.

All is as she wills.

All is as she wills.

All is as she wills.

The second door swung open. A Masked Sister entered. She bowed to me, hands spread. I gestured readiness—*as she wills, as she wills*—and the woman retreated from the room and ushered in her charge.

He was a large man. Not fat, just big, like someone out of perspective in a painting, a figure superimposed from a different scene. Late thirties, with smooth white skin and lank hair. Probably a Minor Quarter dweller, he had that bearing, maybe a merchant or craftsman. The Sisters had exposed him to the herbs for several hours to make him more susceptible to a compulse, which lent his eyes a feverish, wandering quality. He too was naked.

The lock on the door clicked. I saw the man's shoulders stiffen as the compulse took hold.

The Sisterhood had a simple problem, and it had devised a simple solution. Simple, efficient, multifunctional, and the foundation of our rule of Aytrium.

We could not fuck men without the risk of infecting them, but neither could we afford the death of our lineage. Only Sisters were able to wield the lace that preserved Aytrium.

And yet, who would have us? Who would we have? Men who strayed too close to the Star's fire got burned, so what we needed were men to set ablaze.

He staggered toward the bed.

And so, convicts. The only crimes that led to the Wards were murder, rape, and treason. The man before me had committed one of the three. Anything less than that, and he would be hauling rocks in the mines or waiting out a sentence in jail.

The first time, I had cried. Just once, and it had made no difference. After that, I learned to seal off a part of myself. I separated into my body and my mind, and only the body was hurt. Eleven Renewals, eleven men, and I knew the name and crime of every one of them, just as I knew which of them broke down, which embraced their fate with vicious abandon, which cried for their mothers, which begged for mercy. I bore their names inside of me.

One last time.

Compulses were only strong suggestions—they could not control a person entirely. My safety lay in the hands of the Masked Sister behind the bed. And although my body flinched, I never made a sound.

When it was over, they took him away. I shut my eyes. He might have been infected before he ever set eyes on me. The Order made the best use of its resources; a multitude of Sisters could perform the rite with the same man. A few weeks, then the signs would show. Maybe longer, maybe less time. It varied. But whether by my body or another, his degeneration was inevitable. Once he had outlived his usefulness, the Sisterhood would banish him to Ventris. Drop him like a stone into the clouded abyss, so he would never disturb Aytrium again.

The Masked Sister performed the gesture for gratitude and bowed out of the room.

We could not conceive without the rite, without sex, without *this*. We could not just take their seed and bury it in our bodies. That had been tried, over and over, but it seemed that for a Sister to fall pregnant, a man needed to suffer infection.

And so, somewhere below, my father and grandfathers stalked the unknown dark. My victim would join them, and wander, and hunger. Haunts never die.

CHAPTER

EIGHT

HIS NAME WAS Declan Lars, I later discovered. Murderer.

Swallows crisscrossed the sky. They flew low and swift over the slate roof of the dormitory and down to the street, veering without warning. I watched them through the open bathroom window.

Attending Kisme's party was the last thing I felt like doing. I shrank down so that my mouth was submerged by the bathwater. But I would, of course. A bruise cut across my ribs; I traced it with my fingertip. Of course.

Rhyanon's cab was probably already waiting. I needed to pull myself together.

I rose, sending water splashing over the rim of the tub, and wrapped a towel around my chest. My hair had curled into a wild tangle of black ringlets; I tugged it into order with my fingers. Outside my window, I could hear other Acolytes returning from work. Snippets of conversation, the rusted squeak of the front door, raucous laughter from the dining hall.

With a pang of unease, I realised I had last eaten yesterday. Between Rhyanon and the Renewal, it had slipped my mind.

Surely there would be food at the party? If not, I could get something from the Candle on the way home. I pulled on a dress, knee-length and pale blue. My mother had seldom attended these things, and I had never been invited before now.

A group of Acolytes from Judicial Affairs lounged in the stairwell outside my room, chatting.

"Where are you off to, El?" one of them asked.

"Going to see some friends," I replied.

"How nice."

As promised, a carriage waited at the end of the street. The heavy brown cart-horse watched me approach. The driver, apparently asleep, wore his wide-brimmed hat over his face and slouched sideways on his seat, legs dangling over the edge. The air was calm and mild, the faint breeze cooling my still-damp hair. Between banks of pale cloud, the first stars had appeared.

"Excuse me," I said, as I drew nearer the carriage. "I'm not sure . . ."

The man stirred, yawned, and lifted his hat. "Ah, Acolyte Raughn. Greetings."

My stomach sank, and I almost swore. This must be Rhyanon's idea of a joke.

The driver was the same man who had accosted me in the park.

"Huh." He sat up and studied my face with interest. "After last time, I was expecting more of a reaction."

"Just . . . just take me to the party."

"That's what I'm here for." He offered me his hand. His palms were heavily calloused. "Osan Jerone, at your service."

I ignored him and climbed into the back of the vehicle. He slid open the front-facing window.

"Admittedly, we might not have got off to the best start."

"You humiliated me."

"Not really. Everyone else was in on it."

"That makes it *worse*." I fixed my gaze on the road ahead and breathed out heavily. "Look, it doesn't matter. Can we get this over with?"

He looked like he wanted to say something else, but stopped himself. He gathered up the reins. "Sure. Your dress is in the box beneath the bench."

"I'm already dressed."

"Not for a Reverend's party." He clicked his tongue, and we rolled forward.

Rhyanon had misjudged my measurements. I didn't fill out

the bust of the dress, and it hugged uncomfortably tight across my hips. I spread the skirts around me, running my hands over waves of soft green velvet. Even ill-fitted, it was undeniably lovely. Tiny embroidered peonies danced along the shoulders and neckline, like a basket of flowers had been overturned above my head.

"Everything okay back there?" Osan called.

I don't belong in a dress like this. "I'm fine."

"It fits?"

"It's fine." I cleared my throat. "I'll pay her back, but I can't afford it right now. This seems expensive."

He snorted. "You don't need to pay."

I drew back the curtains. He glanced over his shoulder.

"The colour looks good on you," he said.

"What does Rhyanon want?"

"Don't use names in public."

Over the rattling of the wheels and the horse's hooves, I doubted anyone would hear us. "What does she want?"

Osan reached into his breast pocket and pulled out a bronze key. He passed it to me.

"You're looking for the file of someone named Kalis Nortem," he said. "A Herald working as an overseer for the Department of Water and Sanitation. She's fictional."

"Fictional?"

"The account belongs to someone else, and they've gone to considerable trouble to create Kalis on paper. Our friend is trying to determine who, and why."

He brought the horse to a halt, allowing a group of women to cross Forge Street.

"That key unlocks Kisme's office. Second floor, last door on the right. There should be a filing cabinet where she keeps copies of her subordinates' records. Memorise Kalis's account number." He politely nodded to the pedestrians. "Think you can do it?"

I tucked the key into the bodice of the dress. "I'm not sure yet."

"When in doubt, play it safe. If you get caught, you'll be on your own."

In the distance, the bells tolled out the hour.

"I won't get caught."

"That's the spirit."

We rumbled over the road, past other cabs and wagons, below bridges that spanned the broad streets and into the most opulent sector of the city. The Sisrin District of Minor East was occupied almost exclusively by Reverends and their consorts. Most also owned properties outside Ceyrun, but here was where the influential and beautiful came to play. I watched as the manors grew larger and the gardens stretched further.

"Nervous?"

I shrugged.

"Doesn't seem like much scares you."

"Meaning?"

We passed two Enforcers on patrol. More security than pedestrians around here, I thought. What a waste of resources.

"Well, you certainly weren't intimidated by me," said Osan. "Even after I started wielding lace."

I rested my hands on my knees. "That was Rhyanon, right?"

"Could have been." He glanced backwards and smirked. "But, like I said, you didn't seem scared, exactly. Furious, yes."

I huffed.

He laughed. "I was glad to have backup."

I was quiet for a while. Osan let the silence lie.

"Maybe you just aren't that intimidating," I muttered.

He laughed again, more softly this time. "Probably."

Ahead, carriages blocked the road. Harassed-looking porters tried to direct the chaos, and horses shied and tossed their heads.

"That's the place," said Osan. "If you don't mind the walk, I'll wait here."

"Thank you."

"My pleasure, Acolyte."

I opened the door, then paused. "Elfreda. Or just El."

"Just El it is." He slid his hat forward to shield his face. "For the record, I'm sorry I called you a corpse eater."

Kisme's other guests remained in their stationary carriages, waiting to get closer to the gates. I made my way between the vehicles, careful to hold my skirts above the ground. Osan had been right; I did not feel scared. Apprehensive, maybe, and uncomfortable, but the Renewal had left me too weary for outright fear.

When I reached the gates, the doorwoman beckoned to me.

"It's madness," she said. "You had the right idea by walking. Your name?"

"Acolyte Elfreda Raughn." I forced a smile.

She crossed out an item on her list. "Enjoy the evening."

Fine shards of mosaic glass tiled the path to Reverend Kisme's front door. They glittered like a track of crushed ice beneath hundreds of tiny paper lanterns. Suspended by reels of invisible thread, the yellow orbs revolved slowly in the air. I thought that their placement was random, and yet, as I continued along the path, the lights slid into alignment. Constellations of herons in flight, a fawn gazing at the moon, fish leaping skywards—each step I took revealed the complexity of their arrangement. A marvel of mathematical precision, but effortless in appearance. Around me, other guests murmured approval. The lanterns reflected in their eyes and made their skin gleam golden. In silken dresses and the low, warm light, they too seemed part of another world, gods passing through the night.

I shivered and climbed the stairs to the entrance. A band was playing somewhere, a woman singing. I accepted a flute of honey-coloured wine from the attendant in the foyer and swallowed it too quickly. The sweet alcohol stuck to the roof of my mouth like syrup. I gave the empty glass back and moved toward the ballroom.

A wide stairway led down to the dance floor. Sprays of snowflowers, white lace, and strings of amber beads dripped from the dark balustrades. From the landing, I could see the whole hall. The ceiling was high and vaulted, and sheets of saffron gauze swooped between granite joists. Women danced, or watched others dancing, and the band performed on a stage at the far end of the hall. The singer's voice rose above the hum of general conversation; the drums beat slow and seductive. Overflowing plinths of violets and chrysanthemums punctuated the floor, and candles set amongst the blossoms lit skin in dappled, shifting colour.

A couple smiled as they passed me, arms entwined. Never had I felt more out of place; I was adrift and I could not seem to find a sensible place for my hands.

"I find it's best to hold the fabric of your skirt."

I jumped, and the Acolyte laughed. I recognised her—Megane Tersi. Eight years my senior, she used to live in the neighbouring dormitory building—an accountant in the Department of Civil Obligations. With a group of friends, she had once organised a poetry reading for Martyr's Eve. At the time, Millie had been nursing a crush on her, so we had attended. I knew nothing about poetry—and found the evening boring—but Millie assured me Megane's work was excellent.

"At the sides, slightly back," she said, demonstrating. "Not too tight. It'll keep your shoulders from hunching."

"Thank you," I muttered, wishing I could sink into the ground.

"It's Elfreda, right?"

"Yeah."

"Shout if you need a dance partner." She winked, then carried on down the stairs to greet a Herald.

I watched her go. Out of my league, but still . . . I straightened, pushing back my shoulders as she had advised, and strode down the stairs. A hundred different perfumes—jasmine and orange blossom and musk and juniper—mingled into a heady blend.

The band struck up a new song. Old partners broke apart and formed groups of three. A young Herald grabbed my wrist and pulled me over to join her friend. I recognised the song and I knew the dance; it was popular in Major East springtime festivals. Although this version might be more formal, the basic sequence of steps was the same.

The Herald took the lead. Her date looked like a civilian, too old for an Oblate, but no tattoo. I dipped her, spun, and was lifted in turn. In the past, before my induction, I'd danced this with Millie and Finn. In the wavering light beneath the trees on Indigo Avenue, all of us wine-dizzy and laughing, Finn lifting me so easily, his hands warm against my waist, eyes bright, skin flushed.

I pushed the memory away, focussed on my footwork, step, cross, turn, cross, turn. The pace of the dance increased, but my partners never missed a beat. Other triplets stumbled and dissolved around us. Laughter rang through the hall. My chest ached. My eyes burned.

The musicians taunted us, raced ever faster, but we were quick enough, sure enough. The rest of the room was hazy, but within the circle of our three bodies, everything was clear. I was aware that we were being watched, but the other guests seemed far off and unimportant. Dip, spin, lift, all the world a blur around us. I wanted to drown in that moment. If I closed my eyes, I could pretend it was him.

Then Declan Lars's face flashed in my mind, a memory so clear and sharp that I could smell the oil and the herbs and taste the bile in my throat. I missed a step, just as the drums came to a stop.

The other dancers applauded, and the Herald gave a breathless bow. Strands of her hair had slipped free from her headband and brushed her jaw. Her civilian friend clasped a stitch in her side, grinning. There was a ring of open space around us; we were the only triplet to finish the dance. My hands shook, and the small of my back was damp with perspiration. Blood pounded in my ears.

The Herald clapped me on the shoulder. Her cheeks were pink. "You up for the next one?"

"I   I need water."

"Ah, no problem. Make sure you find us later, though."

I nodded, too out of breath for much else. A new song began, and I was alone again. My bruised chest throbbed.

I circled the edge of the floor, skirting the windows. Outside, guests strolled through terraced gardens, between domed gazebos and fountains. Tables with food were set out in the corner of the hall, but I could not eat. Not now. Muttering apologies, I pushed my way through the throng.

The passage beyond the hall was quiet and dim, and I could breathe more easily. A few guests wandered the corridors, speaking in low voices.

I found the washroom unoccupied. Fat yellow candles burned in glass bowls on the basin. I turned the faucet on and let the water pour over my hands. My reflection in the mirror looked ridiculous. This whole subterfuge was ridiculous. I drank from the tap and then shut it off. Who knew what Rhyanon wanted that account number for? I only had Osan's word that Herald Kalis Nortem was a false identity; she could very well be a real person. Rhyanon might intend to defraud a completely innocent woman. Or blackmail one; she clearly had experience in that area. My reflection scowled.

I can get you out of Renewal duty.

I walked with purpose, and nobody stopped me. The stairs leading to the second floor of Kisme's house were roped off. I made sure I was alone, then ducked beneath the barrier and hurried upstairs.

The second floor décor was simpler, wood-panelled corridors and soft green rugs. The floor creaked, but over the noise of the party, I doubted I would draw attention. I passed empty bedrooms and a painter's studio. On the easel rested a half-complete watercolour of leafless trees against a pale sky.

I found Kisme's office in the southern corner of the building, the only room with a lock on the door. I pressed my ear to the wooden surface and listened. No sound from within. I took the key out of the bodice of my dress, unlocked the door, and stepped inside.

Moonlight broke through the gap between the heavy drapes. I shut the door. The office overlooked the gardens; through the windows I could see the intricate constellation of lanterns, and the silhouettes of the city beyond the manor gates.

I could not risk lighting the lamp, so I drew the curtains further apart. Bright enough to read by, if I strained my eyes. The room contained three cabinets and a large desk. A huge ornamental fireplace took up most of the right wall, and a selection of pretty spun glass figurines decorated the mantel.

"Hope you're organised, Reverend," I muttered, and pulled open the top drawer of the closest cabinet.

She was. She had her records sorted first according to rank—one cabinet for Oblates, another for Acolytes, and the last for Heralds and Reverends—and then by name. I riffled through the neat pages, skipping ahead in the alphabet till I reached N. Many of the files were annotated with a cramped, small script; hard-to-decipher notes about a Sister's proficiency or misdemeanours.

Hah.

Herald Kalis Nortem on paper. I sat below the window, angling the file toward the light. No notes on this file; judging by her brief record, Kalis was thoroughly unremarkable at her job. And there, in sharp black ink, was the account number. TBN7825C.

I put everything back as I had found it and locked up the office. I could hardly believe that I had done it. Now all I had to do was return to Osan.

At the end of the corridor, the stairs creaked.

I froze. Swift footsteps, drawing near. I ducked inside the artist's studio and pressed myself against the interior wall, out of sight of the corridor.

"—can talk in private."

"I don't want to talk."

The plastered wall was rough and uneven against my back. I held my breath.

"You involved me in this mess, you don't get to run away from it." The first woman spoke in a low, forceful tone.

"We shouldn't even be here. Let's just go back to the party, okay? Please, Jesane?"

"Explain what you meant in the garden."

The footsteps had stopped; the women stood outside the room. Their shadows lay across the threshold.

"What is there to explain? They need the seat, and there's an easy way to vacate it."

"So murder is easy for you?"

"Don't be ridiculous. It's not murder."

"Sure. Tell me, if I step out of line, can I expect the same?"

"No! Eater, you don't understand at all." The shadow threw up its hands. "I don't like it, but it's necessary. These people will destroy the Sisterhood."

"How many?"

"What?"

"How many martyrs, Ilva? How many accidents?"

A long silence. My heart pounded, and there was a rushing in my ears, growing louder.

"I can't believe this." Footsteps, heading back toward the stairs. "I need some air."

"Jesane!"

I had to be wrong; somehow I had misheard or misunderstood. The band fell silent, and voices from below the floor hummed like a swarm of insects. I stepped away from the wall. My head spun.

The dance hall had quietened when I returned to it; the guests gathered around the stage. Reverend Olwen Kisme, dressed in black, was speaking.

"It has been a privilege and a joy to serve alongside so many of you over the years," she said. Her voice was hoarse. "To be honest, I feel that I could never spend enough time in your company."

I quietly made my way along the back of the hall toward the exit.

"But my time has come," she said heavily, with the intonation of someone who had practised the words for days. "It is an honour, and I take pride in my continued service to our Order and our home."

I paused at the base of the stairs. My mouth tasted of ashes.

"Thank you all for coming," she said, staring over our heads. "May the Star shine brightly on you."

As I left, the image of her unfinished painting haunted me. That pale sky and the blank paper, the bare trees and the shadows that they cast.

CHAPTER

NINE

ALL SISTERS FEARED three things, and the first was falling pregnant.

Oh, we pretended otherwise. We made a lot of noise about honour and duty and sacrifice, but in the secret heart of every Sister lay the knowledge that conception was the beginning of the end of our lives.

Our second fear was of Haunts. Immortal, insatiable, and vicious: they were difficult *not* to fear. The appearance of a Haunt also meant that one of us had broken rank, and a renegade Sister was always bad news.

And then we feared rot.

A little over a year ago, my grandmother began to decay. The infection developed from an incision beside her lumbar vertebrae, which went unnoticed until far too late. An inquiry was held, and the blame was pinned on a negligent Oblate.

As soon as I heard the news, I returned to my mother's house. She had smashed everything, all the plates in the kitchen, bottles, vases; she had torn apart books and clothing; she had ripped the curtains down. In the midst of the wreckage, she stood and glared at me. Her hands bled.

"This wasn't an accident," she said.

And that was how, three weeks after my birthday, I became a full initiate of the Sisterhood. My mother never reached the status of Reverend.

I sat beside her now, in the coolness of the Martyrium, feeling sick to my stomach. Helpless. I could not protect her, and as a result, I could not protect myself. How naïve, to assume that martyrs were sacred, that no one would think to use them for political gain. I gripped her hand. For years, I had believed my mother to be paranoid to the point of delusion, and yet, and *yet* . . .

"Did you know?" I whispered.

And if so, what else had she kept hidden?

I had given Osan the account number on the way back to the dormitories. The journey had been subdued; he must have sensed that I was upset. I changed into my original outfit before the carriage came to a halt, and carried Rhyanon's dress to my room in its box. Now it hung in my wardrobe. A reminder of the risks I was taking.

And already, only two days since the party, Rhyanon had a new task for me.

"I don't know what I'm doing," I said softly. "I wish you could tell me the answers."

My mother's face was unchanging.

"I miss you."

I performed the rite and took extra sacraments in case of an emergency. Then I lingered. The idea of leaving her alone filled me with dread.

But I was no one significant. I set down the scalpel and washed my hands. There was no target on my back. Besides, I could have misunderstood that conversation. I could be leaping to conclusions.

The Martyrium was busy; other Sisters stopped to greet each other on the stairs and left tokens at the feet of the Eater.

Reverend Belia Verje. Account shows huge payments for building materials delivered to her Farasni province estate. Have a look into her secret renovations? Your next R has been cancelled. Keep up the good work.

The note had been slipped under my door while I slept. No signature, no invitation to respond. I wanted to talk to Rhyanon about the conversation I had overheard at the party, but it seemed

I would have to wait. Walking into Civil Obligations and demanding a meeting was probably unwise.

I headed for Major West. Millie expected me in half an hour. Following a Renewal, every Sister was supposed to meet with their counsellor at the Minor West Guidance Centre. Records would show that I had turned up at the offices with clockwork precision for the last eleven months.

In reality, I had only attended three sessions. It was one of the many benefits of having a counsellor who was also my friend; I got let off the hook when it came to formal mental health evaluations. Millie and I still talked, of course, but the Guidance Centre reminded me of the Sanatorium, so I preferred to spend as little time in the building as possible. Today, we were meeting on the stairs outside the Major West Civic library.

When I arrived, Millie was standing with her elbows propped up on the banister, talking to Daje. I hung back. The two of them were caught up in a serious conversation; Millie kept shaking her head, and Daje's shoulders were slumped.

". . . reason with her, but maybe she'll listen to you?" I heard him say.

"I think I'd rather jump off the Edge," Millie replied. "But yeah, I'll try."

She spotted me over Daje's shoulder, and for an instant, I thought that she looked alarmed. Then her expression cleared and she smiled.

"Hey, El," she said.

"I didn't mean to intrude."

"Not at all." Daje turned around. "Here to steal Millie away from me?"

Millie and Daje's relationship had been going, on-and-off, for the past eight years. We weren't exactly friends, but I liked him well enough, and certainly more than I liked Hanna. He didn't seem to mind that I was a Sister either. Maybe he just hid it well.

"If she's available to be stolen," I said.

Millie grinned. "For you, I'm always available."

"In that case, I'll be off." Daje kissed her cheek. "See you this evening."

The library was a small yellow-brick building. Silver-leaf ivy covered the walls, and a neat row of orange trees cast shade over the patchy grass of the adjoining garden. Scholars read at the tables. A woman roasted candied nuts in a skillet and sold them to passersby.

"Sorry about that." Millie's hair was loose today, falling in waves over her shoulders. "I didn't mean to keep you waiting."

"Is everything okay?"

"Fine." She grimaced. "I have an ex who's making Daje's life difficult, that's all."

"Anything I can do to help?"

"Really, it isn't a big deal." She took my hand and started toward the trees, but I shook my head.

"Can you get me a stress pass?" I asked.

Millie's face fell.

Stress passes, issued by counsellors, entitled members of the Sisterhood to paid leave. In the past, I had only ever used two—once after my first Renewal, and once three months later—but I had not asked for them. Millie had made the call on both occasions.

I would not have asked now either, except that I needed to leave the city without the Sisterhood noticing my absence.

"Of course," Millie said quickly, recovering herself. "I'll put in the paperwork tomorrow."

"Thank you."

"Do you want to go somewhere private to talk about it? Maybe my place?"

I shook my head again. "I can't stay for long."

"Oh."

Her obvious disappointment and concern made me feel awful.

"Maybe we could meet in a few days," I said. "It's just not a good time."

"No, I completely understand. But, El?"

"Yes?"

"Is something going on?" Millie tilted her head slightly to the side. "Since Daje's birthday, I've been worried about you. Finn is too. You've been avoiding us."

I laughed. "Don't be ridiculous. I'm fine."

"You disappeared without a word."

"It was just a work thing that came up unexpectedly."

Millie's frown deepened. "You don't have to tell me, but something *is* bothering you. Are you in trouble?"

This was not going at all the way I had hoped. My goal had always been to keep my friends out of Sisterhood business.

"Have you been eating properly?" she pressed gently. "The anniversary must have been hard on you, so I'd understand if—"

I waved my hand, cutting her off. "I really am fine. About my mother too."

"Then what is it?"

I sighed. "I'm acting as a spy for a Herald in Civil Obligations."

She blanched. "You what?"

In a low voice, I explained what had happened. Millie listened in silence, and her face grew increasingly pale, especially when I came to describe my activities at Kisme's party.

"Eater, El," she said. "If you'd been caught . . ."

"It was a risk worth taking if Rhyanon can get me out of Renewals."

"The Sisterhood will skin you if they find out."

"That's inevitable anyway."

She scowled. "You know I hate it when you talk like that."

I made a placating gesture. "It might seem rash, but I—"

"So you need the stress pass to investigate this Reverend?"

I nodded.

Millie pursed her lips and gave me a long, appraising look. I tried to project confidence.

"All right," she said, after a moment. "But if you're really serious about this, then I'm going with you."

"Millie . . ."

"Non-negotiable."

I opened my mouth to argue. She arched one brow, and I shut up.

And that was how, by fifth bell, we were leaving the city together.

CHAPTER

TEN

THE SOUTH GATE, also known as the Main Gate, was the largest of the eight entrances to the city. Framed by the twin bell towers, it rose a hundred feet in the air; a wonder of lacework and architecture, all gleaming polished stone and intricate locks. It could only be opened from the inside, and then only by those with the Sisterhood's blessing.

That wasn't to say civilians hadn't tried to force it open in the past. Four centuries ago, a group of revolutionaries—the Ash Disciples—had made a serious attempt to topple the Sisterhood. Heretical in their beliefs, they had put forward that the Order was founded on lies—that the Sisterhood's domination was a perversion of nature, and the Eater herself nothing but a vicious tyrant. As the true and *rightful* rulers of Aytrium, they were in fact direct descendants of an elevated race of people. One untainted by our bloodline. Pure.

For all I knew, maybe they were right—the Order's pre-Ascension historical records were pretty hazy on the details. And the Disciples' story had a kind of romantic resonance; there was something chivalric and grand about the whole thing, about that exclusivity, about the idea of belonging to a better people. Even now, the story was whispered in certain subversive circles.

Accordingly, in the Disciples' view, the only just course of action was to slaughter half the Order's forces and drive the remaining Sisters into servitude. We were to feed the Pillars in chains.

Despite some flaws in this scheme, the Disciples' rebellion

proved moderately successful; they rallied the rural communities, and together managed to assassinate the Salt Pillar's Head Custodian. But it all fell apart when they tried to breach the South Gate.

With superior numbers on their side, they must have felt confident that they could break through the walls. The Disciples split their forces. Half to take Ceyrun, the rest to eliminate the Pillar Houses' remaining reserves.

In principle, this was sensible; in practice, catastrophic. The sitting Council directed the majority of the Order's forces to provide aid to the Houses. Twenty Heralds and eight Reverends stayed in Ceyrun to safeguard the city walls.

If the Disciples had thrown all their forces against the South Gate, who knows, maybe they would have broken through. Maybe if they had just laid siege to the city and let everyone inside the walls starve, they could have won. But I doubt it. The Sisterhood was never one to contemplate surrender; we would have burned Ceyrun to the ground first. I suspect that the Disciples must have known that too.

Their direct assault on the Gate failed. The walls held, and the victorious Sisters returned to obliterate every one of the surviving men. Caught between the wall and the Order, what hope did they have? There was no chance of escape or mercy.

After the battle, the Council razed the Fields and staked the Disciples' castrated bodies like scarecrows from Ceyrun to Halowith. It had the desired effect; no one had tested the South Gate since.

"Your frown is going to become a permanent fixture," said Millie.

I blinked, my thoughts interrupted. The Fields on either side were a hive of activity; workers were carrying copper pipes to the dig sites. The boreholes had struck water at last.

"I was going for 'brooding,'" I said.

That cracked a smile. "Are you certain you want to do this?"

"I've thought it through."

She glanced at me sidelong. "How do you know this Herald is trustworthy?"

We passed below a small copse of trees at the roadside, where the Sisterhood had set up a water station. Labourers queued in the shade, sweat shining on their faces.

"She's very careful," I said, once we were out of earshot. "And she obviously has the resources to cover her tracks."

"So she could throw you to the dogs at any time."

"She could," I agreed. "But I don't think she would, especially after putting so much effort into recruiting me."

"I don't know, El. That sounds an awful lot like wishful thinking."

"Her competence is reassuring. You should have seen the way she blackmailed me. Masterful."

Millie sighed.

At the crossroads to Halowith, we turned west toward the Farasni Hills. In other years, the valleys had glittered with lakes, and the hills had been green and lush. Many Reverends and senior Heralds held estates in this area, and divided their time between the countryside and Ceyrun.

When I was nine, my mother had taught me to swim at the reservoir on her friend's estate. I remember the oak trees that hung over the deep cold water, the smell of wet grass, and her voice. I remember that she had been happy sometimes, back then.

The road narrowed. Straggly wild lavender grew along the verge, and bees hovered above the flowers.

Reverend Belia Verje's house—more of a mansion, I suppose—sat at the base of a low hill. The yellow-brick residence was three storeys tall, with an ornate gable roof and pretty balconets outside the upper windows. Behind the main house stood cottages for the serving staff and a large barn. A five-foot-high stone wall surrounded the property.

Millie whistled.

"Verje *is* a Reverend," I said. "Not to mention that she's tipped for Kisme's Council position."

She elbowed me and grinned. "Someday you could live in a place like this."

"Sure. Briefly." I glanced down the road, then hoisted myself up the perimeter wall. The stones provided easy footholds and were warm from the sun. "Given the choice, I'd rather stay in the dormitories."

"Come on, think about *me*." Millie put her hands on the top of the wall and pulled herself up with a grunt.

"Are you asking to move into my hypothetical country estate, Millie?"

Her grin widened. "Are you offering?"

We dropped down on the other side, the sound of our landings muffled by the soft, clover-covered earth. Rows of tall trees screened the house from view.

"You sure you want to do this?" I whispered.

"Someone has to watch your back," she replied. "If I can't stop you, then I may as well help you."

The estate was quiet; even the birds fell silent as we drew closer to the house. Rotten figs littered the ground beneath the trees. The mottled purple skin of the fruits had shrivelled, and their juices bled into the soil, sticky under the heels of my shoes. The sweet odour of decay turned my stomach.

Such a waste, I thought. The figs should have been harvested earlier in the season.

Through the branches, I could see snatches of brick wall. Windows like eyes gleamed in the sun, and black smoke rose from the kitchen chimney. Clearly, someone was home. A narrow stretch of lawn divided the orchard from the house; we would get no closer without abandoning the shelter of the trees.

I waved at Millie, motioning for her to stop. The sun beat down overhead, and even the shade was stifling and humid. So quiet. My breathing sounded too loud in my ears.

"I want to look around the back," I muttered to her.

She gestured affirmation. Her cheeks were flushed.

The orchard ended a few feet from the house's rear wall. Beyond was an untended vegetable patch, with tomatoes sagging on their vines and swollen eggplants drooping over the rims of clay pots. The servants' quarters lay further off; the buildings were small and the windows shuttered. Silver fingers of dried ivy crusted the walls. The wooden frames were worn smooth and pale.

I frowned. It was too exposed here; if we emerged from the orchard, we would be entirely visible from both the mansion and the servants' houses.

Millie nudged me. She jerked her head to the left.

"What?"

There's a trench, she mouthed.

I followed her, and sure enough, a deep channel ran along the length of the orchard. We crouched beside it. Rough stones and mortar covered the soil. The trench had probably been used to carry water for irrigating the trees, but now a layer of dry silt covered the base, and flowering weeds poked out of the dirt.

"We can crawl up here to reach the back wall," Millie whispered, and pointed to a cluster of pines growing beyond the rear wall of the property. "Then we'll at least be able to scope out the rest of the place."

I looked at the channel, and then back at the main house. "Do you think it'll be enough to hide us?"

"If we stay low? The rest of this place looks deserted, so I think it will work."

I hesitated, still doubtful, but there didn't seem to be a better alternative. She waited. A film of perspiration gleamed on her forehead.

"Let's try it," I said.

We made our way on our hands and knees, Millie first. The midday sun scorched the back of my neck, blood pounded in my ears. She was right: the estate did appear abandoned. The rotting fruit, the untended gardens, the curtains drawn in the windows of the servants' houses: everything about the place seemed just slightly *off*. If not for the smoke rising from the chimney on the main house, I might have believed no one lived there at all.

A rusted pump stood at the end of the channel, and the faucet slowly dripped onto the moss-covered ground. The temperature was cooler; a draft ran along the perimeter wall, and the ground smelled damp, faintly musty.

Inside the house, a door slammed shut. We both flinched, and I glanced over my shoulder.

A man stood in the channel behind me. He stared right at my face, silent, silhouetted against the sun. He was naked. I jumped to my feet.

Millie swore. "What are you *doing*?"

The man's gaze bore into me. His eyes did not reflect light, but sat deep in his skull, cold as stone. His mouth was slack.

"For fuck's sake, El!" Millie yanked me back to the ground. I struggled to rise, and she gripped my shoulders.

"Tell me what's happening," she demanded.

The man took a step forward.

"You can't see him," I whispered.

There was something inside his mouth, something with legs, an insect or a spider. It crunched under his teeth.

Millie grasped my jaw in her hands and turned my face away from him.

"You're right, I can't see anything." She spoke urgently. "But El, I'm here. I'm right here."

She refused to let go of me. I could see the man in my peripheral vision; he took another step, and his shadow crossed my legs.

"Breathe," said Millie. Her hands were steady and cool, her blue eyes unwavering. "It's not real."

It's not real. It's not real. I inhaled. *It's not real.*

I closed my eyes and breathed out. When I nodded, Millie let go of my face.

"Don't scare me like that," she said.

This was too soon; I had only seen Finn three days ago. And I had never experienced visions while in Millie's company.

I opened my eyes. The man had vanished, although I still felt watched. Dead, vacant eyes. My skin crawled.

"We need to move," I said. "Someone might have heard us."

The trees hung low above the wall. Millie climbed over first, and then I followed. The hillside beyond was wild: nettles and long yellow grass, thorns and dry soil. I crouched, catching my breath.

"You okay?"

"Sorry." I shrugged and tried to keep my voice light. "Must be stress. Let's just finish this and head back to Ceyrun."

Millie hesitated. There was a familiar, stubborn light in her eyes, an expression I recognised from all our previous arguments on the subject.

"The visions are getting worse, aren't they?" she said.

I knew how it would go. Millie, telling me I needed to confess my problem to the Sisterhood. Me, telling her that the Order would sooner martyr me than help. She refused to see that it would be so much less complicated for them to put me to sleep. Less messy, less risky. Besides, even if they didn't martyr me, I'd still be sent to the Sanatorium.

"You're putting too much pressure on yourself," she said.

Millie never needed to think about Renewals, or Haunts, or rites. She could have whatever she wanted. Whoever she wanted. She could joke about country estates and never calculate how many years remained until someone started cutting her apart.

"You have to slow down with all of this," she said.

"I'm fine," I snapped.

She drew back, surprised by my coldness.

"I'm going to do this," I said. "Because you know what really puts pressure on me? Renewals."

"I didn't mean . . ." She bit her lip. "I'm just worried about you, El."

My resentment burned red hot, but I knew that I had hurt her.

"I'll visit Finn when we get back to the city." My voice came out hard and bitter. I swallowed, tried to soften it. "Look, Millie . . ."

"You're right, we should keep going," she said, and got up.

The wall ran straight along the base of the hill. Parts of it were crumbling with age, and long-dead ivy spread across the stones like grey veins.

In the distance, I caught the faint murmur of voices from the house, too indistinct to understand. Another door closing. A sudden cold wind rustled through the leaves of the trees above us and chilled the sweat on my face. Millie peered over the top of the wall.

"Found the renovations," she said.

I stood on my toes, and followed her line of sight. The barn doors stood wide open, but there were no farming implements or animals inside. Instead, mounds of loose earth were piled up next to the building, and the ground inside sloped steeply downwards beyond the door.

"I wonder what she's trying to dig up," Millie muttered.

I could not see much of the pit, but if the excavated dirt was anything to go by, it ran deep. Enormous steel panels lay stacked beside the entrance, shining in the sun.

"Maybe she means to bury something." I did a quick count of the number of panels beside the barn. At least enough to cover the floor of the building. "Something she doesn't want found?"

Millie shook her head. "Then this is far too conspicuous. If your Reverend had bodies to hide, she'd be better off throwing them over the Edge."

As I stared, the vision emerged from the barn. Despite the distance between us, I could hear him breathing. His skin was stained with mud, like he had crawled out of the ground. His eyes found mine, and for a few seconds, he just stared at me. I balled my hands into fists.

He turned away and began rubbing himself against the wall.

"I think we're done here," I said, my voice flat.

We kept to the perimeter wall until we reached the road. Millie noticed I was shaking, and touched the small of my back.

Although I shared most things with her, I would never speak about this vision, or the fact that the man bore a striking resemblance to Declan Lars.

C H A P T E R

ELEVEN

We reached Ceyrun as the sky darkened. Dusty workers queued at the gates, and an Acolyte checked their names off her roster one by one. At the roadside, an ox cart waited for indentured labourers to climb aboard. The convicts would be taken to lodges in the Berai province—their home until the completion of their sentences.

Millie had not said a word since we left Verje's estate. I was miserable, guilty, and increasingly anxious in the wake of her silence. This was unlike her; she was naturally expressive and carelessly sociable, but now her face was closed to me. Should I say sorry? Should I try to make conversation? Every topic that came to mind was either pathetically trivial or hideously self-involved, and while Millie had every right to be angry, I still wished that she would talk to me.

As a result, I was a little taken aback when she stopped at the corner of Swallow Road and apologized.

"What are *you* saying sorry for?"

Civilians passed us; we stood like rocks in a river. A grumbling man moved from one streetlamp to the next, lighting them.

"Oh, I don't know. For being insensitive, mostly," she said. "And for not being able to help you more. With, you know, Renewals. And your mother."

"Oh, come on, Millie."

"No, I mean it. A lot of the time, I kind of forget your situation."

"If anything, you're more patient than I deserve." I rubbed the back of my neck. My face felt too hot. "And actually, I wanted to say thank you. For today. And all the time, really. I, uh . . . I appreciate you."

Without warning, Millie stepped forward and hugged me. I made a small sound. Her grip tightened.

"You don't have to thank me," she whispered. She smelled like grass and dust and sweat, like summer. "But if anything else comes up, make sure that you tell me. Anything else your Herald asks for, I want to know about it."

I suddenly felt flustered by her closeness, acutely aware of her warmth and the softness of her hair. I swallowed. Nodded. She let go of me and smiled.

"Visit Finn, okay?" she said.

"I will."

I watched her until she vanished at the end of the road, feeling the ghost of her arms wrapped around me. She was renting a cheap room in Major West, six blocks from the South Gate. I knew that she could afford better, but Millie avoided spending money on herself. She had been that way ever since her parents died.

For the first time I could remember, I wished that I owned an estate. Maybe someday. Hanna could sleep in the barn.

The streets bustled as I made my way back up Pearl Boulevard. Merchants were setting up stalls for the night bazaar, laying out jade-coloured scarves and bronze jewellery, carved soapstone figurines and blown-glass ornaments. Moon Tide Eve was only a few days away, and business was thriving. Hungry, I stopped at a vendor selling deep-fried bean cakes. The seller dipped her ladle into the shimmering oil and fished out two, then wrapped them up in maize husks and handed them across.

As I accepted the greasy parcel, a quick movement in my peripheral vision distracted me. I looked to my left. The road was full of people, all of them moving, talking, bartering.

"Everything okay?" asked the seller.

"Fine," I replied quickly. "Thank you."

I paid her and hurried up the road. It was probably nothing, but I felt like someone had been watching me. I glanced backwards. Probably nothing.

The Candle was a double-storey bar, with a covered wooden deck that overlooked Milner Road. It had been converted from a run-down bakery eight years ago, and two of the old bread ovens remained to heat the place in colder months. Four large chimneys poked through the shingled roof. The tiles had a distinctive orange gleam, which, in the right light, made the building look like it was on fire.

I entered through the wide front door, sidling past a group of loud patrons. One of them—already reeking of alcohol—attempted to hug me, and I ducked out of the way. His friend reined him back in, calling out an apology. The night had scarcely begun, and already the place was packed. People shouted to be heard.

On the far side of the room, Lucian was working the bar. When he saw me, his expression soured.

"Hello to you too," I muttered, nodding in acknowledgement. A bull-necked merchant's son, Lucian had always disliked me—and since I had started working at Food Management, that dislike had morphed into outright animosity. While I was not personally responsible for taxing his father's business, I *was* the nearest available Sister. Lucian remained only too happy to hold me accountable for the sins of my department.

In all honesty, I didn't take it too personally; it was common for people to resent the Order. I mostly just tried to stay out of his way.

I made my way along the timber wall to the stairs at the back of the room. The air was stuffy; people occupied every one of the trestle tables, and still more were arriving through the front door, yelling to their friends over other patrons' heads. The mood was relaxed, good-natured. I felt prickly and out of place.

A stage filled a corner of the second floor; the sides of the platform stained deeper brown by years of smoke and spilt drinks. A few regulars swayed to the music. I leaned against the wall, out of the way of everyone else.

A wispy woman with black curls sang and beat a slow rhythm on her hand-drum. Finn sat in her shadow, picking at his eight-string with close concentration. His light hair had fallen forward over his eyes, but it didn't matter—he played by touch. Up there on the stage, he never noticed much; not the lights or the clamour, not even other people.

Some of my anxiety eased, and the pressure inside my head faded.

After Sefin Vidar wheezed out his last, spiteful breath, his grandchildren had inherited both his house and bookkeeping business. Neither of them wanted the business; Millie had run away six years earlier, and Finn would probably have preferred to burn the offices to the ground. So instead they sold it and used the proceeds to pay for college tuition. Millie studied counselling, but Finn went into music and philosophy, subjects without obvious practical applications. Which I suppose was the point. We all knew it would have killed Sefin to see his grandson happy.

But the old house, Millie kept. Neither she nor Finn would set foot inside it, but they still tried to rent it out. I wasn't sure if they were successful in finding tenants; when it came to matters related to their grandfather, I tried to ask as few questions as possible. Better not to re-open old wounds.

The song came to an end. The singer bowed, and the audience clapped, a few people cheering. Finn pushed back his hair at last and took a sip of water. The shifting play of the lights made him look gaunt and strange, but he was smiling, enjoying himself. He typically performed three or four times a week, more than that during the festival seasons. His gaze travelled across the room, and his face brightened when noticed me standing in the corner. I lifted the bean cakes in greeting.

It had been a while since I had watched him play. Work had kept me busy, especially as the drought dragged on. I headed back downstairs to wait for him while he packed up for the evening.

The Candle's loud, drunken atmosphere was only getting louder and drunker; the ground floor teemed with people. Someone had shattered a glass over by the door, and Lucian was clearing up the broken pieces. As I tried to sidestep the mess, he looked up and saw me.

"Here to meet Finn again, huh?" he said, with a knowing smirk. "You two seem to spend a lot of time together."

I kept my face neutral. "Hi, Lucian. Nice to see you."

"I heard about the Haunt from the other day." He straightened. "Makes you think, doesn't it? Wonder where he caught it."

"Have a good evening." I stepped out the door. "Pass my regards to your father."

I scored a point there; before I turned away, I saw rage flash across Lucian's face. I smiled grimly. Good. Not that I should provoke him, but after the day I'd had, I allowed myself a small moment of satisfaction.

Milner Road felt pleasantly cool compared to the Candle. A row of magnolia trees grew on the other side of the street, their glossy leaves lit warm yellow in the lamplight. I crossed over and sat down on the old bench under the branches. The sounds of laughter and shouting were muted here; I stretched and leaned back, tracing the weaving flight of a moth above my head. People passed by—couples, lovers, groups of friends. I was half in the shadow, and most of them didn't appear to notice me at all. Strange, how far away they seemed.

I breathed out slowly.

Millie could be right; I might just be under too much pressure. But the vision I had experienced today . . . I didn't even want to put words to it. Sick. Something was very wrong with me. And maybe my paranoia was foolish, maybe I should just ask the Order for help. Maybe someone would actually be able to fix me. Yet, even now, a deep-rooted instinct held me back. I could not shake the conviction that if the Sisterhood found out, they would martyr me.

Finn emerged from the bar. I sat up straighter, but before I could call out, Dajo appeared behind him.

"—question of loyalties," he was saying. "It looks odd, that's all. It's not that they don't trust you."

"And Millie?" snapped Finn. His shoulders were raised; he seemed annoyed. "How is the situation any different for her? I know where my loyalties lie."

Daje made an exasperated gesture. "As I said, I trust you. But you need to realise that appearances still matter. People don't think you're serious."

"Which people? Because if we're talking about Millie's favourite bad choice *again,* I really couldn't care less."

"Just be there, all right?" Daje performed a small gesture, a practised swivel of his left wrist meeting his right fist. "And try to understand where they're coming from."

Finn scowled, but returned the gesture. "Fine."

Careless, out in the open like that. Anyone could see you. I watched Daje turn and walk back into the Candle. Then I stood up.

"Finn?" I called.

He started and turned. Just like when I had surprised Millie earlier, Finn's face went a little pale at the sight of me. Wondering what I might have witnessed, what I might have overheard. *That'll teach you to be more cautious.* But he smiled, covering up his unease, and walked over to the bench.

"Why are you sitting in the dark?" he asked.

"Because it's out of the path of the drunks." I lifted the parcel of bean cakes. "These were probably better hot, but I thought you might be hungry."

"Starving." He gestured thanks and took one, his fingers brushing mine. "I didn't know you'd be coming tonight."

"Spur of the moment decision. That was a new song at the end, right?"

He nodded. "Did you like it?"

"Very much." I took a bite of my own bean cake. Spicy but soggy. Definitely would have been better earlier. "What did Daje want?"

Finn winced.

"What?" I asked innocently.

"It's nothing. Just people being stupid." He took a bite. Chewed and swallowed. "I'm going with him to sort it out tonight."

"So you're saying that you're too busy for me. You'll just take my terrible food and leave?"

His expression was pitiful. I reached out and lightly punched his arm.

"I'm joking."

"I know, but . . ."

"Finn, it's fine. Stop looking so serious." I held out the remainder of my bean cake. "Do you want the rest of this? Because I don't."

He wavered, then took it.

"I'll make it up to you," he said, glancing at me sidelong. The lamplight caught on his cheekbones. "I promise."

It wasn't as if I didn't know what Finn was involved in. I wandered back up the road alone. For his sake, I pretended to be oblivious. Well, maybe it was also a little for my own sake. Being a Sister, what could I possibly say? It seemed kinder to feign ignorance, easier to act like it didn't matter.

I sighed and crossed the bridge to the Wheren District, heading back toward the dormitories.

Eleven years ago, a group of civilians had formed an underground movement seeking to topple the Sisterhood. They were not very successful, creative, or organised, but they were *loud*. Subversive slogans appeared on the walls, department buildings were raided, unsubtle threats of violence hung in the air. It was nothing new; Aytrium had seen hundreds of similar protests. At the time, most Sisters regarded the latest iteration of the "Resistance" with something between exasperation and contempt. With one notable exception.

I remember feeling afraid when my mother broke rank. I'm still not sure how she won their trust, but she started attending a few of the civilians' meetings in secret. Once she even took me with her. I sat in a dark hall, listening to strangers while they talked about justice and tyranny and righteousness, and knew that—while everyone was polite and friendly on the surface—my mother and I were the enemy. Not to be completely trusted, but to be tolerated. Perhaps used.

Then someone in the Resistance poisoned a Herald. And although the Sister survived, the Order's patience finally ran out.

The night of the incident, the Resistance had met in a school hall in Major West. A lamp tipped over. What followed next was never made entirely clear; the Order only reported that flames caught, spread, and engulfed the room.

Not a single person made it out. In one night, Finn and Millie lost both of their parents.

Although it was never publicly acknowledged, my mother later told me that the doors to the hall had been locked from the outside.

CHAPTER TWELVE

After work, I confronted Osan.

Walking to Food Management that morning, I had noticed someone trailing me. They were careful about it, always keeping at least twenty feet away, dissolving into the crowd whenever I glanced backwards. To be certain I wasn't imagining things, I took a slightly more circuitous route to reach the offices. Sure enough, my shadow followed me on a pointless detour through Lokon.

Got you, I thought.

I bided my time. I pretended not to notice them during my lunch hour, or when my supervisor dispatched me to collect a report from the warehouse. When I left the office at seventeenth bell, I took Grove Street and then Lerish, acting like I was heading for the Gardens. Then, two streets away from the Lower-East entrance, I abruptly spun around.

Osan could not conceal himself in time.

"Oh, Just El," he said. "What a nice sur—"

"Why are you following me?"

A quick calculation took place behind his dark eyes. I glared at him. He sighed and stuck his hands into the pockets of his trousers.

"You're a little more observant than I anticipated," he admitted.

"Does Rhyanon think I'll double-cross her? How long have you been stalking me?"

"It's not stalking." He frowned, mildly offended. "I'm supposed to keep an eye on you, that's all. For your own good."

I could feel my blood pressure rising. "For my own good."

"Yes." He paused. "So I can make sure no one else is following you."

"Go jump off the Edge, Osan."

He lifted his hands in exasperation. "Come on, I was only watching your back. It's for your own protection."

"Take me to her."

"That's not—"

"If she wants me to put my life on the line spying on Reverends, the least Rhyanon can do is *talk* to me."

Osan hesitated, and then suggested, valiantly, "I can pass a message?"

I gave him a caustic look.

"Fine, but she's not going to be pleased," he grumbled.

I did not care. Osan led me on a winding route through Major West, past the greenhouses and around the Gardens. He moved quickly, but I noticed the way his eyes roved, his gaze shifting from street corner to alley to shaded doorway, ceaselessly vigilant. He seemed on edge.

Who does he think would follow me? I had done nothing to draw the Order's attention. Not yet, anyway.

"Just up here," he said.

Rhyanon's home was at the border of Minor East. A modest property for a high-ranking Herald, single-storey and rough-plastered. The garden was wild, overrun by oleander and bougainvillea, carpets of nasturtiums. An old dog slept on the front steps; he raised his head as Osan opened the gate, and his tail wagged.

I remembered this place. The name-giving celebration, the sugary sweetness of Rhyanon's gift. The dog sniffed my feet.

"A word of advice?" said Osan, resting his hand on the gate. "Don't involve your friends in the Order's business again."

The hair on the back of my neck stood up. I leaned forward to knock on the front door, and when I spoke, my tone was perfectly controlled. "Why do you care anyway?"

"More people involved, more opportunities for mistakes. More opportunities for someone to get hurt. Think about it, all right?" He closed the gate and stepped back. "See you around, Just El."

"Not if I see you first."

The door opened.

Rhyanon wore a long green shirt and cotton pants. Her hair hung loose, which made her look less severe. Relaxed, she seemed almost pretty. Her features were soft and animated, and she had a distracted smile on her face, like she had been laughing a moment earlier.

The expression vanished the instant she saw me.

"What . . . what are you doing here?" she asked.

I folded my arms. "We need to talk."

Rhyanon peered down the street. Osan had melted away, and we were alone in the evening twilight. "You couldn't have waited? I was going to arrange a meeting for tomorrow."

"You told me you needed information, and I risked my life to get it. Why would I wait?"

She was still flustered, grasping the edge of the door to block me from entering. "I do appreciate your efforts, but now isn't the best time. You shouldn't be here. Tomorrow—"

"People will notice if I keep missing work. I already had to take a stress pass for yesterday."

"I see." But she didn't move.

Annoyed as I was, I couldn't help but wonder at her reluctance. I had expected her to be irritated, and instead she seemed alarmed.

"It won't take long," I said.

She wavered, unhappy, then nodded.

"Yes. Yes, of course. Osan brought you here? I would have expected more discretion from him." She stepped backwards to open the door wider. "Come in."

The entranceway smelled of beeswax polish and sandalwood. Small details drew my attention: fresh flowers in a glass vase, books arranged by colour on the shelf, hand-painted bookends in the shape of stretching cats. Pretty, homely things. Things I wasn't supposed to see. Somewhere in the house, I heard a door close.

Rhyanon's jaw was clenched. She watched me out the corner of her eye.

"Let's talk in my study," she said.

"Mom?"

A scrawny, straw-haired girl, ten or eleven years old, hung in the doorway to the kitchen. She chewed on the end of her ponytail.

"Is everything okay?" she asked.

"Everything is fine, darling." Rhyanon's shoulders were tense. "This is Elfreda; she's a friend of mine. Elfreda, this is—"

"Jaylen," I blurted out as her daughter's name finally came back to me.

The girl regarded me with large moss-green eyes. She had a turned-up nose, and a sharp chin. Unfriendly, unsmiling, steady in her gaze.

Rhyanon interrupted our staring match. "Yes, that's right. Jay, I need to have a quick conversation with Elfreda, and then we can finish the costume. Can you go to your room until then?"

She nodded slowly. "Are you sure everything is fine?"

"Absolutely. Off you go."

Rhyanon's study was a mess. Papers were strewn across her desk and stacked in dog-eared heaps. Mostly financial statements and records of transactions, all bearing the stamp of the Department of Civil Obligations.

She closed the door behind me. "Take a seat."

"Thanks." I cleared a pile of folders off her spare chair and set them on the ground. "Costume?"

"For Moon Tide," she said shortly. She drew her floral curtains across the street-facing window.

"Oh, of course." I found it difficult to imagine Rhyanon sewing. Difficult, and faintly amusing. "You've probably forgotten, but I was at her name-giving."

She paused, still holding the edge of the curtain. "You were?"

"You gave me sweets."

Her brow furrowed.

"I remember Kirane being there," she said. "She was the only person who didn't congratulate me."

Hearing her say my mother's name gave me an odd, out-of-place feeling. I gestured apology. "She could be thoughtless."

"I believe it was the opposite, actually." Rhyanon shook her head. "So you saw my public meltdown?"

"I wouldn't call it a meltdown."

"Everyone else did." She snorted. "Horrendously embarrassing. For years, I was a joke in Civil Obligations. The incident cost me a promotion, you know. Not to mention I got sent to the Sanatorium for a month."

I was silent.

"What, that surprises you?"

"No," I said, stung. I felt defensive, although I wasn't sure why. "Of course not."

"Ah yes, because you're the expert on the San." She smiled, a cold and deliberate movement of her lips. "Have you lost weight since I last saw you?"

She was trying to goad me into losing my composure, to reclaim the upper hand after I'd trespassed on her private life. I looked at her, and I understood her cruelty. I had made her feel vulnerable.

"Actually, I was thinking that you were unjustly treated," I said. "I'm sorry. Truly."

Rhyanon's mouth tightened. For a moment, I thought she would tell me to get out of her house.

Then she looked away and sighed.

"You're quite like your mother," she said, in a different voice. "I didn't see it at first, but sometimes you sound exactly the same."

I tried to affect nonchalance, but couldn't quite pull it off. "In what way?"

"You share a certain forthrightness, I suppose." Rhyanon

leaned back in her chair. "Kirane was my supervisor for a few years. She wasn't always an easy person to be around, but I admired her."

A strange kind of hunger rose up inside me. Now wasn't the time to ask questions; Rhyanon would only leverage my weaknesses against me. And yet I could not help myself.

"At Kisme's party, I overheard women talking about . . ." I hesitated, struggling with the word. "Accidents. In the Martyrium."

Rhyanon said nothing, and my nerve faltered.

"I probably misunderstood."

She breathed out heavily. "I know what you're trying to ask. But I'm not sure how to answer you."

Her voice was surprisingly gentle. My mouth went dry.

"So it could have—" I swallowed. "Someone might have wanted to martyr my mother?"

"It's happened before."

"Does it happen often?"

My mother in the kitchen, telling me that it was no accident. My mother burning with rage, then gone. The quietness of her house. I felt suffocated.

Rhyanon spread her hands. "It's possible, but I don't know. I'm sorry, Elfreda."

"No, it's . . . I don't suppose it changes anything now anyway." I gripped my hands together in my lap, trying to gather myself. Later. I could deal with it all later. I should not have asked in the first place. "The woman I overheard at the party said that someone intended to destroy the Sisterhood. She said that they 'need the seat, and there's an easy way to vacate it.'"

Something shifted behind Rhyanon's eyes: a strong feeling stifled.

"Saskia," she murmured.

"What?"

She shook her head, and the emotion disappeared. "Commander General Saskia Asan. They were probably referring to her seat."

"You're saying that this extends to the Council?" My mind reeled. I held up my hands. "Wait, do they think *we're* the ones trying to destroy the Sisterhood?"

Rhyanon gave me a hard look.

"*Are* we trying to destroy the Sisterhood?"

"Not exactly, but would you have a problem if the answer was yes?"

Of all the heretical, insane things I could have suspected of Rhyanon, this possibility had never occurred to me.

"Not exactly," I said faintly.

She smiled, amused.

"I thought as much," she said. "I'll warn Commander Asan, and we'll take further precautions to protect her mother."

"This is—what are we doing? Who else is involved?" My head was still spinning. "What—"

"You are safer not knowing," she interrupted.

"That's not—"

"If anything happens to me, trust Enforcement. That's all the information you need."

No, you *are safer if I don't know enough to sell you out.* But I bit my tongue. Rhyanon seemed unperturbed by my scowl.

"Do you have anything else?" she asked.

Oh, nothing on the scale of destroying the Order, no.

I shook myself. "Possibly. I looked into Verje's renovations."

"And?"

"She's dug a pit inside her barn, and has sent away all her estate's regular staff. The farm was badly neglected."

Rhyanon looked mystified. "A pit *inside* her barn?"

"Yeah. And there was a lot of metal sheeting stacked outside. Whatever she's doing, it seems unfinished."

She chewed on her lip. "How odd."

"That was my reaction." I stood up and straightened my robes. "Anyway, that's all I had to tell you. But one more thing, before I go."

"Yoo?"

"Call off Osan."

Rhyanon gave a little shake of her head. "And there I thought he would be subtle. I'll talk to him. And good work, Elfreda. This was valuable."

Jaylen watched me through a gap in the curtains as I left the house. When I waved, she vanished. I shoved my hands into my pockets. Children were not my forte. I walked out into the warm evening, mosquitoes droning in the heavy air.

Destroying the Sisterhood?

If they had really sent my mother to the Martyrium before her time, maybe that wasn't the worst idea.

CHAPTER THIRTEEN

THE AIR INSIDE the hothouse was humid. I sank my gloved hands into the tray of dark, loose compost and delved around until I found a grub. The fat white creature squirmed in the sunlight filtering through the glass windows overhead.

Probably ripe enough. I tossed it into the box for processing.

Aside from the earthworms which the Sisterhood distributed to farmers throughout Aytrium, the Vilitir Wormery was also home to sixteen other species of insect. *Easy to breed, easy to feed* was our project's unofficial slogan; the bugs weren't fussy, and we put the city's refuse to good use. In the last six months, the Department of Food Management had expanded operations threefold in anticipation of food shortages, and I had learned a lot about the versatility of insect ingredients. For example, the tiris beetle—the object of my present search—could be ground up in the larval stages to form a sweetish grey paste. We salted the pulp and stored it in glass jars, as a kind of meat spread. Well, bug spread. It didn't taste that bad on bread.

Zenza, my supervisor, was collecting locusts in the next room. Those had yet to win me over. Too many legs. I harvested enough grubs to fill my container, sealed it, and stacked it neatly on top of the other seven boxes.

"Sleep well," I said, and pulled the shade cloth back over the trays.

Next week, we would be visiting the fish breeding tanks outside Halowith. The week after was the mushroom tunnels in Beral. Reverend Somme's new greenhouses were nearing completion, and on top of everything else, we still had all the regular paperwork to file. Progress reports and evaluations for Somme, forecasts and projections for Civil Obligations, applications for increased water supply from Water and Sanitation. To my profound discomfort, the last now needed to be addressed to Reverend Belia Verje. Olwen Kisme had been martyred yesterday.

I tucked my gloves into my belt and carried my grub boxes to the wagon. Zenza emerged from the locust room as I set down the last one.

"Ah, you're done," she said. "How are they?"

"Healthy, but we might want to keep the soil a little wetter."

"I'll put in a request for additional spraying." She picked a stray locust leg out of her curls. "The spurwings have spawned very well. Creepy little bastards."

"They aren't my favourites."

She passed two of her boxes up to me. "It's the red eyes. And the legs. And the weird noises they make when you grab them by the thorax."

Her boxes buzzed ominously. I set them down beside mine, careful to keep the lid sealed. If the locusts got loose, they could decimate our remaining crops. Zenza climbed onto the wagon beside me, and the driver flicked his reins, encouraging the mules forward.

"Are you okay?" she asked. "You've been even quieter than usual."

"Oh, I'm fine."

"Any plans for Moon Tide?"

"I thought I could work through some of our outstanding grant applications."

She favoured me with a look that was part disgust, part admiration. "On your day off? Really?"

"Nothing better to do."

"That's . . . kind of sad."

"Do *you* have plans?"

By the time we reached the city, I possessed a comprehensive understanding of my supervisor's love life and menu plans for the holiday, as well as an update on her opinion of everyone else in the department. I nodded at appropriate points in the conversation, and made various sounds of approval or concern. This was the foundation of my relationship with Zenza; she talked, I listened. We got along well enough. I think she liked me, even if she thought I was a little odd.

The driver brought our wagon to a stop behind a queue of people at the Upper East gate.

"Here for Moon Tide, presumably," said Zenza. "I hope the inspections don't take too long."

Judging by the sour expressions on most of the farmers' faces, I suspected we would be waiting for a while. Not that I minded; the breeze was warm and soft, and it felt good to be out of Ceyrun. I stood and stretched my legs. Ever since my conversation with Rhyanon, I had found the city oppressive. The Martyrium loomed large over everything, and my thoughts spiralled endlessly back toward my mother. Who she might have offended, what she might have done. Outside, at least I felt like I could breathe.

A murmuration of starlings swooped through the air above us. They flowed like silk toward the city wall, a ribbon caught in the wind. Then they smashed into the ramparts.

"Hmm?" Zenza glanced at me.

The birds did not fall. They dotted the top of the wall like darts thrown into a board. Thin steaks of blood rolled down from their tiny crushed skulls.

"It's nothing," I said, and sat down. "Won't you be late meeting Faye for dinner?"

"Probably."

"Then let me take the boxes to the warehouse."

She smiled. "It's kind of you to offer, but that's not necessary."

"I don't mind."

"No, look." She pointed at the queue. "We're moving now

anyway. But maybe you could drop the paperwork back at the office afterwards?"

"Sure."

The starlings' bodies turned silver as we passed under them, gleaming, profane bundles of broken wings and splayed feathers. I kept my eyes on the road ahead. I had to keep my composure in Zenza's company.

Inside the walls, the throng thinned as the travellers dispersed. Three men in overalls were setting up for a fire-dancing show on Bell Square, laying out sand-coloured rugs. One of them caught my eye and waved. I didn't recognise him, but I nodded in return. He grinned.

The warehouses were only two blocks from Food Management's headquarters in Major East. Our driver skillfully navigated the busy roads and took a shortcut through the outskirts of the Crin District, where the streets grew quieter. Shouts and laughter drifted over the rooftops from the direction of Pearl Boulevard.

"I'm amazed that the Council didn't call off the festivities," said Zenza under her breath. "In two months, the Reverends will be eating spurwings with the rest of us."

I snorted. "At least Reverend Somme will get to say that she told them so."

"Over here, Sister?" the driver asked.

"Thanks, that will do nicely."

The wagon stopped and Zenza jumped down. I handed her two boxes. The warehouse was an ugly, square building. No windows on the ground floor, rough-plastered walls, and a deep basement filled with a variety of preserved produce. The best that could be said about the place was that it was secure and dry.

Zenza wedged the boxes on her hip and unlocked the reinforced warehouse door. I lit the interior lamp, revealing a short, low-roofed corridor. We took the stairs down to the basement, where rows upon rows of sterilized glass jars waited to be filled. I left the lamp with Zenza and fetched more of our boxes. Other Acolytes had the unenviable task of processing the insects; we just had to deliver them here.

I brought down the last boxes, and Zenza shook the locusts into their holding tank.

"You're sure you don't mind dropping off the reports?" she asked.

"I'm sure."

She grinned. "I owe you one."

It really wasn't a big deal. I had planned to head to the dormitories afterwards, and our office was only a little out of my way. I waved goodbye to the driver as I left the warehouse. If my visions were flaring up again, I was better off on my own.

I climbed up the narrow, weed-choked stairs to Herts Street. A man dozed inside his soup kiosk, his pot of vegetables simmering gently as he snored. Dogs barked in the distance. The buildings in this district were largely residential, the people who lived here older and less affluent than the merchants of the western quadrants. Small potted plants nestled inside private window boxes: herbs and vines of tomatoes and wilted geraniums. Bird nests and feathers choked the rusted old gutters.

Finn's grandparents had lived four blocks south of here. Back then, the contrast between their house and the rest of the street had been striking. Clean. Nothing out of place. Nothing growing. It had always smelled of lye. An iron trellis ran up the back wall of the building. I had climbed it once, in the middle of the night, but that had been a long time ago now. Millie might have taken it down.

Chester Street curved steeply upwards toward Minor West. Halfway along it, I stopped and turned around.

"I thought I told you not to follow me, Osan," I said.

The sign for a bookshop swayed in the breeze, but everything else was still. A shiver ran down my spine. I had been so sure that I had heard footsteps.

"Osan?"

The offices were only a block away. I swallowed and hurried onwards. With everyone celebrating Moon Tide, the district felt unusually quiet.

There again.

I glanced over my shoulder, quick enough to catch the movement of a shadow at the end of the street. I reached for my lace. It could just be a stupid kid or a stray animal, but the way they were trailing me—out of sight, cautious, from a distance—felt too deliberate. Predatory.

"I know you're there," I called. My voice did not sound as confident as I would have liked.

No one answered.

"Fine," I said, and kept walking. The thread of lace burned inside me.

You are a Sister, I told myself. *No one can hurt you.*

I walked a little quicker.

Except other Sisters.

The Food Management Offices lay ahead of me. The wide steps leading to the main doors were swallowed in shadow; the lanterns at the end of the road had not been lit tonight.

That could not be an accident. In my head, my mother repeated, *not an accident, not an accident, not an accident.*

Ahead, I caught sight of movement in the darkness. My heart stuttered, and I froze.

"El?"

I almost slammed my lace into Finn's chest. I changed the rope's course at the last moment, and the force hit the wall with a crunch.

"Whoa!" He raised his hands. "It's just me."

I clenched my fists. That had been close; that had been *far* too close. I would have probably broken his ribs.

"Sorry," I said tightly.

"What's wrong? Are you okay?"

"I'm fine." I hurried toward him. "What are you doing here?"

"I wanted to catch you after work," he replied, and looked a bit sheepish. "I said I'd make it up to you? For the bean cakes?"

I breathed out. "Right, of course."

"What's going on?"

"I can't explain right now." I steered him toward the security of the offices. If I was being followed, I didn't want my pursuer to see Finn. Osan's warning about putting my friends at risk rang all too clearly in my mind.

"Are you in trouble?"

"It's probably nothing." I unlocked the glass door. My hands were clumsy; I fumbled and dropped the keys. Finn touched my arm, concerned.

"El, you're shaking," he said.

I ushered him inside and closed the door behind us. Through the pane, the street was dark; the lamps cast isolated rings of light on the cobbles at the far end of the road. I locked the door from the inside.

"I've got to file a report and then we can leave through the back." I pushed my hair away from my face and forced a smile. "Hi. Sorry about all of this. Moon Tide blessings upon you."

"Is there someone out there?" He craned his neck to see around me.

"I don't know." I blocked the entrance. "But it doesn't matter now."

"Of course it matters. I could take a look around, see if—"

"*No.* Absolutely not." I took his arm and pulled him deeper into the room. "I'm probably only imagining things anyway."

"You don't believe that. Something's really bothering you." He allowed himself to be dragged along. "And you don't want to involve me, so . . . You think another Sister was following you?"

"I don't think anything." That was exactly what I thought.

"I can take care of myself, you know."

"Yes, of course," I said distractedly, and stopped at the base of the stairs. "Wait here."

He muttered something I didn't catch.

"What?"

"I said, 'Happy Moon Tide to you too.' Go file your report."

I hesitated.

"I'm okay, El." His face was half in shadow. "Really. I hate seeing you scared, that's all."

"I'm sorry."

"There's nothing to apologise for. Go on. I'll wait."

I hurried upstairs. The offices were eerie at night; all the empty rooms and locked doors, the usually bustling corridors silent. I slid Zenza's papers beneath Reverend Somme's door, then crossed over to my own office. There was a new stack of memos in my inbox, yellow slips from the accounting division, nothing urgent.

I shrugged off my work robes and stuffed them under my desk. Beneath, I wore ordinary civilian clothes. Without the uniform, people would not immediately recognise me as a Sister. I returned to Finn.

"Everything under control?" He straightened.

I nodded. "Thanks for coming to meet me."

"No problem. So, about making it up to you—will you let me buy you a drink?"

"Tonight?"

"Yeah."

"Is that a good idea? People might . . . well. I don't know. It is Moon Tide, after all."

"If you don't want to, it's fine," he said gently.

"No, I *do*. Of course I want to. You know that's not the problem." I was flustered. "I'm just worried about what people will think."

"Let them think what they like, El. Besides, no one's going to recognise you. No one important, anyway."

I wavered.

"You have to take a break sometimes," he coaxed. "Have fun. Live a little. Like you said, it's Moon Tide."

I sighed. "You sure about this?"

"Of course."

"Then at least let me buy." I rubbed the side of my neck. "As an apology for the terrible food last time."

Finn grinned. "I guess I can live with that."

C H A P T E R

FOURTEEN

We left Food Management through the back entrance onto Grove Street, and crossed over the Stonelay Bridge to loop around the edge of the district. Only after we reached the line of dark, shining greenhouses did I allow myself to relax. Finn was right; I needed a break. My visions had probably been getting worse for a reason.

He had been quiet for most of the walk, but when I caught his eye, he smiled.

"So, how are your spurlegs?" he asked.

"Spurwings."

"Right. Those."

I tucked my hands into my pockets. "Not too bad. The adults have finished breeding, so they're ready to be harvested, and the new eggs will hatch in about two weeks. We're thinking of increasing the temperature of their habitat; see if it makes them grow larger."

He tilted his head to one side. "Really?"

"It worked surprisingly well for the waxbeetles, but only when we also lowered the heat during their egg and larval stages. That seems crucial; my theory is that the eggs are usually dormant and buried until the end of winter, so early development occurs more naturally in colder conditions."

"Like they hibernate?" he said mildly.

"Exactly! It's quite funny; you should see when they hatch." I found myself laughing. "All of them worm over to the west-facing trays to catch the afternoon sunshine. The manager thought they'd escaped the first time it happened—it was hilarious. And then, six weeks later, they're almost twice as large as their parents. So we try it with the next generation: same results. Obviously we can't let them get too hot either, because that seems to interfere with their reproduction, and they become strangely aggressive." I paused, and my face grew warm. "Feel free to stop me at any time."

Finn broke into a sly grin. "So do you name them?"

"Oh, shut up."

"Make me. How many generations can you breed in a season?"

I tried to look resentful. Unfortunately—as Finn was well aware—I also really wanted to keep talking.

"For the waxbeetles, one, and the spurwings are even slower. But tiris beetles? Two to three." I resisted the urge to launch into a second lecture on the subject of the grubs' favourite foodstuffs. "There are a lot of variables."

"And how much bug jam does that amount to?"

I made a face. "*Preserve,* thank you very much."

"Okay fine. How much 'insect preserve'?"

"We want to fill the Major East warehouse within the next three months."

He glanced at me, noticing the change in my voice. "Will you?"

"There are a lot of variables."

"Like how quickly the other food runs out?"

"Well . . . yeah." I hesitated, then made an effort to sound more positive. "But some of the harvest is still coming in. And the boreholes are now operational in the Fields, which means we might be able to rescue most of the grain."

"El."

I came to the mouth of the Agate Bridge. A steady stream of people flowed past me, heading for the stairs down to Pearl Boulevard. I turned to Finn, and his expression was grave, his usual easy carelessness gone.

"Maybe four months?" I said. "Until our stockpiles are

completely depleted. We have enough drinking water for six months, assuming that there's no rain at all."

He flinched. "That bad?"

"We've been saving for almost a year. It's just . . . there are so many people to feed."

Finn grimaced. "But then why aren't we rationing? How can Ceyrun possibly afford"—he swung his arms wide to encompass the Moon Tide market below us—"all of this?"

Pearl Boulevard was a riot of music and colour. Hundreds of people flooded the road, shopping, talking, watching entertainers tumble and sing and recite crude jokes, modelling for street artists, arguing about prices. Costumes, children, pork fat sizzling in frying pans, hand-embroidered scarves and shirts stained with wine, hawkers shouting, the smell of spiced lamb, smoke from open fires, shrieks of laughter, and in every direction the festival spread and continued, more chaos and more abundance.

"I don't know," I admitted. "It's complicated. Political."

"So the Council is just going to sit on their hands?"

I made a noncommittal gesture.

"What, you support them?"

"Finn, can we not do this? What I think is irrelevant anyway."

His expression darkened. "So what's the plan; they just wait until people are actually starving—"

"It's not that simple—"

"—and then sit in their mansions and feed on the corpses?"

I lost my breath for a second. Finn instantly realised he had made a mistake; he paled and unconsciously raised his hand like he wanted to pull his words back. I turned away from him.

"Oh, okay," I muttered.

"I'm sorry, I never meant—"

"No, of course not." My voice was hard and flat. I crossed the bridge and started down the stairs. Finn had to break into a jog to catch up with me. "That's just how your friends talk. Of course it rubs off."

"What . . . what do you mean?"

I snorted, lengthening my stride.

"El, come on. You know I wasn't talking about you. Why are you so angry?"

"I'm always angry. And by the way, the first food regulations are coming into effect this week. Feel free to pass that along."

"What are you—"

"Eater, enough." I rounded on him. "How stupid do you think I am, Finn? You think I don't notice whenever you start plying me for information?"

"Wait, *what*? I wasn't!"

"Yeah, of course. You're just really interested in beetles." To my dismay, my voice cracked. Finn reached for my arm, and I stepped back.

"I get it." I waved him away, skin crawling. "I get it, I really do. You want revenge for your parents. You want justice and equality and all the rest, everything you feel that the Sisterhood denies you. I know that. But I'm telling you now: if the Order falls, the city *will* starve."

He shook his head urgently. "No, you've got it wrong. That's not what it's about; I'm only involved because I want to help you."

I couldn't help it, I laughed at him. "What, by getting your friends to murder me?"

He stepped closer and spoke quickly. "Listen. One of the Resistance's key goals is bringing an end to Renewals. El, I know how much they hurt you. If we can—"

"If you can what?" My voice was too loud; nearby civilians looked toward us in surprise. I dropped it down to a furious whisper. "Don't you see? It doesn't matter who's in charge. Aytrium will still need Sisters, which means we will still need daughters, and no man is going to be stupid enough to fuck us voluntarily. So what do you propose? There is *no way out for me*."

Finn stared at me, mouth slightly open, as if he was seeing me for the first time. His expression only made me angrier—I didn't want to feel guilty, or awkward, or have to reassure him. We were supposed to be having fun.

"I need space." Bitterness curdled on my tongue. "Meet me at the Candle in an hour."

"El . . ."

"No, I just . . . I can't deal with this right now, okay?" I backed away from him. "Please?"

His shoulders slumped. "Of course."

The crowds swallowed me up. I stopped to buy a cup of spiced wine at a stall. The merchant thrust it out to me, sending hot alcohol sloshing over the rim. I drained half of it in one go. My throat burned.

For a little while, until I had regained my composure, I could not be around Finn. My fingernails bit into my palm. His expression of shock was seared onto my mind. He wanted to help me? He wanted to bring an end to Renewals? The idea would have been laughable if it didn't also make me feel sick to my stomach. I didn't understand how he could possibly be so naïve.

Not to mention that he had come within a hair's breadth of actually calling me a corpse eater. Clearly that was how they all talked behind closed doors. But *him* thinking it, saying it—that cut deeper.

Coming out tonight had been a mistake anyway. I wandered down the boulevard alone. Moon Tide, the Festival of Lovers. What a joke.

I drained the rest of my wine and left the cup in one of the collection bins for vendors to retrieve. The stars were dim through the haze of smoke and light; a fat yellow moon climbed the sky above Martyrium Hill. I cut across to Arbour Street, where smaller stalls and blankets were set out on the pavements. A group of children performed a pantomime on the corner, supervised by a flock of parents.

Someone bumped into me. I apologized reflexively.

"Everything all right?" asked Osan.

"I thought you weren't following me anymore."

He nodded toward the children. "Correct. I'm with the boss. And the smaller boss."

"Oh." I recognised Jaylen in a brown Cat costume, apparently fully committed to her role. Her face was painted white and orange, and she had a pair of cardboard ears. "That's nice."

"The word you're looking for is 'dull.' You seem down."

The child playing the role of the Haunt flexed his fingers into claws. The others mimed terror, clasping their faces and rushing to the opposite side of the set.

"One of those days."

"Fight with Kamillian?"

I glanced away from the performance. "I didn't realise that you knew Millie."

"Not especially well, but we used to move in the same circles."

For some reason, I found the idea unsettling. Like the different parts of my life were colliding, when all I wanted was to keep everything separate and contained.

"No. I haven't spoken to her since your lecture."

"Hm. I made the assumption that you and her . . ."

I shook my head. "We're friends. And she's my counsellor."

"Then you had a fight with someone else?"

"Her brother, actually."

Osan's eyes widened fractionally. "Ah. That would be Finn, right?"

"Yeah." A breeze tugged at my hair. I wrapped my arms around my chest. "Honestly, it wasn't a fight so much as him standing there while I yelled at him."

"Did he deserve it?"

I rubbed my temples. "Not entirely."

"And that's why you look like a kicked dog?"

"Why thank you, Osan. You're making me feel much better."

He laughed. "Hey, at least you didn't try to throw him over a balustrade."

"For the last time, that wasn't intentional."

"But I definitely deserved it."

I sighed.

"Cut yourself some slack." He nudged me. "Apologise. Make amends to your friend. It's better than beating yourself up about it."

"I already have a counsellor, you know." The pack of Cat children danced around the Haunt. "Besides, I don't know what to say to him."

The pantomime ended and the audience applauded. I watched Jaylen as she bowed.

"You'll work it out."

Rhyanon hurried over to her daughter, smiling. Jaylen, eyes wide, asked something. Probably whether her performance had been satisfactory. Rhyanon swept her into a hug.

Osan scratched his head. "I shouldn't ask, but you and Finn?"

I gave him a hard look. "I'm a Sister."

"So it's like that." To my surprise, he gestured regret. Swiftly and formally, as if he were a member of the Order.

I negated his apology with my own hasty gesture. My face felt hot. "No need for that."

"It must be difficult for you. Is it only men?"

"No, I like women fine. Just . . . It doesn't matter. Don't tell Rhyanon about any of this, okay? She already has enough ammunition."

"I won't." He smiled slightly. "She likes you, by the way."

"She likes using me."

"Well, that too." He watched Jaylen and Rhyanon walk toward the food stalls on Pearl Boulevard. "I need to go. Take care, all right?"

"I will. And thanks."

"Anytime."

The conversation had left me calmer, although my sadness persisted. I would apologise to Finn, and then maybe we could just go home. I wandered on down Arbour Street, past jewellers and sweetmakers, merchants hawking timepieces, metal finches and lizards in glass baubles, switchblades with carved handles, enamel bowls. A vendor sold painted wind stones; she waved a wooden fan over the hollowed pebbles, and they produced a reedy whistling.

The smoke of burning sandalwood and rue wafted through the air. Over the heads of the crowd, I could see flaming effigies of the Eater's enemies rising from the ground. Teams of Oblates dragged the flaming icons upright, and the civilians cheered. Straw and hard-baked mud with crude, painted faces, each figure had the mark of the heretic scored into its chest. A Haunt burned between the renegade Sister and the Denier; the lurid features of the Tempter smouldered beside the Thief. Their bodies were adorned with emblems of their sins: bare bones for the Haunt, woven heretic symbols for the Denier, crude wooden phalluses for the Tempter, coins imbedded in the clay flesh of the Thief.

I coughed on the smoke, and edged closer. Six Enforcers stood to sharp attention in front of the pyres. The heat must have been uncomfortable on their backs; I could see sweat beading their hairlines. They held their hands out in front of them, like beggars, and civilians passed over tokens to be cast into the fires. Beyond the effigies, a queue of worshippers took turns to kneel at the plinth before the Eater's icon.

I joined the line to pay my respects. The Eater's opinion of me was unlikely to be favourable at the moment. I seemed, after all, to be working for a sect that intended to undermine the existing Order. Not to mention my attempts to escape Renewal duty. And, well, there was also Finn.

"May your mercy shelter me," I murmured as I reached the front of the queue. I knelt and gestured reverence. "May you teach me humility and grace."

I stood and moved out of the way of the man behind me. Over the crackle of burning wood, I heard the bells ringing. I should head to the Candle.

I am not sure what about her caught my attention. It might

have been that her bearing struck me as out of place: the easy assurance of her posture, the restraint of her movements. She wore civilian clothing, nothing extravagant, although maybe a little warmer than the weather warranted.

Reverend Celane walked quickly over the Orchard Road footbridge and disappeared into the Lokon District of Major East.

I frowned. What was a Councilwoman, the Chief Archivist of the Department of Memories, doing all alone in the low districts? Usually Reverends attended private functions on Moon Tide Eve. I was sure it was her too; that elegantly styled hair was a giveaway.

How very convenient, then, that I was headed in the same direction.

The road narrowed beyond the bridge. I sidled through the stream of people, standing on my toes to see above their heads. At the corner, Celane stopped. I could see her face in profile; she was scanning the crowd. Looking for someone. I averted my gaze toward a stall selling candied plums and hardboiled sugar sweets. Had to be careful.

When I glanced up again, Celane was speaking to a woman with short, slicked-back hair. The Reverend's expression was impatient. She shook her head and repeated something emphatically.

I edged closer. The newcomer had her back to me, but looked like a regular citizen. She rested her hands on her hips. I couldn't see any sign of a Sisterhood tattoo on her wrist, and Celane's arms were covered by her long sleeves. Interesting. The woman motioned toward the city wall.

Over the noise of the crowds, I would never be able to hear their conversation. I slowed, then wandered over to the leatherworks stall on the other side of the street. Whatever Celane's business, she meant to keep it quiet. Councilwomen had every resource and luxury on Aytrium available to them, so she must have been after something that was either illegal or embarrassing.

"You like it?" the vendor asked me.

"What?"

"The bag."

I picked up a satchel at random, still watching Celane out of the corner of my eye. "Very nice. Although I'm not sure I need one."

The stranger walked off toward Pearl Boulevard. Damn. Celane watched her go with narrowed eyes, then turned and headed deeper into Lokon.

"Ah, but you can't have one of such good quality, surely?" The vendor had noted the tattoo on my wrist.

"Probably not," I agreed, and set it down. "Unfortunately, I don't really need a bag, and—"

"Thirty set."

Celane was already at the end of the street. "No, thank you."

"Come on, you're with the Order. It's not like you can't afford it." There was a mean glint in the man's eye. He held out the bag. "Hard times are coming. Some of us are going to struggle more than others."

I wavered, and he saw my weakness.

"Thirty set, Sister," he repeated.

"I'm only an Acolyte," I said. "I don't earn much."

"Ah, but that's all relative, isn't it?"

Celane had disappeared, but I might be able to catch up to her if I was quick. "I'm sorry, I really am. But I can't justify it."

"Twenty-five set, then, but only because I like you."

It was as if I was talking to a brick wall. I shook my head and turned away. "No, thank you."

"You think that you won't need the goodwill, girl?" he said, louder. "Think you're better than the rest of us? You'll see."

"What's that supposed to mean?"

He smirked. "Buy the bag, and you never need to find out."

"She said 'no thank you.'"

Finn rested his hand against the small of my back. I started; I had not heard him approach.

"And while she might not be a high-ranking member of the Order," he continued pleasantly, "she does have the power to revoke your trading licence."

Oh Eater. "I won't!"

The vendor sized Finn up, suddenly guarded. "Who are you?"

"Finn Vidar. Come on, El, you were supposed to buy me a drink."

I let him steer me away from the stall. I could feel the vendor's eyes raking my spine.

"Since when do you let people bully you?" he asked under his breath.

"It was a misunderstanding." I was acutely aware that he still had his hand on my back. "Since when do you threaten civilians on my behalf?"

"He was trying to take advantage of you."

"He was trying to make a sale. Finn, wait." We had reached the outskirts of the market and stood in the shadows of the Gardens once more. I pulled him through the gate and up the stairs to the Chequered Garden so that we could talk without being overheard. "Listen, tonight was a bad idea. I know I crossed a line earlier, and I'm sorry. Let's just go home."

"He was manipulating you." Finn's voice was harsh. "He knew that if he could make you feel guilty or scared enough, you would fold."

"I wasn't scared. He's just a merchant; it really isn't a big deal."

"Until it happens tomorrow. And the next day. Over and over again."

"So what?"

"It gets to you!" He jerked his arm free and came to a stop at the top of the stairs. "And you accept it, all of it. You don't even try to find a way out, because you *are* ashamed."

I wanted to bite back, but words deserted me. Finn glared at me, daring me to argue, and it wasn't fair of him and I should have said, *No, you don't know what you're talking about, you don't know the first thing about being a Sister.* I wanted to say that, but it wouldn't come out.

Did he think I should feel ashamed?

I looked away.

"What did you want me to do, then?" I asked dully.

He was quiet for a while. I carried on toward the trellis of hanging plants, fine-leafed fingers of ivy that dangled from wooden beams. Through the gaps between the slats overhead, the moonlight cut squares of yellow on the bricks.

"I want you to fight." Finn's eyebrows had drawn together, and he stared at the ground as if it might hold the answers he was looking for. "I don't want you to . . . to lie down and accept your fate like it doesn't matter. If you're so angry, then fight."

"I try. But it's not that simple."

"Then let me help you. If what I'm doing isn't enough, then tell me what is."

Osan's warning about involving my friends lingered in my mind, and I hesitated. There was also Reverend Cyde's offer of a place at the Moon House; I could leave, but it was too much to ask for him to come with me.

"Please," he said.

He looked so broken and exposed, so desperate for an answer from me. *I don't know,* I wanted to tell him. There was a pressure in my chest that threatened to crush me entirely, a terrible, helpless aching.

I kissed him.

His lips parted in surprise, and he breathed in sharply. I drew away, an apology half formed on my tongue, but then he kissed me back, hard; he drew me close, and his hands found my waist, trailed up my back, tangled in my hair. Desire burned through my blood.

I broke away from him, my heart racing. "I shouldn't have done that."

Finn touched his mouth. The moon reflected yellow in his eyes. "You kissed me."

"I . . . That was—" I wrapped my arms around my chest. "Oh no."

"El—"

"This can't happen. I'm a Sister, I *can't*—"

"It's okay. There's no one else here." He spoke in a low voice.

What had I done? A roaring filled my ears.

"El, look at me."

The single most important rule for any Sister: men were off-limits. We were poison. I was poison. The toxic mass of my lace curled inside my chest, malevolent and slick. I would infect him, I would turn him into—

Finn brushed a strand of hair out of my face. His fingers felt cold against my cheek.

"I'm fine," he said gently. "Nothing has changed."

"Stop it."

He drew back his hand as if burned.

Millie had warned me. My mother had warned me. And yet here I stood, with no more room for weakness. I had always known my duty; I should have put an end to this years ago. Instead, I had allowed myself to pretend that things could be different.

No more weakness. I raised my head.

"We're done." I looked him in the eyes. Meant it. "From now on, you're going to stay away from me, or I'll go to Enforcement with everything I know about the Resistance."

Finn's body went rigid.

"I have enough to point Commander Asan in the right direction."

"You're lying," he said, breathless.

"And you won't risk finding out." I kept my voice level. "Cut your ties with them, Finn. It's futile, and it will end badly."

He clenched his fists.

"Please don't do this," he whispered. "Please, El."

"Stay away from me." No weakness. No retreat. "Or their blood will be on your hands."

"El!"

I left him standing beneath the arbour. From the festival below, the burning effigies sent curling tendrils of black smoke up into the sky. My throat stung with the taste of ash.

CHAPTER FIFTEEN

THE *Resounder*'s FRONT page featured a lurid artist's impression of the murder. In stark black ink, the faceless assailant raised a dagger above the head of their cowering victim. Blood already splattered the ground between them.

According to the accompanying article, the attack took place in the Lokon District, in the alley dividing Tamber and Herts Street. A resident of the area had stumbled across the scene. The body was mutilated; organs cut out and strewn around the corpse, bones shattered, limbs twisted. The newspaper gleefully listed every gory detail.

Zenza Lenard. Thirty-two years old. Department of Food Management. Herald of the Blessed Star Eater. My supervisor. After I was released from the Sanatorium last year, she had brought cooked meals to the dormitories for me. She enjoyed romance novels and loved her two cats, Pounce and Skitter. She had planned to spend Moon Tide with her wife. Loyal. Funny. Sweet. Dead.

Again and again, I walked Herts Street in my mind. All those deserted buildings with their long shadows. I passed the soup-seller and climbed up the stairs to Chester. Ahead of me, I could see the unlit lamps outside Food Management. I heard soft footsteps, saw a shadow peel away from the end of the road.

When I arrived at the Detainment Offices that morning, I found them in a state of turmoil. Senior Acolytes strode down the hallways, and Heralds yelled orders to their subordinates. I found Commander General Asan in her office, scowling at a map of the city streets.

"What?" she snapped. "Who are you?"

"Acolyte Elfreda Raughn," I said. "I was with Zenza last night."

Her scowl deepened. She looked me up and down.

"Well, shit," she said.

Two hours later, I found myself waiting in the corridor outside the Conclave of Representatives. The emergency inquiry had been arranged at short notice, and the usually austere eastern wing was overrun with notaries and judicial advisors. Two other witnesses sat in the hallway with me: the man who had found Zenza's body and Tenet Poll, our driver. A grim-faced Enforcer watched over us.

"I had nothing to do with it," Tenet whispered to me.

"I know."

"You'll tell them though, won't you? Please, Sister. I swear, when I left she was fine. I never touched her."

"Quiet," the Enforcer said sharply. "Witnesses are not to confer until after the inquiry is concluded."

Tenet's eyes went wide with fear.

They called the first man inside. I closed my eyes and rested the back of my head against the wall. My body felt heavy and sluggish. To my right, Tenet's breathing sounded loud. Perhaps as a gesture of apology, the Enforcer offered him a glass of water.

Time passed. Then he was summoned, and it was just me left to testify. The Enforcer sat down beside me.

"Commander Asan says you should keep it short and calm," she muttered.

I did not open my eyes. "How can I be calm when my supervisor was murdered?"

"Better try. That driver was right to be scared; they're going to want to pin this on someone."

"Should you be talking to me?"

"No."

"Then don't."

Tenet's testimony must have been brief, because a few minutes later the door opened for a third time.

"Acolyte Elfreda Raughn?"

The Conclave looked much the same as when I had delivered Reverend Cyde's missive, but this time a lone hardback chair stood inside the semicircle of pedestals. The Reverends sat beneath their banners, stone-faced. They wore identical blue mourning gloves, the fingers boned by strands of silver wire. Behind me, the Oblate closed the door.

"Be seated," said Commander Asan.

My footfalls echoed on the polished tiles. I avoided eye contact and settled on the chair. The painted map of the island spread out across the floor before me.

"Acolyte Elfreda Raughn, you accompanied Herald Lenard to the Food Management Warehouse in the Lokon District last night?" asked Asan.

"Yes, Councilwoman," I said.

"You arrived at the facility at seventeenth bell?"

"Yes."

"And subsequently, you parted company with Herald Lenard?"

"Yes. After we had made our delivery to the warehouse, I volunteered to file Zenza's paperwork back at the Food Management headquarters."

"Why?"

"She was running late for an appointment."

"What appointment?"

"Her wife, Faye Lenard. They had plans for Moon Tide."

Reverend Somme, head of my own Department, gestured for attention. She looked ill; her skin had a sallow, stretched appearance, and I felt a pang of sympathy for her. She had known Zenza longer than I had. Asan nodded and sat back in her chair.

"I can confirm that the paperwork was filed," said Somme. "I found the reports in my office this morning."

"But that does not give an indication of *when* they were filed," drawled Reverend Verje.

The newly appointed Councilwoman rested her chin on her right hand, gesturing with her left. She had a narrow face and wide blue eyes. Her mouth turned down at the corners, which gave her a subtle, permanent sneer. So this was the woman on whose estate I had trespassed. I had heard stories about Belia Verje, unpleasant whispers, but never met her in person. Seeing her now, I was immediately and instinctively repulsed.

"The papers could have been handed in at any time before your arrival at the headquarters this morning, Reverend Somme," she continued. "Correct?"

"That is correct, yes."

"So there is a period of ten hours during which this might have taken place."

"Acolyte Raughn." Asan ignored Verje. Her strident voice carried over her fellow Councilwoman's with ease. "Do you know where Herald Lenard planned to meet her wife?"

I quickly detailed what Zenza had told me about her intentions for the evening: a concert on Caon Square, dinner in Minor East. Asan took brief notes as I spoke.

"So you and Herald Lenard headed in opposite directions after you made your delivery to the warehouse?" she verified.

"Yes."

"If I might be so bold," said Reverend Jiana Morwin, "it seems very generous of you to perform your supervisor's job for her."

Morwin's voice emerged breathless and reedy, lacking in all force. In contrast to the other Reverends—and especially Asan, who held the podium next to hers—the Head of Public Health appeared oddly diminutive. Although she was of average height, she carried herself with a pronounced stiffness, like she was trying to shrink down into a smaller mold.

"I had no particular plans for the evening," I answered. "The headquarters were along my route back to the dormitories; I thought that I might head home afterwards."

"'Thought that you might'?" Morwin repeated. She glanced at Verje like she was seeking backup.

"I changed my mind after I delivered the reports."

"Why?"

I met her gaze. "No real reason. I decided to visit the markets."

"And this necessitated taking off your robes?" asked Verje.

For a moment, I couldn't make sense of the question.

"According to Reverend Somme," Verje continued, taking advantage of my silence, "a set of robes was found in your office. Yours, presumably. Why did you remove your robes?"

"Because I considered them a little formal for the occasion." A hint of impatience crept into my voice. "Not that I can see how this is relevant to the murder of my supervisor."

"I think you'll find that the Council decides what's relevant. Do you have anyone who can verify your story?"

"No."

"No one you spoke to, no friends?"

"I'm not the most sociable person. I did ask some merchants about prices, but I doubt they'll remember me."

"So it's impossible to know whether your version of events is *true*?"

"Reverend Verje," said Asan, with eyes like daggers. "I'm not sure what your motivation is for discrediting this particular witness, but perhaps you could rein in the amateur sleuthing until such time as she has actually presented her account of the evening."

Verje made a dismissive gesture of acquiescence, and Asan's lips thinned. She turned back to me.

"Could you describe everything you remember from the time you entered the Lokon District until you reached the Food Management headquarters?" she said. "You don't need to detail any subsequent shopping."

Somme rubbed her temples as if nursing a migraine.

I gathered myself. For Zenza's sake. We might not have been close, but my supervisor had been a kind and constant presence in my life. She had deserved to go home to her wife on Moon Tide. Not this. I fixed my gaze on the floor in front of me and, as best as I could, described every detail of the streets and my passage through them. The Council listened in silence.

But when I mentioned that I had been followed, Asan's eyes narrowed. She leaned forward and held up her hand.

"You heard someone behind you?" she asked.

I nodded. "I'm not certain, but I think so."

"This was on Chester Street?"

"Yes. After I filed the reports, I left through the back entrance of the headquarters. Whoever was behind me could have returned to Herts Street in that time. Caught up to Zenza."

"Speculation is not encouraged," said Reverend Morwin.

I fought the urge to shrug. It would have been more disrespectful than I could afford. "My apologies, Councilwoman."

"And you didn't see anything that might identify this individual?" pressed Asan. "Anything at all?"

"I did not."

Asan chewed on her lip, obviously frustrated. I could see other Reverends exchanging glances. My testimony had provided nothing useful, only further questions, more avenues that might lead nowhere. On the night of the most significant religious festival of the year, one of our own had been slaughtered. The Order had to respond.

Then Reverend Celane, unspeaking until now, gestured for attention and asked, "Could you describe your relationship to Herald Lenard?"

Celane's voice was melodious, pleasant. Her hair was swept back from her face into a neat bun, and her expression was attentive. I was struck again by her poise; she was just ineffably *refined*. No trace of the irritable impatience I had witnessed last night; today she was all control and calm.

"She is my supervisor." I paused. "Was my supervisor."

"Could you characterise that relationship for us?"

"I'm not sure I understand."

"Were the two of you on good terms?"

"Enough," said Asan harshly.

Celane rested her gloved hands in her lap. "Commander, you have asked your questions, and now the rest of Council also has the right to be heard. This inquiry is not under the sole jurisdiction of Enforcement." She turned back to me. "Acolyte Raughn, I would like to know whether you bore any kind of resentment or ill will toward Herald Lenard."

Even though I could scarcely believe it was happening, I knew what Celane was trying to do. What she was suggesting. My whole body shook; I felt almost dizzy with anger, helpless with it. The ridges on the wooden armrests carved lines into my skin.

But when I spoke, my voice remained even.

"To Reverend Verje's earlier point, no one can confirm my whereabouts last night," I said.

"I fail to see—"

"And yet this morning, I presented myself to the Detainment Offices of my own volition. I am offering all the information that I can, of my own volition. If I had murdered my supervisor, I would not have marched straight to Enforcement the moment that the news came out. I would have kept quiet. But here I am. I would greatly appreciate it if the Council would stop insinuating that I killed Herald Lenard."

The silence in the room yawned like a chasm.

"Forgive me, Acolyte," said Celane. Her voice was smooth as polished stone. "I understand that this must be a difficult time for you, and my question was not intended to paint you as the culprit. It is simply my assumption that a Sister must have been involved in the crime."

"In that case, Councilwoman"—I laid heavy stress on the word—"perhaps you should explain what *you* were doing in Lokon last night."

I was looking directly at her when I spoke, so I caught her reaction. Although it was subtle—a tightening of her graceful jaw, a new hardness that entered her eyes—it was the final confirmation I needed. The last of my doubts evaporated.

"You are mistaken," said Reverend Verje after a moment of silence. "Councilwoman Celane was at my property, attending a private Reverend function. Numerous Sisters can corroborate this."

I said nothing. It was too late to take anything back. Besides, I was right. It didn't help me at all, but at least I was right.

"Thank you, Raughn," said Asan. "Please wait in the adjoining chamber. I would like to discuss a security matter with you."

I nodded and stood up. My gesture of reverence might have come across as sarcastic, but that would be the least of my offenses today. I crossed the floor past Reverend Somme and stepped into the small adjoining room. Lines of filing cabinets crowded the space.

Rhyanon had warned that my temper would get me into trouble, I reflected.

The Commander did not keep me waiting long. I heard the murmur of voices and the rustling of formal robes as the Councilwomen stepped down from their podiums. The session was adjourned.

Asan opened the door to the antechamber, stepped inside, and closed it behind her.

"Well, that was . . . something," she said.

"I didn't realise that I was your prime suspect, Commander."

She waved her hand with visible impatience. "They were trying to muddy the waters; the other witnesses received similar treatment. Did you really see Yelina Celane in Lokon?"

"Yes."

"You're certain?"

"She was talking to a civilian on Orchard Road. I tried to follow her, but lost her in the crowds."

"Rather reckless of you." Unexpectedly, Asan grinned. "It's true that I saw her at Verje's party, but as our new Head of Water and Sanitation has pointed out, we can't always account for a person's location at all times. I imagine she could have slipped away. Doesn't mean she had anything to do with the murder, but the secrecy suggests that she was up to *something*. And her people are covering for it, which is even more interesting."

"Her people?" An idea dawned on me. "Wait, does that mean Verje isn't—"

A knock on the door. I jumped, but Asan hardly flinched.

"Come in," she said casually and, with the air of someone finalising an arrangement, continued. "This means that a junior Enforcement officer will accompany you to any of the Food Management operations outside the city."

Reverend Celane entered the room.

"Forgive the interruption, Commander," she said.

"No interruption," said Asan. "We had just finished our discussion regarding additional security for Acolyte Raughn. How can I help you?"

"I would actually like to speak to Elfreda."

"Ah." Asan cast me a sidelong glance.

"If she does not object?"

"Of course not, Reverend," I said softly.

"Good."

Asan hesitated, then favoured her colleague with a painfully insincere smile. "In that case, please excuse me. May the light of the Star shine brightly on you."

Over Celane's shoulder, she caught my eye.

Compulse, she mouthed.

A horrible sinking feeling settled over me. I gestured apology to Reverend Celane, and bowed my head.

"I am sorry, Reverend," I said. "I was clearly mistaken when I thought that I saw you in Lokon."

She shook her head. "No harm done. I only regret that I obviously upset you. How are you feeling?"

"Angry, I suppose."

"Understandably so. We are all shocked."

And there—so fine and subtle that I could scarcely detect it—was the compulse. It slid into my thoughts without a whisper; caught unawares, I would never have noticed the faint ache at my left temple. Reverend Celane wanted me to relax. To trust her.

"If possible, I'd like to make up for your ordeal today," she said.

"There's no need—"

"Are you familiar with the game Tryst?" she asked.

I blinked. "I am, although I haven't played it before."

"Ah, that's no problem; it's easy enough. If you're available, a group of Sisters and I are organising a casual dinner two days from now. The games will take place before we eat." The compulse grew stronger. "You said that you aren't a sociable person, but after everything you've been through, I think you need support. To take your mind off things."

"I wouldn't want to intrude."

"Not at all, not at all. I promise it will be very relaxed. Bring along a friend if you like."

The compulse urged me to say yes. How kind and caring the Reverend, how very tired I felt, and wouldn't it be nice to eat together, to be safe and surrounded by my Sisters, by all the women who truly *understood*. I had been through a terrible, traumatic ordeal: I deserved this.

It seemed that Celane was very skilled in this kind of lacework. But maybe that could be used against her. I smiled, allowing my eyes to unfocus a little.

"I would love to attend," I said.

Leaving the Council Building, all my exhaustion and fear and guilt caught up with me. I had allowed the Order's protocols and my own momentum to propel me this far, but now, my obligations fulfilled, weakness flooded back into my body. I rested on the stairs outside the front doors. Not for very long. Just until my hands stopped shaking.

The Martyrium was busy when I arrived. It would be, given the circumstances. We needed to be vigilant.

I performed the rite with little ceremony and stayed with my mother for a while after that, not talking, not really doing anything. She breathed slowly, so slowly; every time she exhaled, I became convinced she would not inhale again. I studied her face. *Would you prefer that? Would death be better?*

I knew I was too selfish. My life depended on hers, as my daughter's would depend on mine. I rested my head on the pallet beside her. My mother breathed in. Could she feel, even now?

Would I still feel? Doctrine said no, but the fear remained. She breathed out.

Much later, I woke to an Oblate touching my shoulder. The handle of the scalpel was still clenched within my fist.

CHAPTER

SIXTEEN

"So the Council believes that you did it?" Millie examined the slim-fitting trousers in her mirror. Her eyebrows knitted together. The colour was wrong.

"Maybe. Probably not. Commander Asan thinks that certain factions want the investigation expanded or diverted."

"'Certain factions' means the Chief Archivist, right? Who you saw in Lokon that night. Doesn't that suggest, you know"—she turned and looked at herself from the back—"guilt?"

I shook my head. "They found Zenza on Herts Street, so she was probably attacked minutes after we parted. I didn't see Celane until nearly an hour later."

"Are you okay talking about this?"

"I'm fine."

We were inside Millie's apartment. I sat on her bed while she sifted through her wardrobe in search of a suitable outfit. Clothes spilled over the shelves and onto the floor. I folded the rejected items and stacked them neatly on the carpet beside me.

Millie pulled off her trousers, tossed them to me, and reached for a different pair. "All right, but if Celane's innocent, why try to pin it on you?"

I averted my eyes to be polite, although Millie was entirely unselfconscious about her body. If anything, a bit of a show-off, actually. "I'm not sure, but I think she was trying to push the idea that only a Sister could have been responsible for the murder. She said so during the inquiry."

A slight pause. "Isn't that the case?"

"Not at all. If a civilian caught Zenza off-guard, she might have been too slow to defend herself." I tried not to imagine how she might have felt, how afraid, how confused. How helpless. "It would have been easier for one of us, but that doesn't necessarily mean it *was* one of us."

"I see." Millie crossed the room to her jewellery box. "Hm. I would have thought it better serves the Sisterhood's interests to blame an outsider."

"Or at least to reserve judgement. I don't know if any of the Councilwomen actually bought Celane's idea, though. Aside from Verje and Morwin, but they're clearly operating as a block." I flopped over on the bed. Millie owned more scatter cushions than I would have deemed strictly necessary. "The only explanation I've come up with is that Celane wants to make the investigation itself impossible. Drag it out, pursue too many leads, drain resources. Anything that makes Commander Asan look incompetent."

"Oh, so it's political."

"Probably personal too. I'm sure the Commander offends most members of the Council."

Millie picked out a pair of red earrings to match the trim on her blouse. "Does this look okay?"

"Looks nice."

"So Celane wants to unseat the Commander and replace her with a different Reverend." She checked her reflection one last time. "But Rhyanon is clearly in with Enforcement, and thus with Commander Asan, who is probably in charge of your faction."

"Probably," I agreed.

"Meaning that your people are under attack."

"Kind of."

"And we're going to Celane's party anyway."

"Accepting the invitation was the least suspicious thing to do under the circumstances."

It was also my opportunity to figure out what Reverend Celane wanted from me. I might have entertained the possibility of her invitation being genuine, had she not tried to compulse me into accepting it. And in spite of what I had said to Millie, her presence in Lokon *had* been suspicious.

Better the enemy you know, I figured. At any rate, tonight I planned to be as bland as Food Management's emergency gruel rations. After my outburst at the inquiry, I occupied a strangely powerful position. On the one hand, I was fairly certain Celane would love to shove me off the Edge. On the other, if I came to any harm, she would instantly become Commander Asan's prime suspect. It wasn't the most comfortable situation, but confronting the Chief Archivist had offered me a great deal of unexpected security.

Osan waited at the end of the road. He stood beside the horses of his cab, feeding them from a bag of withered apples.

"Hello, Kamillian," he said.

Millie, pale at the best of times, went white. Her mouth opened, then closed.

"What's wrong?" he asked. There was a hint of bitterness in his voice, a hard edge beneath his smile. "I know it's been a while, but you seem surprised to see me."

She struggled to speak. "I didn't realise that you worked for a Herald now."

"Hm. How the times have changed, hey?" He presented his last apples to the horses, then hoisted himself up onto the driver's seat. "Let's go. Don't want to be late."

Millie looked shaken. I let her climb inside the cab first.

"You know I disapprove, right?" Osan muttered to me.

"It sort of just . . . happened."

Through her job, Millie had learned of the Council's inquiry, and I had found her waiting outside the dormitories when I got home from work. Relief had broken across her face the moment that she saw me, quickly followed by outrage.

I was, she had swiftly informed me, a terrible friend for keeping her in the dark; how dare I worry her like that, what had I been *thinking*?

And so now Millie was attending Celane's party as my partner.

There was no need for Osan to look so disappointed in me; I felt guilty enough as it was. I stared out of the window as we rolled down the road. Millie would be effective; I didn't doubt her ability to worm her way into private conversations. But I didn't want to make a habit of putting her in harm's way either.

She elbowed me in the ribs. "Relax, gorgeous."

"I shouldn't have brought you along."

"No one's going to pay any attention to me. Well, unwanted attention." She smoothed her hair. "I can handle this."

Celane's city manor was smaller than Reverend Kisme's, a double-storey building at the end of Benevolence Street. Smaller, but still one of the largest private residences in Ceyrun. It sat a few blocks from the dormitories, and three streets from my mother's old house.

As our cab trundled toward the gates, the thought crossed my mind that I had no idea who lived in my childhood home now. After my mother's martyrdom, her property rights reverted to the Sisterhood, along with the credits she had earned with Civil Obligations. In my mind, it was an empty, haunted place; broken plates and smashed glass and angry silences. I couldn't picture other people sleeping where she had slept, eating where she had eaten. Yet the property had belonged to a different Herald before my mother, and another Herald before her.

Osan tugged on the reins, and the horses drew to a stop. He leaned back in his seat.

"All right, I'll be waiting here," he said. "Don't do anything stupid."

"It almost sounds like you care."

"Don't push it, Just El. I'm not done being mad at you."

Millie hopped down and offered me a hand. Her grip was sure and steady.

"Let's do this," she said.

An Oblate, around sixteen years old and looking exceedingly bored, waited by the gate to Celane's house.

"Eater's grace upon you," she said. "Invitation?"

I drew out the small vellum card from my waistband and gave it to her.

She squinted. "Elfreda Raughn?"

"And I'm Lariel Sacor, her date for the evening," said Millie brightly.

The Oblate nodded and handed the card back to me. "There are refreshments in the garden. Go through, it's on the left."

Millie looped an arm around my waist and steered me up the path. She tilted her head and murmured, "I thought perhaps, an alias . . ."

"I'm going to forget what to call you."

"Oh, don't be difficult. You met me at a theatre production, and we've been together for two months."

Eight tables were clustered together at the far end of the garden. Filled wine glasses glinted against white tablecloths, and the afternoon sun cut through the leaves of well-tended cedar trees. An open stretch of grass divided the main house from a small guest cottage, where a group of around twenty women played a ball game. The participants called to one another, trying to gain possession of a plain leather ball, while a few spectators watched from the sidelines. Verje, dressed in a flowing blue dress, was deep in conversation with another Reverend. To my surprise, I also saw Commander Asan slouched at one of the tables, holding a half-empty glass between two fingers. Her eyes met mine, and she raised an eyebrow fractionally. I looked away.

"Which one is Reverend Celane?" asked Millie.

"Over there, in the yellow. I should thank her for the invitation."

"Sounds like a good idea."

We wound down the curving stone path to the tables. Reverend Celane noticed me and smiled.

"Ah, Elfreda! I'm so glad you could make it." Her hair fanned out behind her head like the wing of a bird. She gestured at the wine glasses on the table behind her. "Please, have something to drink."

"Thank you," I said.

"It's only a pleasure." She inclined her head toward Millie. "Hello. I don't believe we've met?"

Millie gestured reverence smoothly. "I'm Elfreda's friend, not a Sister. It's an honour to meet you, Councilwoman Celane."

"Oh, no need to be so formal. I always like to see new faces around here. You are?"

"Lariel Sacor. I work in a theatre in Major West. Assistant set designer, but I'm hoping to be a production manager one day."

A strange expression crossed Celane's face, fleeting and difficult to identify. Her eyes flicked toward me. Then her smile returned.

"That sounds wonderful," she said. "I love the arts; it's part of the reason I chose to work in the Department of Memories. What is the theatre's name?"

"The Jarn Holt Theatre. Just past Coronon Commons, with the bronze sculptures of the Eater's first daughters outside?"

"Ah, I think I've seen it. Perhaps you could tell me about your upcoming productions later this evening."

"I'd be happy to, if you're interested."

"I am, but I'm afraid I need to excuse myself for the moment. There's a friend of mine who has just arrived."

Once she was out of earshot, Millie muttered, "I don't suppose you know what's upcoming at the Jarn Holt Theatre?"

"Haven't got a clue."

"I'll have to continue improvising, then." She picked up a

glass of wine and drank, frowning slightly. "Or hope that she forgets."

"With luck, she won't talk to us again."

"I doubt that. She wanted you here for a reason. Maybe to charm you, get you to rescind that statement about you seeing her in Lokon."

"Not a chance."

"I know. But she doesn't. Not yet anyway." She set the glass down. "I'm going to poke around and talk to some other guests. Can you join that ball game?"

"Why?"

"So that people will see you indulging in some harmless fun. If you skulk around in the background, it'll look like you're up to something."

That made sense, although I found the idea of being watched discomforting. "Okay, but be careful."

She gave me a gentle shove. "Go on."

I wandered closer to the field. Tryst, the game at play, might have appeared rather laidback to anyone unfamiliar with the rules. Participants paused for drinks or to greet their friends mid-match. A few women seemed to have forgotten they were playing at all, and stood in the middle of the field, chatting with their opponents.

But the obvious shows of indifference were a ruse, and integral to the fun. This wasn't a game of physical prowess. Tryst was all about social strategy.

Four teams—yellow, red, blue, and black—competed for possession of the ball. The objective was to catch it while standing within an opposing team's base. Squares of chalk staked out the territories. If one team member held the ball, the rest of her team froze, while all the other players were free to move and block passes.

To score maximum points, a team needed to retain players in all sections of the field. This necessitated forming alliances with opponents, who might at any point betray their promises and steal the ball for their own purposes. And so no one wanted to look too invested in winning. It made negotiating for passes more difficult.

A Herald in the black team saw me watching the game. "Do you want to join?"

"If it's no trouble."

"None at all," she said, amused. "What's your name?"

"Elfreda."

She raised her voice. "Hey, Mirene! We have a new teammate. She's called Elfreda."

A broad-shouldered woman waved from the yellow team's base.

"Mirene's captain, and Ilva and Fresia are also on our side." She pointed them out. "And I'm Guin."

Ilva. I felt a shock of cold. *The woman from Kisme's party.*

"You can just hang around the midfield for now," said Guin. "Try to block passes."

I nodded and walked to the most crowded section of the lawn—the neutral territory between the four base camps. The ball was in the hands of a grey-haired Herald from the yellow side. Her teammates had been cut off by other players.

"Need help, Devlin?" a red player called.

"Eater, no." Devlin threw the ball to a different woman. "I'm not that desperate."

Other players laughed—clearly this was something of a running joke. The rejected woman did not look overly upset by the remark; she only sighed and moved to block a new pass.

My anonymity proved to be a disadvantage, and I soon discovered that my primary purpose was to obstruct frozen players by standing in front of them. Still, on the whole, my teammates worked well together. We had formed a casual alliance with the blue team, who needed help more than we did. They reliably backed up Mirene's manoeuvres.

But Ilva was clumsy. She made bad calls, missed opportunities, and caved too easily when singled out. I could tell that my teammates were frustrated with her.

"Jesane! Hey, come on! Work with me," she called.

The woman in possession of the ball was a Herald in a fitted black dress, with lovely brown skin and thick dark eyebrows.

"No thanks," she said. "I'd rather not."

Ilva's cheeks darkened with anger or embarrassment. I glanced at Mirene, who motioned for me to cover the red player to my right.

"You sure about that? Not even for old time's sake?" Ilva pressed.

"I think I've made it clear I want nothing to do with you."

A few other players winced. Ilva laughed, acting as if Jesane had been joking, but the sound was so forced and uncomfortable that no one joined in.

"You don't seem to have many other options, though," said Ilva. "So do you want to stand around all night waiting for something better?"

It was true. Jesane's own team was completely blocked, and she had no obvious alliances with anyone else. Yet she could not, or would not, lose face by acquiescing to Ilva.

"Someone better, yes," she said.

I don't know why I did it, except that the expression on Ilva's face made me feel like something terrible was about to happen. I stepped sideways to open a path for Jesane to pass to her teammate. She saw the gap and threw.

From around the field, I thought I heard a collective sigh of relief. The tension eased. Ilva continued to smile, teeth bared, but after a few minutes, she abandoned the game. No one stopped her. She wandered over to the drinks table and found herself a glass of cider.

I took over her position inside the black base. The pace of the game picked up; there was less begging now. Alliances had settled and the patterns of play became predictable. The Herald in the tunic dress would always pass to Herald Loks,

Mirene helped whichever side was losing, and Devlin was reliable in returning favours. My team scored twice more, benefiting from Ilva's absence, but it was clear that we wouldn't win the game.

"It's getting late," called Reverend Celane from the sidelines. "Last point!"

Oh well. The ball was two bases away and in Devlin's hands once again. I was unmarked by other players, but too far from the action to matter.

"Jesane," said Devlin, "kindly pass this over to Heide."

She tossed the ball across to Jesane without waiting for confirmation. Jesane caught it, then paused.

"Sorry, Devlin," she said.

She threw hard, and the ball soared over the heads of the other players. Toward me. Despite the distance, it seemed that the ball would still pass out of my reach. I raised my hand, and yes, it was too high, my fingers grazed the stitching, and . . .

It was in my hand.

I blinked. The ball rested warm and solid in my palm. I lifted it.

"Does this mean we win?" I asked.

The women around me looked baffled, but Mirene whooped and punched the air, and then a few people clapped. I clearly had the ball; therefore, I must have caught it. Devlin complained about Jesane's betrayal, but without venom. The game was done.

When I turned around, I caught Commander Asan watching me. When we made eye contact, she swivelled on the spot and marched off up the lawns toward the house.

Millie jogged over to me. "How did you do that?" she asked under her breath.

I looked at the ball again. Innocent, brown, a little scuffed. "I'm not entirely sure. It felt like someone dropped the ball into my hand."

Lace? I wondered. But who would care whether I won or lost?

"More refreshments are available in the parlour," called Reverend Celane.

Perhaps it was just a lucky catch, after all. Millie and I walked up the path toward the house, where warm orange light spilled out the windows. Maybe small good things were allowed to happen to me, every now and again.

CHAPTER SEVENTEEN

CELANE'S PARLOUR WAS spacious and pleasantly cool, with soft red carpets furnishing the floor and wide windows looking out over the garden. Old paintings hung on the dark panelled walls—still-lives of sacred instruments, muted landscapes, and antique maps of the city on stained yellow parchment. Guests lounged on leather couches, playing cards and drinking wine.

"There's the woman you pissed off," Millie muttered out the corner of her mouth.

Ilva stood by a bookshelf, her arms folded across her chest. She was pretending to read the spines, but kept glancing across the room at Jesane, who was engaged in a lively discussion with two other Heralds. No one else paid her any attention, and she looked so pathetic that I almost felt sorry for her. Almost, but not quite.

"I'm going to talk to her," said Millie.

"I don't think that's a good idea."

She just grinned and slipped out of my reach, leaving me alone in the entrance to the room.

"Great," I muttered. *Now* I'm *the pathetic one.*

I fidgeted, my eyes sweeping over the faces of the other women in the room. This was the kind of socialising I was least equipped to handle. Everyone here was so much more established and important than I was, and I had none of Millie's charm—I could not just walk up to the Heralds and start a conversation. Never mind that I would probably have to interrupt them to do so. Even the idea made me cringe.

Time, I decided, to hide in a bathroom.

The corridor beyond the parlour was decorated with a beautiful collection of devotionals to the Star Eater. Each of the traditional verses was written out in red ink, and embossed with small pieces of gold or semiprecious stones. I had not realised Celane was so ardent in her faith, but her passion revealed itself through the obvious care she took in presenting these scripts. Each lovingly framed in cedar wood, each protected by a screen of spotless glass.

Strange, how uncomfortable it made me feel to see even a hint of Celane's private self. I did not like to imagine what lay behind her controlled mask of a face, who she might be in her quiet moments.

I found the bathroom and washed my hands and face. The whole exercise had not wasted nearly as much time as I would have liked, and now I was faced with the prospect of returning to the parlour or waiting here until dinner was announced. Neither option seemed very appealing.

I sighed. Maybe Millie had given up on Ilva by now.

But as I was leaving, I noticed that the door across the hallway stood open. Through the gap, I could see rows of bookshelves and a large leather armchair. Celane's personal office.

I glanced down the corridor. If there was ever a time to pry into the Reverend's business . . . I quickly stepped inside.

The room was cozy, lit by three wicker-covered lamps and pleasantly warm. A window seat overlooked the lawns. Celane's book collection was modest, but well-organised. Judging by the selection of plays and novels on the shelves, she really did have an enthusiasm for the arts and theatre. I ran my eyes over the spines. Also quite the interest in Golden Age lacework applications, the miracles the Order had been capable of in the past. Some of these texts must have been borrowed from the restricted sections of the

Department of Memories; it wasn't the kind of material readily available to ordinary Sisters.

A lone book lay on the pedestal table beside the armchair, multiple velvet bookmarks poking out from between the pages. I picked it up. *Memories of Our Mothers.* Celane's current reading looked cheerful. I opened to one of the marked chapters.

. . . could be viewed as sacred, both in terms of our heritage as custodians of Aytrium, and in terms of our function, that of deliverers-of-the-peace. When those two roles are brought into conflict—such as when violence is demanded in order to fulfil our duty of upholding the continent—civilian unrest inevitably rears its head. Our power, as any Sister knows, is both the well of our custodianship and the furrow that draws endless antagonism toward us.

How, then, to maintain order in the absence of reverence? Why, faith must be performed.

Again this applies in a dual sense. "Performed" in that our actions must confirm and renew faith; i.e., we must actively use power and let such power be witnessed. And then, the second sense, "performed" in terms of spectacle. We must inject theatre, artistry, and ceremony into such demonstrations of power, for therein lies the road to the civilian's heart. Tell them a story and tell it well—power is performance.

Our failings, on those occasions where the Sisterhood lacked the foresight to . . .

A little dry for my tastes. I lowered myself into the armchair and flipped forward to the next bookmark.

Broadly speaking, we have evidence of four discrete phases in the transformation from man to Haunt. More might well exist, but to conduct a study of the farthest advanced stages of infection is beyond our present means. (Chiefly, the issue is of secure containment—to hold a Haunt past the 'adolescent' stage of development imperils all of Aytrium. See Chapter 9: The Cost of Mistakes.)

Stage One, or the Incipient Phase, is characterised by minor changes in physiognomy and mental state. After the subject has contracted the infection, the Incipient Phase may last up to a month. During this period, the subject may experience nausea, an aversion to certain foods, persistent irritability, paranoia, mild insomnia, increased sensitivity to sound and smell, and joint pain.

Stage Two, or Basic Manifestation, sees an escalation of existing symptoms: severe insomnia, aggression, drastic weight loss, depression. This phase may be as brief as a week, depending on the individual. Here, the more obvious visual cues become apparent. Secondary teeth begin to develop, the subject grows taller as his bones soften and regrow, and a distinctive yellow discolouration stains his irises. Frequently, these changes are accompanied by aggravated itching; subjects will often scratch themselves until their skin bleeds. After Basic Manifestation, the subject becomes unsuitable for use in Renewals, and expresses an intense craving for human flesh, most especially that belonging to Sisters.

Someone in the parlour laughed loudly. I jumped and looked up, but the low babble of conversation continued unchanged. Presumably, it was not yet dinner time. My heart rate slowed.

Stage Three, or Adolescence, often blurs with Basic Manifestation. Some symptoms may grow alarmingly more advanced before others even manifest. However, the key characteristic of this stage is that the subject completely loses the capacity to sleep, even with the aid of drugs. Speech becomes increasingly difficult, as does the capacity for empathy, reason, memory, etc. The subject's appearance is wholly changed (see illustration 16B), and he gains a form of preternatural strength, agility, and speed. Sensitivity to smell and sound far exceeds human capacities, and antler-like protrusions emerge from the skull. This phase lasts approximately two weeks.

Stage Four, or Early Maturity, sees the onset of necrosis. Subjects are no longer capable of human feeling, and will not recognise even close family members or friends. Bones regain their hardness, irises are a flat shade of yellow, and secondary teeth are fully developed. Subjects are insatiably hungry and appear impervious to injury. With their prior personalities and natures all but obliterated, a new intelligence emerges in the absence of the old. Researchers have witnessed Haunts using lures to prey upon their victims, and they appear able to accurately mimic human voices. Unconfirmed reports of stranger abilities exist, but perhaps belong more to the domain of fiction.

To be certain, more advanced stages of infection exist in the Haunts of Ventris, and study of these . . .

"Good book?"

I started guiltily. Jesane stood above me.

"You appeared quite engrossed," she said.

"Sorry," I said. "I probably shouldn't be here."

She waved aside the matter. "I doubt Reverend Celane would mind. I just wanted to find you so I could congratulate you on that last catch."

"It was a pretty spectacular throw."

"I had some pent-up aggression, I suppose. I didn't catch your name."

From down the corridor rang a clear tinkling sound, and the murmuring of conversation in the parlour subsided. Time for dinner.

"It's Elfreda," I told Jesane as I rose.

"Pleasure to meet you," she replied.

Delicate chandeliers lit the dining room in pale yellow. Four tables, each seating eight, were laid out with simple white plates and bowls. Sprays of blue flowers rested in slender vases, and condensation beaded the outside of gilded silver flasks. The smells of rosemary and garlic drifted from the kitchen, causing my mouth to water.

Millie caught my eye as I entered. I nodded to the furthest table, where many of the younger and less important Sisters had gathered. Nice and out of the way. But as I reached it and pulled out a chair, a slender hand closed on my shoulder.

"Elfreda, won't you join me at my table?" said Celane. "Lariel was going to tell me about the theatre."

"Oh," I said. Behind Celane's back, Millie looked horrified. "Of course, Reverend."

Maybe she just wants to be nice, I thought, without any conviction. Millie had deployed her best winning smile, always a bad sign.

We took up the seats that Celane indicated. Verje sat on the other side of the table, Celane's Oblate daughter was to Millie's left. Jesane, who seemed equally surprised by her invitation to the host's table, occupied the chair to my right.

I poured water into my glass and, at her nod, into Jesane's.

The kitchen doors opened, and four Oblates appeared carrying trays of steaming bread, halved peaches filled with coloured sweetpaste, and soft riverweed braided into the shape of the Eater's sigil. They carefully set the trays down on each table, bowed, and backed into the kitchen again.

"The star player of the red team," said Millie, leaning forward to speak around me. "It's Herald Jesane Olberos, right?"

"That's me. And you are?"

"Lariel Sacor," said Millie. "I'm here with El."

"Ah, a civilian. How are you finding the party?"

"To be honest, a little intimidating. I've never attended anything like this before."

I accepted a peach and some riverweed, and then passed the tray along to Millie.

"This is rather subdued by the usual standards." Jesane smiled. She picked up her bread and bit off a piece. "I noticed that you were trying to cheer up Ilva. That was kind of you."

"I think she might have had a bit much to drink."

"Quite possibly. I hope she doesn't cause a scene." Jesane frowned, then shook her head. "So, Elfreda, where do you work?"

I swallowed a mouthful of the tangy, salty riverweed. "Department of Food Management. I'm a junior field research officer." At Jesane's blank look, I added, "I'm involved in finding and overseeing production of alternate sources of food."

"Oh! That seems interesting."

"Please don't get her started on the bugs," Millie muttered.

"So you must be quite knowledgeable about the water shortages, then?"

I nodded. "We work extensively with Water and Sanitation."

"Yes," drawled Verje from across the table, "so extensively that sometimes Food Management sees my department as a subsidiary of its own. Or at least, that's the impression I've received from Deselle Somme."

Once again, seeing Verje up close unnerved me. Although her voice was friendly enough, I could not shake the sense that her mannerisms were staged. Too deliberate. As if her actions were telegraphed long in advance and she had only been waiting for the right cue to begin performing them.

I might have been influenced by rumours I had heard about the Reverend, however; whispers that still circulated the dormitories. All Oblates trained in butchery before their induction as Acolytes, mostly working with dead pigs or sheep. It was a grisly education, but necessary.

It would have been over thirty years ago now, but people still gossiped that Verje had delighted in honing her flesh-cutting on *live* animals.

"I don't think that's the case," I said carefully.

The Reverend laughed. "It certainly won't be going forward. I plan to run a tighter ship than Kisme, may the Star light her dreaming." She paused to drink. "I mean, the projects I hear about are insane."

"Insane?"

"No disrespect to you, Acolyte. I'm sure you work very hard, but I don't think toasted locusts are really the way to go."

Under the table, Millie placed her hand on my leg.

"I've tried them," she said, with an easy smile. "I think they'll be quite popular, if there's not much else available."

"There's more than enough food 'available,'" said Verje. "And we're anticipating a change in the weather soon anyway."

Celane cleared her throat.

"I hear about the water problems every day in the Conclave, so perhaps a different subject? Although . . ." She turned to me. "Given the loss of Herald Zenza Lenard, I believe Elfreda will be giving a presentation at the water symposium in her place."

This was news to me.

"But I'm only a junior officer," I said.

"You have important first-hand insight into the issue. I think Reverend Somme was going to issue the invitation tomorrow."

"Oh."

"Jesane, you are also attending, yes?"

Jesane nodded, and the conversation moved on. It surprised me that Reverend Somme had not asked me whether I wanted to take part in the symposium, especially if she expected me to deliver Zenza's presentation. She had always been sensitive in the past; she must know I would find this difficult. But I suppose that the Reverend was also under a lot of pressure.

"Raughn."

I looked up from my empty plate. "Yes?"

"Your name has been bothering me for a while," said Verje. "Raughn, as in Kirane Raughn? She was your mother?"

I felt cold. "She is my mother, yes."

"How old are you now?"

"Twenty-two."

She gave me a pitying look. "Ah, I thought you seemed young for an Acolyte. It's tragic, what happened to her. She was so vivacious too."

The rest of the table had fallen quiet while listening to our exchange. They watched me.

"So sudden," she said. "All martyrdoms are difficult, but for Kirane to join the Eater at, what, forty-eight?"

"Forty-six," I said softly.

"Forty-six. This was a year ago, wasn't it? I remember the inquiry." She smiled. "Oh, but in the old days, Kirane was forever getting into some kind of trouble. You might have been too young to remember, but there was a huge scandal about her involvement in this subversive civilian organisation. All very dramatic. It ended when the organisation's headquarters burned down. Pity there were people still inside, but at—"

Millie's side plate shattered on the floor.

"Oh!" she exclaimed, and jumped to her feet. "I'm so sorry! Oh no, what a mess."

She crouched and began collecting the broken pieces of ceramic. I quickly moved to help her.

"Don't worry about it," said Celane. "The plates are easily replaced. Let me just call one of the Oblates to help you."

Millie, out of sight of the rest of the table, touched my hand.

I will ruin her, she mouthed, then jerked her head in Verje's direction.

I shook my head.

You'll see. Then she got up, and continued to apologize, drawing everyone's attention away from me. An Oblate appeared with a dustpan and swept up the rest of the broken plate. By the time everything had been cleared away, the main course was being served.

Seared fish flavoured with chives and lemon cream, sweet potatoes dusted with pepper and shavings of dried mushrooms, noodles in a clear, salty broth. So much food, all of it beautifully prepared. Thoughtless of expense, careless in generosity. I was unsettled and uncomfortable in the face of the Reverends' easy hedonism, and ate sparingly, without tasting anything.

"Elfreda," said Celane, as she set down her cutlery, "I hear you were something of a master at Tryst. Yet I distinctly remember you telling me you had never played before."

"I hadn't." I tried to smile. "And I only scored one point, so 'master' seems a stretch. It was Herald Olberos's throw that deserves praise."

"Oh, so the pass came from you?" Celane asked Jesane with interest. "Unfortunately, I missed the moment, but I hear it was quite something."

Jesane grinned. "I saw an opportunity, and I took it. Honestly, I'm surprised it worked. Earlier in the game, Elfreda had helped me out, so I . . ." She trailed off, and her expression soured.

Two tables away, Ilva had stood up. Her pale cheeks were flushed pink with emotion or alcohol, and she gripped the back of her chair for support.

"I don't need any of you!" she slurred.

The room fell quiet.

"All of you." Her eyes wandered until they found Jesane. "You think you're better than me?"

The Acolyte beside Ilva said something soothing and tried to make her sit back down. Ilva swatted the woman's hand away.

"Bunch of old dead women. Who cares? Who really cares? And what did I get out of it? Nothing." She laughed. "I hope you're happy now, Jesane."

"Please stop making a spectacle of yourself," said Jesane coolly.

"Spectacle? That hasn't even *started* yet. You have no idea, but I do." She swayed and mumbled something, then spoke louder. "I do."

The Acolyte made another attempt to calm her down, but Ilva stepped out of reach.

"You're all sick." Her voice quavered. "I'm done with it all; I'm leaving now."

She staggered to the door of the dining room, and slammed it behind her. A moment of silence, then a few guests laughed nervously. I felt stricken.

Bunch of old dead women. That could only be the martyrs. To hear Ilva raving—*who cares? who really cares?*—while surrounded by light and wine and luxury seemed monstrous. Like someone had peeled back the skin of a new apple to reveal a core crawling with maggots. It was *real,* as good as a confession. It was right in front of me.

Ilva had probably killed my grandmother.

"Unbelievable," muttered Jesane. She cleared her throat and pushed back her chair. "Please excuse me for a moment."

I was back in my mother's kitchen, all the curtains torn down. *This wasn't an accident.* The broken glass on the floor.

"If there is an awkward situation between the two of you, I can make sure that Ilva gets to her carriage safely," said Millie.

Jesane wavered.

"Really, it's no problem." Millie rose from her chair. She ironed out the creases in her shirt. "Let me take care of it."

"Well, if you're sure . . ."

"Lariel, was it?" said Verje suddenly. "I'll assist you. I don't trust that woman not to steal something on her way out."

The Reverend's voice snapped me back to the present, and I tensed. *Shouldn't leave Millie alone with Verje.* I wanted to stop her, but Millie's mouth was set, and I knew that look too well; she would not listen. Before I could protest, she had squeezed my shoulder affectionately and was following Verje out of the room.

"That was upsetting," Celane murmured. "I wonder what Herald Bosch could have meant."

"Probably nothing, Reverend," said Jesane. "She's just drunk and bitter."

Liars. Both of them. I swallowed. They knew, they all knew. But I could not afford to dwell on any of this right now; I had to rein in my feelings.

Celane shook herself. "Probably. It just made me think of the new condition that Public Health is investigating. It's supposed to afflict some younger Sisters."

Need to act normal.

"What kind of condition?" I took a sip of water.

Celane turned to look at me. Her gaze was sharp.

"Hallucinations," she said.

I was lucky; I could cover my reaction behind the act of drinking. My heart pounded. I set the glass down before carefully replying, "Hallucinations?"

"Yes. Reverend Morwin said that they aren't yet sure what causes the condition, but the individual experiences a kind of intense vision, which she can scarcely distinguish from reality."

"Frightening," I managed.

"Public Health is working on a treatment." Celane was smiling, but her eyes could have cut glass. "Do you suffer from any kind of hallucinations, Elfreda?"

"Not to my knowledge, Reverend."

"I suspected not. Jesane, how about you?"

Jesane frowned slightly. "I can't say I have. Never heard anyone else talking about hallucinations either."

I thought that Celane looked, for an instant, disappointed. Then her expression smoothed over.

"Well, I suppose that's something to be thankful for," she said.

Millie slipped back into the dining room. She had a faintly puzzled look on her face, but smiled when she sat down beside me. The conversation moved on, and I did my best to seem relaxed and engaged, all the while feeling like I might be physically sick.

Celane knew. Celane knew about the existence of visions, and she had known to ask me about them.

Verje returned a few minutes later.

"I paid the driver double," she said. "He still wasn't happy about it, but Ilva had already passed out on the back seat, so he didn't have a lot of choice in the matter."

Jesane looked troubled. "Is she all right?"

"As well as can be expected. Disgraceful behaviour. I'll have to talk to Maternal Affairs about getting her demoted."

"Oh," said Jesane.

After a while, the mood of the dinner picked up again, but Jesane remained subdued. When the Oblates cleared the last plates, she was quick to excuse herself.

"I have to be at work early tomorrow," she said. "Thank you for the lovely evening, Reverend."

"My pleasure, Jesane," said Celane.

"We should be going too," said Millie. She gestured reverence in an endearingly clumsy way. "It has been a privilege to spend time with you all."

"Lovely to meet you, Lariel. I hope to see you and Elfreda again soon," said Celane.

Millie waited until we were out of earshot before whispering, "That was dramatic."

"Tell me about it."

She maintained a firm grip on my waist as we walked. "You okay?"

"Yeah. I was glad you were with me, though. Thanks, Millie."

She briefly leaned her head against my shoulder. "Anytime."

Osan's eyes glinted below the rim of his hat. He straightened in his seat as we approached.

"I was getting worried," he said.

Millie hesitated. "Osan . . ."

"Let's go. We can talk later."

Millie climbed into the carriage. I glanced down the street.

"Just El?"

"Sorry. I was thinking about something." I followed Millie inside.

Osan clucked his tongue at the horses. We rolled forward. Once we were a street away, he spoke.

"How did it go?"

"Bunch of psychopaths," said Millie.

"And the woman escorted out?"

"That was Herald Ilva Bosch," I said. "She had too much to drink. Started ranting about old dead women. Did you see her carriage leave?"

"I did. Reverend Verje spent a long time convincing the driver to take her away."

"Yeah, Verje told me to go back inside." Millie grimaced. "I didn't think twice about it. Presumably a compulse?"

"I'm so sorry," I said. "I was worried about that."

"No harm done." She squeezed my hand. The streetlights passed, turning her face light, then dark, light, then dark. "I should have been more vigilant. Next time."

"Next time?" said Osan.

"I made a few friends," she said. "So I can do a little independent digging."

Osan and I both groaned.

"What?"

"Who did you talk to?" I asked.

"Ilva, for a start. She's clearly vulnerable, and involved in *something*." Millie ran her fingertip along the ridge of the window. "She's lonely and scared. I can work with that."

"Millie, I don't know."

"I do," she said. "It'll be fine."

"She's unstable."

"But not dangerous. Really. I can handle this."

Osan drew to a halt at the end of Millie's street. The horses stamped their feet and snorted.

"Don't get reckless," I said.

Millie leaned over and kissed my cheek. "Same to you."

Osan watched her until she reached the door of her building. Then he turned the carriage around and we headed toward Pearl Boulevard. I slouched back on the bench, quiet for a while.

"What's on your mind?" he asked.

"A lot of things." We passed another cab heading the opposite way. The air drifting through the open window cooled my skin. "I'm thinking that if I'd stayed with my supervisor that night, she might still be alive. Or if I hadn't told you to stop following me. Things like that. Why is Millie afraid of you?"

"I think you can probably guess."

I fell silent. We rattled up the boulevard, the wheels loud in the quiet residential area. The night folded around us.

"You used to be in the Resistance," I said. "And Millie's scared that you'll tell me about her involvement in the organisation."

Osan gently guided the horses across the intersection. The Gardens grew larger on the left, and a layer of dry leaves carpeted the road.

"How long have you known she's part of it?" he asked.

I laughed softly. Osan glanced around and, with irony, I performed an old gesture; a swivel of my left wrist to touch my right fist. The same gesture Daje and Finn had exchanged outside the Candle. It dated back to the Ash Disciples. It meant "we shall reclaim."

"I can't remember *not* knowing," I said.

"I see." He turned back around. "And what makes you think I quit?"

"You work for Rhyanon."

"Could be two-timing her."

"But you aren't. For starters, she's too smart for that. And you care about her."

"And Millie cares about you. That doesn't mean . . ."

"Why did you quit?"

He sighed. I waited.

"Let's see," he said. "There was a man. Renson. He made some mistakes, ended up in the Renewal Wards. As he was an upstanding member of the Resistance, I expected that his friends would attempt to save him. But they didn't. When it mattered, the Resistance proved toothless."

He turned onto Reverence Street.

"That's when Rhyanon came in. At considerable personal risk, she managed to break Renson out of the Wards before he could face any Renewals." He glanced over his shoulder. "About that time, I realised that the Resistance was full of shit. All rhetoric and bluster, no real plans. But Rhyanon, she meant business."

I smiled. "So you joined her instead?"

"It was one or the other." He stopped the horses. "This was about eight years ago, so it's ancient history now."

I climbed out of the carriage. "Were you Renson?"

He shook his head, looking a little sad, a little amused. "No. No, I wasn't. But I did love him. He lives in Portevis now, where he's met someone else."

I put my foot on the driving board and hoisted myself up beside Osan.

"What . . ." His look of alarm vanished when I hugged him. He laughed. "Hey, what's this for?"

"Renson made a bad call if he chose someone else," I whispered.

"You think?"

"I'm certain."

"Uh-huh." He briefly returned the hug. "All right then, but please get down now before you spook the horses."

I complied. He straightened his hat.

"Don't go sentimental on me, Just El," he said. "This is long in the past."

"I won't mention it again."

He nodded, satisfied. "Get going, then."

At this hour, the dormitories were all but silent. I moved quietly down the corridors and up the stairs to my room. A light burned in the passage outside.

I felt exhausted but restless. The evening had given me a lot to think about. A lot to worry about. Not to mention my other lingering concern, but that . . .

A folded piece of paper had been slipped under my door. I frowned, then knelt and picked it up. There were only five words written on the page.

We need to talk.

—Finn

I stared at the message for a minute, before crumpling the paper within my fist. No. I had made myself clear. We were not going to do this again. It didn't matter that I missed him, or worried about him. The memory of his kiss burned bright in my mind.

He kissed me back.

And for a moment, just the smallest moment, I had felt joy.

I tossed the paper into the bin beside my desk and sank onto my bed. I would ask Millie to pass a message to Finn, but I could not face him myself. Especially if he wanted to talk about what happened on Moon Tide Eve.

Tired though I was, I struggled to fall asleep. I felt too hot. When I did eventually drift off, my rest was fitful. Vague, stressful dreams dissolved into nightmares.

I ran through the trees, retracing my steps to the Moon

House, but instead of a vision, Finn was stalking me. Then I was chasing him, and no matter how fast I ran, he was always just out of sight. The forest began to collapse around me, and I was waving goodbye to Zenza while she begged me not to leave her, waving goodbye to my mother as they took her to the Martyrium, then I was inside the Renewal Wards and Declan Lars was on top of me—

I sat bolt upright in bed, breathing hard. My nightclothes were soaked in sweat. I panted, my heart pounding, and waited for the fear to subside. It must have been an hour before dawn; the streetlamp outside had burned out, and the sky had turned a dull shade of navy. My throat was parched. I got up and walked to the bathroom, where I drank straight from the tap. My cracked reflection shivered in the early morning chill.

Just bad dreams. I washed my face, letting the water drip from my neck. The worst since my mother's martyrdom, but still. Just bad dreams.

I returned to my bedroom. The sun had appeared above the hills to the east. The light caught on my windowsill, and it was only then that I saw the lines. Dark, straight, running along each side of the frame.

I touched them and my fingers came away coated in black powder. Charcoal.

CHAPTER

EIGHTEEN

I WAS AT MY desk in Food Management when I heard the news. Acolyte Tahen walked in holding a copy of the *Resounder*. She set it down on the meeting table and smoothed out the pages.

"It . . . it happened again," she said.

According to the article, the carriage driver had escaped from the incident unharmed. Masked attackers had jumped into the path of the horses and, when the driver stopped the vehicle, threatened him at knifepoint. While he protested, the assailants dragged Ilva out the back. Drunk, half-asleep, disoriented Ilva. The Herald had put up no defence.

More enquiries. More Council meetings. I carried a grey, leaden feeling in my stomach for days. I remembered Ilva storming out of the dining room and the uneasy laughter that followed after her. Why hadn't I offered to help? It would have been easy. But instead I watched as she stumbled—drunk and angry and alone—out the door.

"You can't blame yourself," said Millie, later. "How could you have known?"

But the difference was that Millie *had* jumped in to assist Ilva. She had scarcely even hesitated. Unlike me.

And a small, dark voice whispered: *Should I feel pleased?* It seemed very likely that Ilva had sent my mother to the Martyrium. If that was the case, then wasn't this a kind of justice? It didn't feel like justice. It felt like I had wished harm on her, and then someone had immediately butchered her in the street.

Food rationing came into effect two days after the murder.

We could not afford to delay any longer. According to our projections, Aytrium had enough resources to keep the city fed for the next four months, assuming that food was distributed equitably. I knew that was optimistic; two months was more likely.

Unless it rained. If it rained, we might be able to salvage some of the harvest.

In the wake of our announcements, the merchant guilds were in uproar. Of course they were. Access to fresh goods would be more heavily regulated, independent contracts with farmers dissolved, and any excess foodstuffs seized and delivered to Food Management. But in spite of several furious petitions, there was nothing they could do to stop us. The Sisterhood held complete control over access to Ceyrun, and large quantities of food could not get inside the walls without our permission.

The clamour only grew louder when we announced that we were instituting a freeze on all produce prices. Merchants attempting to overcharge would lose their trader's license and find Enforcement knocking at their door.

We weren't stopping business. We were just making it arduous and less profitable. Meanwhile, Food Management would expand emergency stockpiling operations for non-perishable goods in the Field silos. If matters came to the worst, we would establish food depots all over Ceyrun, where citizens could collect daily rations.

In addition—and despite Verje's grumbling—Water and Sanitation had agreed to decrease water pressure within the city, and would start implementing strategic rolling water outages in the next week.

Finally, and on top of everything else, I had to prepare a presentation for the symposium. I found all of Zenza's old files and reports on my desk, along with a note from Reverend Somme thanking me for my help. That bothered me. She could have at least asked.

Nevertheless, I applied myself to the task, collating figures from our alternate food source programs, calculating the volume of water these projects would require going forward, outlining worst-case scenarios and possible outcomes. Zenza had done much of the math already, and I was determined to honour her work. The finished presentation would be accurate and comprehensive, and it might finally be alarming enough to convince Water and Sanitation of the seriousness of the situation.

I didn't sleep much that week. Or eat. I became so absorbed by the avalanche of work and stress that I began to forget about the little things.

"Elfreda?"

I looked up from the file I'd been reading on soil quality. Reverend Somme stood in front of my desk. I hastily gestured reverence.

"Can I see you in my office please?" she asked.

That did not sound promising.

"You aren't in trouble," she added.

"Right." I closed the file and got up. "Of course, Reverend."

Somme's office was tucked into the corner of the second floor; a large, wood-panelled room with a varnished desk, and drapes in the colours of the Food Management insignia: pale orange and mauve. The Reverend's robes hung loosely, and her face had gained a new gauntness, but her hair and make-up remained immaculate.

"Won't you close the door behind you?" she asked.

I did so.

She gestured at the chair across from her. "How are you holding up, Elfreda?"

"I'm fine."

"Are you sleeping?"

"Yes, Reverend."

"I want to tell you to take the week off, but Food Management cannot afford to be short-staffed at the moment."

"I understand. If I might speak freely, Reverend?"

She gestured assent.

"Work gives me something to focus on. If you tried to send me home for a week, I would refuse."

"That's not much of a comfort." She adjusted her glasses. "How would you feel about a promotion?"

The question caught me off-guard.

"Excuse me?" I said.

"This is unpleasant to discuss, but you are the most qualified to fill Zenza's vacancy. If you took over her role, I could assign another Acolyte to your current position."

That Acolyte would almost certainly be many years older than me, and she would regard me as a power-hungry usurper. Taking advantage of my supervisor's murder to scale the Order.

"I'm—I don't know," I said. "I've never held a leadership position before."

"I believe that you could excel, under the right circumstances," said Somme. "But take some time to think it over. I won't pressure you. Eater knows that you've been through enough already."

"Thanks."

"And you are eating, aren't you?" She reached under her desk. "I think I have some wheatcakes here somewhere. Maybe a bit stale, but—"

"I'm fine," I said hurriedly.

"Yes, well, if you're sure. Are you ready for the symposium this evening? I was grateful for your offer to present Zenza's work."

I thought that I had misheard her. "Excuse me?"

"The presentation. You are ready, aren't you?"

"Yes," I said. "Yes, of course. Sorry, I was thinking about something else."

She nodded sympathetically. "At first I was surprised that you volunteered, but now it strikes me as the honourable thing to do. I'm sure you'll do her legacy credit, Elfreda."

"I hope so."

I returned to my work, but found it impossible to concentrate. Somme believed, without question, that I had volunteered to speak at the symposium. But I hadn't. I had never even given an indication that I was interested.

A misunderstanding? That seemed unlikely, but why would it matter to anyone else whether I gave the presentation or not? When the fifteenth bell rang and other Sisters began to leave, I hung back. The thought crossed my mind that I could just fail to show up for the event. But I had told Somme I was ready; it would be embarrassing for Food Management, and very unprofessional on my part.

The stack of audits on my desk dwindled. I cracked my knuckles and leaned back in my chair.

You're just being paranoid.

The symposium was happening in Tivaria, the agricultural epicentre of Aytrium. The town was a few hours from Ceyrun, and the Order had arranged a fleet of horse-drawn cabs to take participating Sisters from the South Gate to the venue.

I had almost reached the end of Pearl Boulevard when Finn called out to me. I tensed, and turned to see him straightening up from the wall of the customs house.

"I thought we were past this, I specifically—" I began, but then I looked at him properly and my anger transformed into alarm.

"I need to talk to you," he said.

A livid bruise darkened the left side of his jaw. He looked drawn and tired, as if he might have been sleeping rough for a few nights. His eyes were ringed by dark circles.

"Have you . . . Did you get into a fight?" I quickly walked over to him. "Eater, Finn. Who hit you?"

"No one." He touched his jaw. I noticed that his knuckles were split. "Well, no one I couldn't handle."

This was unlike him; Finn seldom even got into arguments, let alone fistfights. The bruising stretched all the way down his neck. The only time I ever saw him angry, it was on someone else's behalf.

"What happened?" I demanded.

"It doesn't matter."

"No, tell me. Whatever it is—"

"El, I appreciate the sentiment, but I'm fine," he said shortly, his face closed-off. "I just need to talk to you in private. I wouldn't bother you if this wasn't important."

He spoke to me like I was a stranger. I had no right to feel hurt; I was the one who told him to leave me alone. But it stung all the same.

I breathed out through my mouth.

"All right," I replied. "We can talk, but not right now—I'm presenting at the symposium and the cabs might leave without me. Can it wait until tomorrow?"

"The usual place, third bell?"

"Fine." Behind me, the horses were departing through the Gate. "I should go."

Finn nodded, still cold, still detached, but then something in him seemed to give way, and he sighed.

"Good luck tonight," he said. "Not that you need it."

"Thanks." I turned to go, but in spite of myself, I couldn't help adding, "You are okay, aren't you?"

The ghost of his old smile passed across his face. He nodded again.

"Whatever is going on, just . . . be careful." A cool wind blew down the street, and I drew my robes tighter around me. "I'll see you tomorrow, then."

"El?"

"Yes?"

He averted his gaze. "You're going to be fine."

I quickly walked away. Finn stayed where he stood, alone, his shoulders hunched against the breeze. The bruise on his jaw looked painful, and I hated to see him so hollow-eyed, like the life had drained out of him. It reminded me of the bad times, the years before his grandfather died.

I presented myself to the harassed Acolyte ticking names off a list on her clipboard. She glared at me.

"You're late, Acolyte."

"Sorry," I murmured.

She checked my details off on her register. "Well, you aren't the only one, I suppose. Use whichever cab you want; they're identical."

I nodded and walked over to one of the last remaining vehicles. I still didn't understand why we couldn't hold the symposium in Ceyrun; most of the participants would be members of the Order. True, a large portion of the civilian farming community lived near Tivaria, but anyone with the ability to make policy decisions resided in the city. It seemed a waste of resources to travel so far, as if the symposium was all for show—a performance for the public's benefit.

I climbed into the empty cab and set my bag down on the seat beside me. Through the window, I saw that Finn had vanished.

I wouldn't bother you if this wasn't important.

I drummed my fingers against the bench. It had to be something to do with the Resistance. The *Resounder*'s illustration of Zenza's murder loomed large in my memory, and I shook my head vehemently. No. Not possible. If the Resistance were responsible for the murders, Finn or Millie would have told me sooner. My friends had grievances against the Order, but they would never stoop to *that*.

I opened my bag and delved around for my presentation notes. I was overthinking the situation; tomorrow, I would talk to Finn and find out what had really happened.

The cab door opened. I looked up and found myself face-to-face with Jesane Olberos.

"Oh," she said. "It's you."

The Herald was red-eyed and dishevelled, her robes rumpled like they had been slept in. She clutched a brown folder to her chest, and her fingers left sweaty marks on the leather stitching.

"You're still presenting?" I asked in disbelief.

"Apparently no one else could give the talk." Her voice came out husky and thick. "May I share this cab with you?"

"Of course." Flustered, I crammed my papers back into my bag. "Of course, please do."

She climbed inside and sank onto the opposite bench. Her nails were bitten down to the quick, but she seemed more exhausted than anxious—as if she had worn through her stress and now sat hollow and ill.

"Listen," I said. "The presentation can't be that important, and I could help you to apply for compassionate leave? Maybe a stress pass—"

"Tried that. Denied."

My confusion must have shown on my face, because she offered a weak, humourless smile in response.

"I was also surprised by my supervisor's decision," she said. "But I suppose it was well-known that Ilva and I had broken off our engagement."

I hesitated, unsure of myself. Whoever Jesane's supervisor was, I felt that they had badly misjudged the situation. The Herald looked like a wreck.

"I think you should go home," I ventured. "Stress pass or not."

The cab rolled forward. Jesane shrugged.

"Better to get it over with." Her voice faltered, and she quickly brought her hand to her forehead, hiding her face. "Sorry to burden you. We barely even know one another."

"Can I do anything to help?"

She fell silent. We passed below the South Gate and out into the yellow afternoon of the Fields. The farmhands looked up from their work to watch us ride by. A flock of crows circled over the stunted grain, cawing.

"I had to explain to my daughter that Ilva is dead," said Jesane softly.

"Oh."

"She's five. And Ilva's daughter is only two. They've taken her into communal care."

"That's unfortunate."

"Yeah." Jesane stared fixedly out the window. "I'm probably overthinking something, but will you hear me out?"

The hair on the back of my neck rose.

"Of course," I said.

Even so, Jesane remained silent. She traced the flight of the crows with her eyes. The silence dragged on; I said nothing. When she finally spoke, her voice was scarcely louder than a whisper.

"Do you find it strange that the attack occurred right after Ilva's outburst at the party?" she asked.

So you wondered about that too, huh?

"I guess." I tried to keep my expression neutral. "She was drunk. It made her a more obvious target."

"But she was *inside* the carriage. The attackers wouldn't have known that." Jesane turned and I saw that her eyes burned, not with grief, but with anger. "I keep thinking about it. How would anyone know that a Sister was inside that cab at all?"

"Unless they followed her from the party. Or the driver was complicit."

She nodded.

"It is strange," I said. "Although there is so much we don't know."

Jesane bunched the fabric of her robes between her hands. Beyond the window, the sun was setting, and the light cast her in red and gold.

"Your friend, Lariel?" she said. "Did she say anything to you afterwards?"

"Nothing specific." But Millie *had* assumed that Verje compulsed her. At the time, I assumed it had been a matter of convenience for the Reverend. But if Verje wanted to talk to the carriage driver without Millie hearing, or perhaps to give a signal to someone watching . . .

"Could you ask her about it?" asked Jesane. "Please?"

I nodded. "If you'd prefer, you could speak to her yourself. She won't mind."

Relief washed over her face. "That would be good."

"Is there any reason why Ilva might have been targeted?"

Jesane opened her mouth to answer, then stopped.

"Did what she said mean anything to you?" I pressed. "Her outburst, at the party?"

Jesane seemed frozen. "Perhaps. But you don't want any involvement in this, trust me."

"Does that mean you're in some kind of danger?"

A pause.

"I don't know," she said.

A reckless impulse seized me. I reached out and took hold of her hand. She flinched.

"Go to Enforcement," I said.

"That could make matters worse."

"Then what if I approached the Commander on your behalf? Councilwoman Asan is abrasive, but I believe she's trustworthy. I'm sure she could shelter you."

Her jaw tightened. "She will extract a price."

"You mean information?" I withdrew my hand. "If you have any idea why Ilva was attacked, you need to tell the Commander. She could stop it from happening again."

Stop it from happening to you, I did not need to add. Jesane was furious, yes, but she was also afraid—that she would resort to having this conversation with me was evidence enough of that. But she seemed to realise she had shared too much; she sighed, and the edge of her mouth quirked upwards in an ironic half smile.

"It's probably just paranoia speaking," she said. "My thoughts run away from me; I didn't mean to alarm you. You must think I'm ridiculous."

"Not at all."

"Then you are far too kind." She rubbed the raw skin surrounding her thumbnail, unthinking. "Perhaps I will talk to Commander Asan, after all; it might help to set my mind at ease. Although I suspect she won't be as sympathetic a listener."

"I doubt it could do any harm."

She nodded, distant now.

"I'll think about it," she said.

CHAPTER NINETEEN

THE TIVARIA COMMUNITY Hall was draped with Sisterhood banners for the event. The trees surrounding the building had shrivelled in the heat, the last of their leaves turning crisp and yellow, curling at the edges. A few civilians loitered on the steps outside; college students, a number of merchant guild members. Not a large crowd, but more would arrive before eighteenth bell—the hall's auditorium could seat up to five hundred people. I tightened my grip around my papers. I really hoped that five hundred people did not show up tonight.

Jesane remained hollow-eyed, but seemed calmer by the time we arrived. She had spent the remainder of the journey to Tivaria consulting her notes for the symposium, and I had left her to concentrate. I wanted to believe that she would talk to Commander Asan—not only because she might prove useful, but because she clearly needed help. Her raw vulnerability left me feeling strangely protective.

A few Sisters hung around the foyer of the hall, mostly Enforcement staff, no one I recognised. The evening was settling in, and a draft of chilled air drew goose bumps from the skin of my arms.

"Fewer members of the Order than I expected," said Jesane, echoing my thoughts. "Shall we go through?"

The air inside the main auditorium proved colder still, and smelled distinctly musty. The furnishings were sombre: dark wooden benches and grey carpets. A cluster of Heralds and senior civilian officials stood at the base of the amphitheatre, deep in discussion. Other Sisters sat in the first few rows of benches, reading over their notes before the presentations began. I noticed Rhyanon in the third row from the front. Commander Asan leaned against the side of the speaker's podium. Her gaze hardened when she saw me.

"Is this really it?" Jesane gazed around the room.

I descended the stairs and sidled into a row. "Perhaps the civilian turnout will be higher."

"If I'd known this was a public grievance forum for the farmers, I would have put up more of a fight with my supervisor. What's the point of coming all this way if the Head of Water and Sanitation doesn't even bother to attend?"

She was right—I could not see Verje anywhere. I shrugged. "It seems the Councilwoman didn't regard the matter as important."

"You really dislike her, don't you?"

"She refuses to take any kind of action to save water. I find that disheartening."

"But also on a personal level, you dislike her."

I allowed a small smile. "Is it that obvious?"

"Oh, I feel the same." Jesane sat down and set her notes on the bench in front of her. Her forehead furrowed; I guessed that she was thinking about Verje accompanying Ilva to the carriage. "There's something not right about her, don't you think?"

"Not right?"

"Something snakelike. Coldblooded." She leaned forward, resting on her elbows. "She's ambitious too, or so I've heard."

"That's not exactly unusual, though."

"It is if you're already a Councilwoman. Where to go once you've reached the top?"

I took a seat beside her. "Maybe the esteemed Councilwoman is just late."

Jesane snorted derisively.

I gazed around the auditorium. Even discounting Verje's conspicuous absence, the turnout was poor. From the Sisters I knew on sight, they also struck me as an odd mix. Apart from myself, I could recognise no other Acolytes, and no one else from Food Management. No one notable from Judicial Affairs either, which didn't bode well from a legislative standpoint. There seemed a disproportionate share of Sisters from Civil Obligations and Enforcement, far too few from Water and Sanitation. Why, out of all the Council, should only Commander Asan be present? I drummed my fingers on the bench.

Jesane and I had been amongst the last Sisters to arrive, and now civilians were starting to file inside. They looked grim, grimmer still when they saw the empty auditorium. They had probably expected more than the thirty of us to show up. I cringed. Far from ensuring the goodwill of the farming community, the symposium looked likely to turn them against us.

Then the door opened again and Reverend Jiana Morwin hurried inside. She pushed past the civilians on the stairs, her eyebrows drawn into a frown and her cheeks flushed with exertion.

"Councilwoman Morwin, huh?" said Jesane. "I wonder what's got her hot under the collar."

Asan met her at the podium. The Commander's expression was neutral, but she stood firm when Morwin attempted to step around her. I watched her mouth move. *What's going on, Jiana?*

"I think Councilwoman Morwin wants to address us," I said.

Jesane lifted her head from the bench. "She wasn't on the agenda for the evening. Maybe something's come up?"

Asan's jaw clenched and she stood aside, allowing Morwin to take up the podium. Other Sisters in the room whispered to one another. But I was looking at the Commander, at her tensed shoulders and narrowed eyes, like a caged Cat that smelled blood on the wind.

"May I ask civilians to vacate the hall immediately?" called Morwin.

A ripple of outrage spread through the crowd of farmers. I flinched.

"With haste, please," said Morwin, her reedy voice faltering. "The symposium has been postponed indefinitely."

"What is she *doing*?" I hissed.

"It must be an emergency," said Jesane, although she looked uncertain.

What emergency? It wasn't as if the building was on fire. Rhyanon had turned in her seat and caught sight of me. She blanched, then quickly looked away.

"I don't like this," I whispered.

Morwin gestured for a Civil Obligations Herald to close the door after the departing civilians. The tramp of feet on the wooden floorboards faded, and she waited until the auditorium grew quiet. Her expression was anxious, her face pinched.

"Thank you," she said at last, and adjusted the collar of her robes. "I'm sure you're all confused, so I'll get straight to the point. Just before I reached Tivaria, I was intercepted by a messenger from the Mud House. According to her intelligence, a mature Haunt has been sighted in the Berai province."

There were gasps from across the room. My mind reeled. A *mature* Haunt? But how? Asan rapped the speaker's gavel against the side of the podium.

Morwin spoke a little louder. "The last communication the messenger received, the creature was headed north-west toward Ceyrun. The messenger makes for the city, and will alert the Order to the threat as soon as she arrives."

"And the rest of the Mud House?" demanded an Enforcer in the audience.

"They are safe, having evaded the creature's attention." Morwin cleared her throat and stood taller. "We, however, are not. As matters stand, Tivaria lies directly in the Haunt's path. It will most likely be drawn to us."

My heart rate quickened. It was coming here? The idea seemed faintly ridiculous. How could there possibly be a mature Haunt loose on Aytrium in the first place? Surely there would have been attacks, some earlier indication of its presence, some kind of warning? It could not just appear out of the air.

"You will be divided into three-woman cohorts," continued Morwin. "We will begin binding every entrance to the building."

"That would be pointless," said Asan.

Morwin paused, caught off-guard. She turned slightly. "With all due respect—"

"We don't have the numbers to fortify a building this large. Not without a lot more lace." Asan projected her voice so that everyone in the auditorium would hear her. "I'm guessing that none of the Sisters present brought emergency provisions this evening? Which means that even if we succeed in defending the hall temporarily, the bindings won't last long enough for Ceyrun reserves to reach Tivaria. If a Haunt gets inside the building, Sisters will die."

"We need only hold the entrances, Commander."

"If this Haunt is mature, it will come through the walls." Asan's tone was brutally matter-of-fact. "Not to mention that staying here would jeopardise the safety of the civilians assembled for the symposium."

Morwin had gone red in the face.

"It is our only option, Commander," she said. Her forehead shone with sweat. "Your pessimism is unhelpful."

"I'm not being pessimistic; I'm stating facts," said Asan. "And you're wrong—there *are* other options. Where in the Berai province was the Haunt sighted, and how long ago?"

"We're wasting time—"

"Where, Jiana?"

"The messenger was in an understandable hurry; she didn't stop to brief me on specifics."

"Then she's grossly unprofessional." Asan's brow furrowed. "All right, we will assume the worst. From the Mud House to Tivaria is about five hours' ride by Cat, and the Berai province is an hour to the west. If the messenger left the House immediately after receiving intelligence of the Haunt sighting, then let's say the creature had an hour's head start. The Haunt probably moves at two-thirds the speed of the messenger's Cat. Given the addition of the time between Berai and the Mud House, it should place the Haunt at least an hour and a half behind the messenger. Herald Hayder, are my approximations unreasonable?"

Rhyanon jumped.

"Uh, no, not unreasonable," she said. "If you factor in a few assumptions, that is."

"Those being?"

"Well, the relative speed of the Cat, for a start. But also that Reverend Morwin met the messenger in close proximity to Tivaria, that neither the Cat nor the Haunt fatigued, and that neither party made substantial detours along the way."

"Thank you, Hayder," said Asan. "So, let's imagine the absolute worst and say that we have less than an hour."

"What good can this do?" Morwin burst out. "The Haunt is coming, and we cannot reach the safety of the city in an hour."

"We *think* the Haunt is coming." Asan fixed her with a piercing stare. "You seem curiously convinced of that fact, Reverend Morwin, especially given that one would have expected the creature to head toward the Mud House rather than Tivaria. There is plenty to distract it along the route, far more accessible Sisters to prey on. Why should it fixate on this symposium in particular?"

Morwin's cheeks grew blotchy, and her mouth shrank like she had tasted something terribly sour.

"But you're right, we can't return to Ceyrun in that time," continued Asan. "As far as I can see, that leaves us with three options. The first is staying here and waiting for the Haunt to arrive."

"The hall *can* be defended," Morwin insisted angrily. "If we don't waste time with—"

"The next"—Asan spoke right over her—"is dividing into smaller groups and immediately dispersing across the countryside. The Haunt might not be drawn to the scent of individual Sisters with Ceyrun so nearby; it might ignore us altogether. But if that gambit fails, then whichever lone cohort the creature targets will be practically defenceless."

"You would sacrifice Sisters?" said Morwin.

Asan's expression turned very cold. "I would sacrifice no one, although I suspect that splitting up would still result in fewer deaths than remaining here."

"You have no way of knowing that."

"Our third option is to make for Geise's Crown." Asan folded her arms. "If we push the horses, it should take no more than forty minutes. From the higher vantage point, we'll be able to see the Haunt coming. Instead of binding an entire building, we bind the creature directly. Less lace, more time for reserves to reach us. We light the flares, we wait. No one gets hurt."

"Unless your calculations are off, and the Haunt reaches us in the open."

"I am with Commander Asan."

The auditorium had been listening, rapt, to the Councilwomen's argument, but now they turned to stare at Rhyanon. She held her head high, and a fierce pride was written across her face as she gazed at the Commander. Asan met her eyes, and returned that expression with equal boldness, the same measure of warmth and challenge and possessiveness.

Oh, I thought, stunned. *So that's how it is.*

"I am with the Commander too." Jesane rose beside me.

I looked around, then also stood up. Morwin glared daggers at us, but I kept my nerve. Around the room, others were rising in turn, until almost every Sister was on her feet.

"I suppose that settles the matter, then," said Asan.

CHAPTER

TWENTY

THE MOON CAST a thin sliver of silver above the southern horizon. The air remained warm, and the sky was dark and hazy. I urged the horses down the eastern track, air streaming over my face. Before we had left Tivaria, Asan had instructed all the civilians to remain inside the hall, including our Ceyrun drivers. Alone, we would take the cabs as far as the old farm roads allowed, then cross the remaining distance on foot.

At another time, I might have enjoyed the rush of the moonlit ride. Fireflies swarmed over the pastures on either side, bright glimmers against the shaded fields. I scanned the landscape. The Haunt could come upon us at any time. Every movement of the grass, every night bird swooping through the air and animal rustling in the dark, felt like a threat. Two carriages rode in front of mine and four behind, with Asan leading the procession. Ahead, the solitary rise of Geise's Hill loomed over the countryside.

None of it seemed quite real. The appearance of a second Haunt in less than a month put paid to my dim theories about an isolated case of airborne infection; a renegade Sister had to be responsible. But *why?* One Haunt, one drunken mistake or terrible lapse of judgement, I could understand. The taste of Finn's kiss lingered in my mouth, his fingers tangled up in my hair. I grimaced. I understood that only too well.

But to repeat the crime, to have sex with two different men while knowing the probable outcome? That could not simply be lust. Someone must have infected these men *on purpose.*

Asan reached the base of the hill and drew on her reins to slow the horses. I followed suit. The animals huffed, their sides heaving, their coats shining and damp. I wasn't much of a driver, but Zenza and I had occasionally made field expeditions without a coachman, and I knew the basics. Tonight, the horses were skittish; their ears flicked and they tossed their heads. Whether they smelled something on the breeze or simply responded to our own fear, I could not say. I murmured soothingly and swung down from my perch. The doors to the cabs opened, and Sisters clambered out.

"Quickly," called Asan.

Someone brushed my hand and I glanced sideways.

"Are you okay?" muttered Rhyanon.

I nodded. "You?"

"Worried. I think . . ." Her voice faded. "Whatever you do, don't separate from the group."

"Got it."

"Eater, I hope I'm wrong." She quickened her pace. "Be careful."

"You too," I said, as loud as I dared.

Then she was gone. The other cabs had drawn to a halt, and Sisters were climbing the narrow footpath up Geise's Hill. The fortress at its summit formed a dark rectangle against the star-specked sky. Geise's Crown. I didn't know much about the place, apart from the fact that the Order had used it as a rest stop in the days before Tivaria grew prosperous. The hillside rolled with knee-high grass, but from the Crown we would have a clear view of the landscape for miles around.

Asan reached the perimeter wall and stopped beside the rusted old gate. She laid her hand on the bars. A pause, then the lock clicked and the gate swung inwards with a metallic groan.

"Keep moving." She gestured for the women behind her to file inside. "I want everybody on their guard. We aren't safe yet."

I was fairly sure that no one needed to be told, but then I saw Rhyanon hanging back. She allowed other Sisters to pass her, unobtrusively, but in such a way that she would be one of the last through the gate. A stab of anxiety twisted in my stomach. She was watching Morwin as the scowling Councilwoman tramped up the hill toward Asan.

Don't do anything stupid, I thought.

Asan's eyes glided over me as I reached the gate, cold and focussed and absolutely unafraid. Standing there, she looked like a painting of a hero from the Order's past, like Reverend Auvas holding the city walls during the Ash Disciples' rebellion. The effect was reassuring, but it was probably only a front for our benefit.

The perimeter wall of the Crown stood twenty feet tall and two feet thick, and dead vines clung to the cold stones. Beyond, a narrow stretch of brambles and dry soil ringed the fortress itself. The building had the look of a slab of granite that had been torn out of the earth and moulded roughly rectangular by giant hands. Centuries of rain had worn the stone walls smooth, and the windows gaped like small dark mouths. Four arched bridges ran from the roof to the parapets of the perimeter wall.

"Stop dawdling, Hayder," snapped Asan.

I glanced back to see Rhyanon reluctantly passing through the gate, followed by Morwin and then Asan herself. The Commander closed and locked the gate behind her.

"Right," she said, clasping her hands together. "We've made good time so far, but remain vigilant. I want a watch on the outer wall, eight women on each side. Look out for scorpions and snakes; I don't know what might be living here these days. Domonis, Lien, you're in charge of coordinating this."

Two Enforcer Heralds gestured acknowledgement.

"Hayder, Raughn, Olberos, we're going to light a signal beacon on the roof. Then we'll assess how much lace we have at our disposal and—"

"I will be accompanying you," interrupted Morwin.

Asan breathed deeply, as if she was fighting a losing battle with her temper.

"Of course, Councilwoman," she replied. "By all means. You're welcome to assist us in carrying tinder up from the basement."

I caught the smirks on some of the other Enforcers' faces. Morwin was none too popular among the Sisters present.

"Yes, well," the Reverend sniffed, drawing herself up to her full height and trying to salvage her dignity, "please go ahead."

The main doors stood slightly ajar, and clumps of knifegrass grew between the cracked tiles of the floor. It looked like the interior walls had been plastered once, but swaths of the lime had come away from the stones, leaving long ugly gouges like wounds. Our footsteps echoed. Moonlight fell through the door and cast the room in a bluish, wan light.

Asan removed the hood from a lantern hanging on a hook beside the door.

"The stairs to the basement are on the other side of the fort. Gets pretty dark, even in daylight." She pulled a tinder box from the interior pocket of her robes, and struck her flint against the steel striker. The tinder caught, and the sudden brightness threw our dim shadows long against the walls.

It was as if a switch had turned inside my brain. I was overcome by a dizzy rush of sensation; colours bloomed over my sight, and the smell of flowers overwhelmed me. I saw, for a brief moment, two rooms overlapping one another. The bare, dark fortress shimmered with a honeyed vision of sunlight and silk, a carpet of golden blossoms, and the warm hum of familiar voices. Music, a feeling of anticipation, a hunger . . .

I must have staggered, because a hand closed on my forearm. The vision vanished with a snap.

"I know this place," I gasped.

They all stared: Asan, Morwin, Jesane, and Rhyanon. Their eyes glinted in the dark. A wave of panic rushed over me. I quickly pulled free from Rhyanon, my pulse racing.

"Sorry," I stammered. "I think I came here when I was a child. With friends. I'm sorry, I just didn't realise until now."

"Are you okay?" asked Jesane.

"Fine! I'm fine." My voice came out high. What had I done? *Hallucinations,* Celane had said, with that strange lilt in her voice, that gleam in her eyes. I forced myself to laugh. "I think it's just stress."

"Keep it together, Raughn," said Asan.

"Yes, Commander."

She picked up a second lantern and passed it to me, motioning for me to light it from the first. "Enforcement left a cache of supplies here three years ago. We get what we need, take it up to the roof, light the beacons, and let the Order know where we are."

"Understood," I muttered, my face hot. It was a relief when the others turned away from me, although a faint hint of satisfaction played at the corners of Morwin's mouth. I didn't like that at all.

Deeper into the fortress and away from the windows, it was pitch black. The air smelled dank: wet earth and iron and decay. The lantern light cast streaks of wavering orange over the walls and caught on the edges of small recesses cut between the stones. Offering holds, all empty now. Snatches of the vision still ran over my sight; I could see the holds filled with carved stones and wads of orange feathers, everything dripping with black oil. I fought to control my breathing. The further we walked, the more plaster remained on the walls, and some faded paint still showed in slicks of sickly green and peach. We moved quickly, and our footfalls resounded in the empty corridors.

Asan paused to hang her lantern on a hook at the top of the basement stairs.

"Watch your step," she said.

The stairs ran downwards alongside the wall, carved right out of the stone of the hill and thick with cobwebs. The room below was huge, a vast hall that must have stretched almost as wide as the fort itself. A little beyond the stairs, I could see a shadowed mound—a five-foot-high heap of firewood covered in an oilcloth. The earthy smell grew stronger still.

"There should be cloth sacks here somewhere," said Asan.

She descended two steps at a time. "Herald Hayder, can you pack them with wood while we carry?"

"Of course."

Asan reached the base of the stairs and walked over to the woodpile. She pulled aside the oilcloth and picked up a log. She nodded, grimly satisfied.

"Still dry," she said. "With the smell, I thought we might be in trouble. Morwin, could you take that lantern from Raughn and light another?"

Something about the basement bothered me—beyond the yellow spill of the lantern, the shadows formed a shifting wall. Discarded furniture from the Order's past occupations cluttered the room like misshapen islands. The furthest corners of the chamber remained completely dark.

Still, I did not want to draw any more attention to myself. I took one of the hessian bags that Jesane offered and began stuffing it with tinder. Rhyanon stayed close to me. Did she think I was going to faint or fall apart? Her protectiveness unnerved me, as did the way her gaze kept darting between Asan and Morwin. Her jaw moved; she was grinding her teeth.

"Some foresight on the part of Enforcement." Morwin surveyed the covered crates of blankets and boxes crammed with jars of preserved food. She wandered over to have a closer look. "Keeping all these supplies at the Crown, I mean. Why go to such trouble?"

"Enforcement policy." Asan methodically packed wood into a bag. "The department has a mandate to be prepared."

"Prepared for what, exactly?"

"Circumstances like these." She grunted as she straightened.

"So does that make this your initiative or a typical Enforcement policy?"

"I wasn't aware that you took such an interest in our logistics." Asan jerked her head toward the stairs, and I quickly rose and followed her. "Don't worry, the idea of the caches predates my tenure as Commander. I just ensure they are restocked."

"How many are there?"

"A few. The exact number slips my mind."

"An approximation, then?"

"Really, Jiana? I'd almost think you were more worried about stocks of firewood than our present crisis."

Reverend Morwin huffed, but said nothing else.

Outside, the Sisters had organised themselves. Along each stretch of the parapet walk, women stood and stared out across the moonlit fields. An uneasy quiet had settled over the Crown; from the base of the hill, I could hear the horses nicker and stamp. Poor animals. They were probably safe though; if the Haunt showed up, it was almost certain to ignore them. With a feast of Sisters nearby, horse flesh was no temptation.

Lien, one of Asan's junior officers, was waiting for the Commander at the bottom of the stairs. She squinted in the sudden brightness of the lantern light.

"Nothing so far, Commander," she said, even as her hands flicked through a perfunctory gesture of respect. "We've got the sharpest eyes watching the eastern side. I also ran a quick inventory on the lace situation—only four brought emergency vials, but most of us performed a rite within the last week."

"I suppose that's the best we could have hoped for." Asan sighed. "Not that I'm any better; I'm only running on half power. Morale?"

"Not too bad. A little jumpy, especially the non-Enforcement Sisters."

"To be expected. Try to keep things orderly."

"Yes, Commander." Lien bowed her head.

"Good work so far." Asan started up the exterior stairs to the roof. "Leave the lantern inside, Reverend Morwin. It's going to ruin the watch's night vision."

The roof of the Crown rose slightly higher than the exterior walls; a flat stone rectangle about thirty feet across. The bridges slanted down to join with the parapets, and long years of exposure had worn every surface smooth as ice.

Easy to slip, I thought as I watched Morwin out of the corner of my eye. The Councilwoman never looked away from Asan. A thread of lace, a little shove, and the Commander could be dead on the stones below. It would be a different sort of accident, but not a wildly improbable one. Celane would still get the extra Council seat that she wanted. I emptied my sack of wood where Asan indicated. Maybe Rhyanon's twitchiness was just rubbing off on me.

"Can you stack that up, Olberos?" Asan passed Jesane her tinder box. "Don't light it yet though."

"Understood."

Then, like the last gasp of a wounded animal, the breeze died.

My skin prickled. Something had changed; the atmosphere over the fort grew close and cold. No one made a sound. I stared out into the darkness, aware of the rapid beating of my heart, the chill of sweat against my skin.

"It's here," muttered Asan.

The horses screamed. A moment later, a Sister on the eastern wall gave a shout.

"Ten more women on the east side." Asan's voice rang crisp through the night. "Do not try to bind the target until it's within reach. Conserve your lace."

There was a clamour of footfalls as women from the other parapet walks rushed over to the east wall. Beyond them, I saw a ripple of darkness cutting through the grasses, unnatural in its silence and speed, tearing up the hillside on bone-thin limbs.

"Now!" said Asan.

Ten feet from the wall, the Haunt collided with the lacework net. It stopped instantly, and its body seized as invisible ropes coiled around its legs, arms, torso. Tangled up in our power, it threw back its head and shrieked. The sound was awful, and I automatically took a step backwards, my hands covering my ears.

"Hold fast!" said Asan.

The disease was far advanced; the creature below scarcely resembled a human at all. Every part of its body had stretched like putty rolled thin, its flesh withered away to leave bones that protruded sharply from its mottled skin. Its hands were grotesque—the fingers extended to twice their length, and tapered into claws. Two spurs of bone had cracked through its forehead, and black blood leaked down its face. Its mouth yawned, gums crowded with new teeth, and from the sunken hollows in its skull burned a pair of golden eyes.

"Stay focussed," said Asan, her voice cool and flat. "Carsi, Phea, slowly withdraw your lace."

The two Heralds nodded. I saw the moment they let go of the binding; the Haunt jerked as though discovering some new slackness in its restraints. But the remaining nets were woven tight enough to contain it.

"Good work." Asan's shoulders unbunched, just a little. "We have a long night ahead of us, but the worst is done. No slacking."

A few muted smiles from the Enforcers.

"As soon as your lace starts to run dry, shift the binding on to the next available Sister." Asan nodded to herself. She turned. "All right, Olberos, you can light the beacon now."

Jesane fumbled with the tinder box, her hands clumsy. I felt just as rattled; I had never seen a Haunt like this before. It seemed unthinkable that the slavering, disfigured creature below had been an ordinary man until recently. He could have been Osan. Or Finn.

A spark jumped from the flint, and the tinder caught. Jesane bent close and nursed the fire with her breath.

"I want this beacon visible on the other side of Aytrium," said Asan. "Keep it burning, we'll bring up more wood. Raughn, with me."

When she turned back toward the stairs, Morwin was blocking the way. The Reverend's eyes reflected the flames. There was something oddly smug in her expression.

"Shouldn't you oversee matters here?" she asked. "Surely your talents are better spent keeping the Haunt under control?"

Asan's eyes narrowed.

"I have every confidence in my subordinates," she said.

"Still, for the Commander General to haul firewood while a threat stands just beyond the walls? I don't know, Saskia, it feels like your priorities are skewed." Morwin shrugged. "Unless you have some other reason to accompany Raughn to the basement?"

"What are you talking about?"

"I'm only suggesting that the Acolyte and I are more than capable of finding our way without you."

Don't leave me alone with her.

Asan made an expansive gesture. "If you're so concerned with the Council's good image, fine. Olberos, go help Raughn. Reverend Morwin and I will handle the situation here."

Now it was Morwin's turn to look annoyed. Jesane scrambled to her feet, only too happy to escape, but Morwin still stood in the way of the stairs.

"Is there a problem, Jiana?" Asan took a step closer. Her voice was velvet-soft and dangerous. "Something you would like to say, before I begin to wonder at the source of your newfound courage?"

"Excuse me?"

"It's strange, but you don't seem at all worried about the Haunt. Really, I should recruit you to Enforcement. We don't often see that kind of unflinching bravery."

A muscle in Morwin's jaw twitched.

"And it leads me to wonder if this fearlessness might be related to certain purchases at a back-alley butchery in Ceyrun." The light caught the underside of Asan's features, turning her face lurid and strange. "A few pigs' hearts, a couple of calves' livers."

I thought I must have misheard, but Morwin inhaled sharply. An expression flashed across her face—fury? shame? fear?—but I did not know how to interpret it. The moment stretched, tight as a wire. I felt frozen.

"You really think I'm that stupid?" asked Asan.

I was not certain what would have happened next. Morwin stood with her fists balled and her cheeks flushed, afraid and on the verge of violence. In contrast, Asan was a picture of studied composure, cool, almost indifferent to Morwin's aggression. But I never got to find out because, at that moment, a scream pierced the walls of the fort.

I jumped. The women on the parapets turned around, confused. A second scream rang out. This time it cut off sharply.

Rhyanon, I realised.

Asan recovered first. She shoved Morwin aside, nearly sending the Councilwoman tumbling over the edge of the roof.

"Whatever happens, do not release the binding!" she shouted.

I rushed after her. The Commander threw herself down the stairs, and I struggled to keep up. Below, I saw Lien hurrying inside, and the swing of light as she grabbed Morwin's abandoned lantern. There were footsteps behind me, but I did not look back.

"Hayder?" Asan demanded. "Hayder, what's going on?"

Rhyanon did not answer. Asan swore as she tore around the doorway and into the building. I reached the base of the stairs and sprinted to close the distance between us. The Commander had caught up to Lien and the light veered wildly as they ran, a disorienting lurch of shadow and brightness, glimpses of walls and doorways that were swallowed by darkness seconds later. Visions swarmed and flickered across the stones; I saw mouths stretched wide, human hands reaching from the holds, swollen fruit that burst in flashes of red.

"Hayder?" Asan shouted again.

"Saskia, don't!" Rhyanon's panicked voice drifted up from the stones. She sounded like she was in pain. "There's another one down here."

"What?"

I reached the entrance to the basement. Lien was already at the bottom of the stairs, with Asan right behind her. The lantern hanging from the hook burned steadily; just inside the circumference of its light I could see Rhyanon slumped against the woodpile. Blood darkened her robes, and she clutched her shoulder. Red spilled over her fingers.

"Go back, get more help," she cried.

I hesitated, unsure of the situation. Lien was only a few feet from Rhyanon, but she stopped and glanced at the Commander.

In the deepest reaches of the basement, I heard a faint rasp. Then yellow eyes bloomed in the darkness.

"Get back!" I shouted.

Lien's lantern went out like the flame had been pinched between two fingers. In a blur of speed and teeth, the Haunt leapt clear over the woodpile. It struck her across the chest—a thoughtless backhand swipe—and she flew sideways and slammed into the wall. A claw had sliced her throat open, clean as a knife gutting a fish. Her blood splattered over thc ground. She didn't even have time to scream.

Too late, my lace collided with the Haunt's torso. It stumbled back a step.

"Oh Eater," I whispered. Lien slid sideways and fell over with a terrible, dull heaviness.

The Haunt's legs tensed to rush forward again, but Asan yelled and her lace whipped around its body. I saw its flesh crushed beneath her power, crumpling and bruising black.

"You fucking bastard!" she screamed at its face.

Forcing aside my horror, I stumbled down the last few steps and threw out ropes of lace to support her net, twining my power around hers. I could feel Rhyanon trying to do the same. Asan's lacework had a rigid, precise quality; the web around the Haunt was a work of mathematical intricacy. My mind reeled. How could she weave *this,* soaked in her subordinate's blood and staring down her own death? Asan breathed heavily, her shoulders trembling with rage.

The Haunt growled, a rumbling vibration I felt in the depths of my chest. Blood dripped from its hands, and its antlers spread like a canopy of bone from its forehead. At near ten feet tall, it towered over Asan. Although the Commander stood right in its path, it stared past her. Stared at me, with eyes that glowed like the sun.

I heard footsteps and Jesane gasped as she reached the top of the stairs.

"Get help," I yelled. "We need more lace!"

The Haunt shook itself, and our binding rippled. Asan snarled. I tore my eyes off the creature for a moment, chancing a glance over my shoulder. Instead of running for backup, Jesane was stumbling down the stairs to assist us. Morwin shadowed her.

The Reverend wasn't looking at the Haunt. She was looking, with concentration, at Asan.

It was instinct, more than anything else. I withdrew my lace from the binding and flung a protective net over Asan's shoulders. Morwin's power hit mine and tore through, but my ropes were enough to weaken the blow. Instead of crashing into the Haunt, Asan only staggered forward before she caught herself.

"Fuck!" she gasped.

Morwin made a small sound of surprise; she had not expected resistance. Her eyes darted toward me, and she recognised the shock on my face. In that instant, I think that she looked scared; she raised her hands like she wanted to deny her actions. Then her neck snapped sideways.

I recoiled. Reverend Morwin collapsed. Jesane's eyes flew wide and her hands rose to her mouth.

Morwin's head lolled at an impossible angle.

That was lace, I thought wildly. *And it wasn't mine or Jesane's, it could not possibly have been Asan's, which means . . .*

"What's going on?" Asan demanded. When no one answered, she made a sound of disgust and quickly glanced over her shoulder. She saw Morwin. "Oh shit."

The Haunt pulled against the net, and its arm strained forward, grasping for Asan. It bared its grey needle teeth in a grin Saliva dripped from its jaw.

"Saskia . . ." Rhyanon began. Her voice was faint and her skin bone-pale.

"Stay awake, Hayder." Asan took another step backwards. She was almost beside me now. Perspiration shone on her forehead. "Olberos, get backup. *Now.*"

"Yes." Jesane ripped her eyes away from Morwin's corpse. The Haunt made a strange keening sound, and the noise appeared to snap her out of her daze. "Yes, Commander."

"As fast as you can," said Asan, although Jesane was already running up the stairs.

I shuddered. How had everything gone so wrong so quickly? I could hear Jesane yelling for help, her voice echoing through the dark, empty rooms. I fumbled with my lace, panic and shock turning it slippery in my grasp. I could detect none of Rhyanon's power now, and her eyes had drifted closed. It was just Asan and I.

The Haunt's scent of decay was heavy in my mouth. I could taste it, dense and metallic, like ancient damp earth, like underground water. The creature still watched me.

"We aren't going to last," said Asan softly. "Not long enough."

"Commander?"

"How much lace do you have left, Raughn?" She edged backwards, so that she stood beside me. "How long could you keep up the binding on your own?"

"I don't . . . I don't know . . ."

"Guess."

"A minute? Probably less."

Her foot nudged Morwin's shoulder.

"Eater forgive me," she muttered under her breath. She crouched. "Do it now. I've only got seconds left."

I could hardly breathe.

"Raughn!"

My shoulders shook. The Haunt dragged its weight forward like it was wading through mud. Visions scuttled over the walls, over the floor. I wanted to run, but there was no strength in my legs. All I could see were those lamp-yellow eyes, steady and unwaveringly fixed on me.

I wove together my lace and grasped the threads of Asan's binding tightly, just as the last of her power sputtered out. The effect was immediate; I felt my lace draining like water into dry sand.

Asan didn't bother with further talk. She dropped to a crouch and, with a grunt, flipped Morwin's body over. The Reverend's head flopped against her shoulder; her broken neck turning her face to the wall. I saw the knife in Asan's hand.

"Oh," I whispered.

"Concentrate." She pulled back Morwin's sleeve. For an instant the blade wavered. "Don't watch me, all right? It's this or we die."

I nodded stiffly.

"It's this or we die," she repeated, and for all her brusque confidence, I knew that Asan was trying to convince herself. I clamped my jaw shut.

The Haunt pushed forward another step. Closing the distance between us.

Out of the corner of my eye, I saw her make the cuts. Just like the rite: small, precise, bleeding. But we weren't in the Martyrium; this was nothing sacred. The ground beneath the Haunt's feet pulsed like organs, like a great breathing creature.

Asan swallowed the flesh without gagging. She got up. For a second, a terrified, irrational part of my brain believed that she meant to flee and leave me here alone. Instead she dragged Morwin's body closer to the stairs and out of my immediate line of sight.

"Do not turn around." I heard a sharp rip; she was slicing open the Reverend's robes. "Promise me."

"Yes," I managed.

How long before my power gave out? How long until Asan could wield hers again? I imagined the Haunt's talon scything across my throat, the hot spray of blood. My bones shattered, my head tilted. I clutched my lace like a lifeline, and it dwindled within my grasp.

"I won't let it hurt you, Raughn. Just keep your eyes forward."

"Okay," I whispered.

I heard wet sawing. I heard Asan's breathing turn ragged. My lace stretched like a fraying thread, and half-formed visions danced around me like moths made of shadow. I heard the Commander choke as she tried to swallow. All the while, I stared at the Haunt and it stared back, and we both waited for me to fail.

Then, like someone lifting a crushing weight off my shoulders, Asan resumed her hold on the binding. I sagged, and a sob escaped my mouth.

"No need for that," she said, with unexpected gentleness. "You did well."

Then, with power like I had never witnessed before, she raised the Haunt off the ground and swept it backwards through the air. It hissed, but Asan walked forward, pushing it further into the basement and away from us. Her arms and chest were drenched in blood. In her left hand she held the knife, in her right a slick, dark purple lump of muscle and tubes.

I wanted to leave, but I could not bring myself to look at what Asan had done to Morwin, could not imagine stepping over the body behind me. The Commander walked over to the woodpile and stood above Rhyanon. Her shoulders hunched.

"Rhy?" she said softly. "Rhy, please answer me."

At her voice, Rhyanon stirred. Her eyelids fluttered and she grimaced.

"Sorry," she murmured.

"No, don't say that." Asan knelt beside her. "Help is coming, we'll get you fixed. Just stay with me, all right?"

Rhyanon produced a pained wheeze; she was trying to laugh. "Yes, Commander," she said.

CHAPTER TWENTY-ONE

IT WOULD BE far more efficient for us to completely devour our mothers following their martyrdoms. A better use of resources. After all, the logistics of maintaining and safeguarding a vast emporium of half-alive women required an entire branch of our government. But two factors made this impossible.

The first was that, after death, a Sister's flesh rapidly drained of lace. The extremities first, legs, arms, then working inwards, the head, the abdomen, and finally the internal organs of the torso. The heart lasted the longest. While the power of an ordinary sacrament was lost within a day, a Sister's heart could retain up to forty percent of its lace a week after death, which made it by far the richest and most powerful organ of the body.

Even so, this type of consumption—the killing kind—was wasteful. And the Order could not afford waste. Over the centuries, our power had naturally atrophied. Sometimes Sisters died too young: in accidents, in conflict, struck down by disease. A not insignificant number killed *themselves,* especially before the mandatory counselling program was introduced. And with each death, we lost not just the individual herself, but her bloodline.

One day, some whispered, the Order would run out of lace entirely. And what then?

The second factor was that consuming too much flesh too quickly resulted in certain side effects. We called it gorge sickness. When, during past crises in the Order's history, Sisters forced down more than a few fistfuls of flesh, some of them began to behave erratically. Often violently. Therefore, the practice of gorging was reserved for the most dire of emergencies.

Asan began to show symptoms during the journey back to the city. I was not in her carriage; I only heard about it later. They said it started with the drumming. Her foot tap-tap-tapping against the side of the cab without any regular rhythm, listless, more like a nervous tic than anything else. It grew louder and more insistent.

"Afraid of me," she had muttered. "Everyone saw. All afraid of me now."

She kicked the panel so hard that the wood cracked.

At the time, I was sitting in another cab, answering questions posed by a nurse from Public Health. The Herald was sweet-voiced and matronly, but all I could think was that she was Reverend Morwin's subordinate. Reverend Morwin, who had tried to push Asan into the Haunt's reach. Reverend Morwin, whose body followed us back to the city in a carriage shared with Lien, the curtains drawn over the windows.

I said as little as possible. It was clear that I wasn't physically hurt. The nurse explained, calmly and quietly, that I was probably just in a state of shock. But with rest, plenty of water, a little food—she patted my knee in a reassuring way—I would be fine. There was nothing to fear now; the Haunts had been taken to the Edge.

The journey blurred in my mind. I was dropped off outside the dormitory and told not to discuss anything that had happened. The Sisterhood needed time to prepare an official response, and there was sure to be an inquiry process as well. If I did not feel any better by tomorrow, I should ask for assistance at the Sanatorium.

"Herald Hayder?" I managed to ask, before the carriage pulled away.

"She will be taken care of," said the nurse. I took that to mean that she did not know if Rhyanon was even still alive.

And then I was alone.

The sun streaked the rooftops with orange. A small bird sat on the rafters of the building opposite and chirped. Was this all? After the violence and terror, did it just end like this, with me standing on my own in the cool morning air? I felt strangely outside of myself, not angry or scared, but confused, as if something had gone missing or been taken away from me.

I stood there for a long time, waiting without knowing what I was waiting for. When I grew cold, I turned around and went inside.

Sleep came easy. I laid my head down, and unconsciousness rose and swallowed me. Until then, I had not even realised how exhausted I felt. No dreams, no thoughts, not even the bustle of the daytime street could disturb me. I opened my eyes again and it was midafternoon.

I had fallen into bed without undressing, and the bloodstains splattered across my robes had faded to brown. My skin felt sticky. I sat up and rubbed my eyes. Outside my window, I could hear someone whistling, and the stamp of horses' hooves on the flagstones. Ordinary, unremarkable sounds. I shivered.

What now?

I pulled off my robes, bunched them up, and threw them into the corner. To hell with the expense; I would buy a new set. A few meals skipped and a little of my savings—money well spent if it meant I never needed to scrub Morwin's blood out of my clothes. I got up and walked to the bathroom. If I could just feel clean, then maybe I would be able to think straight. My mother used to tell me to focus on one task at a time, to devote myself to the actions within my control. Well, I could control washing. It was a start.

It was while I was scrubbing my arms with a wet sponge that I remembered that I had promised to meet with Finn. Guilt weighed on me; of course he would understand, if he knew, but this morning it must simply have felt like I had stood him up. I imagined him standing alone in the graveyard and waiting for me.

I wouldn't bother you if this wasn't important.

"Damn it," I muttered.

There was no point, but I went anyway. In some unfathomable way, it felt like a penance. Or maybe I was just lost and lonely, and the graveyard gave me somewhere else to go. I took a cab, heedless of the expense, and sat quietly as the vehicle rumbled over Pearl Boulevard and into Minor East. I knew Finn would not be there, but the graveyard called to me all the same.

"Over here is fine," I said, as the vehicle drew to the end of Rush Street.

A few people stood over grave markers, laying flowers or bowing their heads in prayer. I took my time reaching the usual spot. Weeds had pushed up through the soil over the untended grave; ugly clusters of spinebrush and nettle.

I stared at the marker. I wasn't sure what I had expected. Maybe I had held vague hopes for some kind of message from Finn, but that was stupid—it wasn't as if he would pin a letter to the ground.

I shuffled my feet, crossed my arms. He had looked such a mess yesterday, and his behaviour had seemed . . . off. Something was wrong.

I spat on the grave, and then hurried back to the carriage.

"Can you take me to the Candle?" I asked.

By the time we got there, the sky had grown yellow and pale with the dusk. I did not have enough money for the return trip, so I paid the cab driver and he trundled off in search of new passengers. I would walk back to the dormitories.

Lucian was sweeping out front. Sweat darkened his shirt, and his lip was fat and split. He was smiling to himself, though, until he saw me. Then his face closed off like a slammed door.

"I'm looking for Finn," I said.

Hatred shone in his eyes, but I returned his glare with perfect blankness. He held my gaze, then snorted and continued sweeping.

"Not here," he replied.

"Will he be, later?"

Lucian shrugged.

"What does that mean?"

He shrugged again. "I don't keep track of him."

"I just want to know if he's scheduled to perform tonight."

"No."

"Thank you." I gestured appreciation with a slack, careless twist of my wrist. "I'll look elsewhere, then."

"What's your interest in him anyway, Sister?"

After everything that had happened, I felt worn thin as paper. I did not have the strength for an argument, I did not even want to *talk* to Lucian—especially since he was likely the person who had punched Finn. Judging by his lip, at least Finn seemed to have returned the favour.

"If he turns up, tell him I was here," I said.

Lucian smirked. "Anything else?"

"No." I turned from him.

A street away, I stopped and rested against the wall. Stupid, for me to let someone like Lucian get under my skin so easily; that wasn't like me at all. I should go home before I did anything I'd regret in the morning. No doubt Finn was fine, and what did it matter if he was angry with me? I had told him to leave me alone. Maybe now he would.

I sighed. On the other hand, it wasn't *that* far to Answorth Road. Maybe he was at home. I had never been inside his tenement flat—that would have been crossing a dangerous boundary—but I knew where it was. I could just knock, see if he was all right, and then leave.

The walk took a little longer than I expected, and when I arrived, it was properly dark. The air smelled of cooking oil and smoke. People walked with their heads down.

I looked up at the tenement, a three-storey building with dirty windows and laundry hanging from the rails of the balconies. A few people lounged around outside, playing dice and laughing. I folded my arms across my chest. What was I going to say to him anyway? This was foolish.

I climbed the stairs. Two kids almost knocked me over as they raced past. A woman brandishing a ladle pursued them. Finn lived at 12B on the second floor; these were the stairs he used every day. Did he like it here? He complained about the place all the time, but that was probably just a front—when anything was genuinely wrong, Finn clammed up and said nothing. Neighbours chatted in the corridors. Did he enjoy the sense of community, or did he find it claustrophobic? It was not so different from the dormitories, really, only warmer and less clean.

I stopped outside 12B. I hesitated, then shook my head and knocked. When no one answered, I knocked again, louder.

"He's not back yet." A man wearing a felt cap poked his head out of the door of the neighbouring flat.

"Sorry to disturb you."

"No worries. You are?"

"Elfreda. Finn's a friend of mine." I turned my wrist to conceal my Sisterhood tattoo. "Do you have any idea where he might be?"

"Afraid not." He looked me up and down, apparently trying to decide what manner of friend I might be. He scratched his beard. "That boy's been keeping odd hours these days."

"How so?"

"Moves around a lot during the early hours of the morning." He tapped the wall. "The sound comes right through."

I frowned. "Moves around?"

"Walking, dropping things, who knows? I don't think he means to make a noise, but it's woken me three times this week already. He's driving half the tenants mad."

"Have you spoken to him about it?"

"Of course. And he'll settle down for a day or two, but then it's back to the midnight wanderings. Have a word with him, will you?"

I nodded. "Sure."

The man tipped his cap and retreated back into his flat.

It would be an interesting conversation when I did track down Finn, I reflected. *Hi, sorry that I blew you off—I was being chased by a Haunt. Also, your neighbour lodged a noise complaint with me. Now, what was the important thing you wanted to tell me?*

I trudged back down the stairs. I had tried. There was no point spending the rest of the evening combing the streets for Finn; Ceyrun was just too large, and he could be anywhere. So why couldn't I just let it go?

The smell of wood smoke intensified. Across the street from the tenement, a woman had lit up a coal brazier. She knelt on the ground, where she had spread a large oilcloth, and applied a wicked cleaver to the joints of a pig's leg. *Thunk,* once, twice; she moved with practised skill, and the flesh and gristle gave way. Flecks of blood dotted her arms and face.

Stark, in my mind, Morwin's chest peeled open like the thick rind of a fruit.

I quickly looked away. There was a terrible ringing in my ears, and I felt like I was going to be sick. Even from across the road, the iron-sharp smell of the meat reached me.

"Fresh pork skewers!" she hawked. "Get them hot."

Some of the people playing dice wandered over. The woman speared squares of meat and thrust them onto the griddle over the brazier. Fat sizzled and dripped.

"Most affordable meat in the city," she said. "Place your orders quick."

I crossed the road. The woman noticed me and flashed a greasy smile. "Hungry, hon?"

"Where did you get pork?" I asked.

"My friend delivers it weekly. I promise it's the fresh stuff."

"But the Sisterhood has an embargo on meat products. It's supposed to be seized at the gates."

She rotated her skewers. "I guess he doesn't use the gates, then. You want?"

I shook my head. "It just strikes me as very risky. With the shortages, if the Order finds out that you are trading without a license—"

"Aytrium isn't short on food," she interrupted. "Some just get more of it than others. I'm evening things out."

"The shortages are real," I insisted.

The woman eyed me. "Do you have a problem with me?"

"El!"

I turned and saw Millie hurrying across the road. Her hair was tangled around her shoulders, and her cheeks were flushed.

"So good to see you!" she said loudly, as she seized me by the forearm and steered me away from the brazier. She lowered her voice. "What are you *doing* here? It's late, you shouldn't be out alone."

"It's only just past nineteenth bell." I resisted her; there were further questions I needed to ask the meat seller. "Did you know about this? That people are getting around the embargo?"

Millie affirmed her grip and dragged me onwards with grim determination. "The merchants were always going to find a way. But if anyone here realises you're a Sister, there's going to be trouble. Your wrist isn't even covered."

"Why should I always have to hide what I am?"

"What you are is an idiot."

"Say that again when Aytrium is starving."

"El, your friend got murdered barely three blocks from here."

"I'm well aware of where Zenza died," I snapped. "But that doesn't mean I plan to cower away in my room every time the sun goes down. Ceyrun is my home too."

"Your 'home' will stick a knife in your ribs, toss you into a gutter, and spit on your corpse. *You are not safe.*" Millie emphasized each word while glaring at me, and for the first time I realised how deeply afraid she felt. Millie never chastised me; she never lost patience when it came to my bad habits, when I was stupid or callous. But right at that moment, she looked ready to kill me herself.

The realisation cut through my defiance, and I was suddenly left lost and uncertain.

"It's . . . it's important." I dropped my gaze. "I've spent months trying to find new ways to stretch Aytrium's resources, but it won't be enough, not if the embargos are failing too. We'll never be able to feed everyone."

Millie exhaled.

"I get it," she said. "I know how hard you work, and I know the crisis is real. But you've got to be smarter about this."

"They think the Order is lying."

"They think there's still profit to be made, and they aren't wrong." Her hold on my arm loosened. She took my hand instead. "Let me walk you home. Please."

I felt impossibly tired. What was the point? I had nearly died last night, I devoted my life to serving and protecting Aytrium, and in return its people trampled my efforts to save them into the mud. What did anything matter? I would live, briefly, and then this place would cut me to pieces and devour me.

And I missed my mother.

"El?"

"I just wanted Finn," I said quietly. "You asked what I was doing here. I wanted to find Finn."

Her expression softened. "Oh. He didn't tell you?"

"Tell me what?"

Millie squeezed my hand.

"Finn left Ceyrun this morning," she said. "That's why I was here; he asked me to look after his place. I'm sorry, El."

I shook my head. "Where was he going?"

"He said it was for temp work, a job in Fort Sirus. A couple of weeks, maybe longer. It came up suddenly."

So that was what he had wanted to tell me. I should have been glad to hear he was leaving the city. Maybe if he got away from the Resistance, he could begin to build a real life. Something better, something more stable, maybe with someone capable of making him happy. My throat closed up.

"Good," I said. "Good for him."

CHAPTER TWENTY-TWO

THE SANATORIUM SMELLED of lavender soap and boiled cabbage, of slightly stale air and starched sheets and milky tea. During my stay, I had occupied a room on the ground floor, two doors down from the kitchens. I knew every inch of that room, every stain on the curtains, every detail of the wallpaper. For a month, I had been confined to the facility, and that period was scored indelibly into my memory.

My problems had all started with meat. Not that unusual—after their induction, many Sisters were known to turn vegetarian. But in my case, that preference became a fixation. Soon, I could not eat anything that had come into contact with meat, or even anything that resembled it. Red fruits, berries, I saw blood everywhere. I shied away from kitchens where meat was cooked, from any place where I could smell it, from any utensils that might have touched it.

And then I began to see that I had no way of *knowing,* for certain, that my food had not been contaminated. So, really, I could not safely eat anything at all.

I got away with this for a surprisingly long time, up until I fainted during my orientation at Food Management. That mistake led to the Sanatorium, and once the nurses realised *why* I was refusing to touch any of the meals they prepared, they resorted to drastic measures. They were just doing their job; if they had not force-fed me during those weeks, I probably would have starved. That would have been a terrible waste of a Sister.

But Eater help me, I hated this place.

The foyer was a cheerful hive of activity; Public Health Sisters bustled around with files and stacks of clean towels, clean sheets. Sunshine poured through the windows, casting yellow rectangles over the polished floor. A heavily pregnant Acolyte sat on a cushioned chair in the waiting area and stared into space. She absentmindedly ran her hands over her swollen belly, forming little circles with her fingertips.

Here I am, I thought. *Back in this place of my own volition.*

The Herald at the front desk did not look up as I approached. A heavy book lay open in front of her, some sort of medical reference guide. She traced her pen across the text as she read.

"Can I help you?" she asked.

"I want to visit someone."

Her black eyes flicked up.

"You are?" she asked.

"Acolyte Elfreda Raughn. Food Management."

"And the patient?"

"Herald Rhyanon Hayder. She was injured at Geise's Crown."

A pause. The Herald returned to her reading.

"I'm afraid I can't help you," she said. "Herald Hayder is no longer with us."

I felt as if a bucket of ice had been overturned above my head. "She . . . what?"

The woman looked up again and saw my distress. She grimaced and quickly shook her head.

"No, you misunderstand," she said. "I just meant that the Herald has been removed to another facility. We expect that she will recover, but she's no longer at the Sanatorium."

"Oh!" I sagged. "Hah, that was . . . Well. That's a relief."

The Herald smiled slightly. She made a note in the margin of the book.

"I'm sorry for alarming you," she said. She tapped her pen against the book. Loudly. And glanced down. I followed her gaze and saw what she had written in the margin.

Asan has her.

"Oh," I said again.

"If there's nothing else?" She turned the page.

"Uh, no. No, that was all."

"May the Star shine brightly on you."

I hurried out of the building and down the tree-lined stairs to Pearl Boulevard. My thoughts whirled. It seemed that Asan had overcome her gorge sickness. I had heard the rumours in the dining hall that morning: that she had been secluded in an Enforcement facility overnight, that she had been raving and wild and bloodthirsty. By now everyone in the Order knew about the Haunts, and had some idea of how the Commander had held them at bay.

Of course, only Jesane, Rhyanon, Asan, and I knew exactly what had happened in the basement, that Morwin's death had *not* been the Haunt's doing. There was no solid evidence to suggest otherwise, especially after what Asan had done to the body. Still if the full truth came to light, I suspected matters would get very ugly, very quickly.

That was one of the reasons I wanted to find Rhyanon. If there was an inquiry, we would need to present a consistent version of events. On a personal level, I also just wanted to talk to her for a while. It would be comforting to confirm with my own eyes that she was still alive.

But Asan had somehow already stolen her away.

I glanced back at the Sanatorium. In order to get Rhyanon out of the facility, the Commander must have acted within hours of her own recovery. That would have involved a lot of risk and a lot of resources, especially if she was under scrutiny. It suggested desperation. For whatever reason, Asan must have felt certain that Rhyanon was unsafe in the nurses' care. I shivered. An uncomfortable idea.

It was an hour before noon, and Ceyrun's streets were airless and sweltering. People moved slowly, their faces damp with perspiration. Everyone seemed a little more aggressive, a little hungrier, and a little quicker to anger. Stray dogs followed the shade, sleeping off the heat.

I took a cab to the stairs of Martyrium Hill and began the long, thirsty climb to the summit. I had put off the rite for too long already, and without lace I was vulnerable. Even so, I almost turned back twice before I reached the plaza. Cicadas hissed from the grass verges, and the fabric of my clothing clung to my skin.

I found the Oblate on duty slumped in the shade below the Star Eater's plinth. She looked around sixteen, sleepy and irritable. When she saw me, she scrambled to her feet with a start.

"Not many Sisters today, huh?" I said, gesturing for her to relax.

"It's the heat." She brushed off her robes, embarrassed. "My apologies, Acolyte. I should be, um, more alert."

"No harm done. It seems to me that the least Maternal Affairs could have done is offered you a shade cloth."

She smiled shyly. "Oh, it isn't so bad. Someone has to keep watch at all times, and I prefer this to the night shifts."

She took down my name beside the door and ushered me inside. Entering the building was like passing from summer to winter; the air within was mercifully cool. Motes of dust hovered in the rays cut by the skylights.

"I'll be here if you need anything," said the Oblate.

After she closed the door, I spent a moment staring up at the tower of alcoves overhead, the glimmering play of light on stone and flowering vines.

I sighed. Waiting would not make this easier.

My mother's hair was freshly washed and cut. Just above her ear, I could see the half-moon scar left by her martyrdom. A delicate process, so I had been told. I could smell the oil that the nurses had rubbed into her skin.

"It's me," I said softly.

I sat beside her and lifted the shroud to find her hand. Her skin was cool, like she had spent a long time submerged in cold water.

"Back again." I slipped my fingers between hers. They were

slack, but I held tight enough for both of us. "And mostly in one piece."

Morwin's body flashed through my mind, and I shuddered. No, I could not afford to think of that now. I leaned my forehead against my mother's shoulder, breathing in her familiar scent. Below, I heard the doors of the Martyrium open and the murmur of the Oblate's voice.

"Finn's gone," I whispered. "Rhyanon's missing. And it isn't fair of me to keep running to Millie with my problems. It's just that I don't know if I can handle this on my own."

"Kill me."

I stumbled to my feet so quickly that I knocked the chair over. For a heart-hammering, terrified second, I was convinced that my mother had spoken. Then I realised that the words had emerged from the Martyrium walls.

"*Kill me,*" the vision repeated.

The voice was toneless and echoing. I clenched my fist around the handle of the scalpel. Pale globes bulged from the ceiling above me, swelling out of the plaster like raindrops.

"*Why is it so dark?*" whispered the walls. *"Why can't I move?"*

"Elfreda?"

I spun around. Reverend Celane stood in the entrance to the alcove, her head tilted slightly to the side in perplexed concern.

"Is something the matter?" she asked.

I felt like the ground had dropped away beneath my feet. Of all the Sisters in the Order, here stood the woman who scared me the most. Here she stood, blocking my only path of escape from the vision.

"Honoured Councilwoman." I gestured reverence, trying to conceal the shaking of my hands. "You startled me."

The globes swelled and dropped from the ceiling, landing on the floor with a wet sound. Eyeballs. Different sizes, but the irises were all the same colour, a brown so dark it could have been black. The long threads of optic nerves trailed behind them, and they pushed themselves along the stones like caterpillars.

"I thought I heard a noise. Is everything all right?" asked Celane.

"Oh, I just knocked over the chair."

The Reverend stepped inside the alcove, and I flinched. She should not be here, she should not be inside my mother's *space.* Excepting the Martyrium staff, only the martyr's daughter was permitted to enter her alcove. Celane coming inside without so much as asking permission constituted a huge breach of propriety. Even through my haze of fear, I felt outraged.

"You were a speaker at the symposium," she said, still advancing. "Which means you were at Geise's Crown when the Haunts attacked. What an awful shock that must have been. It's little wonder you're on edge."

"So long in the dark." The irises contracted and expanded like mouths. *"No one can hear me."*

I forced myself to breathe. In and out. No panic, not now, not in front of her.

"I'm fine." My voice emerged rasping and faint. "I'm here to restore my lace, that's all."

"Yes, of course." Celane nodded sympathetically. "I heard that Commander Asan ran everyone dry trying to keep the Haunts contained."

"She did what was necessary."

"Yes, I heard about that too. Shocking, truly shocking."

The eyes crawled toward one another, tangling and sliding together into a bundle of white, red, and black. Celane's compulse tightened around my thoughts like a silken noose.

"Elfreda, I have to know," she said. "What really happened that night?"

Eater help me, I needed to get out of here. My head burned like I had a fever, and it was taking every ounce of self-control I possessed not to betray my panic. The Reverend watched me with those kind, intelligent brown eyes while the force of her lace strangled me.

"I'm not sure I understand," I said.

"I have concerns," she said gently.

"Concerns?"

"What Commander Asan did, well, it's unspeakable. Necessary, you said, but even so . . . I need to hear your account of what occurred that night."

The eyes drew tighter and started to fuse together, bubbling and melting like metal in a crucible. The sound they made was hideous. I swallowed. *Let me not pass out, let me not fall to pieces now.*

"Were you there when it happened?" asked Celane.

"The Commander was protecting us," I said. "She didn't want to do it. But the Haunt—"

"So you were with her? And the Haunt?" Celane's voice held a hint of eagerness now. She moved closer, her foot almost touching the twitching mound of the vision. "She shielded you?"

"She . . . she stopped the Haunt from leaving the basement." The back of my knee knocked into my mother's pallet as I tried to keep my distance from Celane. "Reverend, from what I saw, the Commander only acted with the Order's best interests at heart."

"Who else was present in the basement?"

"I—I don't know," I fumbled. "A Herald was killed, another badly injured. Morwin—"

"Was Herald Olberos with you?" she interrupted.

"Jesane Olberos? Yes, she called for help."

"You and Olberos, Asan specifically singled the pair of you out to accompany her?"

Someone else has fed her information, I realised. I wasn't sure what Celane was trying to uncover, but it dawned on me that she had not yet asked a single question about Morwin. As if the death of the Councilwoman was not her concern at all.

"*What has been done to me?*" asked the vision. With newfound weightlessness, it drifted into the air and slowly revolved, pale and quivering. "*I am stretched so thin.*"

"Elfreda?"

I strove to keep my gaze on the Reverend. "You know,

Commander Asan did say something odd that night. It probably isn't important, but it confused me."

"Was this while you were in the basement?"

"No, she was talking to Councilwoman Morwin on the roof of the fort." My heart thudded. "She asked if Morwin had bought any pigs' hearts recently. Do you know what that means, Councilwoman?"

It had been a fumbling stab in the dark, but my instincts proved sound. Celane's mouth hardened, and she grew stiff.

"The question seemed to come out of nowhere," I continued. "And Reverend Morwin reacted very strongly to it."

"I have no idea what the Commander might have meant. Did she say anything else?"

"I'm not sure." I controlled my breathing. *Don't look at the vision, don't look at the vision.* "Maybe. I would have to think about it some more."

Celane's expression was inscrutable. "Are you available to visit my house later today? I think we should continue this discussion."

I nodded. Anything to end this conversation now, anything to get her away from me.

"Tonight, nineteenth bell?" she suggested.

I gestured assent. Behind Celane's right shoulder, the vision had morphed and reformed into a new shape. A foetus, a half-formed creature with eerie, flat features. I could see its heart beating through the thin membrane of its skin.

"Tonight," I said.

As Celane turned to leave, she passed through the vision. At her touch, it dissolved in a swirl of fine grey mist.

CHAPTER

TWENTY-THREE

MILLIE'S FRONT DOOR sat slightly skew in its frame. The wood was worn pale around the lock, and the brass handle had dulled with age.

An old woman in the neighbouring building watched me from her window, lips pursed in suspicion. I could hardly blame her—I had been hovering outside the door for almost ten minutes already. Despite walking halfway across Ceyrun to reach Millie's flat, I could not seem to bring myself to knock.

She might not even be home. Maybe I was standing outside an empty apartment, skin scorching under the sun, for nothing. I studied her door like the battered wood might provide answers.

Foolish, I thought. *Enough of this.*

I knocked. For a moment, I heard nothing from inside, and a guilty relief surged through me. This was a sign, she was not here, I should leave—

The door swung open.

"El? What are you doing here?" Millie squinted against the sunlight.

I wanted to say something, just something funny or lighthearted, but the words evaporated from my mind. I gestured clumsily, a kind of helpless shrug. Millie's eyes widened.

"Come in." She reached out and took me by the arm, ushering me into the cool darkness of her living room. The abrupt change of temperature made me feel lightheaded. "Tell me what happened."

Her place was a mess, as usual. A stack of books lay beside

her couch, and there were plates and glasses piled high in her kitchen sink. A dusty red dress draped carelessly over the pedestal table, as if she had thrown it off once and then never picked it up again. All the curtains were drawn over the windows to keep out the heat.

"El, you're scaring me," she said. "Please say something."

"I'm fine," I muttered.

She sat me down on the couch, shoving aside scatter cushions to make room.

"I'll get you some water," she said, and hurried to the kitchen. She found a glass and thrust it under the tap. "Did you walk here?"

"Yes."

"You can afford to pay for a cab sometimes, you know. It's baking out there." She returned with the glass and pushed it into my hand. "Talk to me."

I looked down at the water. "I was planning to work my way up to the topic."

She sat down. "That bad?"

"Depends." I ran my finger over the rim of the glass. "Millie?"

"Yes?"

"How do you . . ." I stopped. "How do . . ."

I could not do it. *How do you feel about me?* I drank from the glass, unable to look at her. If Millie turned me away, I would have no one left. The idea was intolerable.

"Hey now," she murmured. "Calm down, it's just us here. Everything is okay."

I shook my head.

"Has something happened? Or is this about Finn?"

"It's not Finn," I said.

She rubbed my back with her fingertips. Her touch drew goose bumps over my arms, and I drank again. This was so much worse than I had anticipated. How could I possibly risk losing her friendship? Fear made it difficult to even speak.

She brushed my chin, turning my face toward her.

"Listen, I can tell you're frightened," she said. "And that you want to say something to me."

"Sorry."

"Just take your time. I'm not going anywhere, all right? I promise."

I breathed out. Then, with care, I set the glass on the floor and folded my hands in my lap.

"How do you feel about me?" I asked.

A pause.

"I love you," said Millie, with almost unbearable gentleness. "I should think that's obvious."

"As a—as a friend? Or—"

"If you're asking whether I'm romantically attracted to you?" She sighed. "It's more complicated. Which I think you already know."

"Does it have to be? Complicated?" I tried to smile. "I mean, Hanna and I could probably find a way to share you. And Daje thinks I'm okay."

"It's not them." She leaned back on the couch. Her expression was pained.

"Then it's me?"

"Here's the thing." She picked at the loose stitching on the armrest. "I know you're in love with Finn."

I shook my head.

"I'm not saying that's wrong," she said. "Or that you ever meant for it to happen. Given the opportunity, I'm sure you would change your feelings, but you don't get to make that choice. No one does."

She pulled a thread and the hole in the upholstery grew wider. The stuffing peeked through. I wanted to tell her to leave it alone, but I stayed silent.

"So that's why it's complicated," she said. "Because if we started something, I would always know I'm the person you settled for, instead of the one you truly wanted." Her voice dropped. "I'm not strong enough for that, El. Please don't ask it of me."

"Of course," I said. "I'm sorry, I should never have—"

My throat hitched. Instantly, Millie leaned over and wrapped her arms around my shoulders. I tried to push her away, to tell her I was fine, just being ridiculous, but she did not let go. She stroked my hair, and I felt like a child, lost and confused and overwhelmed.

"I can't handle this alone," I whispered.

"Hush." She held me tighter. "I'm still here. I told you, I'm not going—"

"Millie, I'm pregnant."

Her hand stopped moving across my hair. There it was, out in the open, out of my mouth and irrevocable. The words hung between us like they possessed a physical weight. I buried my face in my hands.

"I'm two weeks late," I said through my fingers.

"It could be stress."

"I'm never late." The vision in my mother's alcove haunted me. "I wanted so badly to be wrong, but I'm not, I know it."

"Has the Order tested you yet?"

"Maybe it will be a boy." I pressed my hand to my mouth, fighting a rising tide of nausea. "But the idea of it growing, all those months, only for the Sisterhood to just . . ."

I could not finish; it was too horrible to say aloud. And it would be no better if I bore a girl, a daughter who would grow up to suffer the same fate as me, as my mother, as all of us. Who would consume me.

Buried away in my memory was a scene from my childhood, which returned to me sometimes in dreams, sharp and clear as glass. In it, my mother stood at her bedroom window in the dark, and outside I could hear music and laughter, see the flicker of festival lights.

Why are you crying? I asked.

She turned away from the window and looked at me, and her eyes were black holes.

I wish you'd never been born, she whispered.

Those words—the way they were spoken—had broken some part of me. I could not blame my mother, I could not hate her, but the words remained, like a small creature had burrowed deep inside of me and then died, its body left to rot.

"El." Millie's voice intruded on my memory. Her tone was strange—distant and yet firm. "I asked you if the Order had tested you yet."

"My appointment is at the end of the week," I said. "Four days."

She stood up abruptly, and I flinched. There was a new tension in her shoulders and the set of her jaw, and her skin had paled. In the shadowy room, she had an almost ghost-like appearance. She walked over to the kitchen, then back again, as if she could not bear to be still.

"All right, I'm going to say something," she said. "And if you don't like it, I'm going to need you to forget this conversation ever happened. Will you promise me that?"

I nodded.

She bit her lip, unsure, and then spoke in a rush. "If you could end the pregnancy now, without the Order ever discovering it, would you?"

"What?"

"Answer me."

I gazed at her helplessly. "Of course I would, but it's not possible. The Sisterhood's checks are too thorough. They'll know if I mutilated myself. Enough Sisters have tried it, tried all sorts of—"

"Are you certain you don't want to have the child?"

"No Sister *wants* to have a child." Knowing what it cost to conceive, remembering who the father was, the constant living reminder of what I had done? I clenched my fists. "Even without martyrdom, none of us would choose that."

Millie crouched before me, taking my hands. Her skin was cool against mine.

"There's a way," she said. "But if the Order ever finds out, people are going to be executed. You and I included. I'm willing to take that risk, but you have to be sure about this, El."

Her grip was uncomfortably tight.

"You could stop it?" My voice came out faint.

She nodded. "If I asked the right people, they would find me a remedy."

"A . . . remedy?"

"Yes. It's vicious, but it's also very quick and leaves no trace after a day or two. Scarcely any different from a late period." Millie released my hands. "It's been around for centuries, but the women who provide the herbs are very, very quiet about the practice. If the Sisterhood *were* to uncover the truth, the repercussions would be crushing."

I felt dizzy. "Because the Order would have to make an example."

"Yes. So you must understand that me telling you this, trusting you with this . . . No one else can ever know."

"It's too much of a risk for you."

"I said I was willing. I can get the remedy, and I can hide you here for a few days. But if you want this, we need to do it now." She touched my face.

"Millie . . ."

"It's no one's choice but yours," she said softly. "What do you want, El?"

I told her. And once she had left, promising to return before nightfall, I sat alone on her couch and cried.

CHAPTER

TWENTY-FOUR

It tasted sweeter than I had expected. The paste had a grainy consistency, like poorly milled flour mixed with thick oil. I suspected it was derived from a kind of tuber or nut, grown perhaps in a remote region of Aytrium. I imagined stooped old women harvesting roots from hidden gardens and parcelling them out to scared customers who came knocking in the dead of night. Maybe that was sentimental of me; maybe the stuff was cooked up by some flint-eyed merchant—a trader who spied an opportunity to fleece the desperate with a furtive solution.

I swallowed it.

"You okay?" Millie asked.

Was I okay? Maybe. I felt guilty, to be sure, and afraid. I was worried that we would get caught, and terrified about what that would mean for Millie. A lifetime of the Sisterhood's teachings rang in my ears, litanies about sacred duties and purpose, about the gift of motherhood.

But I also felt, for the first time in a very long time, that I was in control. And that felt like it was worth a lot.

"I think so," I said.

I began to notice the effects after an hour. I grew shivery and restless; I paced around the kitchen, one moment cold and the next too warm. When I caught sight of my reflection in the window pane, my eyes were bloodshot. The whites had turned entirely red, and brilliant bursts of colour dyed my eyelids whenever I blinked. I drank glass after glass of water, but remained thirsty.

Then the pain set in.

I lay on the couch and gasped for air. It felt like someone was carving through my abdomen with a rusty hacksaw. I threw up, begged for water, threw it up again. Millie's hands were freezing on my forehead when she tested my temperature. Her face shimmered like a mirage.

"This is the worst part," she said. "After this, it gets easier."

"Okay," I whispered.

She stayed with me and helped me to drink. The pain abated by degrees. Eventually, I stopped vomiting and fell into an exhausted doze, wrung out and wretched. A little after nightfall, I was dimly aware of Millie speaking to me saying something about needing to talk to a friend of hers. I opened my eyes when she kissed my forehead.

"Don't leave me," I croaked.

She smiled. "Not for long. Just sleep, you'll be fine."

I did. She had not returned by the time I woke up again, but I did feel better. A little unsteady, I walked to the kitchen sink and drank straight from the faucet. Through the curtains, I could see the glow of the lamps outside. What time was it? I rubbed my eyes. My skin was sticky with old, sour sweat, but it was cooler now; the heat of the day finally broken. A moth beat against the inside of the window, powdered wings fluttering. I opened the latch and cupped my hands around the creature to usher it free.

Someone pounded on the front door.

I froze. Like I had been drenched in ice water, fear flooded my veins. The Sisterhood? How could they have found me so quickly?

The knocking grew louder still.

"Open the door, Elfreda! I know you're in there."

It took a second for me to recognise his voice. I breathed out shakily, then staggered over to the door and unlocked it.

"Took you long enough, you—" Osan caught sight of me and broke off, startled.

"This is not a good time," I rasped.

"What happened to *you*?"

"It's personal."

"You look like death." He shook his head. "I'm sorry, but we need to go. Now."

"Do I look like I'm going anywhere?"

"It can't be helped. Where's Kamillian?"

"She left earlier." I sagged against the door frame. "What's going on? What are you doing here?"

"The other side is making their move." Osan's usual laidback, unflappable demeanour had vanished; he stood taller and his face appeared grimmer than I had ever seen it. "They're looking for you."

"What?"

"And your friend Jesane Olberos, but we've already managed to hide her. I'm going to take you somewhere safe, all right?"

I held the door for support. *No,* I wanted to tell him, *no, I'm safe here, you're mistaken.* And what about Millie? What if she were to come back and find me gone? Osan saw my reluctance.

"You have to trust me on this," he said. "Staying here will place Kamillian at risk too."

I ground my teeth together. "Why are you so sure they're looking for me? What do they want?"

"If I knew, I'd tell you. Rhyanon can probably explain, but we don't have much time to reach her. They've already searched the dormitories; it won't take too long before they start asking around for your friends' addresses."

I shivered, my resolve wavering. Osan glanced over his shoulder, like he expected trouble at any moment.

"Okay," I said in a small voice. "Okay, let's go."

The streets were quiet, and a cool breeze swept over the still-hot cobblestones. I felt feverish and weak; my muscles ached right down to the bones. A few people wandered around, stumbling home from the bar or off on some late-night escapade. Osan sized each of them up surreptitiously.

"I've got lace," I muttered.

"Good to know." He looped his arm through mine. I suppose that we must have looked unremarkable—a couple out for a midnight stroll. "Although we aren't going too far; there's a cab waiting four blocks from here. With luck, we'll make it without any trouble."

"And Rhyanon is all right? She's recovering?"

"She's fine. I heard you went looking for her at the San."

A sudden wave of dizziness caused me to stumble. Osan prevented me from falling.

"You know, you're really quite a mess," he said, but he sounded worried.

"Just sick."

"That came on pretty quickly if you were running around the city this morning."

"Heatstroke," I muttered.

He shifted his grip from my arm to my waist. I leaned on him heavily. My pulse was erratic and my chest burned.

"Sorry," I said.

"Don't mention it."

We cut down the alley behind the district clinic, moving toward the industrial sector of Major West. There were fewer people here. A scrawny rat fled down a drainpipe as we passed, and the lamps guttered low and faint, the panes streaked with years of old soot. Perspiration gathered at my hairline.

"Almost there," coaxed Osan. He guided me toward another alley. "I wanted to avoid drawing attention to Kamillian's place. If I had known the state you were in, I would have brought the cab clos—"

He staggered as something hit his back, and we both fell hard against the brick wall of the building. I scraped my arm bloody trying to stop myself from crashing to the ground.

"Osan!" I cried.

He breathed heavily and reached up to touch his shoulder. A slender iron bolt jutted from his skin, and his hand came away red.

"Oh." He swallowed. "Not good."

Another bolt hissed through the air and missed his head by inches. His knees buckled, and he slid sideways to the cobbles.

No, no, no. I wove lace around the wound. The head of the bolt had sunk deep into his shoulder, and blood seeped across his shirt. I tried to draw the skin tight, to stop the bleeding. "Osan? Oh Eater, please, Osan—"

"On the roof," he gasped.

I turned in time to see the glint of the lamplight catch on a third bolt, just before the shooter pulled the trigger on their crossbow. I threw up a net over our heads. The bolt clattered to the ground, and the person on the roof cursed. They ducked out of my line of sight.

"Hang in there." I tried to pull Osan's uninjured arm over my shoulders and stand, but I couldn't do it; he was too heavy and I was too weak. "Please, you have to help me, I need you to get up."

My lace would only last so long; we had to find help before I ran out. Osan panted, his face screwed up with pain. He leaned on me, using my shoulder as a crutch to lever himself off the ground. Another bolt shot straight toward him. My net repelled it, the threads turning slick in my grasp, but Osan still recoiled instinctively and slipped back down.

"More than one of them up there," he said through gritted teeth. "Can you pull them off the edge of the roof?"

"If I could see them, maybe."

He closed his eyes. "We have to be aggressive, or they'll just wear you down. Run for the emergency stairwell, face them up there."

I shook my head.

"Come on, you know it's—"

"If I leave you exposed, they'll kill you."

"If you don't do anything, they'll kill me too. And you."

Two bolts hit my net, and I felt it buckle a little under the force. Maintaining a shield strong enough to repel the projectiles was draining my lace at a frightening rate; I did not know how much longer I could hold it up.

"Stop!" I yelled. I spread my arms wide to shield Osan. "Stop shooting!"

Silence, except for Osan's pained breathing and the beating of my heart. I shook with anger and fear, my eyes scouring the rooftop for the shooters. But no more bolts were fired.

"They don't want to hit you," Osan whispered.

I could hear movement in the alleyway to the right of us. Careful to keep Osan in my shadow, I picked up a fallen bolt. The metal was cool. I coiled lace around it like a spring.

"Tell me what you want," I called. "I'm willing to talk."

Shuffling on the roof. I threw the bolt toward the sound, packing my lace behind the motion so that it shot forward with unnatural speed and power. All the same, it was a vain hope. The bolt hit the top of the wall, harmless.

"Or I will hurt you," I lied. "No more warning shots."

In response, a fist-sized rock flew toward my net. I stumbled backwards and tripped on Osan's leg. A man jeered from above.

"They've got us pinned down," I said.

Osan struggled to rise, but as soon as he moved, a bolt slammed into my lace. The last of my power trickled away and the net dissolved like smoke in my grasp. I lurched sideways to cover him again, and he caught my expression.

"No more lace?" he asked.

I nodded. "I can't hold the—"

A stone grazed my left temple with a bright flash of pain. I cried out and clutched my head. The skin had split and blood trickled over my fingers, dripping onto my cheek.

"She's out," called someone on the roof. I heard footsteps in the alley.

Get up! I forced myself to my feet again. If I did not have lace, I would have to find another weapon, find another way to defend myself. My head ached fiercely. Had to fight. I picked up the sharp stone and held it tight in my fist.

Two people emerged from the alley, both hooded. One was shorter, a woman, and the other had broad shoulders and a heavy cloth sack tucked into his belt.

"Get rid of her friend," said the woman.

My stomach dropped. I planted myself between the newcomers and Osan. "You don't have to do this."

The man walked toward us. There was a knife in his hand, an ugly old thing, a blade meant for butchering livestock.

"This is about me, right?" I said urgently. "Leave him out of it."

I tried to grab the knife from him, but he gave me a contemptuous shove. As he did so, his hood gaped open and I saw his face, his swollen and split lower lip.

"Lucian?" I said in disbelief.

He stiffened.

"You?" I stammered. "How can *you* be doing this?"

I didn't see the blow coming, not quickly enough. I was still too confused, too shocked—I'd known him for years, and now he was standing there with murder in his eyes. My reaction was slow; I only managed to turn my face away before his fist collided with the side of my head.

Like a flame doused in water, my vision went black. I collapsed. For a few seconds, I lost track of the world; there was a powerful ringing in my ears, and I could hear Osan swearing, but experienced the words only as vague, disconnected noise. Pressure around my neck, and I blinked. Blurred patches of light and shadow, yellow lamps, buildings, and then I found myself looking at Lucian's face. He held me up by the fabric of my shirt.

". . . new order is coming, corpse eater," he said. "And there's no room for your kind in it."

"You bastard," Osan hissed.

"She's to be delivered alive," said the woman impatiently.

Lucian's lip curled. "I'm only tenderising their meat."

My body had grown impossibly heavy, and my head felt like it would split open, but I was also dimly aware of a heat in my chest, a strange flickering feeling. I could taste it in my mouth too, coppery and golden and sweet, as if the sensation had taken wing from my lungs and now drifted out my lips and into the air.

I exhaled, and for a moment I thought I could almost see it—glimmering crystal beads like water in sunlight. Then Lucian screamed and let go of my shirt.

I fell, landing on my hands and knees. The world echoed strangely around me; Lucian's howls reverberated in rippling waves. *There's something very wrong with me,* I thought. I lifted my head. Lucian was clutching his hands to his chest, and I could see his skin had swollen and blistered. His knife lay within my reach. I stretched out for it, shaking.

"She still has power," Lucian yelled. "She burned me with her magic, she *tricked* us. Filthy bitch, I'll kill her!"

"You will *not,*" said the woman.

I closed my hand around the handle. Overhead, there was some kind of a commotion; someone on the roof shouted a warning. Running footsteps. The woman cursed. Lucian was still stumbling around—his hands curled up like claws—when someone swift and pale crashed into him. They both went down.

Everyone was yelling, but the wild tumult of sound and movement seemed far away. My own breathing was much louder; each inhalation caused black flowers to bloom at the corners of my sight.

"Finn," I said.

Lucian had always been taller and heavier-set, but tonight he was outmatched. White as a sheet and furious, Finn slammed Lucian's head into the ground.

"Stop," I whispered.

Lucian's ruined hands desperately clawed at Finn's face and neck. Finn drove his own fist down hard. I heard the crack of a broken nose.

He's going to kill him, I thought.

The woman shouted at Lucian, but she seemed reluctant to risk jumping into the fray. The crossbows on the roof were equally useless; they could too easily hit the wrong man.

The woman's head turned toward me, and I gripped the knife tighter. She did not care, I realised. Lucian was nothing to her.

Through the clamour, a whistle rang out shrilly. The woman jumped.

"Enforcement's coming," Osan rasped. He had managed to stand, and now he leaned against the wall for support. His back was dark red with blood.

The woman cast a last look at Finn and Lucian. The two of them seemed oblivious to the lookout's warning. Blood poured from Lucian's face; he thrashed like a cornered animal. Finn looked completely focussed, as if all his attention was devoted to just this one task, as if he could not see or hear anything else.

The woman muttered to herself. From her pocket, she drew out a thin black rod the length of a pencil. With a deft twist of her wrist, she snapped it in two.

The effect was immediate and grotesque. Like a branch beneath an invisible boot, Lucian's spine bent backwards and broke.

I shut my eyes, but the image was burned onto my mind. Finn swore. I could hear a soft whimpering sound, and realised it was coming from my own mouth. The woman's footsteps rushed past me, back down the alleyway.

Please make it stop. My head burned. *No more. Please no more.*

"El?" Finn was beside me, wrapping his arms around me, cradling me to his chest. "El, I'm here. I'm so sorry. I'm here."

I heard horses and wheels on the cobbles and Finn saying my name, and he had lifted me up, and he was still speaking to me and then I passed out.

CHAPTER

TWENTY-FIVE

SENSATION WAS SLOW to return. I awoke from dreamlessness, rising up through the dark. The first thing I knew was the coolness of a damp cloth on my forehead, and the smell of spiced tea.

Pain was next. I groaned.

"Are you back with us?"

I cracked open my eyelids and light flooded my brain. That hurt. I immediately shut them again.

"Do I have to be?" I asked.

Rhyanon chuckled.

"Well, not right this second, I suppose." She carefully wiped my forehead. The cloth smelled of lavender. Felt nice. Somewhere close by, I could hear birdsong and the wind rustling through trees.

"Osan?" I murmured. "He was badly hurt."

"Saskia took care of him. She's very deft with that kind of lacework. And with needles, but the lacework helps."

"Is he—"

"I spoke with him earlier this morning, and he'll be fine. The problem was mostly blood loss; the bolt didn't hit anything vital."

"I see." I breathed out slowly. "That's good."

Her clothing rustled as she moved closer, and I let myself relax, let her smooth my hair and rest the cloth, so wonderfully cool, on my forehead. It stirred old feelings, old vulnerabilities. Rhyanon was acting like my mother. This sort of entanglement could not end well, and yet I clung to the illusion all the same—that she cared, that I was safe, that everything would be okay.

That maybe, just for a little while, I might be allowed to lean into her kindness.

"How are you feeling?" she asked.

I raised and lowered my shoulders fractionally.

"That bad?"

"No," I muttered. "No, I'm fine. But I was worried about you."

"I heard. Apparently, you went barging into the Sanatorium and demanded to see me."

"I wouldn't say *barging*."

"Still. Rather endearing of you, if a bit stupid." She took away the cloth. "Nightmares aside, I really am fine now. Look."

I grimaced. "It's too bright."

"Come on."

Reluctantly, I opened my eyes again.

Green linens covered the bed. I lay in a yellow-walled room overlooking a leafy garden. The view through the window was screened by delicate beech saplings, and a breeze wafted the gauze curtains like the breath of a sleeping animal. On the pine sideboard rested a pot of tea and a plate of buttered bread.

Rhyanon sat on a cushioned chair beside the bed, a bucket of water on the ground next to her. Bandages covered her arm and shoulder, but her cheeks held a healthy colour and her eyes were bright. She smiled at me, pleased. It was a different smile, more straightforward, more honest. As if matters between us had settled into a new configuration.

"Not so bad, huh?" She gestured to her bandaged arm. "Wouldn't you say I'm in better shape than you?"

"Possibly." I studied her with a critical eye. "But you had an obvious advantage there."

"Oh?"

"Given that you're the expert on Commander Asan's ministrations, I'm sure you received extra care."

To my delight, she blushed.

"All that bed rest," I continued, a grin spreading across my face, "seems to have done you a lot of good."

"Were you never taught to respect your elders?" Her skin had turned a truly vibrant shade of pink now. "Eater, Elfreda, mind your own business."

"Quite a catch though."

She spluttered. "Enough!"

I laughed, although it made my head hurt. With effort, I sat up a little straighter and grunted when the movement triggered a whole host of smaller aches and pains. Not just my head either—my stomach cramped sharply. I pulled a face, and Rhyanon offered me a begrudging smile.

"Well, all right," she said. "Have your fun. But this stays between us, okay? It's safer for the Commander if our relationship remains private."

"I understand. And I approve, for whatever that's worth." I toyed with the edge of the bedspread. "Good for you."

"You're unexpectedly sweet sometimes," said Rhyanon, and it was my turn to blush. I covered my embarrassment by pretending to take an interest in the rest of the room.

"So where is Commander Asan?" I asked. "And where am I?"

Rhyanon leaned back in her chair. "Saskia's working. And we're at the city manor of a provincial Reverend. From the outside, the property looks unused; it's just the groundskeeper coming and going, keeping things in order."

"But?"

"A couple of years ago, a group of Sisters constructed a hidden tunnel from the neighbouring building into the manor's cellar. Awfully convenient if you need somewhere to hide."

I rubbed my eyes. "Who lives next door?"

"No one. It's one of the city's new greenhouses, which made the mysterious quantities of excavated earth a little easier to explain away."

"Huh. Clever."

"Do you want tea?" She levered herself to her feet. "I figured you might be thirsty."

While she poured, I tried to sort my thoughts. Judging by

the shadows cast by the trees, it was still early morning, so I had probably only been unconscious for a few hours. The cut on my forehead had been taped up with soft gauze, and I wore clean clothes, a loose blue tunic dress.

Memories of last night's attack hovered like a dark cloud at the edge of my thoughts. I did not want to consider too closely what had happened, but my present fears could not be ignored either.

"There was a—a friend of mine," I said, trying to keep my voice light. "Do you know—"

"Finn, yes?"

I nodded quickly.

Rhyanon handed me a cup. "He helped Saskia bring you here, but left before the sun came up. Something about needing to tell his sister what had happened."

I nodded again and looked down at my tea. "Right, of course."

"I'm sure he'll return."

But why was he even in Ceyrun?

"Maybe. Doesn't matter." I wrapped my fingers around the cup, absorbing the warmth into my hands. I glanced at her. "I have a lot of questions."

"Yes." She sighed. "I'm sure you do."

Her weariness amused me. I drank from the cup and smiled slightly. "Wishing I was still asleep?"

She did not return the smile; if anything, she seemed to grow more solemn still.

"Elfreda, before we have this conversation, I need you to understand that neither Commander Asan nor I intend to harm you," she said.

I frowned and set down the cup. "Okay."

"It's . . . Well. Just try to keep that in mind." She adjusted the edge of the bedspread. "Please?"

My unease grew; I didn't like Rhyanon's tone. "You're starting to scare me."

"I know this is going to be difficult, that's all." She breathed out heavily. "You suffer from hallucinations, don't you?"

I froze. All the feelings of security and warmth evaporated; my heart boomed in my ears like waves crashing down on my head. I suddenly wanted to get up, to get out of the room and away from her.

"Elfreda—"

"Why do people keep asking me that?" I demanded harshly. "What makes you think I have hallucinations?"

She kept her voice low and calm. "Because they are a defining symptom of a condition that you are likely to suffer from."

"So you think I'm sick? What condition?"

"We think—" She broke off, corrected herself. "We are almost certain that you are what's known as a Renewer."

"Which means?" I was still too clipped, too aggressive. I had let myself grow complacent around Rhyanon, and now my anxieties emerged as anger. I wanted so much to trust her, but I was afraid.

"Well, that's . . . complicated." She seemed unusually unsure of herself too; she rubbed the back of her neck and continued slowly. "As I understand it, Renewers are Sisters who hold unusual concentrations of lace in their bodies. They appear every third generation or so, about seventy years apart each time." She grimaced. "Please stop looking at me like that."

"Like what?"

"I don't know, like you're trying to work out whether you could still outrun me in a foot race."

I swallowed a retort and instead leaned back on the pillows. My head had begun to pound.

"It's okay," said Rhyanon. "I knew this would scare you, but you can trust me, Elfreda. You can."

I shut my eyes.

"So," I said, "a Renewer?"

The chair squeaked as Rhyanon shifted in her seat.

"At Celane's garden party?" she said. "You were playing Tryst. And thirty women saw you catch a ball that should have been out of reach."

"That's it?"

"No. But it was strange enough to draw notice. To you, of course, but also to Jesane Olberos for throwing that pass."

"Why?"

"Because a Renewer is apparently capable of warping reality in subtle ways. Not consciously, and yet the world seems to . . ." She sought the right words. "*Shift* to their benefit. That's according to what I've been told, anyway."

I snorted. "To my benefit, you say?"

"Hm. Perhaps to your instincts, then."

"All right, so let's say this is true." I let out a slow breath and opened my eyes again. "Which means I'm apparently unusually good at ball games. Why should anyone care?"

Rhyanon gave me a sad look.

"Because the Renewer is a queenmaker," she said. "I said you held an unusual concentration of lace in your body? That power, historically, has been enough to completely reshape Aytrium. Each time the Order's lace begins to wane, the Renewer appears. She restores the Sisterhood. She ushers in a new golden age."

"But I'm *not* powerful," I said in exasperation. "My lacework skills are average at best, so I can't be this—this mythical lace wielder."

"It's not about your abilities." Rhyanon studied her hands, avoiding my gaze. "It's your body that matters."

Like the last piece of a puzzle clicking into place, I understood her.

"Oh," I said, suddenly cold. "So it's about who martyrs me."

Who eats me.

"Yes," said Rhyanon.

I drew the covers of the bed up over my shoulders, pulling my knees in.

"Elfreda, this wasn't—"

"Why didn't you *tell* me?" I asked. "You knew! All this time, you knew—"

"I didn't!" Rhyanon got up and sat on the bed, but I shrank

backwards from her. "I had no idea, not until Saskia mentioned that game of Tryst, and even then, it seemed like such a remote possibility. Why should it be you, out of everyone in the Order? We only realised the truth at Geise's Crown."

I pressed my lips together. Rhyanon hesitated, then laid her hand on my shoulder. I flinched, but she did not draw away.

"It's going to be okay," she said. "And I'm sorry that I haven't been more open with you before now. That was a mistake."

"I thought I was going mad." My voice came out hoarse. "For a *year.* And now you tell me that the visions are just some symptom, some indication that I'm . . . I'm meant to . . ."

"No one is going to hurt you again," she said. "You'll see—we'll get you out of Ceyrun and away from the Order. Everything is under control."

"They're going to martyr me," I whispered. "Every Reverend in the Order must be searching the city. And when they find me—"

Rhyanon shook her head. All of a sudden, she looked distinctly uncomfortable.

"Saskia faked your death," she said.

I stared at her. "She . . . what?"

"This is going to take some explaining." She reached over and picked up the plate of bread. "Here. Eat, it might help."

"I don't want to."

"Eat," she said firmly.

I stared at Rhyanon a moment longer, then slowly lowered my knees and straightened up. I took the plate. The bread was toasted, and the butter glistened, yellow and melting. I broke off a corner.

"It might be a bit dense," she said, watching me. "I was distracted while baking."

I had not eaten since breakfast yesterday. I crumbled the bread between my fingers and put the pieces in my mouth.

"No," I muttered. "It's delicious."

"There's more if you want it." She got up and walked over to the window while I ate in silence. She was right, food helped; the immediate swell of panic faded, and I could think more clearly again. Absentminded, Rhyanon ran her fingers across the gauze netting.

"Celane's faction wants to maintain the Order as it currently exists and for that they need the Renewer's power." She let her hand fall back to her side. Her shoulders were tight. "The Sisterhood is in crisis, possibly on the brink of falling apart entirely. And in the service of salvaging the Order, these women are willing to go to desperate lengths." She turned back to me. "We knew that, of course. But we underestimated their ruthlessness."

"Ilva?" I asked quietly.

She nodded. "Yes. And Zenza Lenard."

I had known already, or at least suspected. I looked down at the scattered crumbs on my plate. "Then the murders were Celane's doing? I realise Ilva might have been a liability, but Zenza . . ." I swallowed and lifted my head. "Why?"

Rhyanon's forehead creased. She looked aside.

"You were probably the intended target," she said. "I think they uncovered that you were working for our side."

"So because I got away, Zenza was just—they just killed her instead? I don't understand."

"The easiest way to consolidate the power and loyalty of the Sisterhood is to make us afraid of an external threat." Bitterness bled into her voice. "That's part of it. But they also wanted—needed—a great deal of lace in case their plans went awry."

I felt lightheaded. "Ilva and Zenza were killed for their lace?"

"Yes."

"But their bodies were—" I struggled, almost too sickened to say it. "Their organs were still there. Cut up, but nothing missing. If this was about lace, why leave so much behind?"

"For cover." Rhyanon returned to her chair. She looked tired. "When Zenza Lenard died, who did you immediately assume was responsible?"

"Another Sister, I guess."

"Until you heard that the bodies had been left on the street."

I nodded.

Rhyanon drummed her fingers against the arm of the chair. Her skin had paled; she seemed to find it difficult to keep talking.

"Bodies," she said, and stopped. Tried again. "Bodies with organs removed and arranged around the victim. It seems heretical, doesn't it? Like a message directed at the Order: look at all your power now, wasted." She breathed out. "But whose organs?"

It took a second for her words to reach me. My stomach turned.

"Saskia worked it out, of course." Rhyanon spoke more quickly. "A pig's heart looks similar to a human's. Less round, fewer major veins, but if you put it next to a woman's butchered body, those details are easy to miss."

I turned my face away. Zenza. It could have so easily been me, cut apart and left in pieces that night.

"Then Celane and Morwin and Verje gorged? They just . . ." I gestured helplessly.

"We think so. I'm sorry, Elfreda." Rhyanon folded her hands in her lap. "And it's also why Saskia's gorge sickness came on so quickly—consuming Morwin's heart, when Morwin herself had already gorged? Practically toxic."

It was hideous, but it made sense. Celane was responsible after all. And a tiny part of me felt relieved—at least it wasn't the Resistance, at least Finn and Millie weren't tied up in the atrocities, even indirectly. I rubbed my head. The left side was swollen where Lucian had struck me.

"What does this have to do with my . . . death?" I asked.

Rhyanon picked up her cup of tea, and offered me a wry smile.

"Played their own trick against them," she said. "Saskia arranged it. Between Osan's blood and the dead mercenary, there was already plenty of evidence of a struggle on that street. She simply ornamented things. Animal organs, a set of stained Acolyte robes, a few messages in blood. *Down with the Order, Death to the Corpse Eaters,* that kind of thing. You get the idea. Then she took a statement from your friend, saying you were supposed to meet him but never showed."

My chest tightened. "Finn testified?"

"I would rather Osan had done it, but he wasn't in a state to talk much."

"But—but the people who attacked me will just tell Celane that I survived," I said. "Not to mention the fact that Enforcement chased them off."

"Of course they will, but *think,* Elfreda. What can Celane do with that information? Yes, she knows that you survived and can probably guess that we have you, but where does that leave her? She can't exactly reveal *how* she came upon this information; that would be as good as confessing to the previous murders. 'I know that Elfreda Raughn is still alive, because the people I sent to kidnap her told me so.'" Rhyanon shook her head. "Currently the only thing that's stopping us from exposing her is the absence of hard proof. But she's on the back foot; the stakes are too high, and she can't call Saskia's bluff without drawing attention to herself. A single mistake, and all her plans go up in smoke. That doesn't mean that she'll give up, not by any means, but her priority will be trying to find you. Which means that all *we* have to do is keep—"

The door burst open.

Rhyanon moved faster than I would have expected. She leapt to her feet, spun to face the entrance, and raised her uninjured arm to shield me.

"—absolutely have *no* right!" snarled Asan.

"El!" cried Millie.

She had a sickly, haggard look, and her clothing was rumpled. Her eyes swept the room and found me, and she took three strides toward the bed before colliding with Rhyanon's lace. She froze and her eyes flew wide with alarm.

Rhyanon swayed slightly and gripped the back of her chair. I saw Millie's gaze dart around the rest of the room, taking in the tea and empty plate, the bucket of water and cloth, and for the briefest of moments, I felt embarrassed—as if she had barged in on something deeply private, something intimate that no one else was supposed to see, something small and important that I wanted to keep between Rhyanon and myself.

"Don't hurt her," I said, struggling to get up. Blood rushed to my head, and I almost toppled over onto the floor.

But Rhyanon had already released the lacework binding. She sat down heavily on the bed beside me.

"Sorry," she said. "She startled me."

Millie stayed in the middle of the room like she had been rooted to the spot. Her breathing was shallow.

"This was all my fault," she said.

Then she burst into tears.

CHAPTER

TWENTY-SIX

Rhyanon offered Millie her chair, and then gently excused herself. In the doorway, she murmured something to Asan.

The Commander nodded in response. "You should be resting anyway. I'll take care of it."

Rhyanon glanced back and gave me a weary smile. I wanted her to stay, I realised. There were so many questions I still needed to ask, about Renewers, about what would happen next, but most of all, I craved reassurance from her.

I pushed aside my feelings. When I gestured thanks, she turned away. Asan ushered her out into the corridor.

"There's been a development," I heard the Commander say.

Millie sat with her knees hugged to her chest. Her skin had turned an ugly, blotchy red, and she seemed small and drained. Completely unlike her usual self.

"I really should have left a note for you," I said.

"I'm so sorry," she whispered.

"For what?"

"I left you alone. I poisoned you, and then I left you all alone. Could have put off paying for the stupid stuff until later."

"Millie," I said quickly. "Come on."

She shook her head. I hesitated, then patted the bed beside me. "Sit closer? Please?"

Millie unfolded from the chair and moved next to me. I found her hand, laced my fingers between hers. Her palms were clammy, and she had bitten her nails down to the quick. She hunched her shoulders, and I could tell she was trying hard not to start crying again.

"Look," I said. "I'm all right. Everything is all right. Really, all that happened was that I got punched in the head. You've done nothing wrong."

"But those people could have killed you," she said hoarsely. "And now Finn's locked up, and the Commander's telling everyone you're dead—"

I straightened. "Wait, *where* is Finn?"

"Judicial custody." Asan walked back into the room. "Don't look so alarmed, we worked out a story together. As long as he sticks to it during the inquiry, they'll let him go by tomorrow."

"Rhyanon never mentioned that." My heart quickened. "Is he at the Detainment Offices?"

"No, he was transferred to the Judicial Affairs holding quarters to await official questioning." She leaned against the wall. "This is all standard procedure, and your friend is perfectly fine. He went there of his own accord."

I looked to Millie for confirmation. She rubbed her eyes with the back of her hand, then nodded.

"After Finn told me how to find you, he said he needed to return to Enforcement," she said. "He seemed exhausted, that's all. Not hurt."

Even so, I hated the idea of Finn being interrogated by the Order. I still couldn't understand what he had been doing in Ceyrun in the first place, but with Asan present I felt uncomfortable raising the issue. The Commander sensed my disquiet.

"He knows what to say," she assured me. "Judicial Affairs has no reason to doubt his testimony, especially since he's being so cooperative."

"But what if they do?" I asked.

"They won't."

"And what about the people who know he's lying? You don't think they'll try to discredit him?"

She looked at me, reappraising. "*Will* they know he's lying? All he's claimed is that you never showed up for drinks with some friends. Could be true, as far as they're concerned."

"The people who attacked me saw him."

"It was dark, and they saw *a* man. City's full of them. Listen, Raughn, all your friend is doing is placing you on the right street, at the right time, to be murdered. The rest is on me. Besides, if my esteemed colleagues want to take him down, they're going to need to provide a better story. They're aware that I'm looking to hang them, so I can't see them risking that kind of exposure."

I tried to shake off my unease. What she said made sense, and yet it all seemed to rely on presumptions and chance—that Celane would not find fault in Finn's story, that none of her hired killers would tip her off to his role in the attack, that she would be too afraid to test Asan's mettle. The Commander made it sound simple and risk-free, but it wasn't.

And the worst part was that I felt certain she knew that too. Asan had probably not meant for Finn's involvement to go beyond providing a statement to Enforcement.

But it was too late to change anything now. I turned to Millie.

"Can you go to him?" I asked. "Tell him I—tell him a mutual friend said thank you. And to be careful."

"I'll try, but I don't know if they'll let me in."

I forced a smile. "I've always had complete faith in your powers of persuasion."

To my distress, Millie's eyes reddened. I awkwardly opened my arms, and she lurched into the embrace, burying her face in my shoulder.

"Hey now," I murmured. "This isn't like you."

She hugged me tighter. Her hair was soft as cat fur against my cheek, and smelled of soap. I relaxed a little, glad to have her near me.

"I was so scared," she mumbled. "Didn't know what to do with myself."

"You should talk to a counsellor about that. I can recommend one."

She sniffed. "Don't be ridiculous."

"I happen to think mine is wonderful," I said. "Although she is making my shirt kind of wet at the moment."

Millie drew away from me with a sound somewhere between a laugh and a sob. "I'll talk to Finn."

"Stay out of trouble," I said.

Asan waited for Millie to leave the room. Then she straightened and stretched her shoulders.

"You know, she turned up at the Detainment Offices on her own," she said conversationally. "Flat-out refused to leave until she could speak to me. There aren't many people who try shouting me down, least of all civilians."

I winced at the thought, and Asan smiled slightly.

"Tears aside, she's quite formidable," she said. "I'll keep an eye on her while you're recovering, make sure she doesn't come to any harm. Did Herald Hayder explain your situation?"

I nodded.

"Then you're taking it better than I anticipated." She reached into the pocket of her robes and drew out a small brown sachet. She tossed it to me. "Here. That's for the swelling. It'll also probably put you to sleep."

"I feel fine."

"You certainly don't look it." She glanced out the window. "I have to return to work before my absence is noted."

Alone, I opened the packet. The powder inside had a pungent smell, like crushed mint and something deeper, earthier. Not unpleasant, exactly, although not appetising either. I stared at it, and my hands began to shake.

Then you're taking it better than I anticipated.

"Yeah, right," I muttered.

I poured the powder into my mouth and washed it down with the last of my cold tea. Then I lay back and gazed at the ceiling.

They were going to martyr me.

They were going to eat me alive.

My thoughts churned, spiralling between Finn and Osan and Millie, dead bodies cut apart for lace, my mother, the remedy I had taken, Millie asking what I wanted, the idea of a child, Rhyanon stroking my hair, Lucian's burned hands and the woman breaking that rod, the feeling of a leather ball falling into my hand like a gift. And my own future—to be hunted and consumed for the sake of Aytrium.

I woke chilled and thirsty. The windows still stood open, but it was dark outside. I got up and found that my dizziness was gone, along with the lingering pain in my stomach. When I touched the side of my head, it felt tender but much less swollen, so whatever Asan had given me seemed to have worked. I crossed the floor and closed the windows quietly.

A lamp burned in the room at the end of the corridor. I padded down the hallway on bare feet, wrapping my arms across my chest to keep warm.

Osan slouched on a kitchen chair with a cheese sandwich and a jug of water in front of him. He had no shirt on, but his shoulders were entirely bound up in gauze and bandages. He jumped when a floorboard squeaked under my heel.

"Hello," I whispered.

"Oh, it's you." A smile broke across his face. "Just El, back from the dead."

"You're one to talk." I walked over to the shelf and found myself an empty glass. "Wasn't Commander Asan sticking you full of needles?"

"Hah. Not exactly my idea of a good time, but she put me back together all right." He leaned forward. "How are you feeling?"

"Hm." I sat down opposite him and poured water into my glass. "Has Rhyanon told you?"

"About you? Yeah, earlier this evening. She filled Kamillian in at the same time."

I drank and set the glass back on the table.

"I'm terrified," I said.

"I can't really blame you."

"And I'm angry."

"At?"

"Everything."

"Fair enough."

"The Order has Finn in Judicial Custody. Commander Asan says it's nothing to worry about, but I think she's lying. Osan, if something happens to him—"

"He'll be fine," he said, although he sounded a little too confident, a little too quick to be entirely believable. Ever since that first ride to Kisme's farewell party, Osan had spoken straight with me, no pretence, no ceremony. No bullshit. Now he was . . . acting. My eyes lingered on his bandages. Had his feelings changed after last night? Or did he see me differently, knowing what I was? I dropped my gaze to the table.

"Yeah," I said quietly. "Of course."

"You're not going to stop worrying, are you?"

"No." I rubbed my arms, and glanced up. "So Millie came back?"

"Earlier this evening, but she didn't want to wake you. She's gone again now."

"Do you know if she managed to speak to Finn?"

He shook his head. "She might have, but I don't think so. Sorry."

"No, that's . . ." I hesitated. "Osan, are you—are you sure you're okay? I didn't expect you to be up so soon."

"I'm a whole lot better than dead." He smiled again and made a gesture of dismissal. "Rhyanon says I got off lightly, all things considered."

A low creaking sound issued from the pantry, and I looked around in alarm.

"Just the Commander, I think," said Osan. "The entrance to the cellar's through there."

A few seconds later, Asan appeared in the doorway. She was still dressed in her Enforcement uniform, and carried a heavy bag over one shoulder. She seemed surprised to find both of us sitting at the kitchen table in the middle of the night.

"Is Hayder asleep?" she asked Osan.

"As far as I know, yes."

"Good. You should be too." She hefted the bag higher on her shoulder. "Raughn, a word? In private?"

"Of course." I got to my feet. "Is something wrong, Commander?"

"It's just a personal matter."

"In that case, I'll head back to my room." Osan stood up. He moved far slower than before, and the image of the bolt protruding from his shoulder flashed through my mind, the blood soaking his back. "Good night to both of you." He wavered, and then added. "Elfreda . . . I owe you one."

"For what?"

He trudged out of the kitchen. "For staying by my side last night."

So that was it, the source of his new awkwardness. I wanted to tell him not to be stupid, anyone would have done the same, but he was already in the corridor. Asan picked up the lamp from the table.

"Let's talk in the central conservatory," she said. "No chance of being overheard, and it's a little more comfortable."

The mansion, I discovered as I followed her through a sumptuous sitting room filled with upholstered chairs covered in pale dust sheets, was grander than my guest bedroom had suggested. The furniture gleamed in the shifting lamplight, polished hardwood and gold finishes, embroidered velvet and silver piping. Opulent, certainly, but the whole place possessed a curious air of sterility—as if no one had ever really lived here. Which I suppose was true, if the Reverend who owned it resided outside Ceyrun.

The conservatory was ensconced between two wings of the house, shielded by double-storey walls on two sides and adjoining the main foyer to the south. Through dusty glass roof panels, the thin moon shone like the edge of a knife. Bright-leafed creepers ran up elegant trellises on the walls; pomegranates and grapes, flowering sweet peas. A line of low couches ran beside stone-topped cabinets. It was warmer in here; sunlight had soaked into the marble floor tiles during the day, and now the heat gently radiated up from the ground.

Asan walked over to a cabinet and crouched before it. I trailed after her. She rummaged around and pulled out a dark bottle from the lower shelf.

"Probably shouldn't mix alcohol and medication, but after the week you've had . . ." She proffered a metal tumbler. "Hold this."

I took it from her uncertainly. She returned to searching the cabinet.

"I figured we probably won't have many opportunities to talk," she said. "Cclane's increased the number of people tailing me. Real fucking pain in the ass. It's almost impossible to slip away during the day now."

"I'm sorry to hear that."

"What can you do?" She found a corkscrew and jammed it into the top of the bottle. "You seem much better. That's good."

"May I ask a question?"

She pulled out the cork. "Sure."

"Why aren't you martyring me?"

She snorted.

I kept my voice measured and calm. "Rhyanon said that you don't intend to harm me, and I believe her. I'm just not sure that your decision makes much sense."

Asan motioned for my tumbler. I held it out, and she filled it.

"Sit," she said.

I lowered myself onto one of the couches. The Commander remained standing. She had not poured a drink for herself.

"When we brought you here last night, your eyes were blood-shot," she said. "You seemed severely dehydrated, and when I spoke to Osan, he mentioned that you were feverish and weak before the attack. You told him it was heatstroke." She sat on the edge of the cabinet. "That was a lie, wasn't it?"

I shook my head.

She sighed. "You started bleeding while you were unconscious."

"I have no idea what you're talking about."

"You have terrible timing, Raughn. Not that you could have known." She finally filled her own tumbler. Drank. "Kamillian Vidar helped you get hold of the remedy, didn't she? No one would ever sell it directly to a Sister."

"There was no remedy," I snapped, my voice too loud. "Leave Millie alone."

Asan nodded to herself. She drank again.

"You're probably aware that I don't have a daughter." She set down her tumbler. "That's always been a blot on my reputation. The old guard love it—my barrenness as a sign that I've offended the Eater. You must have heard that?"

I gripped the tumbler tightly within my fist and said nothing. Asan could play whatever games she liked; I wasn't going to betray Millie. She seemed to read that from my face; she smiled slightly and shrugged.

"You have," she said. "Sisters talk; it doesn't bother me. But what you might not know is that I did have a son."

I tensed.

"Very briefly, of course," said Asan. "I never even got to hold him."

"I—"

"And after that experience, I vowed never again," she continued. "So I took steps to make sure of it. At first, only the emergency solutions. Then a more permanent one."

I looked down, shaken. "You should not be telling me this."

"You're supposed to be dead, Raughn. Who are you going to share my secrets with?" She looked aside. "Listen, we never need to talk about what you did. That's absolutely fine. But if you should *want* to, I might just be the only Sister who understands. No judgement, no repercussions."

I turned the tumbler around in my hands.

"Does Rhyanon know?" I asked.

"She does."

I should not say anything. I had promised Millie. But there was a hard ache in my throat, and all my feelings were pressed up so suffocatingly tight, that I could not quite help myself.

"Was it the right choice?" I asked. "If you could go back, would you have changed your mind?"

"Never."

I raised my eyes. Asan met my gaze evenly.

"I can only speak for myself," she said, "but if I think about what I lost and what I gained? It was right for me."

She wore such a serious expression and spoke so directly that I could not doubt her. I lowered my head again.

"I see," I said.

She gave me time to think, letting the silence stretch. Imagining Asan as an Acolyte, as someone who had faced the same fears and made the same choices, brought me an odd kind of relief. She might have been far stronger than I was, but perhaps strength could be learned. Perhaps I could be that sure of myself one day.

Eventually, Asan sighed. She stuck her hand into the pocket of her uniform and took out a vial.

"This is for you," she said. "Osan told me that you were out of lace."

The sacrament glistened dark red.

"Who does that belong to?" I asked warily.

"Which martyr? My mother."

"I can't accept it."

"Don't be ridiculous." She pushed herself off the top of the cabinet and held the vial out to me. "Do you want to face another attack without the means to defend yourself? No? Then take some basic precautions."

"But it's yours."

"I doubt this will make you feel better, but I recently consumed a huge amount of lace that 'belonged' to Jiana Morwin's daughter."

I swallowed.

"Consider it recompense for failing to reach you before last night's attack," she said.

I took the vial unhappily. "Thank you."

"It's nothing. Hopefully you won't even need it."

"Commander?"

"Yes?"

I felt apprehensive about broaching the topic, but she had alluded to it herself.

"Rhyanon told me that she realised I was the Renewer at Geise's Crown." I quickly pressed on, my words coming out in a tangled rush. "I just—what did she mean? How did she know?"

Asan grimaced. "Ah."

"I understand that you probably don't want to talk about that night."

She made a dismissive gesture. "It's fine, this is just a very ugly affair all round. We knew it was you because of the way the Haunt behaved in the basement. They always target whoever has the most lace. That one never took its eyes off you. I'm sure you noticed."

"I did." I shifted on the couch. "So that was it?"

"Seems too easy, doesn't it?"

I didn't know if I would have described anything about that night as "easy." "Which meant that Morwin would have realised too. That I was the Renewer."

"Yes." Asan smiled without a trace of humour. "Joining the dots, Raughn?"

I thought of the book I had read in Celane's library. Thought about her reading it. All the marked pages.

"A Haunt, that mature?" Asan took another drink. "It *planned*. It knew to wait until its friend showed up so that our forces would be divided. It knew to use Hayder as a lure. It anticipated us, and we waltzed right into its trap. That's not typical Haunt behaviour; they aren't supposed to strategise."

"A new intelligence emerges in the absence of the old," I murmured. Pieces slid into place. "The Order should have found that Haunt sooner. If it was so far gone, it would have attacked someone long before the symposium."

"Exactly."

"Unless it could be contained." My voice dropped. "Locked away and kept secret. Somewhere out of the way, somewhere private and secure, where it could develop unnoticed." I clenched my fists. "Like Verje's barn."

Asan spread her hands in acknowledgement. "Like Verje's barn."

My mouth twisted. I had missed it. All along, I had missed that Verje was concealing a monster, even though it had been right in front of my face.

"Hide away your Haunts until they're fully turned." Asan leaned back. "Then, under a reasonable pretext, gather both your enemies and the two Sisters most likely to be the Renewer. Release the monsters, watch who they run to, let the carnage unfold. Snatch your prize out of the Haunt's claws at the last moment."

"After you and Rhyanon are dead."

"It's a very convenient tragedy, and almost impossible to link back to the perpetrators. Celane wasn't even there, so her hands stay clean. Luckily for me, Morwin miscalculated when she tried to force her little accident." Asan shook her head bitterly. "Clumsy, really. With that much lace at her disposal, she could have pushed much harder."

I remembered the look on Morwin's face when I had stopped her lace. She had not believed it would take more power. Why should she? Asan had made a point to tell Herald Lien that she had not performed the rite recently. The Commander should have been defenceless.

"You made sure that Morwin would underestimate you," I said.

Asan sighed. "To be honest, I thought Jiana might try to knock me off the roof. I wanted to force her into the open before the Haunt demanded my attention."

"You had a protective net in place the whole time?"

"Only on the roof. After that, I was, well, distracted. Hayder says that you shielded my back in the basement. Thank you for that."

"But . . . but did she really think she could hold off both Haunts on her own?"

"Raughn, you need to understand—the lacework that Sisters currently wield? Pathetic, compared to the works of our predecessors. But gorging gives you a glimpse into what's really possible with sufficient raw power. It's . . ." She paused. "It's completely different. Frightening, but the sense of invincibility is more than a little intoxicating. I mean, just consider the fact that, all those centuries ago, the Eater lifted *all of Aytrium* into the sky. Imagine having that kind of power, imagine what you could—"

She noticed my expression and stopped talking. The fervour faded from her face.

"But then there's the cost," she said softly. "And the question of who must pay it."

I smiled thinly. "From what I can gather, payment is the Renewer's responsibility, Commander."

She pressed the back of her hands together in the gesture for vow-taking, a sign usually reserved for commitments to the Eater.

"Not while I have anything to do with it," she said.

I was too taken aback to react, then quickly gestured negation. "There's no need for that, I was only joking."

She reaffirmed the gesture, then lowered her hands.

"I will not see you martyred, Raughn," she said. "Not just

because it would be a terrible and cruel waste, but because it goes against my most ardently held principle."

"What principle?"

Asan smiled wryly. "That we can be better than this."

CHAPTER

TWENTY-SEVEN

SIX DAYS. I did not see Commander Asan again during that time, although I knew that she had visited at least twice at night. She left food in the kitchen, and once woke Osan to check his stitches and replace his wound dressing. He was recovering well; he moved more easily and appeared cheerful enough, although I suspected that some of his good humour might have been put on for my benefit.

I, on the other hand, could not keep Finn from my mind.

"Saskia is doing what she can," said Rhyanon, not taking her gaze off the balance sheet in front of her. In the early hours of the morning, Asan had delivered a stack of files from the Civil Obligations offices, and Rhyanon had been scouring them for suspicious activities in Reverends' financial affairs, any evidence that could be used to incriminate Celane or her associates.

"But on what grounds are they still detaining him? It doesn't make any sense." I stood up. We were in the western study, a light, airy room on the second floor of the mansion. Through the windows, I could see the long sweep of the yellowed lawns, the red-brick perimeter wall in the distance. "And Millie was supposed to be here already."

"I'm sure both of your friends are fine."

I paced to the windows and back again. "And you're certain the Commander didn't say anything else?"

"Only that the inquiry is moving slower than she expected. Celane and Verje are being obstructive."

You told me that they would be too afraid to cause any trouble.

I drummed my fingers against my thigh. As uneasy as I felt, I didn't want to drive Rhyanon away. It hadn't escaped my notice that my visions had been absent since the attack, and I suspected that the lull was mostly due to her company. She made me feel safe.

I mumbled something about stretching my legs, and left her to work.

Outside the study, Jaylen sat cross-legged on the floor. She had been intently focussed on a math problem written out in her notebook, and jumped when I opened the door.

"Sorry," I said. "I didn't mean to startle you."

She blinked at me owlishly. For a ten-year-old, Jaylen didn't speak much, although I had the distinct impression that her silences weren't a product of shyness. She just seemed very self-contained, as if she preferred to keep her thoughts to herself.

"Did your mother set you that work?" I asked.

She nodded. "If I improve my mathematics, she said that I might be able to help her with the ledgers."

"That seems reasonable." I crouched. "May I check your calculations?"

She handed across the notebook. While I scanned the page, she fidgeted, pulling on the end of her plait.

"Do you know how long we'll have to stay here?" she asked.

"I don't, although you could try getting an answer out of Commander Asan." I pointed to a subtraction error. "That's close, but check it again."

She took back her book and peered at the numbers. I thought of Rhyanon crying over her crib, the taste of caramel sweets. Jaylen carefully crossed out her answer and corrected it.

"That's better," I said, and was rewarded with a hint of a smile.

It was sometime past seventh bell. I wandered down a corridor of the mansion, restless and unsettled. Through the windows, the sun beat down. The weather had grown even hotter, although the temperature remained bearable inside the house. Bad news for the harvest. I wondered how Food Management was coping with the situation, whether they had appointed a new Sister to my position yet. The idea of being replaced brought me a strange pang of sadness. My old life, my time as Field Researcher Elfreda Raughn, was over. Whatever plans Rhyanon and Asan had for me, I knew I could never go back. It would be a tough blow for the department to lose two Sisters within the space of a month. Reverend Somme would take it hard.

I reached the end of the passage and gazed out of the bay windows at the parched garden. Had anyone at work discovered that civilians were breaking the meat embargo? I could alert the Commander, ask her to pass it on. Not that I wanted the street vendors to get in trouble with the Order, but if the merchant guilds were behind it—

I squinted. Someone was climbing over the property's locked gate. The intruder struggled to scale the high metal bars, almost toppling. With a rush of dread, I recognised her.

"Oh no," I whispered.

I flew down the stairs and through the passage, across the living room and into the sweltering heat of the conservatory. From somewhere behind me I heard Rhyanon calling my name, but I did not stop, I raced through the rows of sunlit plants and into the foyer. The front door leapt open for me.

Millie stumbled up the path to the house. She was deathly pale, her expression wild.

"El!" she gasped. "You have to stop it. He confessed."

I reached her. Millie's clothing was doused in sweat, her hair plastered to the sides of her face. She was shaking. I gripped her by the arms.

"Confessed to what?" My pulse raced. "Millie, what's going on? What did Finn say?"

"He told the Council he murdered those Sisters." Her voice cracked. "El, he told them that he killed you."

For a brief moment I could not make sense of her words, and then they hit me like a blow to the chest. I released Millie and took a step backwards, shaking my head.

"They've taken him to the execution grounds." She swayed. "El, you can't let them do this. Oh Eater, please don't let them do this."

"Why would he say that?" I whispered.

"What are you doing?" Rhyanon's shoes crunched on the dry grass as she hurried toward us. She clutched her injured shoulder. "Get back inside before anyone—"

With a crack like thunder, the windows of the mansion exploded. Glass rained down on the lawns, and Rhyanon and Millie both flinched, shielding their heads.

"*Why would he say that?*" I shouted.

My skin felt cold, but inside I burned. A buzzing filled my ears like a furious swarm of winged insects, and the dark twitching silhouettes of visions flickered over the grass and across the sky.

Rhyanon grabbed my wrist.

"Elfreda, listen to me. *Listen* to me!" Her voice came out harsh. "You have to calm down. We can work this out, but if Celane's people discover you're here, then we're all as good as dead."

I pulled my arm away. "You told me Finn would be *safe*!"

"Saskia is there to protect him, she won't let—"

"Commander Asan already tried to stop the sentencing," interrupted Millie. "She wouldn't let the guards take him away, so the other Councilwomen arrested her."

The blood drained from Rhyanon's cheeks, and I saw her swallow. Behind her, Osan hurried down the path toward us.

"Even so," Rhyanon managed. "Even so, it's still my duty to keep you safe, Elfreda. Come back inside. Let's figure this out together."

I shook my head.

"Please, you're smarter than this," she begged.

"I'm sorry." I turned from her.

"Elfreda!"

I had barely gone ten paces before Rhyanon's lace coiled around my shoulders and brought me to a stop.

"They're going to cut you apart," she said desperately. "If they catch you, it's over. We won't be able to save you again."

I sliced through the bindings with my own lace, and stumbled onwards.

"I'm sorry," I said, my voice raw. I reached the gate and set one foot on the metal bars to hoist myself up. "I'm so sorry."

Osan caught up with me. He grabbed my waist roughly, pulling me back down, and his face twisted in pain when the movement jolted his shoulders.

"Stop it," he said.

I pushed him away. "He needs me."

"Would he want this? Would Finn want this? Running straight to his rescue is exactly what they're expecting you to do."

"Osan," I said in a low, dangerous voice, reaching for my lace, "if you believe you owe me anything at all, then get out of my way. Now."

He opened his mouth to argue, but something about my expression stopped him. He glared at me, then cursed instead.

"Fine," he said, "but I'm coming with you. Two streets east there's a stable with a cab ready for emergencies. It'll be faster than running."

"No!" said Rhyanon.

He turned to her. "Take Jaylen and get out of here. Kamillian, help her."

Millie shook her head. "Finn needs—"

"Just do it! Elfreda and I will deal with your brother." He turned back and pulled a ring of keys from his pocket. He shoved one into the lock on the gate, and it swung open. "Major East safehouse, Rhyanon. I'll find you there."

He pushed me through the gate and onto the tree-lined avenue beyond. The street was deserted, heat shimmering above the paving stones.

"Do you have a plan?" he demanded.

I did not answer. All I knew was that I had to fix this. I started running. Celane could have me, but not Finn—she had won, but it did not matter so long as they let him go.

"Dammit, El," snapped Osan. "Answer me!"

"Get me to the execution grounds."

He made a sound of frustration, but kept up. His breath emerged ragged, and a sheen of sweat covered his face.

The stables were quiet; a single stable hand watched over the drowsy horses. Two animals stood within the harness of a black cab, heads low in the heat, brown coats dark and shining with perspiration. The stable hand recognised Osan before we had even reached the doors, and rushed to secure the traces to the vehicle.

"I'll drive," I said.

Osan leaned against the side of the cab heavily. "No."

"You're in no condition—"

"Well, you should have thought of that earlier. Get in and stay out of sight." He pulled himself onto the driver's seat and snatched the reins. The horses stamped their hooves anxiously.

I clambered into the back and slammed the door shut. My heart thudded; my breathing came fast and shallow. With a jerk, the cab lurched forward.

One small action, then another. Fix this. If the mansion bordered one of the greenhouses, then we could not be far from Minor West; it should only take a few minutes to reach the execution grounds. I gripped the edge of my seat. Time felt like water slipping through my hands. Through the front-facing window, I could see blood seeping through the fabric of Osan's shirt. Cold sweat beaded the back of my neck.

Eater, let Finn be safe, I thought fervently. *Please, let him be okay.*

The cab jolted across the bridge spanning Pearl Boulevard, then swung right at the bend in the road. Someone yelled, angry or alarmed, but Osan ignored them and kept us moving, dangerously fast.

"Come on," I muttered. "Come on, come on."

I smelled smoke before I saw it, plumes of dark grey rising

above the roofs of the buildings to the north. Osan cursed, but urged the horses down Calamite Road all the same. Ahead were the red-brick walls of the Renewal Wards; beyond lay Steel Street and the execution grounds.

The smoke grew denser, catching in the back of my throat. Osan dragged on the reins, and we slowed.

"I can see robed Sisters up ahead," he said. "They'll be looking for you. You do realise that?"

"Doesn't matter." I fumbled with the door. Osan stopped the horses and swung down to block my way.

"It *does* matter," he said. "You're going to stay close to me and keep your head down, because it will do Finn no good if you're caught before we even find him."

There was a large crowd facing Steel Street; white Sisterhood robes mingled with civilian clothing. People held strips of cloth to their faces, warding off the smoke. They muttered amongst themselves.

"I need to get closer," I said.

Osan scowled and pulled a knife from the back of his belt.

"There's a change of clothes under the seat," he said. "Give them to me."

While I rummaged beneath the bench, he pulled off his bloodstained shirt and deftly ripped two strips of fabric from the waist. I shoved a new shirt into his hands, and he tugged it over his head.

"Wrap this around your face," he said, thrusting one of the rags out to me.

The crowd was pressed tight, with civilians craning their necks to see what was happening ahead of them, and even more people gathered further along Steel Street. I started to push my way through the throng, but Osan grabbed my arm and wordlessly dragged me toward the Maternal Affairs offices. A set of stairs ran up the side of the double-storey building. He climbed, still holding my wrist.

"Let's see what's happening first," he muttered. "From the

balcony, we'll have a better view. You might be able to use your lace if necessary."

I nodded and pulled ahead of him, taking the steps two at a time. A few people seemed to have struck upon the same idea; two Judicial Affairs Acolytes stood on the balcony with their hands on the railing, their faces obscured by scarves. Beyond them, over the heads of the crowd, I caught a glimpse of the broad stone platform where mass executions had taken place during the Order's darker days. A pyre blazed on top of the dais, black smoke billowing into the air.

I shuddered. This was like a sick kind of theatre, the crowd all gathered to watch the Sisterhood perform. Judicial Affairs officers surrounded the platform, their ordinary grey uniforms replaced by black dresses and featureless silver masks. I stepped around the Acolytes, trying to get nearer, to see better.

"El," said Osan suddenly. "El, stop."

The smoke stung my eyes. I could see Reverend Somme near the platform, her expression fixed and cold, and Reverend Bremm of Maternal Affairs standing stiffly beside her.

Osan laid a protective arm over my shoulders.

"El," he spoke gently, "let's go now, okay? Don't look."

I shook my head. The flames of the pyre shifted like a living creature. At their heart stood a thick vertical beam.

"Don't look," he said again, still with the same awful gentleness. "Let me get you out of here."

"I'm not leaving without Finn," I snarled.

The two Acolytes were watching me and whispering, but I ignored them. I swept my gaze over the crowd. Finn had to be here. Osan tried to draw me away from the railing.

"I'm so sorry," he said, his grip tight around my shoulders, his fingers digging into my arm. "Please, please just come with me now."

My eyes were drawn irresistibly back to the pyre. In response to a hidden signal, four of the Judicial Affairs officers turned in unison to face the platform. They raised their hands and the fire guttered out instantly, drowned in a complex web of lace. Smoke obscured the dais; through the shifting haze, I traced the edges of the smouldering wood, the blackened beam, the manacles, until finally I was staring at the tortured husk bound to the pole.

It wasn't Finn. That split, charcoal skin was not his. The peeling flesh and scorched limbs, the blood and the smoke, that wasn't him. I needed to tell Osan there had been a mistake, but I could not seem to form the words. He wrapped his other arm around me, turning me away from the pyre. *Stop it,* I meant to say, *stop it, I have to see, I have to find Finn.* Osan held me tightly.

I made a sound, and it was swallowed by Osan's body, my face pressed to his chest. This could not be real, this could not be happening. I struggled against him, and I was screaming, obscenities pouring from my mouth, fuck him and fuck Rhyanon and fuck the Sisterhood, they had already taken everything from me, they could not do this, they could not have him too, they could not have *Finn.* My best friend, my refuge, the one person I could not live without, the one person who had loved me without caring about the consequences, the person who had loved me even as I failed him over and over again. They could not have Finn. They could not have Finn. They could not—

The strength in my legs deserted me, and I slumped against Osan. A few people were starting to look toward us—the latest spectacle, the next act in the show. Let them burn. Let the pyre consume them all. The walls glowed like amber in sunlight.

"El, don't," said Osan urgently.

Finn laughing, his whole face lit up and animated. Finn, his hair falling in front of his eyes as he concentrated. And then Finn burning, fire raging across his skin. Below, I heard exclamations. The walls shone brighter.

Someone else screamed, and Osan stopped short.

The woman's voice cut through the hum of whispers.

"He's not dead! He moved!"

I wrenched free, running back to the railing. Hope flared wildly inside my chest. For a moment, everything fell quiet, and we all stared at the body tied to the stake. There was no way he could still be alive, but I desperately searched the wreckage of Finn's face all the same.

His head rose slightly, he lifted his sightless eyes toward the rooftops and his chest fluttered. From the back of his throat, he produced a quiet moan.

Impossible.

Below us, noise built up in a wave, the tide of a hundred voices rising in disbelief.

"Finn?" I whispered.

Osan recovered first. He dragged me toward the stairs, past the stunned Acolytes, and down to the street. I did not resist. My mind was paralysed; I stumbled after him as the clamour grew ever louder.

Finn was still alive. And that could only mean one thing.

CHAPTER
TWENTY-EIGHT

THE LOFT WAS clean and dim. A small window set into the roof admitted a shaft of pale afternoon sunshine; outside, the sky was uniformly white. Storm weather, humid and close. A thin layer of cloud stretched from horizon to horizon, softening the contrast between brightness and shadows.

On one side of the loft was a narrow staircase, leading to a concealed entrance on the first floor of the Major East house. On the other side was an old mattress, a bookcase, and a small couch where Osan and I sat. He watched birds through the window. I threaded a needle with gut twine.

"Did you sleep with him?" he asked.

A bowl of water stood on the floorboards next to me, murky with blood. Beside it was a cheap bottle of brandy.

"No," I said. "Of course not."

Osan glanced at me over his shoulder. "Everyone will believe that you did."

"I can't blame them. I would have assumed the same thing in their position."

Some of Osan's stitches had torn and the skin surrounding the wound looked bruised and ugly, but it could have been worse. Much worse. This was only a setback in his recovery; before our mad rush to reach the execution grounds, the wound had been almost healed. I peered closer, straining to see in the low light.

"Could there have been another Sister he was interested in?"

"You mean, could Finn have had sex with another Sister?"

"I was trying to be sensitive."

I pressed the needle through Osan's skin. He held still, although I noticed his fist clench. I swallowed. I wasn't squeamish; I just knew that I was hurting him.

"Finn might have slept around," I said. "It's possible. I just struggle to imagine him being that stupid."

Unless he didn't realise she was a Sister. Or if he wasn't given a choice. I pulled the twine through and stuck the needle into Osan's skin again. My fingers were slippery with blood.

"So you didn't know of anyone else?" asked Osan through gritted teeth.

"No. I assume he contracted it from the air, from being close to me. We grew up together; he was always at a much greater risk. And if I'm a Renewer, well, that probably pushed up the odds. More lace. More of a chance of making him sick."

"You know, I always thought 'airborne infection' was a Sisterhood euphemism."

"It still happens, very rarely." But maybe that was just what I wanted to believe.

He hissed as I drew the twine tight again.

"Sorry," I murmured. "Almost done."

"At least you're more sympathetic than the Commander," he said, strained. "For the record, I don't recommend being shot."

I tied off the last stitch, cut it, and picked up the bottle. "Okay, brace yourself."

Osan nodded. I poured brandy over the wound. His muscles went tight, and he made an agonised sound. I set the bottle down. Blood and alcohol seeped across his back, and I gently dried the mess with a towel.

"Done," I said.

Osan groaned, fists clenched around the edge of the couch. *A setback,* I told myself. *Could have been worse.* I leaned back against the cushions, giving him time to compose himself.

After we left the execution grounds, he had brought me to this place. I assumed it was where he lived. The loft struck me as a little sad—although it was secure, it seemed bare and lonely;

there was no evidence of sentiment, nothing of his personality here.

He had departed soon after that, only to return a few hours later, haggard with pain. Rhyanon and Jaylen were safe, and Asan had been released from custody. As far as he could tell, no one had followed him.

It was all too much, the risks he had taken on my behalf. And how could I convey my gratitude, when I required still more from him? He sighed when I picked up the roll of gauze and some tape from beside the water bowl. I carefully wiped his shoulder dry and laid gauze over the wound.

"I expected you would be more upset," he said quietly.

"I am."

"And yet?"

I shrugged. "Would you prefer it if I fell apart? And at least Finn's not dead."

"He's a Haunt."

"Yes." I taped the gauze in place. My voice dropped. "And I'll take that over dead."

Osan sighed again.

"He's not going to remain the man you love," he said.

"I know. I know it's selfish. It just seems . . ." I stopped. Busied myself with the tape.

Osan didn't say anything. I handed his shirt to him.

"I get it," I said. "Wishful thinking."

"Men don't come back once they're infected. You of all people should know that."

I shrugged.

"Elfreda—"

"He's still human now. Let me have that." I submerged my hands in the bowl of water, washing them clean. I softened my tone. "I'm sorry for dragging you into this. And for getting you hurt again."

"I wasn't dragged anywhere."

"No, I'm . . . I would never have managed without you." I glanced across at him. "Thank you."

"In that case, you're welcome." He pulled the shirt over his head. "So, what now? Rhyanon wants you to join her at the new safehouse and wait until the situation calms down."

I shook my head.

"Yeah, I told her you wouldn't like that. So?"

I stood up. "Can you find Daje Carsel?"

"I could. But what do you want with him?"

I explained my idea. Osan's expression grew grimmer with every word, but he kept silent. When I was done, he did not tell me that my plan was insane, although he must have been thinking it. Even I could see the multitude of ways that this scheme could come crashing down around me, and even if it worked, what would I really gain?

On the other hand, how much did I still have to lose?

"Are you sure about this?" he asked at last. "I can still take you to Rhyanon. There might be another way."

I smiled at him.

"No," I said. "I have to break Finn out of the Renewal Wards myself."

CHAPTER TWENTY-NINE

OSAN HAD RETURNED the cab to the stables, so we crossed the city on foot. I wore a scarf around my hair, and he had dressed like a labourer. Not much of a disguise, but he said it would be inconspicuous enough. We travelled the labyrinth of backstreets through the dimming twilight, quick and unspeaking.

I hadn't wanted him to come. After he had returned from delivering my messages, I told him to go back to Rhyanon; be safe, I would do the rest by myself. But Osan had only brushed me off irritably.

"Don't be insufferable," he said.

Getting inside the Food Management warehouse was easy enough; everyone in the department knew that a spare key was hidden in the gap under the loose paving stones beside the door. Osan kept watch on the street while I descended to the basement.

The dark room was full of fluttering, the rustling of wings—someone had brought in a new batch of crossmoths. I took two empty jars down from a shelf, and then a third, just in case. Small, sterile, with polished tin lids. I wedged them inside my rucksack; using the jacket Osan had lent me to cushion them. I could not afford for the glass to shatter.

As I turned to leave, I noticed the markings on the wall. Smudged black letters, just above the insect holding tanks. I frowned and moved closer.

taken everything from me

That was all, just those four words scrawled in charcoal. Yet the sight of them unnerved me; I was sure they had not been there the last time I visited the basement. The letters spiked and lurched unsteadily, like whoever left the message had been shaking. Familiar. My eyes lingered over the angular cut of the "f" and "y."

This was my own handwriting.

A dog barked in the distance, and I snapped out of my daze. I hurried back up the stairs to Osan.

From the warehouse, we made our way up through Major East to the main thoroughfare. A couple of citizens still strolled along Pearl Boulevard, but it was getting late. By the next bell, it would be more difficult to blend into the crowd. Across the street, a hawker was selling the last of his half-price copies of the *Resounder*. "Murderer's Execution Takes Unexpected Turn!" read the headline.

A street away from the Martyrium stairs, I pulled Osan aside.

"This is where we say goodbye," I whispered. "After dark, there's a lacework web around the Martyrium. It triggers an alert when civilians approach the building."

"So I can't come with you."

I tried to smile. "I'll be fine. You've taken me this far."

He scowled, seeing right through my bravado. His obvious concern warmed me, and I felt a painful twinge of affection for him. *What did I do to deserve your help, Osan?* Something of my feelings must have shown on my face because he made an annoyed noise.

"Oh, for Eater's sake." He pulled me into a one-armed hug. "I'll see you later, all right?"

I nodded.

A faint breeze blew over the hillside, cool and damp. Alone, I climbed quickly, my nerves tight. When I glanced backwards, Aytrium looked curiously small. In the darkness, the streetlamps and windows formed tiny pricks of flame, a glowing patchwork of stars.

I breathed deeply. I could do this. I *had* to do this.

About twenty feet from the top of the stairs, I stepped off the path. The statue of the Eater loomed up ahead, great and terrible, her sightless eyes accusing me. I crept through the undergrowth, climbing around the side of the hill. The soil was stony and dry beneath my shoes. Noisier than I would have liked.

I inched closer to the Martyrium. I could see a lamp burning outside the entrance, and a woman slouched on a chair beneath it. The Acolyte stared off into space, her arms crossed behind her head. She looked young. Probably at the bottom of the Maternal Affairs pecking order if she had been given the night shift. I crouched down and studied her carefully. She seemed drowsy, and the light was an unexpected piece of good luck—she would be blind to anything beyond the glow of the lamp.

Nothing else for it. I picked up a stone and tossed it in the direction of the stairs. The clatter made the Acolyte jump. She sat up straighter.

I took a deep breath and stretched my lace toward her.

Outside of three mandatory training sessions, I had never compulsed anyone. The act was deeply intimate and intrusive, a violation, and even now I struggled to do it. Compulsing was also an incredibly delicate art, and the difficulty lay in the balance—I had to make the Acolyte *want* to take action, but without her finding the urge itself suspicious. For this reason compulsing other Sisters was especially tricky. If we paid attention, we could feel the lace at work.

Nothing to be scared of. I brushed against her thoughts. *Probably just an animal. No need to feel too anxious, you shouldn't raise the alert over nothing. That would be embarrassing.*

She squinted out at the darkness.

"Is someone there?" she called uncertainly.

I held my breath. The grass waved in the breeze. Up here, away from the city, it was disconcertingly quiet.

I counted to a hundred, watching the Acolyte relax. Then I threw another stone.

This time she could not dismiss the sound quite as easily. She got to her feet, clearly nervous, her shoulders tense.

Still probably nothing, I soothed. *A rat? Some kind of bird? Maybe you should take a look, to be absolutely sure. Just to set your mind at ease. It would be the responsible thing to do.*

She wavered.

You could take the light with you. Don't be silly. You aren't afraid of the dark. Just a quick look around.

She hesitated, then reached up and unhooked the lamp. I felt a surge of triumph, but quickly suppressed it. Not yet, I had not won yet. The Acolyte walked to the edge of the stairs.

So hard to see. Didn't it sound like the noise came from further down? May as well be thorough.

A pause. I did not dare push her any harder. It should be enough; the seed had been planted. I willed her forward. If this failed, all my plans would be wasted; I needed to get inside the Martyrium.

The Acolyte stood perfectly still, her lamp held up high. Listening.

Then she sighed.

"Stupid rats," she said.

She carried on walking, swinging the lamp from side to side as she descended the stairs. I let her take a few steps, then slipped toward the plaza. Once I reached the paved square, I raced for the Martyrium door.

It opened before I even touched it. I dashed inside, quickly pulled the door shut behind me, and backed away.

Five seconds passed. Then ten. I strained my ears. Had the Acolyte heard me? I could see the lamp through the misted glass panes of the door. It moved slowly, weaving a little, but not drawing any closer.

A giddy rush of relief came over me; I held the stairway railing for support. The spiral of alcoves glowed above my head; each calm, undisturbed, lit by a single candle. I let my pulse steady. I was inside. Getting out again would prove its own challenge, but at least I had made it this far, and one step closer to Finn. I closed my eyes, breathing deeply.

I'm coming, I thought. *Just wait for me.*

The air inside the dome was rich with the smell of night blossoms and incense, the curve of the walls stretching toward the dark sky. My boots were quiet on the stairs; I trailed my fingertips over the vine-covered balustrade as I walked. At the entrance to my mother's alcove, I washed my hands and picked up the scalpel.

"Hi, Mom," I murmured.

No visions tonight. She slept peacefully, her face relaxed, mouth slightly open. The candlelight softened her features and turned her skin a warmer shade of bronze. I approached the bed.

"This is going to be goodbye. So we have a little time."

Her body radiated warmth; even just standing near her, I could feel it. I gripped the knife tighter.

"Not long, just . . . just a little while." My throat tightened. The laugh lines around her eyes, the soft angles of her face—I needed to fix all of it in my mind. Keep her, preserve her. I swallowed, looking up at the ceiling.

"I'm sorry," I said.

And even though she was right next to me, I missed her. I had missed her every day since her martyrdom, even though it was meant to get easier with time, even though we had been broken from the start.

"All I ever wanted was to make you proud, you know?" I wiped my cheek roughly. "I wanted to hear you say it, just once. That you were proud of me."

Stupid, all the things I had demanded of her. That I still, impossibly, tried to demand of her now. I lowered myself onto the bed beside her. Touched her hair. The scalpel lay between us and I knew what needed to be done, but all I wanted was to curl up beside my mother and let Aytrium burn.

"It's not fair," I whispered, and the words stuck in my throat. I shook my head. "I—"

Like a viper striking, bands of lace whipped around me. My limbs seized, and I cried out. The ropes tightened, pinning me to the spot.

"That was very touching, Raughn," said someone behind me. "I'm almost sorry to interrupt."

I wrestled with the invisible bindings, and they shrank painfully around my arms and legs. Too strong, far too strong; I had never encountered this kind of power before. The lace had a humming, seething quality, like water under immense pressure.

Abruptly, my body swung around so that I faced the doorway, my legs forced straight to hold me up. Verje grinned.

"I'd have thought you'd be in more of a hurry," she said, stepping inside the alcove. "Well, to be honest, I'd have thought you would be eager to flee the city entirely, Renewer."

"Get away from me," I said. It was difficult to breathe.

"Asan must be spitting mad that you slipped through her fingers. Where was she keeping you anyway? We'd reached the stage where we were considering releasing an inmate of the Renewal Wards to sniff you out. Eater, that would have been a mess."

"Like the Haunt you released from your estate?" I hissed. "Did you infect him yourself?"

"Don't be crude." Verje glanced over her shoulder, as if she had heard something. Clearly, she was on edge. "Besides, you're hardly one to talk, are you? Finn Vidar probably has some opinions about the topic of infection."

"Get his name out of your filthy fucking mouth."

"Touchy." She walked closer, and lowered her voice. "He was very uncooperative. Celane and I paid him a visit in Judicial Custody, you know. Compulsed the life out of him, but he still wouldn't tell us where you were hiding. He just kept repeating Asan's story over and over."

I lashed out at her with my lace, but it struck her protective net and rebounded harmlessly.

"In the end, Sacor gave us the tip we needed." She picked up the scalpel I had dropped. "About his sister? Be a shame if Enforcement found out she was leading the murderous insurgents. That could end very badly for her."

"Liar," I snarled. "You killed those Sisters, and Asan knows it."

Verje lifted up my left arm and pushed back my sleeve. Her lace drew tighter.

"We still couldn't get a word out of him on your location." Although her tone was almost conversational, her eyes had a feverish light: a hunger. "But he *was* willing to go down for treason and murder, and we could use that. Celane thought a public show might draw you out. Seems she was right."

Rage had smothered my fear, but the sight of the scalpel was enough to bring it roaring back. I wanted to shrink from Verje, from those cold, reptilian eyes. She set the blade to the back of my forearm.

"But I was the only one to consider setting a watch on the Martyrium," she whispered. "Just in case you decided to take the fight back to us. Mistake, Raughn."

She pressed the scalpel down. I screamed as it sank into my arm. The metal felt shockingly cold; the pain electric, biting. She withdrew the blade.

"Please," I gasped. "Don't. Please stop."

She cut again, and I screamed until my voice choked off. Hot blood ran down my elbow, dripping onto the floor. Verje drew out the soft severed notch of my flesh, slicing through the last strands of muscle fibre to free it. I shuddered uncontrollably, wanting to retch but unable to move, unable to even look away. The wound burned.

Verje held my flesh between her fingers, but did not move to eat it. She was watching my face.

She's insane, I realised through a red haze. *She's . . . she's relishing this.*

With slow deliberation—her eyes never leaving mine—she transferred the flesh to her mouth. Blood smeared her lips. She swallowed.

"And now I get to keep you for myself," she said with satisfaction.

I spat, but she stepped back. Her fingers curled around the handle of the scalpel.

"I have a place for you." The candlelight glinted in her eyes. "Out of the city, where Celane won't know to look. Our own private martyrium."

"Go jump off the Edge," I panted.

She grinned again, wider. Her teeth were bloody. My blood. Then an expression of wonder dawned on her face.

"Oh, I can feel it now. This is your lace? Eater, it's like *gold*. And from so little . . ." Her skin flushed, and her lips parted. "Let's see."

Pain shot through my head—not the ordinary dull ache of a compulse, but an explosion of caustic command.

Raise your arm.

The lace binding my body made it impossible to follow the order, but I tried, straining desperately. The pressure built, but I could not obey; I was trapped. My head felt like it was going to split open.

"Please," I gasped.

Verje laughed. "Please what?"

Darkness gathered at the edge of my vision. "I . . . I can't . . ."

The binding around my left arm relaxed, and I immediately lifted it above my head. Fulfilled, the compulse stopped hurting. Blood trickled down my arm. It dripped onto my ear and collarbone.

"All this time, we thought we had power, but this?" Verje held out the scalpel. "*This* is what it's meant to feel like."

Take the scalpel.

"No," I said hoarsely.

Take it.

My fingers trembled as I reached out. The blade was slick. I knew what Verje would make me do next; it was written on her face—the way she was smiling like a child pulling the wings off butterflies.

"Put all the martyrs together, and it's still only a fraction of the power of one sacrament," she said, eyes shining with glee. "And it's all mine. You are all—"

Thunk.

The bolt pierced Verje's windpipe. The tip protruded from the skin above her collarbone, while the shaft remained wedged in her neck like some kind of grotesque jewellery. She blinked rapidly and raised her hand to touch the iron spike.

The scalpel dropped from my fingers, clanging on the floor. My thoughts were frozen. Verje made a gurgling noise and acted like she wanted to cough, her hands fluttering over her throat. Her lacework dissolved around me. I sagged, my legs giving way.

Millie finished reloading the crossbow, aimed, and put a second bolt through Verje's head.

The Reverend crumpled. Millie stood still for a moment, poised, watching for any sign of movement. Then she dropped her weapon and pressed her hand to her mouth.

"Oh," I said. "Oh Eater, oh *shit*."

"No kidding," she whispered.

I tried to get up, and Millie rushed over to me. I clutched her, pressing my face into her shoulder, trying to block out the body on the floor. My chest heaved.

"She was going to eat me alive." I could hardly get the words out. "Millie, I couldn't stop her. She was going to make me—"

"I'm here, I've got you."

"I couldn't do anything. I couldn't do anything," I repeated, and she held me tight, half crushing me in her embrace. "She said she would lock me up. No one was going to find me. And she . . . she . . ."

"I won't let her hurt you again," Millie said fiercely.

"You *shot* her."

"Eater, you're bleeding so much." She drew back to look at

me. "I should have been quicker, you're such a mess. But I'm here now, and I'll never let any of them touch you again."

She was going to make me cut myself. She was going to make me feed her.

Millie wiped blood off the side of my face, and I could tell that she knew. I didn't have to say it aloud.

"How did you find me?" I croaked.

"Daje said that Osan had talked to him, that you were going to help Finn." She kissed the top of my head. "Knew you'd need lace, so I came here. I think we should wrap up your arm, sweetheart; it looks so painful."

I squeezed my eyes shut. My heart hammered.

"It's over, she's dead," Millie murmured. She brushed my cheek with the back of her hand. "Is it all right if I use your mother's shroud?"

I exhaled. Nodded. Millie leaned across and picked it up. When the silken fabric touched my gouged flesh, I jumped.

"Look what she did to you," muttered Millie.

I forced myself to hold still.

"Better than what you did to her," I said.

Millie laughed. Even though the sound had a bite of hysteria, I felt better. I tried not to react when she pulled the makeshift bandage tight. Red soaked through the material. She tied it and briefly rested her forehead against mine.

"I'm sorry," she said.

I shook my head. My pulse had slowed, and I took a shaky breath. "We need to get out of here. When civilians climb the hill, it triggers the alert. The Acolyte outside will have summoned her superiors."

Millie's jaw tightened. "The Acolyte outside was dead."

Eater. That explained why Verje had not worried about my screaming. Millie helped me to my feet. Blood specked the walls and floor of the alcove, pooling red-black beneath the Reverend's body. Her glassy eyes stared at the wall.

My voice came out as a strained rasp. "Can you wait on the stairs?"

Millie frowned. "Wait?"

"Yeah." I averted my gaze. "I need to do a terrible thing, and I don't want you to see."

"El—"

"It's okay. Just . . . I can only do it if I'm alone. Just for a little while?"

She hugged me. "Of course. I'll wait."

In some ways, this was a relief. A kind of gift. I picked up the scalpel. Verje had given me a way out of what needed to be done: a simple, brutal alternative. Not an easy way out, by any means. I knelt beside her still-warm corpse. But at least it didn't have to be my mother.

I thought of Asan at Geise's Crown. *It's this or we die.*

Verje's blood ran thick and hot.

When I was finished, I packed the jars back into my rucksack. I washed my hands in the basin. Then I sat down beside my mother once more and spoke to her in a low voice. Words for just the two of us, things I would never say again. In my mind was a lake in summer, and water on my skin, and the sound of her laughter. I imagined she could hear me.

With a small, gentle pull of lace, I finally let her go. Her chest rose, fell, and did not move again.

CHAPTER THIRTY

The Acolyte lay prone a few feet from the door. Her eyes were shut like she was merely sleeping, her jaw slack. I knelt to check her pulse, although I knew it was pointless—she wasn't breathing. Another casualty, another Sister dead, but this murder struck me as especially cruel. She had just been given the wrong shift.

"May the Star shine brightly on you," I said quietly. "And I'm sorry."

In the distance, the bells tolled. I stood up.

"Will you be all right?" asked Millie.

I nodded. "Let's go."

My whole body felt tight with power; it seeped through my skin and burned iron-sharp on my tongue. While Asan had warned me that gorging was unlike consuming an ordinary sacrament, nothing could have prepared me for how profound the difference felt. Suffused with lace, I was left with the sense of being slightly off-balance, like I was standing somewhere high up and the wind was blowing. Millie kept shooting concerned glances my way. She knew what I had done. Of course she did—I wished I could have obscured the truth, but emerging from my mother's alcove covered in Verje's blood had made that rather difficult.

At least she didn't seem afraid. That would have wrecked me.

"Millie." I gathered my courage. No sense in putting this off any longer. "About Finn . . ."

She quickly looked away. We were halfway down the stairs.

The wind had picked up and grown cold, and the clouds blotted out the stars and moon.

I forced myself to continue. "I'm probably the one who infected him. But it wasn't . . . it wasn't like you're thinking. There was no sex. I just thought you should know." Her silence flustered me, so I carried on. "That doesn't make anything better, and it's still my fault, but I wanted you to know anyway."

"El, I *already* know that."

"Oh."

She looked at me and made an effort to smile. "Finn can be irresponsible sometimes, but you aren't, not where he's concerned. I've always known he's safe with you."

"Except clearly he wasn't."

Her shoulders hunched. "Yeah. What a cruel joke. Some kind of airborne infection?"

"Unless he was seeing another Sister."

She snorted. "Not a chance."

We came to the base of the hill. Pearl Boulevard was mercifully empty—although I had managed to wash the worst of the blood off my clothes in the Martyrium, my arm was still bleeding through the shroud cloth, and we could not afford to draw too much attention.

"Something has been bothering me for a while," I said as we hurried down the first side street into Minor West. "And I thought it might have been in my head, but Verje mentioned the name again. Who is Lariel Sacor?"

Millie stiffened. "What?"

"Sacor. Verje said that Sacor had tipped them off. You used the same name as an alias at Celane's party, and I thought that the Reverends reacted strangely to it then too."

The blood drained from her face.

"Oh no," she whispered.

"Millie?"

"Tipped them off?"

"Yeah, that Finn would—" I changed my mind, lied, "That

Finn was concealing something. Verje wasn't too clear. Why did you choose that name as your alias?"

She scowled. "Because if things went wrong, I hoped it might somehow land Lariel in shit. No good reason. Stupid vindictiveness, nothing more."

"Who is she?"

"An old associate of mine." She was definitely anxious, almost defensive. "But I don't see how Verje would have ever met her in the first place, never mind anything else."

"Why not?"

"Because Lariel hates the Order, passionately. Always has."

Which gives her an obvious connection to the Resistance, I thought. *And would probably mean that she knows everyone else involved. But in that case, why betray them? And why does Millie hate her so much?*

The dark streets lay empty and eerie; even now, I could taste the smoke in the air. I felt watched; with each building we passed, I was sure someone was peering through the gaps between their curtains. Every step toward Steel Street filled me with a dull sense of foreboding. I knew the pyre was gone. I knew he was still alive. Yet in my mind's eye, I could still see the stake on the dais and Finn's skin burned tar-black. The way his head moved, blind and stiff, searching for something. I felt—although I knew it was only in my head—that I could smell charred flesh on the wind.

The Renewal Wards waited at the end of the road. I stopped. Millie looked sick, her eyes drawn toward the bare execution grounds.

"Come on," I said. "He's waiting."

We reached the entrance to the building. I silently motioned for Millie to stay behind me.

Then I took a deep breath, wove a net, and blasted the door open.

To her credit, the Acolyte on duty reacted quickly. She threw up a defensive web of lace and reached for the alarm bell, but my power ripped right through hers. My lace slammed into her before she could pull the cord. I swiftly yanked her upright to stop her from toppling.

"What is the meaning of this!" she demanded, outraged. "What do you think you are *doing*?"

I waited until she had exhausted her power trying to break my bindings. Then I strode across the room, opened the door to the first cleansing chamber and propelled her inside.

"Sorry about this," I said.

"Hey!"

The Renewal Ward keys were stored in the top drawer of the front desk. I found them, walked into the cleansing chamber past the furious Acolyte, locked the interleading door, returned to the foyer, and locked the second door. The Acolyte hammered on the other side, swearing at me.

Millie whistled. "That was, uh . . ."

"Let me out of here!"

"She'll be fine."

"Sounds mad though."

"The cells are this way," I said. "Keep close."

The Renewal Wards were dark; only the foyer was lit. Strips of streetlight filtered through the windows in the first floor corridor. I had never been in this part of the building at night. I flipped through the keys and unlocked the door leading to the stairs. The hinges creaked.

Millie had paused before the door leading to the final Renewal Chamber, a strange expression on her face.

"It doesn't look the way I imagined, somehow," she said. She shook her head. "Sorry."

The Wards comprised three floors and a basement. I headed upwards. My heart quickened. Now that we were so close, I was filled with dread. I wanted to see Finn, more than anything, but I also wanted to run. What if he was no longer himself? The smell of smoke seeped from the walls. What if he was still that burned-out wreck, what if he was mad with pain? I knew that Haunts' flesh regenerated quickly, but to recover from *that* . . . I did not feel prepared to face him. I was not sure I ever would be.

The second floor was filled with soft murmurs and moans, the low breathing of men within individual cells. The Wards could hold up to a hundred prisoners, but seldom housed more than forty. Each man had his own room, padded and sparse, a mattress on the floor and a thin blanket. There was a large metal grill set into every door, so that inmates could be safely monitored. Once the prisoners were past use, too far gone to partake in Renewals, they were transported to the Edge. Well, apart from the ones down in the basement. They were kept for demonstration purposes, for training.

The moment I took my first step into the second floor corridor, the sounds of breathing stopped. They had all woken up.

"El?" Millie whispered.

"Check the right side," I murmured. "I'll check the left."

"Hello?" A gruff voice emerged from the room ahead. "Who's there?"

I put a finger to my lips. Millie nodded. It was darker here, and I could hardly see her face. Down the corridor, someone giggled. The sound choked off.

"Hey. Who's there?" the first man snapped. "What's happening?"

I could see very little inside the first cell. I leaned closer to peer through the grill.

"You smell good," the prisoner inside whispered.

I jumped. He was right on the other side, pressed against the door. Close enough for me to feel the warmth of his breath. His eyes glinted in the darkness.

"I'm starving," he said.

I backed away silently, heart in my throat, and moved to the next door. The man inside slammed into the frame, senseless to pain. Not Finn either. This was so much worse than in daylight. There was a manic quality to the prisoners at night, something more feral, less natural.

Or, I realised, they were reacting to the smell of a Renewer.

The man grunted and collided with the door again, so hard that the impact sent vibrations through the floor. Another prisoner was sobbing, babbling to himself, a string of words I could not quite understand, a kind of profane prayer.

"I really don't like this," said Millie, her voice small.

I reached for her hand. "The cells are secure."

"It's not that, it's that this whole place feels *wrong*. Unstable."

I understood what she meant. The presence of so many half-turned men lent the atmosphere a vertiginous quality; reality turned slippery and slick. An intense feeling of dread was building inside my chest; even though I knew the doors were plated and near impenetrable, to my eyes they looked thin as card.

"It *is* wrong," I muttered. "In more ways than one. But after tonight—"

"You. Speak to me," ordered the rough-spoken man. "Tell me what's going on."

"Nothing that concerns you," I said softly.

"Oh, it concerns me, all right." He punched the grill. It rattled, but did not give. He punched it again, and we both flinched at the sound of crunching bone. "You know what it's like, living here? Waiting for my turn?"

"Stop it!" snapped Millie. I tightened my grip on her hand.

"Millie?"

My heart performed a weird jolt. The uncertain voice came from one of the last cells on the right. Millie snatched the keys from me and ran to the end of the corridor. I followed her, although it was as if my limbs moved through treacle, each step a war between the part of me that was terrified and the part of me that yearned to hear him speak again.

"Where do you think you're going?" the rough-spoken man called, but his words were far-off and unimportant.

Millie tried one key after the next, swearing to herself. Then one fit. She turned it and flung the door open, staggering through and throwing her arms around Finn.

He looked different. Even in the low light, I could see that. His hair had been burned away, which made him appear vulnerable, strangely naked. He was taller too, not much, but noticeable to me. The transformation had already begun to stretch his spine. But his skin was smooth and healed, like the fire had never happened.

I could not speak. I just stood there, rooted to the spot.

"What . . . Millie?" Finn sounded confused. "You shouldn't be here."

"Stupid, stupid, stupid, stupid," she said fiercely, her voice muffled against his shoulder. "Last family I have left, and I was ready to kill you myself for being so stupid."

"Sorry to disappoint you, but that's not really . . ." He trailed off as his eyes found mine. "Possible."

I remained mute and frozen.

"You shouldn't . . . You should go," he said, faltering. "I'm infected. You know that. I don't understand why you're here."

How long, I wondered, had I known? The signs had been there for weeks, but I had refused to acknowledge them. So what if he wasn't sleeping well? That could have meant anything, or nothing at all. So he had looked sick, too pale, what of it? The bruise on his jaw that had already disappeared the night I was attacked? The fact I knew he had been hiding something? All of it could have been my imagination. He had still been Finn.

"When did you work it out?" I asked.

It took him a moment to reply. "Moon Tide."

The same night that I had kissed him. It had been me, I was responsible, I had infected him. Not in that moment, but it had still been me. A splinter of ice worked its way into my heart, a cold, bright needle of pain.

"I didn't want you to know," he said.

My voice sounded like it belonged to a different person. "You didn't sleep with another Sister, did you?"

"What?" He shook his head. "No, of course not."

I had done this to him. The full weight of that knowledge

settled down on me. The ice grew harder, colder, made it difficult to even breathe. I nodded slowly, my head heavy.

"We need to go," I said.

"El, there's nowhere for me to go."

He pronounced the words in such a matter-of-fact way, so calm and resigned, that they took a moment to penetrate my brain. Millie started to say something angry. I spoke over her.

"I will not let you stay here." I turned around. Couldn't look at him. "I will not let the Order use you to Renew other Sisters, because I know exactly what that means and what it is like. You will come with me because no matter what happens, no matter what you say, I will *not let you stay here*."

Silence. I was trembling and could not stop.

"Do I have to drag you out of the building?" I asked.

Soft footsteps behind me. Finn placed a hand on my shoulder. Even through my clothing, his skin felt icy.

"I'll come," he said.

I shrugged him off and walked quickly toward the stairs. I did not trust myself to say anything else. Millie whispered to him, urging him to follow. Around me, the prisoners shouted and moaned, but I ignored them.

I did this to him.

I did this to him.

I did this to him.

The words echoed in my footfalls, pounding against my skull. I kept my eyes on the floor in front of me, down the stairs, past the Renewal Chambers, into the foyer.

"I have to speak to Commander Asan," I said. "Stay out of sight and wait for me at your grandparents' house."

"Elfreda?" said Millie, alarmed.

I pushed the front door open and kept walking. I would find them later. I ground my teeth together so that I did not scream.

CHAPTER THIRTY-ONE

Alone, I moved faster and with less caution. Power coursed through my blood and begged for violence. It would feel good to wield it, to give in to all the anger and lash out. I could crush anyone.

But the cold night air blew through me and cooled my head. One step, and then another. I had known all along that Finn was infected. It should not shock me now.

There's nowhere for me to go.

I scowled.

I had hardly even looked at him. I was such a coward, after everything he had been through. I had interrogated him about his sex life and then threatened to drag him out of the building. At least Millie behaved like she actually cared; I hadn't even said I was sorry.

Seeing him in front of me, the truth right there and him so infuriatingly *calm* about it, I had been forced to recognise my own helplessness. Finn was infected. No way to undo it, no way to stop it. The knowledge terrified me, and so I smothered my grief with anger and ran away from him.

Next time, I would have to do better. I owed him that much, at least. Eater, but I didn't know if I had the strength. I tried to put it out of my mind.

Coromont Street bordered the Slate District in Minor West, not far from the Detainment Offices. I had chosen it because, in theory, it would be easy for Commander Asan to reach. When I had discussed my plans with Osan, he had agreed.

"Asan's retreated to her office," he had told me. "Locked herself in and won't speak to anyone but her immediate subordinates. She'd be able to slip away unnoticed, I think, although I'm not sure for how long."

The alleyway smelled of sour wine and urine, and the light from Coromont Street did not fully illuminate the narrow passage. Broken glass glittered on the dirty flagstones. Daje was already waiting when I arrived, dressed in dark clothing and a hat which shadowed his face. He greeted me with a terse nod.

"Thanks for coming," I said.

"Any time," he said, although he sounded resentful. His eyes flicked to my bandaged arm. "Millie went looking for you. Do you know where she is now?"

"She's with her brother."

"Really?" He lifted an eyebrow. "Then you already broke him out? How?"

"Brute force, to be honest. Millie's fine, they're both fine." I lowered my voice. "Look, I don't have much time. I'm sorry to bring this up so suddenly, but I need to know: Is Lariel Sacor a part of the Resistance?"

He took a step backwards, and his face closed off.

"Daje—"

"Why are you asking me?" he growled.

"Because, unless I'm mistaken, you're in charge."

"Is this some kind of joke? What did Osan tell you?"

"Daje, please. Sacor. Who is she?"

He glowered at me. "I always told Millie you weren't to be trusted."

"Yeah? And I could have sold you out years ago, but here you stand. Un-executed." I reined in my anger. I felt hurt, although I had always sensed that, beneath the friendly veneer, Daje disapproved of me. Didn't matter now. "I'm not trying to get you in trouble, but I need to get to the bottom of this. It's important."

He gave me a flat look. I met his eyes without flinching.

"Who is she?" I repeated.

He made a sound of frustration. "Lariel and Millie, they were—they broke up years ago."

Of all the answers I had expected, this one had not occurred to me.

"And yes, she was involved with the Resistance. *Was.*" Daje buried his hands in his pockets and hunched his shoulders. "Even by our standards, Lariel was an extremist. We cut our ties when she started talking about culling Oblates and uninitiated daughters."

I breathed in sharply. "She suggested killing children?"

"You asked, El." My reaction must have annoyed him, because Daje scowled. "What did you expect the Resistance would be like? People are justified in hating the Sisterhood. And, in all honesty? You're not someone who should be talking about child murder."

A wave of cold swept across my skin. I grew very still.

"What did you say?" I asked.

Something about my expression made him swallow. He glanced toward the street, aware that we were alone here. That it was dark.

"I'm sorry; that was low of me," he said hurriedly. "Look, if you ever gave birth to a boy, I know you wouldn't give him up willingly. Please forget I ever said anything."

He had been talking about the Order's practices. I breathed out slowly. My skin crawled; I realised my fists were clenched tight, and I relaxed them. Forget he had said anything? Even if it hadn't been meant as a personal slight, the remark made it abundantly clear what Daje thought of my kind.

"Sacor?" I said stiffly.

He looked relieved, if a little guilty.

"Lariel's rhetoric only swayed a couple of people before we asked her to leave." He shifted uncomfortably. "That was a few months ago. She's since formed her own movement, although sometimes she still tries to recruit from our numbers. It's just talk, but people like Finn don't take kindly to suggestions of assaulting Sisters."

That explained the bruises, then. I tried to keep Finn out of my mind. "So Sacor *could* betray you to the Order, if she wanted to?"

"Sure, but why would she? If she sells us out, we'd only return the favour."

"Do you know if she was behind the murders?"

"What?"

"The murders of Zenza Lenard and Ilva Bosch. The two dead Sisters."

"You think Lariel did *that*?"

"Based on what you've told me, it seems likely. If she was happy to threaten children—"

But Daje was shaking his head. "She was just a lot of talk, El. I know the Order would love to pin this on the Resistance, but that's not how any of us operate."

"But say it *was* her," I insisted. "You wouldn't be able to tell Enforcement without putting your lives on the line. Right?"

"Well, yes. But—"

"A week ago, I was attacked by civilians working for Reverends on the Council of Representatives," I interrupted. "Tonight, one of those Councilwomen mentioned the name Sacor."

He looked winded. "Why would Lariel ever work with the Order?"

"I don't know. Money?" I waved away the matter. "You said that people hate the Order. Is it so much of a stretch to believe that this woman would take a paid opportunity to murder us?"

"Yes, actually. The way those women were cut up? It's too vicious. I've known Lariel since we were kids."

"Kids grow up. Come on, at least concede that it's a possibility." I ground my teeth. "I mean, don't you see? She's *safe*. The Reverends would have promised her their protection. So long as they hold power, Lariel Sacor can betray you with impunity."

He still looked unconvinced. "There could be many Sacors in the city."

"You're the one who kicked this woman out of your organisation in the first place!" My temper flared. "Finn only confessed because the Councilwomen threatened to go after Millie. Because they knew she was in the Resistance. Who else would have told them?"

Daje's face fell. "Is that why Finn said that he killed those Sisters? Does Millie know?"

"Not yet, but she'll figure it out soon enough."

Daje rubbed his forehead, grimacing. I knew how he felt. I could only imagine how Millie would react when she learned that Finn had tried to sacrifice himself for her sake.

"Sacor *is* responsible," I pressed on. "And if I'm right, that means there are people in the Order who know your name. And Millie's. That's why we have to resolve this quickly. These women can crush you whenever it suits them—whenever you cease to be a useful scapegoat for their crimes."

"They have no proof."

"Did that matter when they tried Finn? You'll dance to their tune, and the truth won't matter one bit. The Resistance is dead."

He bristled. "It's not dead until we are."

"Yes, pretty words." I made a savage gesture. "I'm sure that will inspire your people, but I want Millie to remain *alive*."

"Then what do you propose?" He was also losing patience. "If you have everything all worked out?"

I could hear swift footsteps approaching, Enforcement boots on stone. Relief surged through me, and I smiled.

"A compromise," I said.

Asan appeared at the mouth of the alley. The Commander looked worn, and sported a livid bruise just below her left cheekbone. At the sight of her, Daje went rigid.

"Raughn?" Asan's eyes travelled between us, and narrowed in suspicion. "I'm glad you're not dead. Want to explain what this is about, before I haul you off to a safehouse?"

I gestured respect. "Good evening, Commander. I heard you were arrested."

She shrugged. "Correct. It's been kind of a shit day. Talk quickly."

"El?" said Daje in a strangled voice.

"Not the best day for me either," I replied evenly. "Commander, this is Daje Carsel. In exchange for your protection, he is going to tell you everything he knows about the people who murdered Zenza Lenard and Ilva Bosch. Daje, this is the Commander General of Enforcement, Councilwoman Saskia Asan. Although I suspect you already knew that."

Daje was backing away toward Lavais Street, shaking his head. I brought him up short with a rope of lace.

"You have similar goals," I said. "You might not necessarily see eye-to-eye—"

"You're a real piece of shit, El," snarled Daje.

"But I think working together would serve both your interests."

Asan eyed Daje like a cat stalking a bird. "Mr. Carsel knows the people who were hired to carry out the killings?"

"Yes," I said. "Catch them, tie them back to the Council, you'll have all the evidence you need to take down Celane. Once the truth comes out, the rest of the Sisterhood will turn on her."

"I doubt it will be quite that simple. And in exchange, Mr. Carsel wants . . ."

"Amnesty from prosecution on treason charges. For himself and his associates."

"*Treason?*" said Asan.

"I am not helping the Order," said Daje angrily. "Go jump off the Edge."

"You each have something that the other desperately needs," I went on with greater urgency. "It doesn't have to be a close partnership, but at least consider it. When I asked for this meeting, I didn't even realise all the ways that you could help one another."

"Get to the point, Raughn," said Asan.

"The Order needs to reach out." I was speaking too quickly, but I had to make them understand. "There need to be conversations now, or else we're risking a whole city of hungry, angry people turning on us."

"You're making the generous assumption"—Asan gestured toward Daje, who was glaring at me with seething resentment—"that your insurrectionists want to talk."

"It's going to take some trust. But it can be done. It needs to be done, before things fall apart."

Asan sighed. "What kind of treason are we talking?"

"Sedition."

"So, the 'Resistance,' then." She grimaced. I could see her weighing up matters in her head, her eyes raised in thought. After a moment, she nodded.

"All right," she said. "My protection, provided no violence was involved. And only if I receive his full cooperation in finding the killers."

I turned to Daje eagerly. "Well?"

He remained tight-lipped and silent. His eyes were stony.

My hope wavered. Had I miscalculated so badly? I had thought that, even if he was angry, Daje would see sense. *What did you expect the Resistance would be like?* Like Finn, or Millie, or even like Daje himself, although I realised now that I scarcely knew him at all. Before tonight, I had thought the Resistance might hate the Order in an abstract way—that even if they opposed our methods, they might still recognise Sisters as ordinary women. Might see that we had the least choice, the least room to breathe.

Maybe, if I was truly honest, I had thought that citizens should actually feel a little more grateful for the fact we protected Aytrium at the cost of our own lives. That I endured my role, that I fulfilled my duties, so that people like Daje could play at being heroes and tell themselves stories about how righteous and honourable they were in comparison. Brave scions of rebellion. The glorious lost people, reclaiming their birthright. A pity that their fantasies were built upon the bones of every martyr who had ever served Aytrium.

I released the lace binding him.

"If you want to disappear, start running," I said. My voice was toneless. "I can hold off the Commander long enough to give you a head start. But when the Order finds you, I want you to remember that I warned you, and I gave you a way out, and that you made this choice anyway."

"It's not a choice!" he burst out, throwing up his hands. "You never asked me whether I wanted this until it was too late to escape."

"It's as much of a choice as I've ever had." I pointed at Lavais Street. "You get to decide whether to run, or work with us. And no, I haven't placed you in any new danger; ever since Sacor sold you out, you've been standing within the Order's line of sight. The fact you were unaware of the danger doesn't make it any less real."

"Cooperate or die, is that how it is?"

"Two women were murdered in cold blood, and you might know the person responsible. Where is their justice, Daje?"

He glared at me, and it looked like he was going to argue more. I returned his stare without flinching. If this was what he wanted, I would make him own it.

He took a deep breath and shook his head.

"What do you want from me?" he asked Asan.

The Commander had been observing the argument, a thoughtful look on her face. She tilted her head to the side.

"Come to the Detainment Offices in an hour," she said. "I'll need a proper statement, but first I have to take care of Raughn."

He nodded. "Fine."

"Daje?" I said.

He looked at me.

"Thank you," I said.

His mouth twisted downwards, displeased.

"I know you mean well, El," he said. "But I'm still not on your side. This is for Millie's sake."

As much as I could hope for, I supposed. Daje turned and quickly walked away, disappearing onto Lavais Street. I had done what I could; at the very least, Millie would be safer than before. There was no sense in feeling guilty.

"Well played, Raughn," murmured Asan.

"If he actually shows up in an hour's time to make the statement."

"I think he will. But we'll see." She rubbed her jaw and glanced at me sidelong. "Osan told me what happened after my arrest."

I lowered my eyes. "About Finn?"

"I'm sorry that I failed to protect him. Deeply, deeply sorry." She bowed her head. "The responsibility was mine. This might not bring you much comfort, but in light of the fact that he confessed, Deselle Somme managed to convince the Council that he should be drugged before the execution. He would have been unconscious."

I shut my eyes for a moment. The flames flickered behind my eyelids.

"I know you tried," I said. "And you were not responsible; he confessed. What else could you have done?"

"I promise to get him out of the Renewal Wards at least."

"That won't be necessary."

Asan frowned. "Even if he's already infected, we can still spare him that experience."

I knelt and opened my bag. "I have something for you."

"Unless, of course . . ." She groaned when I lifted out one of the jars. "Oh fuck, you've already done it, haven't you?"

The lump of flesh inside the glass glistened wetly. I had cut Verje's heart into four pieces, consumed one, and placed the others into separate jars.

"What did you do?" Asan demanded. She raked her hands through her hair. "How did you get hold of that?"

"I broke into the Martyrium." I held out the jar to her. "Reverend Verje caught me, there was a fight, she lost."

"That's Belia Verje?"

I nodded.

"Fuck."

"I didn't plan it this way."

"Of course you didn't, but there's still a dead Councilwoman lying in the Martyrium." She rubbed her temples. "Is that what happened to your arm?"

"Verje cut me." Bile rose in my throat, the taste of iron and salt. "And she . . . ate. In front of me."

Asan looked repulsed.

"Eater," she muttered.

"They're getting more desperate," I hurried on. "If you bring witnesses against Celane, I don't think she will go down quietly. But with more lace, you can level the scales."

She scowled. "I've suffered gorge sickness once this month, and I'm not eager to repeat the experience. Let's just go to the safehouse. We can discuss this later."

I dropped my eyes, and shook my head slightly.

"What now?" she snapped.

I set the jar down on the flagstones at my feet.

"Take it or leave it," I said. "I'm not coming with you."

"Oh yes you are." Asan squared her shoulders. "What, you think I'll risk Celane tracking you down? Verje proved how far these women are willing to go for the Renewer's power."

"I know." I gestured regret. Gratitude. "But there are things I have to do, and I can't allow Celane or her associates to stop me."

"And if *I* try to stop you?"

"I hope that you won't."

Asan was silent for a moment. I readied my lace. Just in case.

"This is stupid," she said at last.

"Probably."

"But you are sure?"

I nodded.

"Rhyanon's going to kill me," she muttered. The tension went out of her, and she sighed. "Fine. Go. But don't you dare let them catch you."

CHAPTER THIRTY-TWO

THE EMERGENCY MUSTER sounded as I reached the edge of Major West. The bells clanged, ringing out over the sleeping city.

Had someone found Verje or the Acolyte? Or had the Sister at the Renewal Wards escaped from the cleansing chamber? Either way, the Order would be rushing to fortify Ceyrun's defences. I kept my head down as I hurried along Swallow Road. That might make matters more difficult for me. I shouldn't have spent so long talking to Asan.

The windows of the old house were dark. Dried-out weeds poked through the steps leading up to the front door, and mounds of sand marked where termites had started to burrow. The property looked deserted, and the sight of it caused a flicker of worry to stir inside my chest. I had assumed that no one would think to look for us here, not even Osan—it seemed like a safer location to regroup than Millie's or Finn's place. On the other hand, it was a long way from the Renewal Wards. Plenty of opportunities for them to run into trouble.

I glanced down the street in both directions, then quickly walked up to the door. But before I could try the handle, it swung open. Millie put a finger to her lips and ushered me inside.

The faint smell of lye lingered in the entrance, as if the house itself exhaled it. I blinked, letting my eyes adjust to the darkness. Millie shut the door behind me, and the key ground in the rusted lock.

"You took so long; I was worried," she whispered. "Where were you?"

"I was talking to Commander Asan. Told her about Verje."

"Eater, El, that seems awfully risky. She's still the Head of Enforcement."

"I didn't mention *your* involvement," I said, trying to keep the bite out of my voice. Daje's words were all too fresh in my mind; I was oversensitive, trying to come to grips with Millie's association to the woman who had murdered my supervisor. I would not be bitter; I would not hold it against her. And yet the faint voice at the back of my mind would not shut up either. What *had* existed between her and Lariel Sacor? For years, I had taken it for granted that Millie cared about me. That, in some way, our relationship was special. Its own category. Sure, she had other women in her life—she had Hanna—and occasionally I would get jealous and stupid when I saw them together, but it was fine. If Millie didn't desire me, that was okay, because what we had still mattered.

But Sacor? Sacor was not Hanna; this was different. If Millie could be with someone who murdered Sisters, if she could overlook that, then . . . Then what else didn't I know about her?

"Asan can be trusted," I said, a little too forcefully. "Besides, it's done now. Did you have any problems getting here?"

She shook her head. "No, we were fine. Come through to the basement, Finn's already down there."

The walls in the passage were bare, and the panelling stained with old mould. Millie had tried renting out the building, but the place had a bad reputation in the neighbourhood, and none of the tenants stuck around for long. People said it was haunted, that old man Vidar still lingered here and his dogs continued to whimper in the cellar at night. Which was a lot of nonsense, but even so it was strange how unhappiness seemed to cling to the building like a second skin. One set of stairs led up to the bedrooms on the second floor, a second down to the basement. From below, I could see a faint orange light.

"I expected it to be dustier," I remarked. "When was the last time you had tenants?"

"Couple of months ago." The stairs creaked under Millie's feet. "They cleaned things up a bit."

I kept one hand on the banister as I descended. A year before Sefin Vidar passed away, Millie's grandmother had fallen down these stairs. She cracked her skull open and died.

At age twelve, Finn had fallen down these stairs too. He broke three fingers on his right hand, but suffered no other injuries—not a single scratch, not a bruise, nothing. Although he refused to talk about it, I knew that only a day earlier he had first—shyly—voiced the desire to study music.

An unhappy coincidence, of course. In public, Sefin Vidar knew how to smile and sweet-talk, how to make everything sound like it had been blown out of all proportion. Anyone who knew the first thing about the man would have seen through that act, but to the Order? He showed every sign of being a respectable citizen; he was charming and funny and reasonable. When he wanted to be.

As soon as my mother heard about Finn's fingers, she had intervened. She made certain that his bones were set straight, and demanded that he and Millie be transferred to communal care. I had seldom seen her so angry, so coldly focussed. But it wasn't enough. The Order wanted more evidence, and the case was eventually dropped by Judicial Affairs.

Kids trip. They fall down stairs.

For years after that, my mother made a habit of dropping by the Vidar residence unannounced. Her visits were always short, terse, to-the-point. She made it clear to Sefin that he was being watched. He was smart enough to fear her, because Finn never came to any kind of obvious physical harm again. Millie ran away when she turned fifteen.

What I never understood was why Sefin didn't just hand his grandchildren over. Some kind of warped pride, perhaps, some sense of ownership. He had frightened me, this big, red-faced man with his low, rasping voice and fists knotted with blue veins. I hated the way that he loomed over my mother, and how quiet and small Finn became during those years.

Finn's head brushed the ceiling now. He stood beside the rutted wooden dining table in the basement, arms folded, on edge, his jaw tight. A single lamp hung from the wall and lit the room in dim orange. When he tried to catch my eye, I pretended not to notice and turned my gaze to the floor. Cheap furniture crowded the small room, a moth-eaten mattress, a pine bench, a rusted stove. Next to an old chest of drawers was the door to the wine cellar. I avoided looking at that too.

"You said that you had no trouble getting here?" I asked, before either of them could speak. "Do you think anyone might have followed you?"

Millie cast a glance at her brother. "I doubt it. But what now? You heard the warning bells outside. Do we try to wait it out down here?"

I shook my head. "The Order's going to tear the city apart looking for Verje's killer; we need to get out of Ceyrun fast. The trouble is that they'll have already secured the gates."

"Can't you just . . ." Millie made a pushing gesture. "Do what you did at the Renewal Wards?"

I smiled weakly. "Too conspicuous. Ideally, they shouldn't even realise that we've left."

Millie leaned against the table. The lamplight illuminated her face from the side, throwing her features into sharp relief. "So what are you thinking, then?"

The seed of an idea had been nagging at me all evening, like a stone caught inside my shoe. In truth, it had been planted far earlier, but the sound of the bells had brought it to the forefront of my mind.

"Do you remember the meat seller, on the night I went looking for Finn?" I asked.

Millie nodded.

"When I asked how her supplier was getting meat through

the gates, she told me that he wasn't using them. Which means there *must* be another way in and out of the city, one that the Order doesn't know about."

Millie chewed her lip. "There are people I could ask who'd be able to point me in the right direction. I'd have to go alone, though."

"Ceyrun's on high alert; it's going to be chaos out there."

"And yet I'll get nowhere if you're with me."

"What if—"

"Don't make me use my counsellor voice, El."

I spluttered. "What?"

"I won't be long. Just wait here, and I'll see what I can find out." She looked at Finn again, who shifted uncomfortably. "Besides, there's probably a conversation you need to have."

"Millie . . ."

She brushed my hand on her way past.

"Leave it to me," she said.

Her footsteps were light and swift on the stairs. I slumped. She was right; I should trust her. It had been a long night, that was all. Too much happening far too quickly, too much that felt beyond my control. The front door creaked and then closed with a muffled click. And now it was just Finn and I, with nowhere to run and nothing to distract me.

I set my bag down on the bench. This moment had been inevitable.

"So," I said heavily. "About the way I behaved earlier, that was . . . It was callous. I should have been kinder, after everything you've been through."

"You're hurt," Finn murmured.

"What?"

"Your arm."

I turned around, meeting his eyes for the first time. Although he looked so strange, his eyes were the same, blue and clear and sharp. But his hair. I'd always loved his hair—soft, messy, straw-coloured, the way it curled at the nape of his neck and around his ears. And it was all gone. I could not look at him without remembering the stake and the fire.

"It's nothing serious," I said.

"What happened?"

"I said it's nothing serious. Doesn't matter." I sank down onto the bench. "It's nothing at all next to . . . well. You know."

He was still standing in the middle of the room, with the top of his head grazing the low ceiling. How could I have failed to notice that he was growing taller? How could I have refused to see the changes before now?

"I'm so sorry," I said.

There, a faint smile. The way he was looking at me—with such open gentleness and worry, without accusation, without a trace of resentment—cut far more deeply than any rebuke.

"You say that all the time, you know." He ran his fingers absently across his scalp. "Have you tried not blaming yourself for the things you can't control?"

"But I *could* have controlled this." I swallowed the lump in my throat. "It's my fault."

"You did nothing. All along, I was the one who tested the limits, and you were the one who enforced the boundaries. We got unlucky, but if anyone was to blame, it was me."

"No."

The shadows under his eyes made him look sick.

"Please don't do this," he said softly. "I don't want you to feel responsible."

I balled my hands into fists. "I could have told you to leave me alone years ago. I knew this could happen, but I was too selfish to care."

"It was my choice, El. And besides, I helped with the visions, didn't I? That was important."

By making me feel safe while I poisoned him. By caring for me while I ruined him.

"Stop it," I said.

He looked down, and his voice dropped. "You were always so

lonely, and you never admitted it. I wanted to be there for you. Wanted to make you smile, sometimes."

"Stop," I repeated. My blood pounded in my ears.

"Stop what?"

"I infected you. *I* did this to you." *Don't you dare cry!* "Why can't you just hate me?"

He stood there, looking down at me with that stupid expression on his face, pale and sick and exhausted, and shook his head.

"I don't know how," he said.

It was suddenly all too much. I shrank, arms wrapped around my own shoulders, trying to stop myself from making a sound. Finn crossed the room in three strides and crouched in front of me.

"El, don't do this," he said. "Look, I've had time to get used to the idea."

"You never said anything," I choked.

"I tried. Couldn't find the right time. At some point, I realised it might be easier if you never found out at all."

"Don't lie. I refused to listen to you."

"I could have made you hear me, if I'd really wanted to. This was just . . . less painful."

I shook my head. No, it wasn't. Finn lifted one hand like he wanted to comfort me, but I flinched.

"This wasn't your fault," he said. "El, you have to believe me. It was never your fault."

The kindness in his voice broke something inside me, and all the strength, all the rage and terror and grief that had kept me moving forward, kept me from facing the truth—was gone. I let go of my arms, dropping my hands to my lap. The undersides of my fingernails were scored with dried blood.

I needed my anger back. This emptiness gnawed right through me.

"I saw you," I whispered. "At the execution."

His reaction was close to imperceptible, but I noticed his jaw tighten.

"Commander Asan said you were unconscious." I tasted ash.

"But I saw you move. Every time I close my eyes, the memory returns to me. The way you looked back there."

He touched my cheek. His skin felt like ice, like cold metal. I trembled.

"It was only a bad dream," he said quietly. "I woke up in the Renewal Wards. Before that? Only flashes of memory."

"I saw you."

"And you can see me now too." He placed a finger under my chin and drew my head up, made me look him in the eyes. "Just a bad dream. Nothing more."

I made a small movement with my head, whether to move away or closer to him, I wasn't sure. How could he feel so cold? I traced the familiar lines of his face with my eyes. Him. Not him. Frozen. Burning.

"I have to fix this," I whispered.

For a fleeting moment, I saw longing in his eyes. A hope he could not quite crush, that maybe I *could* undo this, that he could still be saved. Then it died, and he gave a very small shrug.

"Getting me out of the Renewal Wards was enough," he said.

I shook my head and gently pushed his hand away from me. At my touch, a hint of colour returned to his cheeks. He looked at the floor.

"I'll find a way," I said. "Whatever it takes."

"You'll only make things harder for both of us."

"When I thought I'd lost you at the execution, it was . . . I can't go through that all over again. Please, just trust me."

"But this isn't something we can stop."

"I know it's not reasonable, and I know I'm not being fair. Finn, I'm asking you to try, that's all. Don't give up yet."

He looked pained.

"One step at a time." I heard the pleading, desperate edge in my own voice. "We get out of the city, we find a place to hide, and then we work together to come up with a solution."

He shook his head. "Of course I'll try. What's the alternative?

But I won't delude myself, and neither should you. If there's a risk that I might hurt you or someone else—"

"We'll deal with that when the time comes."

Finn sighed and walked over to the table. He was only humouring me, I could tell. But I could not bring myself to be angry about it—any more than I could bring myself to accept that I would lose him again. He sat on the table, and for a long time he was quiet. I watched as his gaze drifted to the cellar door, expression inscrutable. Then he shivered and looked away.

"You were lying to Millie upstairs," he said. "What did you tell Commander Asan?"

"You could hear our conversation?"

He nodded.

"I wasn't really lying. I just wasn't sure if you'd talked to her yet." I hesitated. "About why you confessed to the Order."

"Oh." He winced. "About that—"

"I know you did it to protect Millie, but she should hear it from you first."

He rubbed his forehead. "How did you work it out?"

"Reverend Verje told me. It was Lariel Sacor who betrayed you, wasn't it?"

I could see him wavering over what to say; his shoulders bunched, and his jaw went tight. Then he breathed out.

"Everything," he said softly. "Lariel told them everything. At the time, claiming responsibility seemed like the only way of fixing things."

And they compulsed you into it. But he had probably realised that by now. The wound in my arm ached, and I dug my nails into my palms. *He was very uncooperative,* Verje taunted. She had been terrifyingly strong even without the Renewer's power. The thought of her smiling as she wrapped her lace around Finn's thoughts, breaking him, forcing him to confess, was enough to make my blood run cold.

And Celane would have been right beside her. Celane, whose compulses flowed smooth as silk, as light as breath.

"Was Lariel the same woman who killed Lucian?" I asked, trying to get the picture out of my head. "The night I was attacked?"

Finn nodded. "She couldn't risk him talking to Enforcement."

I swallowed. I knew we were both thinking about the way Lucian's spine had snapped in two. The clean, precise *crack* ringing in the air.

"I don't understand why she didn't just use that weapon on me," Finn muttered.

"If it was laceworked, the instrument might have been specifically tied to Lucian's blood."

If anything, Finn looked more uneasy. "You can do that?"

"Me? No. I wouldn't even know where to start, wielding lace that complicated. But other Sisters"—I thought of the books in Celane's study—"have more resources. I guess the rods were meant to be used as a last resort if anything went wrong. Lariel must have been instructed to silence her own people."

Finn fidgeted, not meeting my eyes. When he spoke again, his voice came out strained.

"Until that night, I didn't know Lariel was behind the killings," he said.

"I know," I replied, a little too quickly.

"I need you to understand that we would never have been complicit in that." His tone grew more forceful. "Not me, not Millie. Never."

"Finn, I know." But a small, anxious part of me *was* reassured to have him say it aloud. I think he heard the relief in my voice; his mouth turned bitter, and he ran his hand over his scalp.

"I screwed up," he muttered. "Should have told the Commander everything, but if she found out about the Resistance, I thought . . ." He made a frustrated sound. "I thought I could handle it all myself, as soon as I was released from custody. I was so stupid—I should have at least told Millie about Lariel, but I knew she would react badly. And when the Commander *asked* me if I knew who was responsible—"

"Finn." I quickly put up my hand to stall him. "It's fine. I've explained everything to Asan. She's offered the Resistance protection if they help her track down Lariel."

"What?" He looked baffled. "That's why you were gone so long? That's what you were doing?"

I nodded. "The Commander isn't so bad. And she's far more preoccupied with taking down the rogue Councilwomen than chasing after the Resistance."

Finn shook his head in disbelief.

"You're a miracle," he said.

The way he said it, the way he was looking at me—my face warmed. I lowered my gaze.

"I'm not," I said. "It's only a chance, nothing is set in stone."

"But it's *something*. The Commander—"

Finn stopped abruptly. His expression clouded.

"What is it?" I asked. "Is something wrong?"

"No. Millie's back, that's all."

I had not heard anything, but a few seconds later, the front door creaked. Finn straightened.

"Don't make her ask," I said under my breath.

He grimaced. "Yeah. I'll talk to her."

I heard Millie's feet on the stairs as she took them two at a time. I stood up when she reached the basement. A broad grin was spread over her face.

"Smugglers' tunnels," she said triumphantly. "Under the western wall. I know where to go."

CHAPTER THIRTY-THREE

FINN LED THE way through the dark streets. It must have been past midnight, but the city felt alive and tense. Lights burned inside the houses we passed, and the sound of raised voices travelled down the busier thoroughfares. Every now and again, he paused and then quickly changed direction, cutting through narrow alleys and forcing us to double back on ourselves. I wasn't sure, but I think he might have been able to hear—or perhaps smell—people nearby. The thought unnerved me. There was also something uncanny about the way he moved, a new kind of fluidity or cunning, something fox-like and predatory. He made very little noise.

The Sorsin District lay beyond Major West's industrial sector. It was filled with squat, crumbling buildings, all packed claustrophobically close and permeated with the smells of old cooking oil and refuse. Unlike the rest of the city, Sorsin came alive at night—we could not pass through it without being seen. Older men lounged around, leaning against low, broken walls; talking, watching. None of them seemed to be doing anything in particular. I grew acutely aware of the fact that, apart from Millie and myself, there were no women on the street.

"You're too tense," Finn muttered.

I shrugged and loosened my neck. Inside one of the buildings, an argument broke out. Shouting was followed by a thud and the shatter of glass. In no hurry, a bearded man got up from the street corner and moved to investigate.

"She stands out," Millie whispered to Finn. "We all do."

"Can't be helped. We must be nearly there, right?"

"The directions were vague, but I think so."

There were no street names in this part of the city, and shoddy alterations to older buildings sloped out into the roads, blocking passage or forcing pedestrians to squeeze between mud and wormwood walls, slanted roofs patched with posterboard and glue.

"Ah," said Millie. "That's the place."

The hostel was a triple-storey edifice propped up against the city wall. The foundations had sunk, and jagged cracks ran up the brickwork. The left side was rough-plastered, the right raw brick and lime, like a creature half skinned.

"There should be a shaft below the floor of one of the back rooms," said Millie. "It comes out in the Fields."

"And no one will object to us using it?" I asked.

"Well, I wouldn't say *that.*" She glanced at me askance. "But you could convince them, if the need arose. Right?"

I nodded.

Finn seemed distracted; he kept turning to look at the street behind us, frowning. Millie nudged him and he started.

"Everything okay?" she asked.

"Yeah." His expression cleared. "Yeah, sorry. There's a lot going on around here, that's all."

"Well, maybe stop eavesdropping, then. Come on."

Millie entered the hostel first, and I followed. The interior smelled musty, and the floorboards creaked beneath my feet. A sullen teenage boy sat on the edge of a rutted bench beside a splinterboard door. He scowled at us.

"What d'you want?" he asked.

"For you to mind your own business." Millie flipped a coin at him. He caught it out of the air.

"I've never seen any of you before," he said, casting a dubious eye over Finn. He stuck a thumb toward the splinterboard door. "Still, it's nothing to me. That way."

"Thanks," I said.

He gave me an odd, appraising look, and I regretted having spoken. Millie stared at him, her face hard.

"Millie?" Finn muttered.

"Hm." She reached into her pocket and flipped the boy another coin. "For your trouble."

The door stuck, and the hinges groaned when it swung open. The corridor beyond was dim; dark mildew stained the walls and shifted in the unsteady lantern light. From the upper floor, people's footfalls sounded loud and heavy.

Finn touched the small of my back, and I jumped. His expression was troubled.

"What?" I murmured.

He shook his head. "I don't know. Never mind."

"Room eight. There's supposed to be a hatch set into the floor." Millie hurried ahead of us down the passage, scanning the brass plates above the doors. "It's probably concealed, in case the Order ever came knocking, but I can't think it'll be too hard to access."

"Wait," said Finn suddenly.

A floorboard creaked. The splinterboard door swung shut, just as Millie pushed open the door to room eight. Finn shoved me behind him, shielding me against the wall with his body.

"Kamillian," said a new voice. "I was hoping you'd turn up."

I whipped a lace shield around Finn and threw out a cord to yank Millie back toward us. A second later, a woman with short black hair stepped out from room eight. She had a crossbow trained on Millie's forehead.

"Lariel?" said Millie.

I didn't hesitate; I threw out another rope of lace, meaning to rip the weapon out of the woman's hands. But my power dissolved when it came within a foot of her body.

The woman saw my expression and smirked.

"It's Elfreda, isn't it?" she said. "Is something the matter?"

I had never felt anything like this before. It wasn't that my lacework had been blocked, or had run dry. My power had just evaporated like water on a hot stone.

"I guess you're Lariel Sacor, then," I said slowly.

She shrugged. "Might be."

"What are you doing to my lace?"

"Ah, that would be the new crossbow bolts. They absorb lace, so if I were to pull this trigger"—she gestured with the crossbow toward Millie—"you wouldn't be able to stop the bolt from cracking her skull open."

Finn made a guttural sound in the back of his throat. I heard footsteps; more doors opened, and three men emerged, crossbows loaded. Millie edged closer to me.

"What's this about?" she asked.

"Didn't Finn tell you? He definitely saw me last time."

"Last time?"

"Oh." Lariel raised an eyebrow. "He *hasn't* said anything. That's interesting."

"Shut up," growled Finn.

"What's going on?" Millie's eyes darted to her brother. "What is she talking about?"

"Then he really did keep it secret from Enforcement." Lariel shook her head in wonder. "I know you decided to take the fall, Finn, but to not even tell the Resistance *why*? That seems stupid."

"Finn?" said Millie. "What secret?"

He spoke through gritted teeth. "That Lariel was behind the murder of the Sisters. She committed the crimes that I was sentenced for."

The men fanned out behind us, blocking off our way out.

"You can't be serious," said Millie.

"I mean, why else did you think he confessed?" Lariel moved closer, and Finn flinched. "He knew full well he would end up dead or in the Renewal Wards."

"I don't understand."

Lariel gave her a pitying smile.

"None of this makes sense," said Millie. Her voice grew louder. "Why would he take the blame for *you* of all people?"

"Oh, he certainly didn't."

"But—"

"Finn did it for you," said Lariel.

Millie paled.

"I told the Councilwomen all about your involvement in the Resistance," said Lariel. "All about Daje, all about your little plans."

"No, Millie, listen," said Finn quickly, "the situation was complicated—"

"They gave him an ultimatum," continued Lariel. "Claim responsibility for the crimes, or have them pinned on his sister."

"It wouldn't have made a difference!" Finn's words came out in a rush. "I already knew I was infected. The Councilwomen showed me the list, and everyone was on it, everyone in the Resistance. But if I said I killed those women, I could at least keep you safe. I didn't have anything to lose."

"How could you?" Millie's voice was gravelly and soft. For a moment, I thought that she was talking to Finn, but then I realised her eyes were fixed on Lariel, burning with anger. "You heartless *bitch*."

Lariel's face revealed nothing. She adjusted her grip on the crossbow.

"You betrayed us? You were the one who framed my brother?" Millie took a step forward. "You murdered those women and cut them apart?"

"It's no more than they do to each other."

Millie swore viciously.

"At least I killed them *before* slicing them into pieces." Lariel's mouth formed a hard line. "Don't act like it's so much worse."

My protective net began to thin; I pulled it tighter around us. *Think!* If I couldn't use lace against these people directly, then I was all but defenceless. Could I try collapsing the building? I probably had enough power, but even if I shielded Millie and Finn with lace, we would still be buried under the rubble. I clenched my jaw. Had to be smarter, had to keep them both safe.

"What do you want?" I asked.

Lariel snorted. "Trying to negotiate, corpse eater? If you come with me quietly, I'll forget I saw the Haunt. Does that sound reasonable?"

Finn bared his teeth, and he seemed suddenly larger and more threatening. The men surrounding us tensed, but Lariel only shook her head.

"Don't test me, Finn," she said. "This won't end well for you."

He spoke in a low, dangerous voice. "I can't die."

She studied him, and her expression turned surprisingly thoughtful.

"It's a shame, really, about the infection," she said. "Death would have been easier for you."

"Save your sympathy."

Her face hardened. "Well, you brought it on yourself. Tell me, what is it like to burn alive? How did it feel?"

"Enough," I snapped. "I'll come."

Finn grabbed my arm and pulled me close, shielding me against his body. He kept hold of my wrist; I could feel his heart hammering through his chest.

"Don't," I said under my breath.

"They can shoot me first," he replied fiercely. "I don't care."

"I'm warning you now," said Lariel. "Old times' sake? It isn't going to stop me from putting a bolt through your head."

Millie stepped into the line of her shot.

"Will it stop you from putting one through mine?" she asked.

Lariel's crossbow wavered.

I used my lace to drag Finn's arms open and stepped free. "Stop this! I already told you I'd come."

It was as though Lariel did not hear me. I saw her finger tense on the trigger, and I knew she would pull it. My mind went blank. Deep inside my chest, I felt something snap.

All the light in the passage vanished.

"Millie!" I screamed.

Noise, all around me. Sounds of confusion, men fumbling through the dark, Lariel swearing. Finn knocked into me and wrenched me to the floor. A bolt hissed above us and thunked into the wall.

"Stay down!" he hissed into my ear.

I heard harsh breathing and then a crash. Finn jumped up and lunged away into the pitch black darkness. I crawled forward. *Not Millie, not Millie.* I had seen Lariel pull the trigger, but then the darkness had swallowed everything up. A bang, muffled gasps. The door hinges screeched behind me—it sounded like at least one person had escaped.

A heavy sliding thump, a body falling.

"Finn?" I scrambled to my feet, panicked.

"I said stay down, El!"

Not him, then. His voice was further away than I expected; he seemed better able to navigate the darkness. I could not tell what was happening, but I stumbled toward the place where I thought Millie should be. Gargling sounds, choking.

Eater, please, I prayed, reaching blindly ahead of me.

I felt the air move as someone rushed past me. A gasp from ahead; maybe Lariel. More knocking against the floorboards. Then stillness and only the sounds of heavy breathing.

"Millie? Finn?" I whispered.

"It's okay," said Finn. "She's just winded."

I felt the edges of a door frame. Finn caught my hand and guided me inside. Millie was wheezing.

"I knew something was wrong," she rasped. "The kid outside made it far too easy. Never checked for Sisterhood tattoos."

I found her, my hands searching her arms and back. Was she hurt? The moment before darkness swept through the room, I had been certain Lariel pulled the trigger. It was as if the bolt had vanished midflight.

"Finn?" Millie coughed. "Is Lariel . . . ?"

"She's still breathing. Just unconscious."

"I think her head hit the wall."

"Are you hurt?" I demanded. "Did she hurt you?"

"Nothing serious." Millie pushed away my anxious hands. "El, stop it, let me catch my breath."

She would have shot you! I wanted to say. Finn stood up and took a few steps to my right. I heard shuffling, the sound of fabric moving.

"What are you doing?" asked Millie sharply.

"I'm taking her bolts. I don't want them used against us later."

"Yes. Good." She took a deeper breath. "Sorry."

I wove my lace into thin strands and extended them like feelers into the darkness. By sensing where they dissolved, I could get a picture of where Lariel and her associates lay. Or, at least, where their weapons lay.

"There are at least four sets of bolts," I said. "I've never encountered anything like them before."

"No kidding," Finn murmured as he moved to collect them.

This had to be Celane's doing; where else would mercenaries have acquired this kind of weapon? I shivered. The Reverend must be insane, giving that much power to someone like Lariel. It left every Sister wide open to attack. Not to mention the rod that had broken Lucian's back. Exactly how many of these tools had Celane been working on?

"I guess we'll hang on to the bolts for now," I said, forcing myself to focus. "You'll have to carry them; they prevent me from using my lace."

"El," Millie started, then stopped.

"What's wrong?"

"You . . ." She faltered. "What Lariel said about me being in the Resistance? It's not what you're thinking."

If the situation were different, I could almost have laughed. "Don't worry about it."

"We would never have hurt Sisters like that."

"I already know. Daje said the same thing."

"Oh," Millie said, and then went quiet, probably wondering

when I might have spoken to Daje. Wondering how much I knew, wondering how I really felt. Overhead, I could hear urgent voices, shouting from the street outside.

"We can talk about it later," I said. "It doesn't matter anyway."

A rustle of movement. Lariel moaned.

"I'll carry her to the entrance," said Finn.

"Asan needs her," I said.

"And the Commander will find her. Frankly, if Daje has the rest of the Resistance searching, Lariel will be lucky to last until the morning. She's betrayed a lot of people; there'll be no safe haven for her in Ceyrun."

Millie made a sound.

"What is it?" asked Finn.

A pause. Then her voice emerged low from the darkness, little more than a whisper.

"She's defenceless."

He breathed out hard. "Mill, she just tried to kill you. She would have handed El over to the Order."

"I know." She sounded pained. "But if it's true, if she betrayed everyone . . . they're going to tear her to pieces."

Finn was silent.

"You know they will," said Millie.

"And she'll deserve it," he said harshly. "What do you want me to do? We can't go back out there, we can't take her to Enforcement ourselves. Believe me, Lariel was happy enough to throw you to the Order's mercy, and she wouldn't hesitate to do it again."

"I know."

"Do you? She pulled that trigger on you, and you're still worried about what might happen to her?" His voice grew hoarse; he was struggling to keep his temper. "Come on, get a grip. Either I take her to the entrance, or we leave her here in the dark."

"Or we take her with us," I said.

Finn paused as if unsure whether he had heard me correctly.

"We do what?" he asked.

"Lariel can't confess if she's dead. By taking her with us, we ensure that she stays alive." From beyond the passage, there were more sounds of movement, raised voices. "There isn't much time. Finn, please?"

"This is lunacy."

"You're more than strong enough to carry her." I felt my way to the wall and searched the floorboards, looking for any kind of latch or hinge. "We'll deliver her to a chapter house outside the city."

My fingers met what felt like an old rug. I pushed it aside and ran my hands across the boards below. Uneven, loose. I wormed my fingers into the gap between them and tugged. The plank came away easily.

"El, she's a murderer." Finn sounded strangled. "She killed your supervisor. She tried to kill *you*."

"No, she didn't. She tried to take me to the Councilwomen."

"That's worse!"

"This isn't about her; she's just a tool." I stuck my hand into the recess below the floor and found a handle. I pulled, and the hatch opened toward me. A draft of cooler air wafted upwards. "We need her."

He swore.

"You know I'm right," I said.

I heard him tramp across the floor and the rustle of Lariel's clothing as he lifted her off the ground.

"We're *definitely* going to regret this," he said.

Millie reached out in the darkness and found my hand. She squeezed it gratefully.

The shaft smelled of dust and iron. It was disconcerting; in the absolute darkness, there was no way of knowing how deep it ran. I descended first. The metal rungs set into the side of the chute were icy under my hands, but solid. Whoever had set this up had meant it to last. My backpack brushed against the side walls, and loose dirt pattered around me.

My feet found the ground.

"It's about fifteen feet deep," I called and stepped back. "Drop the bolts so I can move them down the passage, or they'll interfere with my lace."

There was a thump as the bolts hit the ground.

In the direction of the city wall, the passage shrank, wide enough for one person to crawl through at a time. Still pitch black; I could see nothing. It was an eerie feeling, like if I wandered too far, the darkness might swallow me—I had the irrational sense that I might somehow lose my way. Shadowy fingers pressed against my eyelids. I tossed the bundle of bolts down the crawlspace and returned to the base of the shaft.

"Okay," I said. "If you lower her slowly into the shaft, I'll be able to pick up her weight with my lace."

Millie and Finn manoeuvred Lariel through the hatch, and I wove a net to lower her down. Using my power blind was tricky; I had very little sense of her weight, only a slight strain against the ropes. I reached my arms up and felt for her feet.

"All right, I've got her," I said. "Be quick."

Distantly, I heard the sound of alarmed voices. It seemed the darkness had been discovered. I propped Lariel up beside the entrance to the crawlspace, listening hard. Hopefully the phenomenon would buy us a little more time, although the fact that one of the men had escaped the hostel posed a threat. Word of us leaving the city might get back to Celane.

Dirt showered the base of the shaft, and a few seconds later, Millie reached the ground. She tapped my arm and leaned close to me.

"He's going to struggle," she muttered. "It's pretty cramped down here."

Finn was descending after her. "I *can* hear you, you know."

"Stop listening, then."

"You make it sound like a choice." He paused, and his movements fell silent. "Sorry. Give me a moment."

Millie crouched and dragged Lariel into the entrance of the crawlspace.

"I'll go ahead," she called, and then to me, much quieter: "Try to talk him through it."

I slipped past her and returned to the base of the shaft. The light pitter of falling dirt fell quiet again.

"I'm beginning to think blasting through the South Gate might have been the easier option," I said.

Finn snorted.

"Are you okay? I should have taken this into account."

"It's fine." He descended another rung; I heard his shoe against the metal. "Did you do this? The darkness?"

"Not intentionally. But I think so."

"A product of your visions?"

"Kind of."

"And they're why the Reverends are so interested in you."

Sharp as ever. "A part of it, yes."

A longer pause.

"Sorry," he said. "I'm taking too long, aren't I?"

"It isn't much further."

"I really am fine. It's just the dark, you know? Makes it feel smaller."

"Of course." I reached out and touched his ankle to let him know where I was standing. "Take it easy."

"It really isn't a problem."

He had stopped moving.

"Finn? You're doing well, I promise."

"No, I'm not," he muttered. "Shit, why do I have to be so stupid about this?"

"You can't help it."

"Yeah, but I wish you weren't here to see it. Eater, it's like the walls are closing in around me."

I wanted to reassure him, but I didn't know where to start. The image of the cellar door in the basement was burned into my mind.

"If it's any consolation, I can't actually see you," I said.

He scoffed.

"Can I do anything?" I asked.

"No. I'll manage, it's just . . . difficult."

"I know."

It had taken two years before he was able to talk about the cellar. The space where he had been locked up for hours, sometimes full days, hungry and alone, until his grandfather released him. Lightless, airless, cramped. He had never really recovered from those childhood years, and they haunted him even now in small, irrepressible ways. He hated the smell of wine. He couldn't stand closed spaces. He always left a light burning at night.

Finn descended a few more feet.

"You're almost here," I said gently. "Come on."

I caught the barest yellow gleam as he turned his head my way. Against the blackness all around, his irises glowed. I swallowed.

"What's wrong?" he asked.

He can hear everything. "Just worried about you, that's all."

He shuffled down another rung.

"Do I scare you?" he asked.

"No. Except when you do stupid things."

"Frequently then."

"More often than I'd prefer. But we'll get through this, I promise."

His feet touched the ground.

"And after that?" There was a raw vulnerability in his voice, fear tangled up in hope, and hearing it made my heart ache. I reached out and found his hand.

"I'll think of something," I said.

His ice-cold palms were sweating. To my surprise, he pulled me close and wrapped his arms around me. His heart beat right beside my ear.

"Thank you," he muttered.

I returned his embrace. I was still unused to his new height, but he smelled the same and sounded the same, and my feelings for him continued unchanged, quiet and fierce and warm. Then, because it felt like the right thing to do and because no one would see, I tilted my head upwards and kissed his cheek.

"You mean the world to me," I whispered. "You know that, don't you?"

He buried his face in my hair.

"I can feel myself changing," he said. "It's happening faster now."

"We'll fix it."

He gripped me tighter, like I was all that was keeping him from drowning. "What if I hurt you? Or Millie? What if—"

"It won't come to that."

He shuddered. I drew back from him a little, still holding his hand. The chill of his body lingered on my skin.

"Come on," I said. "We have to keep moving."

He breathed out shakily.

"Compulse me," he said.

I stiffened.

"I can't do this." He let go of my hand, defeated. "I'm not going to be able to crawl through there. Compulse me."

My arm burned, and I found myself shaking my head. No. No, I would *never* do that to him. Verje's eyes, shining with delight. That helpless, all-consuming terror as I took the scalpel from her. For me to do that to Finn—no. Never.

"El, please."

My voice was distant. "You don't know what you're asking."

Celane, Verje, they had already hurt him. Compulses belonged to them, to the Renewal Wards.

"If it's you, I don't care." He sounded broken. "The Reverends already did it to me, right? If I could handle that—"

"No." I took another step away from him, and my back hit the wall. "I won't."

"If it's you," he repeated, softer, "then it's okay."

I screwed up my face. It was a violation, it was crossing a line between us. He did not understand; he could not grasp what it *meant* to compulse another person. Not only for him, but for me. In bending his mind to my will, in doing this to *him*, I would prove myself to be just as monstrous as the Resistance believed.

"I trust you," he said, so exposed and so crushingly sincere. "Help me."

"You don't want this. If you understood—"

"El, I know what I'm asking for."

Stupid, obstinate, reckless idiot! With a cry of anger, I stepped forward and stretched my lace toward him. But instead of meeting resistance, my power melted into him; he welcomed it, he let me in. We stood in the dark, and although I could see nothing, I could see him.

"Finn," I breathed.

He was smiling. Scared, but smiling.

"Told you," he said.

It felt so different. I moved tentatively, barely letting my lace touch him at all, but he leaned into the compulse, impatient, as if he wanted me to hurry up, like he was pulling me in. This was Finn, familiar but so strange, and I was blisteringly aware that he was looking right back at *me*.

"Everything okay over there?" Millie's voice drifted out from the far side of the crawlspace.

"Yes," I replied, flustered. I felt my way over to the tunnel. It seemed that Millie had managed to drag Lariel through to the other side. "Just fine."

Finn knelt beside me. His breathing was unsteady. I gently increased the compulse, my power washing over his fear like ripples on the surface of water.

"You go first," I murmured. "I'm right behind you."

The tunnel was short; I could hear the rhythmic metal clangs of Millie's shoes on the rungs of the far shaft. My lace tied me to Finn, I let my feelings brush against his mind, and his echoed back to me—trust and anxiety and concern; even now, he was concerned about me. *Don't be afraid,* I willed, crawling forward on my hands and knees. *I'm here, I'm here, I'm here.*

He reached the end of the tunnel, and the space opened up around the base of the second shaft. His relief flooded my mind, and I smiled to myself. Wiping dirt off my hands, I straightened and let go of my lace.

"You made it seem easy," I said.

Finn laughed. My sense of connection faded, and I experienced a strange pang. I wanted to remain joined to him a little longer.

"I think the hatch is locked," called Millie from above us. "I can't get it open."

I snapped out of my distraction. "Let me try, then."

Millie returned to the bottom of the shaft, and I sidled around her, almost tripping over Lariel.

"Good job," she muttered.

"Mill, for the last time, I can *hear* you."

She huffed in irritation.

The air grew colder as I climbed the ladder; outside, I could hear the wind howling. The weather had changed swiftly; it sounded like a storm. Maybe that would work to our advantage. The cold rungs prickled under my hands, rusted and slick with moisture. I extended my hand overhead, and my nails scratched the underside of the wooden hatch.

I channelled my lace upwards. With a splintering crack, the trapdoor flew open.

Instantly, rain lashed my face. The water was driven sideways in the high wind, fat drops stinging my skin. I pulled myself out of the shaft. Even though the moon was low and dim through the clouds, the darkness here was ordinary. I could finally see again.

The smugglers' tunnel emerged at the border of the Fields. Behind me, the lights on the city wall floated like yellow beads on a string. Maize tossed drunkenly from side to side. In the storm, we would be invisible to the night watch.

I wiped rain off my face and smiled. They would pursue us: Celane, her associates. Their hunt had scarcely begun, I knew that. But by the time they caught up, it would be too late to stop me.

CHAPTER

THIRTY-FOUR

THE HANDLER AT the Cat stables was surprisingly cooperative.

"Right away," she said, nodding vigorously.

I had demanded the use of two Cats. The young Oblate had heard the emergency muster, she knew there was a crisis—if I was here at a time like this, it could only be with the approval of the highest authorities in the Sisterhood. After all, the gates were locked. Anyone leaving the city would need express permission and a very good reason. I name-dropped liberally.

She lapped up every word with wide-eyed alarm, then hurried to organise my request.

"Why two Cats, though?" she asked, as she brought the saddled animals to the door of the shelter.

"I'm meeting a superior in Halowith; she'll need one too," I said. "Unfortunately, I can't tell you more than that."

"Understood." She offered me a leg up.

"Thank you so much for your help," I said with sincerity. I found myself thinking of the dead Acolyte outside the Martyrium, and couldn't help adding, "There's a lot happening in the city. Keep yourself safe, keep your head down."

"Yes, Acolyte."

She walked the Cats out into the rain. They were not impressed by the weather. My animal, a short-haired female with a black coat, skipped from paw to paw. Her brother yapped. The handler smacked his rump, and he settled into a sulk.

"May the Star shine on you," she called, over the hissing rain.

"And on you."

I met Millie and Finn a few hundred feet down the road. We were all soaked; the downpour continued to flood the Fields and path, gushing over the baked soil. An end, finally, to the drought. Lariel hung across Finn's shoulders, her short hair stuck to her forehead. I didn't know what we were going to do when she woke up. I hadn't really planned for that.

The Cats growled when they smelled Finn.

"Easy," I said, digging my heels into the female's ribs. Millie grabbed the male's harness and made soothing noises. The animals knew the scent of a Haunt.

"I'll take Lariel," I said. "You two ride together."

Finn slowly edged around the Cat's huge jaws. The fur at the scruff of the animal's neck stood on end, and his head swung around suspiciously. Finn patted him. Confused and already miserable, the Cat shivered and mewed plaintively.

"You sure?" he asked. "I could ride with her."

"You take care of the bolts. I can bind her if necessary."

Finn set Lariel down and hoisted himself into the saddle before offering a hand to Millie. She swung up in front of him. They paced a few feet forward, and I used my lace to lift up Lariel.

We made swift progress through the dark. Beyond the Fields, I could see the blurred lights of the fishing towns in the distance, and the deeper black shadow of the hills beyond Malas Lake.

Lariel's head jolted drunkenly in front of me as we rode. Her hair was matted with blood above her left ear, and the rain washed red streaks down her neck. At least her body helped to keep me warm; I could feel my hands and feet growing numb, my back chilled from the rain. In spite of my discomfort, I felt drowsy; the swaying strides of the Cat and the relentless cold dulled my brain.

How strange and terrible to think that Finn's execution had occurred less than a day ago. When my eyes drifted closed, frozen images flashed through my mind. Verje bringing my flesh to her lips, Lariel pulling the trigger on the crossbow. Finn burned and dead, the Renewal Wards, Declan Lars and Finn merging into one pale, shambling . . .

I forced myself awake.

"Millie?" I called.

She turned her head toward me.

"It's too cold. Don't doze off, okay?"

"No risk there," she said. "Not with this ice block stuck to my back anyway."

"I resent that," said Finn.

We had reached the top of the hill. Below lay the orchards, and the Moon Pillar woods. I strained my eyes. I couldn't see any light ahead; the valley was buried in shadow. My teeth chattered.

"It'll be better under the trees," I said. "At least they'll offer a break from the wind."

My mount padded down the muddy road, and I nudged her toward the woods with my knees. The wind whipped over my skin. Although she joked, Millie looked a mess; her lip was split, and her face had turned wan and bloodless. Finn might be impervious to the cold, but it was obvious that we needed shelter, or at least more warmth. The Cats would help; even wet, their bodies remained hot. If we could escape the wind and the worst of the rain, we would be okay. I hoped. Sunrise was only a few hours away.

We came to the edge of the woods. The trees groaned and dripped. I lifted Lariel down and climbed off my Cat, rubbing my arms to restore circulation. My hands had stiffened gripping the saddle. I grimaced and stretched my cramping fingers. Finn helped Millie to the ground.

"I don't think we've been followed," I said. "If we're lucky, the Order will focus their attention on the city for now. Buy us some time."

"Time for what?" asked Finn.

I made a vague gesture. He leaned down and picked up Lariel, easy as lifting a small child. Her head moved, and she moaned.

"Back with us so soon?" he asked.

She did not answer.

I led my Cat deeper beneath the trees, and the wind eased. I was shivering violently. The Cat nudged me with her snout, and I stroked her head.

"El?" said Millie.

"Find a place to shelter, and keep Lariel quiet," I said. "There's something I need to do."

"We should stay together," said Finn.

I wrung water from my shirt. "I won't take long. But I really do need to be alone for this."

"You won't even tell us what you're doing?"

"It's . . . personal, I guess. A decision I want to make on my own."

He looked unhappy. "Be careful."

The ground was soft and slick, sucking at my boots with each step. Droplets of water trickled down the back of my neck. The gloom made it difficult to see, but I kept to the path, winding my way deeper into the woods.

As I walked, I played out the arguments in my head. My mind was sluggish, and my thoughts got caught in familiar ruts. The rain lightened; the sound quietened to an even hush on the canopy roof.

We can be better than this.

Could we? Could I? Maybe Celane, for all the terrible things that she had done, held the right line of thinking. She wanted to protect the Order. The Order protected Aytrium. There was a balance at play, and who was I to upset it?

The trees opened up to the clearing. The moon hung overhead, spreading a feeble white glow through the clouds. The platinum-bright names carved into the Pillar gleamed and faded, gleamed and faded, in time with my breath.

Long grass brushed my legs as I approached. I touched the granite surface of the monument. Warm. A susurration of power flowed from the rock, responded to my own. My fingers tingled and I withdrew them. The clouds shifted, causing the boughs of the Anchor Tree to glow white.

"So I hear you are the Renewer."

I spun around and flung a net of lace. It tangled around Reverend Shaelean Cyde, fixing her to the spot.

She did not struggle. She stood at the entrance of the grove, her expression calm.

"I wish I had known sooner," she continued.

"Don't you all?" I snarled.

"Commander Asan managed to pass a message to me a few days ago," she said. "She indicated that you were safe, but I gather circumstances have changed since then."

Cyde remained composed, despite her paralysis. I was unnerved. I glanced around the clearing.

"I'm alone," she said, reading my mind. "Elfreda, I'm not here to hurt you."

"You're working with the Commander?"

A faint smile. "You *have* been staying in my house for the past week. What happened? Is Asan in trouble?"

"No." I shook my head. "At least, I don't think so. The mansion was yours?"

"Yes. I lived there while I was Chief Archivist, and the property remains under my name." She frowned. "Were you discovered?"

"Not exactly, but it seemed wise to leave."

"Wise to leave on a night like this?"

I said nothing.

"You do not trust me." She nodded to herself. "I understand that."

"How did you know I'd be here?"

"The Pillars are better defended than most Sisters are aware. Your presence triggered certain alarms."

I should have anticipated that. "And yet you came alone."

"Not all of my subordinates can be trusted. Until I knew who you were, it seemed better to be discreet."

I did not release my binding. Cyde simply stood and watched

me; her eyes glinted in the moonlight. She had been a friend to my mother, but still. I could not let my guard down.

"Do you know *why* I'm here?" I asked.

"I can guess."

"But you aren't . . . scared?"

She weighed the question. "Would it matter if I was?"

"I don't know. I'm about to do something terrible. If you were scared, I think I might lose my nerve."

"Would you? Haven't you already come too far for that?"

My stomach twisted. I looked down; I did not want Cyde to read my face.

"Explain why you want to do this, then," she said.

"So you can talk me out of it?"

"So I can understand."

It was difficult to put my feelings into words, to express the bone-deep urgency that had taken root inside of me. I kept my eyes on the ground. The grass shone like razors.

"If Aytrium is to remain airborne, then the Sisterhood is indispensable," I said.

"Yes," Cyde agreed.

"And if that's the case, then . . ." I wavered. Glanced up at her. "Nothing can ever really change, can it?"

Water dripped from the branches, trickling over the dark ground, down into the soil.

"It costs us too much," I said. "What we do to men, what we do to each other, it's . . . it's too much."

Cyde's face was unreadable.

"And if the price of change proves to be our lives?" she asked.

I could not answer her. The names on the pillar grew brighter, casting their light over my skin.

"If you make this choice, you make it for us all," she said.

"I know."

"And here you are."

I hesitated, torn between fear and lingering loyalty and the conviction that this was right. Right, just, and necessary.

"I know what I'm risking," I said, placing both palms flat on the surface of the rock. "But I don't think I can turn back now."

I wrenched.

The power of thousands of long-dead Sisters rose up in defiance, layer upon layer of webs and nets and ropes pulling tight in resistance. A dull, ominous rumbling emanated from the Pillar. I stood firm and pulled, let the old magic stretch to breaking. Lace drained from my blood, the world turned red before my eyes, and the rumble transformed to a roar.

Something snapped.

I lost my balance as the ground rippled. Branches broke off the trees, and flocks of panicked birds took flight. With a crack, the Pillar split and fell apart, tearing the Anchor Tree's roots from the ground.

Then everything fell quiet again. I held my breath. For a moment, nothing happened.

Then I felt a faint vibration, the tiniest jolt of downward motion.

Aytrium was sinking.

CHAPTER

THIRTY-FIVE

THE PATH WAS narrow and overrun with deep green crawlers, thorns that pricked my soles. Music—was it music?—echoed through the chamber, high and wordless and strange. Light fell in silver wheels through the circular windows set high in walls; trees grew through the floor and strained their boughs toward the daylight.

"Save me."

"Let me die."

"Save me."

"Let me die."

I didn't know where the voices came from; their argument continued in toneless whispers as I moved through the chamber. I was unafraid. This place felt as familiar as my own body; I remembered the days before it was abandoned and overgrown, the days when I was whole.

I was . . . ?

—whole. And here they had walked, my children, my beloved ones, and they laid wreaths of flowers at my feet, and I made them whole.

Where was I?

The stairs leading to the altar were set with jewels, an intricate mosaic. Spirals of topaz and ruby, onyx and clear quartz.

"Save me."

"Let me die."

The body upon the altar wore her—my?—face. Her eyes were closed, and she looked to be asleep. As I watched, her skin began to glow diffusely, light bled from her veins. The sight repulsed me, for she was not one of mine, she was an outsider. A defiler. A thief.

I did not know where I began and ended, my thoughts stretched obscenely. The voices grew louder. I looked down and saw that my feet had vanished beneath a river of blood.

I sat up in bed, gasping.

Fat drops of rain skittered over the window pane. The sky outside was dark grey; the shadows of the trees swayed in the wind. I rubbed my eyes. The walls of the guest chamber were covered in burn marks, occasionally coalescing into words: *save me, let me die, save me.* And, written large over them all, *TAKE THE PATH OF GRACE.*

I worked to control my breathing. After a while, I slid out of bed and walked to the window. My feet sank into the pile of the carpet, muffling the sound. It was sometime before dawn, and although the wind had calmed somewhat, the rain showed no sign of stopping.

Ever since I had seen the words on the wall in the warehouse basement—*taken everything from me,* in my own handwriting—I had been turning over an idea in my mind. Thinking back to the graffiti that had appeared, for months, in the alleyway outside the dormitories.

Let Aytrium fall.

All along, had that been me?

There was a soft knock on the door.

"El?" Finn said softly.

"You can come in."

He opened the door.

"Are you all right? You were talking in your sleep." He stopped and took in the burn marks on the wall. "Uh, that's . . . bad."

I smiled to cover my unease. "One way of putting it. It's a vision thing."

He touched the marks. "'Let me die?'"

"Don't worry. That's not . . ." I paused. "It's not me. Just a dream voice. Is Millie still asleep?"

"Yeah. Lariel's awake, though. I think she's trying to find a way to break out of her room. Not very successfully, at this stage."

"I'm sorry I asked you to carry her."

"She only tried to have me executed. No big deal." He sat on the edge of my bed. "Besides, you were right. She's Millie's best chance of survival."

I returned my gaze to the rain. The outpost cottage hunkered in the woods to the west of the main Moon House complex, concealed by a wall of dense foliage. Reverend Cyde had left us here and promised to return as soon as she could—she needed to send word back to Ceyrun. I wanted to trust her. If she had coveted the Renewer's power, she could easily have taken it by now; my lace had run dry in my effort to break the Pillar. She could have cut me apart right there in the clearing. After what I had done, that might even have been justified.

"Did I make the right choice?" I asked, without looking around.

Silence. My breath left a cloud of condensation on the glass pane. I could, if I concentrated, sense the island descending. The other Pillars strained to stop Aytrium's fall, but they weren't enough. Five hundred years of history, and I had torn it all down in an instant.

"It was brave," Finn said quietly. "And kind of noble, I think. I just don't know what will happen now."

"Aytrium falls." I traced circles on the misted glass. "Although if they martyr me, they could still fix it. Raise us back up. Maybe that would be better."

I started as Finn's arms closed around my shoulders. He hadn't made a sound crossing the room. He hugged me from behind.

"No," he whispered. "It wouldn't be."

I swallowed hard. "You say that now."

"I'll say it every day, for as long as it takes for you to believe me. Don't speak that way, El."

I leaned back against him and shut my eyes.

"You're cold," I murmured.

"You know, that's been mentioned a few times."

"Hm."

He smoothed my hair. "Do you remember when we were kids, and you swore you were going to run away from home? Because if you stayed, they would turn you into a Sister?"

I shook my head. I didn't remember.

"I think you must have been about eleven. It was late in the afternoon, and we were sitting on the stairs outside my parents' house." He continued gently combing back my hair. "For months afterwards, I was terrified that my best friend was going to disappear. You had sounded so sure of yourself."

I remembered *wanting* to run away, fantasising about escaping to somewhere remote and secure, a place where no one would know I was a Sister. I just couldn't remember ever telling Finn about it.

His fingers grazed my forehead, cool as river water.

"Then the fire happened, and everything fell apart," he said. "Millie tried her best to protect me, but, well . . ." He shrugged. "I was a burden."

"She never felt that way."

"She did. And it's okay; I always understood her feelings. Didn't blame her."

I tilted my chin up to look at him. He smiled, fond and sad, not hiding anything.

"So everyone else disappeared," he said. "But not you."

I looked down again. "Finn—"

"A few months after the fire, you sneaked out in the middle of the night to see me. Do you remember that?"

Of course I did. I had crossed three districts to reach him, and my mother had been incandescently furious when she found out—angry in a way that I later understood was fear. If Sefin Vidar had discovered me climbing through his grandson's window at midnight, he might have killed me. But I had been very young and very stupid, and I had missed my friend.

"You talking to me that night?" Finn's voice was soft. "It was the first time that I felt normal again. That I felt safe. And you told me—"

"That I wouldn't run."

Finn lowered his hand from my hair.

"You do remember," he said.

I had obsessed over what to say to him: promises of justice and retribution, apologies, pleading insistences that I wasn't like the Order, I was different, I was still the same. In my mind, Finn already hated me. I would be inducted as an Oblate in a year, and then he would never speak to me again.

"I told you I was going to become a Sister," I said heavily, "and that I would either fix the Order or burn it to the ground."

Of course I remembered. And here we were.

Finn's lips brushed my hair. He drew back from me.

"You should try to get some more sleep," he said. "I'll keep an eye on Lariel."

"Don't go."

"El . . ."

My forehead was cool where he had touched me. "There are things I should tell you."

"They can't wait?"

I shook my head. "No, I don't think so. Do you want to sit down?"

It took a while, but we had time. Finn listened while I told him about being a Renewer: about why Celane was hunting me, the murders, my work for Rhyanon, what had happened with Verje. He didn't say anything, and I was grateful; false assurances or shock would only have made it harder. And he knew that, he knew me—although when I described what Verje had done, his carefully controlled expression slipped.

When I finished, he sighed.

"You aren't as surprised as I was expecting," I said. "About the whole Renewer thing, I mean."

He rubbed his jaw, studying the floor. "I already knew you were different from other Sisters."

"My sparkling personality?"

He snorted, but said nothing else. I turned back to the window. The rain gushed down in silvery curtains.

"Finn, how did you find me on the night I was attacked by Lariel?"

Nothing.

"Either you were following me, or you had a way of knowing where I'd be. And if you were following me, you'd have intervened sooner."

"I could smell your blood," he said reluctantly.

I nodded slowly, glad that he couldn't see my face. After the reactions of the men in the Renewal Wards, I had already suspected as much. Still disturbing to have it confirmed, though. "So I smell different to other Sisters?"

"This is a weird conversation, El." Finn shifted on the bed, uncomfortable. "Yes? I mean, everyone smells different, but you have a much stronger scent, floral, kind of sweet. It gets more potent when you're scared."

I turned. "Then I smell . . . nice?"

He made a face. "Don't say anything. I know exactly how bad all of this sounds."

"I'm glad you showed up when you did."

"Yeah, well . . ." He waved away the issue. "That's how I found you."

I smiled, amused by his obvious embarrassment. Finn glanced at me, then sighed and looked away again.

"Out of everyone, it really had to be you, didn't it?" he said.

"I would have preferred otherwise."

The corner of his mouth twitched. "But you've managed until now."

"Not very well. And my visions are getting worse; I can't even sleep without this kind of thing happening." I gestured at the writing scrawled across the walls. "As soon as I'm alone—"

"Then I won't leave you alone," he interrupted.

"You're not listening."

"You deny I'm a Haunt, and I'll deny you're haunted. Seems fair." He saw my face and raised his hands defensively. "El, come on. You're tired and you're scared. Give yourself a break."

"Haunted?" I said in exasperation.

He stretched—too tall, he seemed to grow by the hour—and stood.

"If you're having a nightmare, I'll wake you," he said. "But try to sleep, all right? I think it will help."

The room felt larger and emptier without him. I gazed around helplessly. Everything was slipping out of control; I wanted to scrub the burn marks from the walls, erase the evidence. Let me die. Save me. Let me die. Eater only knew what Reverend Cyde was going to think when she saw this.

"Haunted," I muttered to myself.

I lay down, and I must have drifted off, because when I opened my eyes again, the sky had grown lighter. Rain continued to pelt the roof of the cottage, and dripped darkly from the branches of the trees. I looked around the room blearily. All the marks on the walls had vanished.

I guess I got what I wanted, after all, I thought. *Small mercies.*

I rose and returned to the window. In the east, the sun stained the storm clouds a deep red. Water streamed over the ground between the trees, running off the hard-baked soil. The weather should cover our tracks, buy us more time to get away from here. It wouldn't be long before the Order arrived, if they hadn't reached the Moon House already.

I felt a stab of guilt. Cyde was going to take the fall for the broken Pillar; it had been her responsibility to protect it. And yet she had let me destroy it. If anything, she had seemed *eager* for me to tear it down, which made no sense at all.

A loud thump issued from downstairs. I started and cast around for my bag. I still had Verje's sacraments, lace if I needed it. I snatched my backpack from the chair beside the door and hurried onto the landing. Millie's muffled voice drifted up from below. She sounded angry.

". . . my brother, and you dare ask for *favours*?"

I slowed. An argument, not a crisis. I walked down the stairs and found Finn standing in the corridor outside Lariel's room. He looked strained.

"She's provoking Millie," he said.

"It seems to be working."

"Yeah," he said. "I didn't want to interfere, but it's getting out of hand."

I pushed open the door. The room beyond was tiny, and held reed wash baskets, old crates of papers, and a couple of moth-eaten pillows. There were no windows. Lariel stood leaning against the far wall, and Millie faced her, fists balled.

"Ah, the corpse eater's back," said Lariel lazily. "Along with her Haunt lover."

"Don't you say a word to either of them," Millie snarled. "We should have let the Resistance kill you."

"Right, yes." Lariel nodded. "I forgot that I'm supposed to be grateful. In your infinite kindness, you're handing me over to the Order instead. The Sisterhood: known for their gentle and forgiving care of prisoners."

"You'll be treated fairly," I said.

"Sure I will, corpse eater."

"If you cooperate?" I shrugged. "I'm not saying there won't be repercussions. But if the Councilwomen pressured you, it might mean prison instead of execution."

She laughed.

"What's funny?"

"Pressured me?" She sneered. "What a joke. I killed those women because I *wanted* to."

Millie stepped forward, raised her fist, and punched Lariel in the face.

Finn got over his shock fastest; he lunged past me and grabbed his sister by the forearms, lifting her clean off the floor as he pulled her away from Lariel. I hastily stepped out of the way. Lariel clutched her nose and staggered, bracing herself against the wall. Her shoulders shook. Then she started laughing again, the sound wheezing and high and out of control.

"Do whatever you want, Kamillian!" she gasped. Blood trickled over her fingers. "But don't act like I owe you anything. You're the one who sold out first."

Millie was breathing hard. She shook off her brother and stormed out of the room. Finn grimaced and followed her, which meant I was the only one who noticed that Lariel had started to cry.

CHAPTER

THIRTY-SIX

Reverend Cyde returned at midday. From the upstairs bedroom window, I saw her approaching the cottage. She held a wide umbrella over her head, and wore dark grey travelling robes. She came alone.

"There will be a cab waiting on the south-western road." She folded the umbrella as she reached the doorway. In the dull light, her face was haggard, her eyes bloodshot. I received the impression she had not slept, but she looked composed nonetheless, professional even in her exhaustion. "I also had two of my girls ride your Cats to Portevis and leave them outside the chapter house. I doubt the ruse will work, but it seemed worth a try to divert attention. Any trouble here?"

"Sacor caused a small disagreement, that's all."

"I've sent word to the Commander that the mercenary is in our care. For now, we won't be able to risk handing her over to the Order; she knows too much about your movements." She smiled in a self-deprecating sort of way. "And about my assistance to you, obviously."

My heart sank. "So we can't use her to convict Celane?"

"I said 'for now.' The situation isn't ideal, but it's salvageable. We'll hold her until circumstances change."

Maybe it doesn't matter anymore, I thought with a hollow pang. *What good could a trial do now? What are we even doing here?*

"You could martyr me," I blurted out.

Cyde seemed taken aback. "Excuse me?"

"I've made a terrible mistake, but there's still time to repair the Pillar and halt the island's fall. With the Renewer's power, you could do it."

Her face softened. "Oh, Elfreda."

Why didn't you try to stop me? "There might be nothing down there, nothing but Haunts and death. This was my doing, so it's only right that I pay the price."

She made a gesture for calm, but I swiftly negated it. Cyde had to see, had to understand—this went so far beyond me, or her, any of us. With each passing hour, each slow moment of our descent, my feeling of panic grew stronger.

"Maybe I," I swallowed, my mouth bone-dry, "maybe I don't even need to die. You could amputate—"

"Enough," Cyde interrupted firmly. "I am not going to eat you, I am going to help you. Now, please tell your friends to get ready to leave."

Finn was already waiting inside. He looked like he wanted to speak, but I couldn't bear being chastised or offered empty consolations. I brushed past him to collect my bag.

The woods smelled of mulch and sap, dry earth turned wet. We set out from the cottage and took a path around the western hillside. The track was so overgrown that it was hardly visible. Earthworms slinked through the new mud, and birds rustled their wings and chirped. I drew my borrowed coat tight around my chest as the wind buffeted us with sheets of rain.

Cyde led the way, with Millie walking beside her. The two of them spoke in low, serious voices; heads bent together. Lariel followed behind them, with Finn and me bringing up the rear.

To my surprise, Lariel had put up no struggle. She walked quietly with her head down. Probably just biding her time, waiting for an opportunity to make a break for it. But still, she looked pitiful in the grey light, shivering from the cold, her shoulders stooped. I thought about Zenza, about the bolt that should have struck Millie's head. My sympathies dwindled.

The woods ended close to the edge of Aytrium. The southwestern road looped along the curve of the island's perimeter, with nothing but an old farm fence separating the land and the drop. Beyond was only cloud, too dense for my eyes to penetrate.

"There," said Cyde, pointing at a black spot further up the road. It grew larger as we watched; through the veil of rain, it resolved into a large, two-horse cab.

"How do we know that's the right one?" asked Finn.

"Not many people take this road," said Cyde. Her eyes narrowed, and she nodded to herself. "And the flag's up."

A scrap of sodden blue fabric was tied to the driver's perch. Cyde stepped out onto the road. The vehicle slowed and came to a halt. The driver jumped down.

"Osan!" I exclaimed.

He offered me a smile, although it seemed forced. I quickly walked forward and hugged him. He was soaking wet and shivering.

"You know, you're getting downright clingy nowadays," he said. "Stop before you embarrass me."

"Are you okay? Is Rhyanon okay?"

"She's fine. Furious, but fine. The Commander told her what Verje did to you." He glanced at my arm, now neatly bandaged, then spoke to Cyde over the top of my head. "I came as quickly as I could. Asan says Celane's going to use the confusion around the Pillar incident to try to make her move. You should get back to the Moon House before they come looking for you."

Cyde made a dismissive gesture. "I'm hunting down the vandal. If anything, my absence might convince them of my devotion."

Osan looked doubtful, but the Reverend was already moving toward the cab.

"Well, your martyrdom, I suppose," he muttered.

It was a close fit with all of us crammed inside the cab, so Millie sat up on the driver's seat with Osan and held Cyde's umbrella over both their heads. We rolled down the muddy road, south along the edge of the island. I was fidgety and anxious, and I could feel the pressure of my visions building like a storm in the air. The rain continued.

"Where are we going?" I asked Cyde.

"Somewhere more secure," she said, watching the clouds through the window. "Less obvious."

"And then?"

She did not answer me. Finn caught my eye and gave the faintest of shrugs. It might have been my imagination, but I thought his irises looked more green than blue. Beside him, Lariel sat with her head bowed, hands clamped together. She seemed ill and cold.

Murderer, I reminded myself. *She was the one who sent Finn to the pyre. She deserves to suffer.*

Osan drove us inland again, into a valley where the roads grew rockier and the horses moved more slowly. I guessed that we had crossed into the Rutese province; I wasn't familiar with the area, I'd never travelled this far west from the city. The miles crawled by, and I tried my best not to think, not to imagine what was going to happen next.

The road came to an end at a circular clearing below a sheer rockface. Coarse grey thorn brush surrounded us. Osan stopped the horses and climbed down from his seat. Cyde opened the door.

"Where are we?" I asked.

"Officially? Nowhere." She walked over to the thorny bushes at the base of the cliff, and swept them aside with her lace. Hidden behind the dry branches was a narrow passage cut into the rock. "The Ash Disciples built this place four hundred years ago during their revolt against the Order. While serving as Chief Archivist, I came across a mention of it and decided to investigate whether the passages were still intact."

The entrance was high enough to accommodate a tall man, although Finn still needed to stoop. Water dripped loudly and a strong animal musk lingered in the air. It was pitch dark ahead.

"Apart from a small cave-in, the main passages were untouched," said Cyde. "Remarkable, really, that it survived."

"So the Order doesn't know about this place?" asked Millie.

"Outside of the people I've told, no. We should be safe here until Celane is forced to play her hand. That gives us time to prepare."

Prepare for what?

Finn helped Cyde light the lamps, and the passage brightened. To my surprise, the room ahead was large and ornate. Intricate mosaics covered the walls—the patterns looked familiar, the abstract curves and swirls of the designs curling like vines. I had seen these designs elsewhere. I noticed Cyde was watching me.

"The Ash Disciples didn't build this," I said slowly.

She nodded.

"The mosaics . . ." I walked over to the wall. "They match the ones in the Martyrium. This is Sisterhood insignia. Old-fashioned, but still very similar."

"It is, yes."

"But how can that be?"

"I have a theory. I'll explain after I've shown you where you'll be sleeping."

I trailed my fingers over the tiles. Strange. I was certain this could not be the work of insurgents—why adorn their hideout with the enemy's symbols? why decorate at all?—but neither could the Sisterhood have built the place and then simply forgotten it existed.

The mosaics continued in the next room, a larger hall where it was drier and the sound of the rain diminished to a soft hushing. Three other passages led off deeper into the hillside.

"There's dried meat and preserves over there, lantern oil in the canisters, and blankets in the next chamber," said Cyde, pointing. "You should be comfortable enough, but use the food and oil sparingly; it might be difficult for me to bring more supplies over the coming days."

"Speaking of which," said Osan, "I should take you back to the Moon House. You're going to be missed, Reverend."

"Much as I appreciate your concern, I need to speak with Elfreda first."

"I can wait," I said hurriedly. "If it would be safer for you to go back now, you should."

Cyde shook her head. "It won't take too long. Shall we speak in the cab?"

With reluctance, I relented. Osan looked nervous. I could only imagine the Order descending upon the Moon House to discover that its Head Custodian was missing during the hour of the Sisterhood's greatest crisis. Cyde ushered me back outside.

"It would be better if your friends didn't hear what I'm about to tell you," she murmured. "I think the rain will dampen Finn's senses somewhat."

I climbed up into the cab, and Cyde shut the door after us. She brushed the rain off her face and gave me a reassuring smile.

"Don't look so worried," she said. "I dealt with the Council for years before taking up my position out here."

"With respect, Reverend, you never had to explain a broken Pillar during that period."

She gave me a reproving look. "Then I'll just have to rise to the occasion, won't I?"

Although she spoke lightly, there was an undercurrent of steel in her voice. It was the same streak of self-possession I had witnessed in Asan, only it took a different form with Cyde: more reserved, scholarly, cool where the Commander burned hot. She did not appear at all afraid.

"What is it you wanted to tell me?" I asked.

"Several things." She reached beneath her coat and drew out a brown envelope from the interior pocket. "Firstly, this is yours. Kirane asked that I wait a few years to give you time to grieve her, but we might not have that much time."

My name was written on the outside of the envelope. I recognised my mother's handwriting: the square, scratchy penmanship, the way she looped her *L*'s. My hands shook when I took the letter from Cyde.

"These probably aren't the circumstances she had in mind," said Cyde, her voice kind. "But I hope she would understand."

I fingered the corners of the envelope. I wanted to rip it open right there, but I also wanted to just hold it, or hug it to my chest, or bury it away somewhere safe and never read it at all.

"Thank you," I murmured.

"I wish I could have done more for her. And for you."

The paper felt cool in my hands. I thought of my mother's lifeless body in the Martyrium, and was unable to look at Cyde. "What else did you want to talk to me about?"

The rain pattered against the roof. The horses stamped their hooves.

"Your friend, Finn Vidar," said Cyde. "He's infected. His condition is only going to get worse."

Her bluntness crushed me, but I said nothing. I knew what she wanted to suggest: that I say my goodbyes now, that she take him to the Edge, that I stop denying the inevitable. That I should let Finn go.

But instead she said, "There's a chance you could save him."

I felt as though I had been punched. For a moment, I could not even speak; I just stared at her.

"Only a very remote chance," she said, gaze direct. "And it comes at a cost."

"Tell me," I breathed.

A strange expression flashed over her face, a mixture of uncertainty and regret and something else. Relief? She folded her hands in her lap.

"How much have you been told about Renewers?" she asked.

I could not think straight. I just wanted to know how to fix Finn: no delays, no explanations. I fought to keep my head. "That my body holds more lace than other Sisters'. That Renewers appear every seventy to eighty years. That plenty of people want to martyr me."

"Then it wasn't explained what *we* wanted to do with the Renewer?"

"Not martyr me?"

"Yes." Her face stayed smooth. "Elfreda, I understand your impatience, but you will need this context."

I nodded stiffly. Cyde leaned back on the bench.

"While I worked in the Department of Memories, my particular focus was pre-Ascension history," she said. "It's a controversial field of study, bordering on the heretical, and the few surviving texts from that period are highly classified. In the course of my research, I uncovered details about the Order's origins that are incongruent with official doctrine. Tell me, what did the Star Eater eat, that she could raise Aytrium?"

"A . . . star? Not literally, but some kind of original source of lace."

"Yes, correct, an original source. But not, I believe, 'a blessed fruit of the heavens.'" A bitter turn at the corner of Cyde's mouth. "Records suggest that the real Eater was a group of up to fifty people, women *and* men."

"Men?"

"It's likely that they actually outnumbered the women."

I felt disoriented, disturbed in a way that I could not quite articulate. It was as if the ground beneath me had become less stable. Cyde watched me, black eyes piercing below her long lashes.

"Do you know what the Ash Disciples believed?" she asked.

"That they were the true inheritors of Aytrium, that the Eater stole their birthright. That Sisters are a . . ." My voice dropped. "Perversion."

Cyde was silent for a few seconds.

"'Athwart waters black and wild divided, endless we did drift,'" she said. "'Forsaken, forsaken, in loss seeking new lands to arrest, a place not god-taken and unspeakable.' That's from one of the Order's oldest texts. It suggests our ancestors did not always inhabit Aytrium, our predecessors were from elsewhere, further away."

"The Disciples were right?" I whispered.

Cyde shook her head.

"No one who tries to slaughter children is right. But there are elements of the Disciples' accounts that may be *true*." She gestured toward the entrance to the caves. "The mosaics on the floor of the Martyrium, the walls of these passages? They are not decorated with the Order's insignia—our ancestors adopted those designs and claimed them as their own. They predate us."

Then the Disciples *had* been the true founders of Aytrium. And we, Sisters, were the tyrannical outsiders after all. Just as they had always claimed. I shook my head, staring at the floor of the cab.

Cyde placed her hand on top of mine. Her skin was calloused and cool, her fingers strong.

"You are no perversion," she said, her words reaching into the heart of me. "And the Disciples' myths don't provide a complete picture either."

My voice sounded far off. "Then what is true?"

She gently removed her hand.

"There's no certainty to history," she said. "But from what I could piece together? Our ancestors came to this land before it was raised and begged for aid. They were rebuffed by the people already living here, and so, desperate, they turned to violence."

Millie and Finn knew the Disciples' stories. We had never discussed it, but now it felt like a gulf lay between me and my friends.

"The precise details of what happened are hazy." Even as Cyde spoke, she seemed to be taking careful note of my reactions. "There are repeated mentions of a betrayal, after which our ancestors found and consumed the 'Star' of the local people. 'In fury righteous and bright-flamed, we rent asunder the Star and did her in full entirety devour, her shining blood to ours evermore stain'd.'"

Her words dragged me out of my reverie. "Blood? The Star was a person?"

"Possibly. She certainly had a body. Amongst her own people, she was worshipped as a divine leader."

There was a sour taste in my mouth. "And we ate her."

Cyde pressed her lips together, then sighed.

"Yes," she said. "Our predecessors devoured the Star, gained some measure of her powers in the form of lace, and used those powers to take Aytrium for their own. That's how I understand it."

This was my heritage, the legacy my entire life was built

around. I should have felt betrayed, but instead I was hollow. All along, through centuries of duty and sacrifice, our faith had been . . . empty.

My mother had died for this.

"And then?" I asked.

Cyde gazed out the window for a moment. Her expression was distant.

"Then came the Star's retribution," she said. "Men began to turn into Haunts. First those who had consumed the Star's flesh directly. Then the husbands and lovers of the women who had been a part of it. To save themselves, the remaining Eaters lifted Aytrium into the sky, and purged the island of their former loved ones. And thus the Order was born."

I sat in silence. The wind whistled through the grey bushes. Rain pooled like quicksilver in the ruts of the road.

"What does this have to do with saving Finn?"

It seemed, briefly, like Cyde had not heard me. The Reverend continued to stare into the distance. Her fingers drummed against her leg.

"You suffer from hallucinations?" she asked, her voice low.

I nodded.

"How would you characterise them?"

I was unsure about the sudden change of subject.

"Frightening, I guess," I said.

Cyde gestured for me to go on. She was not quite looking at me.

I tried again. "Personal, strange? They vary. Most often, they're like nightmares brought to life. Like I'm being . . ."

I trailed off.

"Elfreda?"

"Like I'm being haunted."

The rain eased, and I sought Cyde's eyes. Her face was blank, perfectly controlled.

"Is that it?" I asked, and everything around me suddenly seemed unstable and unreal. "Am I haunted by the Star?"

She sat very still, like I was an animal she feared spooking.

"I only have the accounts of other Renewers to rely on," she said, "but I think that you're experiencing manifestations of the Star's dreams. Your fears bleeding into hers and brought to a kind of half life."

"But she's dead!" I cried, much louder than I meant to. My body shook. "You just told me that we killed her."

She shook her head slightly. "I said that we *devoured* her. Her lace lives on in us. Most of it resides in you. And with that lace, some trace of her consciousness and desires."

"No."

"On three occasions in the past, Renewers evaded the Order longer than you've managed to. Do you know what they had in common?" She did not wait for my answer. "They all tried to leave Aytrium. The second Renewer tried to launch a scouting expedition, the fifth wanted to build lacework wings, the sixth joined an insurgency movement and, like you, went after the Pillars. But none of them ever made it back to Ventris; the Order always found them. The cycle continued. Until now."

Wrong, this had to be wrong.

"You didn't decide to break the Moon Pillar on your own. You were compelled to follow the Star's wishes, you were pushed or guided—"

"Stop!" I shouted.

Cyde fell silent, but it was too late, I could not help but recognise the truth. That alien instinct that had possessed me the night we escaped Ceyrun, the voice in my dreams, the pulling sensation that I felt even now, as if I were a magnet dragged toward the Edge and down to the darkness beyond.

"I wanted to break the Pillar," I said forcefully. "For better or worse, the choice was *mine*."

Cyde's mask of studied calm slipped; beneath, I could finally see her guilt, the sadness that she had tried to conceal from me. Her pity.

"I know," she said. "But perhaps you needed a final push to follow your convictions."

I wanted to dismiss her words, but couldn't. Because of course, I *had* experienced that sense of compulsion, that crushing need to tear down the Pillar, even though a part of me had wondered, why not wait? Why not let Asan or Rhyanon help me to leave the city? And the simple reason was that I had felt it would take too long. If I delayed, someone would stop me.

A dark chasm yawned inside me. How much of myself belonged to me alone?

"What does she want?" I asked, throat tight. "Vengeance?"

Cyde gestured uncertainty. "Maybe."

"Then shouldn't you be trying to stop me?"

She was quiet for a moment, and again, she was no longer meeting my eyes.

"The fifth Renewer. Galain Myde," she said at last. "Before her martyrdom, she reported hearing the Eater's voice on the wind. That experience disturbed her more than any other hallucination she had suffered; in her final days, she grew so erratic that her friends feared she would walk right off the Edge. Or kill them in their sleep."

Was that going to be me? I gripped the edge of the bench. Driven insane, swallowed up by visions. Was that my future?

"A friend turned her over to the traditionalists in the Order," said Cyde. "But before she was martyred, Myde insisted that there was 'a debt of blood' that only she could pay, and that doing so would put everything to rights. She spoke of a cleansing, a sacrifice. A 'sundering.' She said that, in fulfilling her duty, she would rid our people of Haunts."

My dream lingered in my mind; the temple and the tide of blood washing over my legs.

"So that's why none of you will martyr me," I said with dull certainty. "Because you're hoping I'll sacrifice myself instead."

Cyde started to gesture apology, and then lowered her hands.

"I don't know," she said quietly. "When I think of Kirane,

I . . . But this isn't my decision. All I can do is protect you, help you, and allow you to make your own choices. Informed choices. If you don't want to do this, that's fine."

"We'd just all sink down to Ventris together?"

"Yes."

I gave her a contemptuous look. "And you expect me to believe that?"

"Take me at my word—I'm not going to martyr you, and I won't ask you to sacrifice yourself. But I believe that you deserved to know about the possibility of curing your friend."

I ground my teeth together. Bullshit. Cyde had laid the trap with Finn as bait and waited for me to walk in. She was no better than Celane; she only wanted me to take the knife to my *own* throat. Against that, the grief in her eyes meant nothing.

She saw my anger and bowed her head. Accepting it.

"You may resent me," she said. "I deserve that. But know that Commander Asan and her associates were only aware of the Renewer's potential to purge Haunts; I never told them the rest. They didn't deceive you."

"You lied to them?"

"Yes."

I remembered Rhyanon's hand on my forehead, stroking my hair. She would have told me, if she knew. She would never have been part of this.

With difficulty, I pushed aside those feelings. "If I do what the Star wants, it could save Finn?"

"A small chance."

I had promised to fix him. Any chance, no matter how small, was better than giving up. No matter the cost. I took a deep breath.

"I'll do it," I said.

Cyde nodded solemnly. "Then I'll make sure you reach Ventris unharmed."

CHAPTER

THIRTY-SEVEN

THE PASSAGES WERE filled with flickering shadows. I lay in the dark and traced the dim outlines of the mosaics over the wall. The coloured tiles fit together like snake scales, cold and smooth and ancient. The longer I stared at them, the stranger the patterns grew: the swirling curlicues and looping spirals transformed from familiar to alien before my eyes.

So the Ash Disciples had it right all along. Our blood was tainted, our power corrupt. And my whole life devoted to preserving a myth. What a stupid waste. Although I guess it didn't really matter—even if everyone had known the full ugliness of our origins, Sisters would probably have ended up performing much the same role. We would still serve and protect and sacrifice. We would still do good, and evil, and whatever else it took to get by, just to carve out a small space for ourselves and call it meaningful. Maybe telling a kinder story had made that duty easier to bear.

I closed my eyes.

Are you there? I thought.

Silence in response. I tried to listen deeper, to feel out which corners of my mind were foreign—the not-me parts—but it was like trying to identify which of my limbs belonged to someone else.

Do you want to hurt me?

Nothing.

Can you help him?

It was like calling out into a dark room; if the Star could hear me, she gave no sign. I hadn't really expected a response. And, of course, there was always the possibility that Galain Myde had been delusional.

"El?" said Millie.

I wanted to pretend that I was asleep, just so that everyone would leave me alone. Talking to my friends was impossible; I could already anticipate their reactions. Finn would outright refuse to listen, while Millie would be unable to admit she wanted me to save her brother no matter the cost. Confessing to that would kill her. Well, not literally. Apparently dying was my job.

And if I told them about the Order's origins, what then? Of course, there was no *guarantee* they were descended from Aytrium's original inhabitants, but on some level, it didn't even matter. In their hearts, I knew that they would lay secret, furtive claim to that heritage. A better, purer people. Not like me.

Perhaps I could have told Osan if he had stayed. He would have been more objective about the whole thing. I needed that; just calm clarity, just a balanced account of the costs and benefits. But he had returned to the Moon House with Cyde.

"Won't you talk to me?" asked Millie.

In the next room, Finn sat and guarded Lariel. Anything I said, he would hear. I rolled over to face the wall.

"Nothing to tell you," I replied, without opening my eyes.

Millie stayed quiet for a minute. I could hear her fidgeting, and I wished she would go away. I didn't want to be counselled, and I definitely didn't want her to lie to me. What could she say? Finn was her brother, her last remaining family. Of course she would be protective, of course she would value his life above mine, but the last thing I needed was to hear her rationalising those feelings. Behind every assurance, she would be asking me to die.

"Are you angry about the Resistance?" she asked.

"No."

"You can be honest."

"I am."

Another pause. "It wasn't like what you're imagining, we're not like Lariel. I would never have been part of—"

"It's not about the Resistance, Millie!" My voice cracked, and I sat up. "I don't care that your stupid little organisation plotted to kill my friends and colleagues. I don't care that your girlfriend murdered my supervisor. I don't care that you sat around and discussed how terrible Sisters are, how you're all so much better, and then acted like my best friend the next day. *I don't care.*"

Millie stared at me, her mouth slightly open and her eyes wide. She struggled to speak, but I got up and stalked out of the room.

"El!" she cried after me. "El, it wasn't like that!"

I kept walking, back through the musty corridors, and away from the lantern light. I didn't want any of this. Lariel was laughing; the sound echoed through the passages so that it seemed like a hundred women mocking me. Finn spoke sharply, and she stopped.

I slowed at the entrance. By now the rain had petered out, and the clouds were moonlit and shining. The thorn bushes glistened where the light touched them.

I breathed in, and cold air filled my lungs. Not Millie's fault, none of this was her doing. But why did she have to look so utterly crushed? It was like I had slapped her. All I wanted was space, a little time to come to grips with the fact that I needed to die. Was that too much to ask? Why couldn't she have just left me alone for once?

Because she doesn't know. Because you're too scared to tell her.

I crouched down and rubbed my eyes. Already, I regretted the outburst. I'd really done it this time too; once I'd started speaking, the words had rushed out like grain spilling from a ripped sack.

And I hadn't even meant what I said, not really. I was just angry and tired and scared. I'd known about the Resistance for so long, and it hadn't bothered me. It shouldn't have bothered me. Civilians had good reasons to hate the Order, and Millie and

Finn could associate with whoever they pleased. I could handle my feelings, and anyway, it was none of my business and it wasn't personal.

I knew they didn't hate me. I knew that.

The cold wind swept over my skin. I grimaced. Better to say sorry now; Millie would be hurt. She deserved better than me taking my frustrations out on her.

I straightened and turned back to the passage entrance, only to find Verje blocking my way.

The Councilwoman had been standing inches from me. Her limbs hung slack and her chest yawned open, revealing a cavity where her heart should be. When she spoke, white light poured from her mouth.

"It hurts," she croaked. "Give it back."

I staggered, almost tripping over my own feet. Around Verje, the darkness changed shape, forming creeping fingers of shadow, lips that gaped wide to reveal rows of red teeth. My head pulsed with pain.

"Look what you've done," she moaned.

I could not tear my eyes away from her. Verje's skin was the colour of ash. Small blue flowers grew between her ribs, bursting into bloom as I watched. Green shoots pushed through the dark swell of her lungs.

"I will take what's mine." Her voice was awful, rasping and broken. She lurched toward me. "I will be whole."

I shook my head, unable to speak. Invisible hands crushed my throat. Verje's arm shot forward and she grabbed me by the hair. Her skin was wet and hot. She pulled me closer. The light from her mouth burned like a naked flame where it touched my cheek.

"Follow the path of grace," she hissed.

"El!"

I could smell her, jasmine and blood and molten metal. I jerked my head away from her, but she held fast. Her eyes bored into mine, glowing with malice.

Finn broke through the vision. Verje vanished with a shiver of light, and then his arms were around me. I sagged against him, all the strength in my legs deserting me.

"Are you okay?" he asked urgently. "El? El, say something."

"I'm sorry," I whispered.

"Just breathe. You're safe, I've got you."

"I shouldn't have let myself get so upset."

"No, it's fine, come on now. Are you hurt?"

I shook my head. He hugged me tighter, and then let go.

"It's all right," he said. "Let's go back inside."

My skin ached where the vision had touched me, and my head continued to throb. Was this how the other Renewers had felt? I was never going to make it; the nightmares threatened to drown me even here. How could I reach Ventris like this? I swayed, and Finn took hold of my elbow.

"You're going to be okay," he said.

Millie appeared at the entrance to the passages, a little out of breath.

"What happened?" Her skin was pale in the moonlight. "Finn ran so quickly; I thought—"

At that moment, Lariel made her move.

Finn saw the threat before I did. He lunged toward his sister with a warning shout. Not fast enough. Lariel grabbed Millie from behind, locked one arm across her chest, and shoved the point of a stolen crossbow bolt up against her windpipe.

"Stay where you are!" she shouted.

Finn froze. My stomach clenched—I had no lace; I had not restored my supply since breaking the Pillar.

"Don't move." Lariel looked unstable and weak. Her eyes were bloodshot. "I don't want trouble, and I don't want to hurt anybody. I just want to leave, okay? So go back inside and wait; I'll take her—"

Millie drove her elbow into Lariel's ribs. The sudden movement dragged the bolt across her neck, drawing a shallow gash. Blood welled from the cut; I cried out and involuntarily took a step forward. Lariel yanked Millie back into a chokehold.

"I told you to stay back!" she yelled.

I raised my hands helplessly. In my mind all I could see was the sharp metal spike of the crossbow bolt piercing Millie's neck, the dark bloom of her blood. *Don't hurt her, don't hurt her, don't hurt her.* But Millie continued to struggle, heedless of the danger.

"You're too much of a coward to do it," she panted. "Because if I'm killed, who's going to protect you from Finn? Didn't consider that, did you?"

"Shut up!"

"You never did think further than the step right in front of you. That's how you ended up working for the Councilwomen, wasn't it? That's how everything starts with you."

"I said, shut up!" Lariel dug the tip of the bolt into Millie's skin.

"Please don't," I said desperately. "Please, we can work this out."

Millie stamped down hard on Lariel's foot.

"You are not going to take me anywhere," she snarled, eyes blazing. She wrenched her arm free and grabbed the bolt, dragging it right out of Lariel's grip. Lariel scrabbled to keep purchase, but instead lost her footing and fell over. Millie turned on her, teeth bared like an animal.

"I am *done with you,*" she hissed.

Lariel started to get up, her expression stricken. But then she seemed to lose all conviction. The change was shocking: her ferocity disappeared like a fire doused in mud. Her shoulders slumped, and she sagged back onto her heels.

"Don't give me to the Order," she whispered. "I'm begging you."

For a moment, none of us spoke. Millie loomed over Lariel, her breathing loud. She threw aside the bolt, and it clattered against the passage wall.

"Did your victims beg?" she demanded. "Did you ever listen to them?"

Lariel hung her head. "Their deaths were swift."

"That does not absolve you of anything!" Millie balled her fists, her expression anguished. "*Why,* Lariel? Why did you have to do this?"

"Millie," Finn began, but she silenced him with a withering look. I found that I was holding my breath.

When Lariel spoke, her voice was hollow.

"Because there are never any consequences for Sisters," she said. "I could spend my whole life under these women's heels, and they would still demand gratitude for not crushing my neck completely."

"And? You think the rest of us are any different?"

"No. And you're right, I never intended to take it so far." Lariel shrank, curling her arms around her body. "But I had power. For a little while, I meant something to them." Her gaze drifted to me. "No matter which Councilwoman comes out on top, the Order will show me no mercy."

"Do you think you deserve mercy?" I asked quietly.

"What would you know?" Lariel shook her head, defeated. "Are you aware that Kamillian left me because of you?"

"Keep her out of this," snapped Millie.

"Say what you will about the Resistance, she'll always come down on your side."

Millie looked like she wanted to hit Lariel again, but Finn placed a hand on her shoulder. He muttered something I failed to catch. Millie glanced up at him, and the tension left her shoulders. She gingerly touched the scratch on her neck.

"I'm fine," she said. "It's not deep."

"Still. We can handle her."

"I'm really fine."

"I know. You always are."

Millie scowled. Finn waited, and after a moment she sighed.

"Yeah, all right." Her voice dropped. "I'll take a walk."

I should have said something. I wanted to tell her that I'd been wrong and stupid, and that she should sit down and let me take care of her, that she had scared me to death, but words deserted me. Millie walked past, stiff and bleeding and avoiding my gaze, and I did nothing to stop her.

All the while, Lariel watched my face. I don't know what she saw there; her own expression was unreadable. When Finn turned to pick her up off the floor, she flinched. But her eyes stayed on me.

"You shouldn't overexert yourself," I said. "The injury to your head was serious."

Finn glanced over his shoulder with a slight frown. I gestured for him to leave her.

"Mocking me?" asked Lariel.

"If you'll let me look at it, maybe I can help you."

"Why bother?"

I shrugged.

"What's it to you, corpse eater?" She tried to sneer, but her voice quavered. "When you intend to trade my life for Kamillian's, what does it matter?"

I took a few steps toward her and she scrambled backwards.

"I don't need your help," she snapped. "You disgust me."

"And that's fine." I crouched and offered her my hand. "I get it. But please come back inside now."

Her lip curled. "What is this? Are you trying to prove a point?"

"Not to you, no." I kept my hand outstretched. "You killed one person I cared about, badly injured another, and sent a third to his execution. You tried to help Celane martyr me *twice*. There is nothing in the world I need to prove to you."

"But?"

"But that doesn't mean I want you to suffer either. I've seen enough people die recently."

Her eyes flashed with anger. "You pity me?"

"I think you're in pain. And I think you're scared."

She slapped my hand away.

"Do you truly regret none of it?" I asked.

"Of course I regret it," she snarled. "I'm here, I'm fucked, and

I have nothing to show for my efforts. But don't you dare pity me, corpse eater. We both know there's nothing I can do to redeem myself."

Maybe that was true. I could not look at her without thinking about Zenza. About Osan telling me to leave him behind. About Finn burning. About the moment that she pulled the crossbow trigger on Millie. Death swirled around Lariel like a vortex, and if she felt any remorse for her actions, she hid it behind a mask of scorn. I knew I should hate her, but I didn't, not really. She seemed so alone.

Besides, in that moment I desperately wanted—for my own sake—to believe in mercy and salvation and the hope of forgiveness.

"You could try," I told her.

CHAPTER

THIRTY-EIGHT

FINN SAT ON the ridge of the hillside, staring into the distance as dawn spread over Aytrium. His skin was bleached of colour; it made the redness of his lips appear painted. Thinner, taller, he looked noticeably less human in the morning light. His scalp glittered with pale stubble.

"I'm getting worse," he said, without turning to look at me.

His arms were scratched, and the underside of his nails dark.

"I can't sleep," he said. "I've had insomnia for weeks, but now? Nothing since they drugged me for the execution. It's like my body's forgotten how."

He blinked less often. His eyes were bigger and liquid-bright, a night predator's. I climbed up the slope and offered him a bread roll. He looked at it with a strange, almost childlike uncertainty.

"Eat," I said.

He reached out and took it. His fingers lingered over mine.

"I don't think I have much time left," he said.

"I promised I'd fix you. Trust me."

He searched my face.

"And when I lose control?" he asked. "Because I will. And you're going to be the closest Sister when it happens."

"We aren't there yet."

He looked down at the bread in his hand. He took a bite of it, and I caught a glimpse of white behind his incisors. More teeth, newly grown. He swallowed.

"I think Reverend Cyde is returning," he said. "I can hear someone on the road. Go inside for now, in case it's not her. And El?"

"Yes?"

"Restore your lace."

I made my way back down the hillside, skin crawling. I should have guessed that Finn knew about the jars hidden in my bag; no doubt he could smell Verje's flesh. He must have known all along. And it was true, I had been putting off gorging again. Every time I thought about it, I saw Verje's lifeless face in my mind and felt the hot rush of her blood over my hands.

Look what you've done, the vision moaned in the back of my head.

My rucksack was propped against the wall inside the first passage. When I picked it up, the jars clinked together softly. Heavier than I remembered. I passed Millie and Lariel—both still sleeping, the latter bound with rope—and took their lantern. Then I pressed deeper into the passages in search of privacy.

While I had tried to appear calm for Finn, his decline had accelerated far more quickly than I anticipated. Seeing him now had lent the situation a fresh sense of urgency. In an unexpected way, it also made it easier to accept what Cyde had told me. I would do this. I had no choice but to do this, because I could not let him down.

The remaining two lumps of Verje's heart rested within their jars, dark and clotted with old blood. I selected the smaller sacrament. When I unscrewed the lid, the smell hit me and I gagged, my stomach roiling like waves in a storm.

No, focus. I took a few careful breaths. *Just meat. Just chew and swallow.* I had left this too long; I risked the flesh spoiling. Already, there might have been a hint of putrescence to the smell, but I tried to dismiss that thought. This was necessary.

Using a small paring knife, I sliced off a section. Then I shut my eyes, raised the sacrament to my mouth, and bit down. The flesh was cold and slippery: the slick texture of cured fish. My stomach turned. *Don't think about it.* I breathed through my nose and forced myself to swallow. If I had done this once, I could do it again. With this lace, I would reach Ventris. I cut a second piece, put it in my mouth, and commanded the muscles of my jaw to work. I would fix everything.

Power bloomed inside me, rich and sweet, and I felt some of the tension inside my chest unwind.

Millie had woken up by the time I returned to the entrance. She was peering outside, and jumped when she heard my footsteps.

"Is it Reverend Cyde?" I whispered, crossing the room to join her.

"I think so," she replied under her breath. "But Finn will give a signal."

Lariel groaned in her sleep, and her eyelids fluttered. We both flinched and looked at her. Millie bit her lip.

"Eater, if she screams and it isn't Cyde . . ." she muttered.

I heard horses' hooves, and the rumble of carriage wheels. I waited, holding my breath. Then a bird call, high and fluting, echoed over the hillside.

Millie exhaled.

"That's him," she said.

Behind us, Lariel stirred. She opened her eyes and for a moment seemed confused, alarmed. She tried to sit up, and the movement jostled her bound wrists. She grimaced. I walked over to her, and gestured for her to lift her arms.

"Just leave her tied up, El," said Millie tersely.

Lariel gave me a sweet smile. She offered her hands like she was praying.

"Oh, don't you know?" she said. "The corpse eater has decided to take pity on me."

"Stop calling her that."

I loosened the knots and slid the ropes over Lariel's hands. Her skin was chafed raw, and her fingers had swollen slightly. I said nothing. From outside, I heard voices and quick footsteps.

"Doesn't that sound like trouble to you, oh benevolent one?" whispered Lariel.

I rose as Cyde entered the passage. The Reverend's uniform

was creased from travel. When she gestured greeting, her movements appeared laboured; she was clearly exhausted.

"Reverend?" I said. "Has something happened?"

Her gaze travelled over Millie, Lariel, and the rope in my hands. Her lips thinned. "Possibly. Collect your belongings quickly; we might need to find another refuge."

There wasn't much to collect; aside from my backpack, there was only the sack with Lariel's bolts. Millie grabbed it, and we followed Cyde outside. The sky was the colour of pewter, dyed red to the east where the sun was rising. Osan, his expression dark, stood beside the horses. Finn hurried down the hill to join us.

"I'll get to the point," said Cyde, turning around to face me. "According to intelligence from Commander Asan, Celane has escalated her efforts to find you."

"What does that mean?"

"During the confusion following Finn's escape, a second inmate vanished from the Renewal Wards. I take it you didn't release anyone else?" She didn't wait for my confirmation. "If Celane has a Haunt, she will use him to track down the Renewer. Finn, forgive me for asking, but from what distance would you be able to detect Elfreda's scent?"

Finn's mouth twisted.

"A few hundred feet? Maybe more?" He looked down, shamefaced. "It depends."

Cyde seemed surprised. "So not from Ceyrun, then?"

"No, definitely not that far. But I . . ." He struggled. "But I would be able to find her anyway."

"How?"

"Even when I can't actively sense her, I always know where El is. She's like a magnet; she's pulling me all the time. The distance doesn't matter."

"The man that Celane released, he would experience the same pull?"

He nodded. "I'm sure of it."

"Then we need to move," said Osan. "Right now."

Cyde returned her attention to me. She saw my unease, and her face softened.

"I'll admit I'm not as prepared as I would have liked to be." She offered a tired, self-deprecating smile. "This is sudden, I know, but if you still want to travel to Ventris, now is the time."

Finn made a sound of alarm. "What? No, that's insane; there are hundreds of Haunts down there."

My hands shook. I clasped them together to stop the trembling. "Aytrium is sinking anyway. It's only a matter of time."

"El, you can't feel—" He broke off. "The Haunts below are different. Worse."

"I will accompany you," said Cyde.

I gestured negation. "No, other Sisters rely on you."

She held my gaze. "And we are all relying on you. If we are to live or die by your success, I must do everything I can to help you."

"No, *listen* to me," implored Finn. "Going down there will be suicide. El, please, this is the worst mistake you could make."

"Whatever we're doing, we need to *move,*" said Osan.

I turned to Finn. "I can't outrun the Order forever, and I can't hide. Ventris is the only escape for me."

He shook his head. He was scared, more so than I had ever seen him. I wasn't certain what had gotten under his skin, but it went beyond a natural fear of the dark and unknown lands below us. Something had shaken him so badly that he could not even speak about it.

"El," snapped Osan.

Forgive me. I broke Finn's gaze and crossed the distance to the cab. *Eater knows I don't want this either.*

"Wait," said Millie.

I swallowed, unable to look at her, and pulled myself up. Seeing her face now might shatter me—I didn't want to think that this might be the last time we spoke.

"El!" she said angrily.

"I have to do this," I said.

"Then I'm coming with you."

"Don't be stupid."

"I'm not." She took a step toward me. "El, look at me. You're right—I betrayed your trust. You don't have to forgive me, but let me help you. I can still do that."

"I'm not mad at you, you moron!" The words got stuck behind the lump in my throat. I raised my head. "I don't want you to come because I love you."

Millie's face crumpled. I quickly averted my eyes again.

"Just stay here," I said. "Please."

Shaking her head, she marched to the cab door.

"Millie, you are *not*—"

She pushed herself inside. I fell back against the seat.

"You'll need me." Her mouth was set and her cheeks flushed. "And this time I will be there."

I felt lost for words, but I had to convince her, had to stop this. She folded her arms, glaring at me.

"Millie, please," I whispered. "I don't want you to get hurt."

Osan muttered under his breath and hoisted himself up to the driver's perch.

"Have the argument while we're moving," he said. "Everyone get in; we're taking far too long here."

Using her lace, Cyde wordlessly dragged Lariel to the cab and bundled her inside. I leaned past them, seeking Finn. He stood with his fists clenched, rooted to the spot. His expression was tortured; I knew that he was grasping for a way to talk me out of leaving.

Come on. I willed him. *We both knew it was inevitable.*

As if he had heard me, he lifted his head and cursed the sky. Then he stalked over to the cab. Osan offered him a hand up to the driver's seat.

"Thank you," I murmured.

We clattered back down the road in the direction of the Moon House, none of us speaking: Lariel mutinously angry, Cyde composed, Millie pale and stubborn. I gripped the edges of the bench. All I could think about were the men inside the Renewal Wards. Those voices in the dark. The whispering, the pleas and threats. That was what lay ahead, but this time there would be no walls to protect us. Millie clutched the bag of crossbow bolts to her chest, and her frown deepened when she noticed that I was watching her.

"Don't try to stop me," she warned.

"I want you to be safe."

She shook her head. "My mind's made up. Besides, there's Finn to think about."

"You're all welcome to jump off the Edge," hissed Lariel, "but you will *not* drag me down with you."

"Nor will we attempt to," said Cyde. Even now, she held herself with calm poise. "Osan will deliver you to the Commander; I believe that she was headed to the Moon House in any case. You'll be able to plead your case."

"Great," said Lariel. "I'm thrilled."

"How are we descending?" I asked.

Cyde turned her attention to me. "Once we learned that the Renewer had been found, a small group of us started building a vehicle based on Golden Age designs. While our version doesn't fly, we should be able to control the way it falls."

Millie stared at Cyde. "You planned for El to go down there all along?"

There was an awkward silence. Millie looked to me for an answer, but I shook my head. Not now. We could have that conversation if we survived long enough for it to matter. Even thinking about Ventris made me feel physically sick, and the idea of talking about it seemed worse. What the Star wanted, what she expected me to do—all of it was hazy and shifting. Eater, I didn't even know *how* I was supposed to die. A handful of fractured visions and vague instincts was the only guidance I had received, and it amounted to nothing if I didn't know where to go. I drummed my foot against the floor.

"Reverend," I said. "Have you ever heard of the path of grace?"

Cyde looked mystified.

"No," she replied. "Do you think it's significant?"

"Maybe. It's recurring in my visions, at any—"

The horses screamed and Osan swore. The cab jolted to a stop, and I smacked my forehead into the door. One of the animals reared, almost upsetting the vehicle. An inhuman shriek pierced the air.

Haunt, I thought dizzily.

Something collided with the exterior of the cab. Finn leapt down from the driver's perch, landing hard on the road. I readied my lace and pushed open the passenger door. We had stopped less than a hundred feet from the edge of the woods. I jumped out of the cab.

The man was taller than Finn and heavier-set, but he moved with weightless ease. He raced forward, bare feet hardly touching the ground, every violent fibre of his being focussed on me. I threw my net into his path. He collided with it and came to a shuddering stop. With him paralysed, I could see his face clearly.

"No," I whispered.

Declan Lars was wild-eyed and covered in scratches, his spine curving like a hook. His bright gold eyes found mine, and through the haze of bloodlust, he recognised me. He grinned obscenely, then threw back his head and screamed again.

"No," I moaned. "No, not him, not him."

Finn stepped between us, his teeth bared at Lars. Lars stopped shrieking and his mouth worked; I thought that he was trying to speak. Between his lips I saw rows of teeth, the glisten of his saliva and blood. My head pounded; I was in the Renewal Wards and the smell of oil and herbs filled my nose.

"Don't release him," shouted Osan. He jumped down from the driver's seat.

I wanted to run away from Lars and his shining eyes and the memories rushing through me. My lace twisted in my grasp, fraying and losing shape.

"I can't," I stammered. "I can't hold it. He's going to kill me."

Cyde touched my shoulder, and I jumped. Her lace twined through mine, smooth and controlled; she reinforced the net. Behind her, Millie rushed to grab the horses' reins.

"It's all right," said Cyde. "I'm here to help you."

I shuddered. I felt like I might throw up or pass out; my chest was so tight that I could hardly breathe. Osan stalked past us, face grim. There was a knife in his hand.

"What are you doing?" I asked, my voice high. "Osan! Get away from him!"

"Don't look." He moved swiftly, circling behind Lars. "And keep your lace up."

"No, don't. Osan, please don't—"

He drove the blade into the back of Lars's knee. Blood splattered the earth. Lars's eyes went wide with pain, and he writhed, struggling against my lace. I clamped my hand over my mouth. Osan, careful but unflinching, drew out the knife. When he raised it to sever the tendons in Lars's other leg, I looked away. Lars howled.

"Stop it," I whispered.

Osan stepped away from Lars. His expression was fixed.

"He must have escaped Celane and her associates, but they won't be far behind." His voice was steady and matter-of-fact over Lars's shrieks. "Get back in the cab. This will only slow him temporarily."

Cyde steered me back to the vehicle. She was speaking, but I could not seem to piece together her words in any meaningful way. I held the strands of lace around Lars together. As the panicked horses pulled at the halters, I saw him begin to crawl after us. One hand over the other, lamp-yellow eyes filled with hunger.

Finn hunched beside me. Although it was cramped inside the cab and he was too tall, he did not touch me. We both stared at Lars as he receded outside the window.

"That's going to be me," he said.

His voice was strange and hoarse. I think he was only talking to himself; I don't think he ever meant to say anything aloud, because after a second he blinked and seemed to snap out of his daze.

"We're nearly there," said Cyde.

I could imagine the flesh and tendons of Lars's legs fusing back together as he dragged himself through the mud. I closed my eyes.

"I'm sorry," I said faintly, although I wasn't sure who I was talking to or even what I was apologising for.

It had started raining again; a thin, bleak drizzle that pattered against the roof of the cab. In the distance, I heard the yips of anxious Cats. Lariel swore under her breath.

"They're gaining on us," she said.

Out of nowhere, Finn laughed.

I opened my eyes and looked up at him. His face was temporarily animated, his expression verging on gleeful, and then it fell into blankness.

"It's over." His voice was like wind through old trees. "What are we trying to do?"

"Finn?" said Cyde carefully.

While the rest of his body remained preternaturally still, he turned his face toward her.

"Nowhere is safe," he said. "No one is safe. The island is sinking now, and I can hear them."

"Hear who?"

He blinked slowly, and his blue eyes gleamed the yellow of ripe corn.

"The Old Ones," he said. "They know she is coming."

Then he shivered and his gaze lost its weird, feral intensity. His breath rattled, coming out in short, suppressed bursts, like he had just surfaced from water.

"Let me out," said Lariel.

I could think of nothing to say. Finn looked like a wreck; he gripped his knees and his shoulders shook violently. Cyde stared at him in incomprehension.

"Let me out!" said Lariel. "I'll turn myself over to Enforcement, I swear, just let me go."

I reached out and placed my hand on top of Finn's. He flinched. His coldness radiated through my palm, so intense that it almost seemed to burn.

"Stay with me," I said softly.

The cab jerked as Osan pulled the reins hard. The horses stopped. We had reached the end of the road. I heard women shouting in the distance. The Sisters following us must have seen our cab.

"Come on," said Cyde.

The Edge was the Order's primary site for disposing of Haunts. I had never attended a drop; until now, I had only seen the platform from a distance. The dock protruded from the island like an accusing finger, and below stretched the vast expanse of Ventris. Aytrium's looming shadow cast a swath of deeper shadows over the undulating hills, where faraway lakes shone like dull metal.

At the end of the dock stood a wooden-slatted cage: roughly square, about twelve feet across and shrouded by enormous white sheets. It sat on four sets of rollers.

Osan swore again. I turned and saw Cats tearing down the road behind us. Eight Cats, eight Sisters. More than Cyde or I could hope to handle alone.

"Run!" said Osan.

We raced for the Edge. The wet ground was slippery; my bag bounced against my back and I almost stumbled, but Millie grabbed my hand and kept pulling me on. Osan reached the cage first. He set his shoulder to the slats and heaved. It rolled a few inches closer to the drop. Finn joined him, and their combined efforts drove it forward.

"We're descending in *that*?" Millie shouted, aghast.

Behind us, the horses snorted with fear. A coil of lace caught me by the neck, wrenching me backwards and away from Millie. I choked, found my own lace, and slashed through the rope restraining me. The moment I severed it, another appeared. I broke free again and turned around.

Cyde, a few feet away from me, struggled to defend herself. Her breathing came out harsh, and her eyebrows were drawn together in concentration. The Cats drew nearer, their riders closing the distance to the Edge.

I struck back and the closest Sister toppled off her mount with a scream. Had to be aggressive, had to break away before they overwhelmed us completely. A net wrapped over my legs, pinning me to the spot. Another collided with my shoulder.

I was so focussed on fending off the lace attacks that I had forgotten about Lariel. During the chaos she had remained hidden inside the cab, but now she jumped out and sprinted toward me, her expression furious.

My lace dissolved.

"Go on, corpse eater," she snarled, shoving me toward the platform. The nets around me vanished as the crossbow bolts in Lariel's fist drained their lace. "Move!"

"What—"

Cyde cried out as a bone in her right leg snapped. She staggered and fell. I moved to shield her, but Lariel shoved me backwards.

"I can deal with a bunch of old women," she snapped. "Go."

Cyde's face had turned bloodless, and she spoke through gritted teeth. "Channel your lace into the sheets."

"Reverend—" I began.

"We're all relying on you," she said. "Make it count, Elfreda."

Millie snatched my hand again and pulled me away. Osan and Finn had rolled the cage almost to the edge of the platform. Over my shoulder, I saw Lariel step in front of Cyde, planting her feet wide.

"All right, corpse eaters," she shouted. "Who wants to take me on *without* your blood magic, huh?"

I tore my eyes away from her and scrambled over the railing of the cage. Millie followed me.

"Finn!" I gasped. "Stop pushing."

He jumped into the cage. Osan copied him, and then caught my eye for a split second as if daring me to argue. *No, not you as well,* I wanted to say, but we had run out of time. I extended my lace and felt for the weave of power meshed with the sheets. I fed the web and the fabric billowed upwards. The cage lurched over the rollers and toward the yawn of the abyss beyond.

"What are you doing, Sacor?" I heard Celane shout.

I took a deep breath and poured my lace into the sheets. With a last jolt, we slid forward and off the platform.

The last thing I heard before we dropped was Lariel's defiant voice.

"You should have paid me better, bitch!" she yelled.

CHAPTER THIRTY-NINE

I BURNED THROUGH MY lace like wildfire, feeding the sheets to slow our descent. Aytrium loomed over us, too colossal to understand, hideous and misshapen. Updrafts rocked the cage and threatened to smash us into the cliffs. I steered us away, but the extra effort bled my power.

Millie stared at the platform as it shrank above us. "Why?"

My forearms felt bruised where Lariel had shoved me. The situation had fallen apart so quickly, so brutally.

They're dead. A creeping coldness stole across my body. Lariel, Cyde, neither of them stood a chance against that many Sisters. We had left them to die.

"Is anyone hurt?" Osan looked sick. "El?"

I shook my head. "I'm fine."

In truth, I felt lightheaded; acutely aware that only my lace prevented us from falling. The cage's wooden supports creaked in the wind, and the sheets flapped and strained ominously. A heap of bags and crates was piled near the railing. We had no other resources, nothing and no one to help us. I fought off my mounting sense of panic.

"Why would she do that?" asked Millie.

Finn slowly walked across the floor and crouched beside his sister. She shrank away from him.

"She never even said sorry," she said. "Never apologised for anything."

Finn spoke to her in a voice I could not make out over the wind, and laid an arm around her shoulders.

The landscape below grew larger; the faraway patches of shadow and light resolved into plains and valleys. Streaks of low-hanging cloud touched the summits of hills. My dizziness increased; the cage seemed a paltry shelter from the sickening drop below us. If I made the smallest of mistakes, if I ran out of lace, if I lost my composure, we were all dead. Osan, his expression grim, made his way over to me.

"Are you sure you're okay?" he asked, softer than before. The wind whipped around us. "Their lace hit you pretty hard."

"Fine," I said, breathless. "Need to concentrate."

Thousands of mossy channels scored the sheer face of Aytrium, where rainwater cascaded over the stone and into the open air. We glided downwards, a feather caught on a draft. The cage's rolling motion made me want to throw up. I swayed, and Osan quickly reached out and steadied me.

"Is there anything I can do to help?" he asked.

I bit the inside of my cheek, using the sharp pain to focus my mind. "Unless you can suddenly wield lace, no."

He squeezed my arm. "I haven't mastered that yet, I'm afraid."

"Osan?"

"Yes?"

"I don't know if I can get us to the ground."

The wall of rock drew away as it tapered inwards; the underside of Aytrium rippling with inverted mountain ranges. Until now, I had never been confronted with the island's full impossible scale, and I could not entirely countenance the horrific enormity of it all. My whole life, I had lived on this mass of earth and soil and stone. And yet standing before Aytrium, I was nothing—a mote drifting in space. Streamers of algae dangled from the cliffs like river weeds, and colonies of bats flew out from hidden crevices in the rocks.

"You can only try," said Osan.

"You shouldn't have come."

"Didn't have much of a choice, under the circumstances. Besides, Rhyanon made me promise that I would take care of you."

My throat hitched.

"Hey, none of that." He forced a smile. "I'm barely holding it together myself. But I trust you, Just El. I believe that you can do this. You aren't scared of anything, remember?"

Forget the terror, forget the cost of failure. Lace flowed out of me like water. I nodded.

Then we dropped further and for the first time, I saw the crater. It gaped like a maw in the earth beneath Aytrium, the depths veiled by mist and shadow. The place from which the Eater had first dragged Aytrium into the air. The experience was like staring up at the night sky; from above, the crater appeared bottomless.

"Eater," Osan whispered.

I pushed us away from the chasm. No matter what happened, I would not risk us drifting down into that awful scar. Rather crash into the ground, rather die where the sun could still reach us.

Finn cried out and clutched his head.

"Finn?" I said in alarm.

He slumped over sideways, and Millie caught him. His back arched as if electricity coursed through his body, and his muscles went rigid. His mouth opened in a silent scream.

"Finn?" said Millie, panicked. "What's wrong? Finn!"

The vision struck without warning. The world inverted; the sky burned black and the earth melted into a sea of white. I floated in space, suspended and unable to move. In the distance, the mountains shimmered oily and slick with mother-of-pearl iridescence, and from their base a bright red ribbon burst from the ground. It cut across Ventris, unfurling toward us over the hills.

Follow the path of grace, boomed a voice inside my head. Enormous pressure filled my chest. Over the surface of the ribbon, I saw thousands of people walking, and I knew they were dressed with flowers, I knew they were coming for me.

I gasped and staggered, and felt hands close around my arms.

"El!" shouted Osan.

Reality snapped back like a spring released. Osan held me up, his face bloodless.

"Pilgrimage." I coughed. My ears were ringing. "The pilgrims' road, the path of grace. She was trying to tell me."

"What are you *saying*?"

The cage tilted dangerously; I had lost my grip on the lacework. My stomach lurched, and I threw out ropes to catch the flailing sheets. For a few awful seconds, I fumbled and we were truly falling. Osan's hands crushed my arms.

I caught the nets. The shock wrenched my lace violently, almost enough to drag the sheets out of my grasp, but I held fast. The fall slowed and the floor levelled.

My breathing was ragged. Too close. Much too close.

We were only a few hundred feet above the ground now. The red ribbon remained seared across my vision, coiled like a snake. Millie helped Finn to sit up.

A sudden crosswind battered us toward the chasm and I stumbled, knocking my knees into the wall of the cage. The darkness loomed and fear surged through me. *Come on, come on.* My remaining reserves of lace dwindled as I poured power into the nets. It might have been my imagination, but drawing on my lace felt different: less smooth, less clean, denser somehow.

I drove the cage away from the crater. The hillside ahead was barren; I could see the cracked earth and dead grass, a few scattered shrubs with grey leaves. Closer, closer, the ground rushing closer far too quickly.

With one final effort, I yanked the nets upwards. The platform slowed and, with a shudder, we coasted onto the rock-strewn earth.

Silence.

I had done it.

My limbs turned liquid, and I collapsed against Osan. He held me up and began to laugh, his shoulders and chest shaking.

"See? I told you so," he said. "You had it all under control."

Bright spots danced across my vision. "I *never* want to do that again. And I think I'm about to be sick."

Osan guided me to the railing, and I promptly vomited over the side of the cage. He rubbed my back as I heaved. The taste of meat lingered in my throat. Again, I caught the smell of rot.

"Finn?" I straightened shakily. "Are you okay?"

Blood rolled down his chin; he had bitten his lip during the fit. "I'm fine."

"What happened to you?"

"I don't know." He wiped his mouth. "But whatever it was, it's stopped."

For now. A symptom of the infection? I had never heard of men suffering from seizures during their transformations. And if it had occurred once, was there anything to stop it from happening again? Even now he seemed disoriented, not altogether present—his eyes wandered across the landscape to the crater.

"So long as you're okay," I said uncertainly.

He nodded, but I had the sense he wasn't really listening. Millie was also watching him now, a slight frown on her face. She hugged her arms over her chest.

"So now what?" she asked. "Is this really Ventris?"

I understood her reaction. I hadn't been sure what to expect either, but this unassuming brown hillside felt curiously underwhelming. As if there should be something revelatory here, but instead there was just . . . nothing. I turned around. Behind us I could see no end to the crater, only a thin bar of daylight in the distance, curving with the line of the horizon. Aytrium blotted out half the sky.

"It's so quiet," said Millie.

None of us moved or spoke. The sheets fluttered in the breeze, and their rustling was the only sound in the empty wilderness.

Osan shook himself and walked over to the pile of bags and crates.

"Reverend Cyde packed provisions," he said, leaning down.

"We'll have to hope there's food and water somewhere ahead of us, but this should last for at least a few days."

"Do you think there's any chance that they—" Millie stumbled. "That the Reverend and Lariel survived?"

"It's not impossible," he said, but by his voice I knew he was trying to be kind. Millie recognised it too, and her face fell.

"Right," she said. "Of course."

Osan busied himself with sorting the supplies. I joined him. Leather shoulder bags bulged with provisions; I looked inside one and saw fire-starters, water canteens, preserved meats, and dried beans. Two crossbows and some blankets nestled between the crates.

"Cyde told me that she hadn't done enough to prepare," I said. "But she still thought of all this."

Osan glanced at me, then away. "We'll only be able to take what we can carry."

Millie picked up one of the bags, testing its weight. She slung it over her back and rubbed her eyes.

"Celane would have wanted to question the Reverend and Lariel," I said with false confidence. "And Cyde mentioned Commander Asan was heading to the Moon House, so maybe help was already on the way."

"Maybe," said Osan. "At this stage, we have no way of knowing."

"Finn?" said Millie.

Her voice was strange. I looked around.

Finn stood at the edge of the chasm, staring into its depths. He had been beside us only seconds before, and I had not seen or heard him move. My heart quickened. His stance—on the balls of his feet, every muscle coiled, leaning forward over the emptiness—disturbed me. Like a dog that had heard something in the night, he watched the darkness: alert, unmoving, absolutely still.

"What are you doing?" called Millie.

He was silent. Millie caught my eye. A draft stirred the fabric of his shirt.

"Finn?" I said.

A long pause. I climbed out of the cage and slowly moved toward him.

"No," he said.

I stopped. "No?"

An infinitesimal shake of his head.

"Finn, you're scaring me."

Wind rattled the dried grass and fell still again.

"There's something coming, and I don't think I can stop it," he said, his tone curiously flat. "You need to run."

A patter of falling stones inside the chasm, out of sight. I took a confused step backwards.

"Go," said Finn.

"But what—"

The Haunt leapt out of the chasm. It moved like an insect, emaciated limbs bending at all the wrong angles. Huge antlers, stained with age, branched above its gaunt face and its lips peeled back in a grin, revealing rows upon rows of needle-thin teeth. Twice Finn's height, but hunched and scuttling, it shot toward me in a blur of bone-white limbs.

I recovered from my shock and threw a web of lace into its path. The Haunt tore through my ropes like they were spiderwebs. It closed the distance from the crater before I even had the chance to move.

Finn crashed into it, sending them both to the ground in a furious tangle of limbs and claws and teeth. He held fast to the creature's shoulders.

"Run, damn it!" he shouted.

I bundled up my lace, coiled it around the Haunt's neck, and pulled. The creature cried out in surprise—a dry, rasping caw—but its neck did not break. It was as though I was trying to snap a steel rod. I pulled harder.

"El," Finn gasped. "I can't—"

The Haunt bucked, trying to dislodge him. Finn had the creature pinned, but it was obvious that he couldn't hang on much longer. For all his new strength, he was never going to match the Haunt in a fair fight.

A glint of metal flashed in the air. A dagger landed in the dirt beside the creature's head.

"Stop it from moving!" yelled Osan.

Without hesitation, Finn seized the weapon and drove it down through the Haunt's shoulder. It shrieked and swiped at him, its long talons raking across his chest. Blood bloomed through Finn's shirt. He grunted and stabbed the creature again.

"El, don't just stand there!" he panted. "Get *moving*, you idiot."

I could not leave him like this. He was bleeding; he could not fend off the Haunt alone.

"El!" he snarled.

I swore and I forced myself to turn away. My heart thundered in my ears. *Run*. The hillside sloped upwards beyond the cage. Millie crouched below the railing, fumbling as she loaded one of the crossbows. Osan had the other ready and trained on the Haunt.

"Go," he said. "Quickly."

I raced up the hill, and adrenaline pulsed through my blood. Where was I running? I could never hope to flee from the Haunt; as soon as it escaped Finn, it would be on my heels. My lace was spent. I was helpless.

Why was I abandoning my friends?

The landscape shimmered and I cursed. Not a vision, not now. I reached the top of the rise. In the valley ahead, the ruins of an old wall rose from the dead soil, the stones tumbled and scattered across the ground. A reddish track snaked into the distance beyond the wall, before disappearing into a thicket of skeletal trees to the south.

I glanced back to see the Haunt throw off Finn. The creature was gouged with stab wounds to the arms and chest, and its blood coursed black over its paper-white skin. Its head swivelled toward me and it crooned.

Osan fired. His bolt slammed into its right leg, but the creature hardly paused. It zigzagged up the hill after me, eyes fever-bright and ravenous.

I ran. Grit and stones skittered under my feet as I flew down the hillside. Around me, ghostly figures rose up from the earth. They whispered and reached out to grab me, but their touch was like smoke and their voices were indistinguishable from the roaring inside my head. The Haunt was closing in behind me; I could hear the uneven rhythm of its footfalls beating against the ground.

My muscles burned, but I pushed myself to move faster. If I fell now, it was over. Fear raged like an electric current through my veins, and the landscape blurred in my peripheral vision; all I saw was the red stones of the path ahead. I was falling or flying, my feet barely touched the earth.

I leapt over the broken wall and landed hard. All at once the figures fell silent. I whirled around, heart thumping. If I was wrong, if my instincts were flawed—

The Haunt stopped.

I sagged to my knees and gasped for air. The creature stared at me, yellow eyes gleaming, no pupils, just flame-bright circles of gold. Black blood dripped from its fingers.

"Can't touch me here, huh?" I whispered, clutching my side.

Its lips parted in an ugly sneer, but it came no closer to the path. Without blinking, it grasped the bolt stuck in its thigh and yanked it free. I flinched. This close, I could smell the Haunt, that cold, earthy scent like damp soil.

An ululating howl rose from the hills to the south. The sound chilled me to the bone; it was like multiple voices screaming in unison, both shatteringly high-pitched and low enough to make my diaphragm vibrate. I clasped my hands over my ears, but it seemed to make no difference—the sound sank through my palms. In front of me, the Haunt bent forward—almost prostrating itself—and its antlers dragged furrows through the earth as it shook its head from side to side. It snapped at the air, teeth clicking together. Was it scared? Reverent? I wasn't sure, but the display unnerved me.

When the sound finally faded, the Haunt's movements slowed and came to a stop. It remained crouched and staring at the dirt, so still that it might have turned into white stone. I lowered my shaking hands from my head. With its body bowed, I could see each of the creature's ribs jutting up against the skin of its back, the tracery of veins spreading darkly over its spine.

This was a man once, I thought.

As if hearing my thought, the Haunt lifted its head. I took an involuntary step backwards, but it only glared at me. Then, with a malevolent hiss, it turned and loped off in the direction of the hills. I stared after it, convinced this was some kind of trick, but no, it kept moving, limping slightly. It gave the track a wide berth and slunk away into the grove.

I was alone.

"Millie? Finn?" My voice emerged hoarse. "Osan?"

It was quiet again, and I felt watched. If I left the path, if I let my guard down, the Haunts would be waiting.

"Finn!" I shouted, louder.

"El!"

Millie appeared at the top of the hill, and my heart leapt to my throat. She stumbled down the slope, almost tripping in her haste.

"Where is it?" Her eyes were wide with fear. "It moved so fast, I thought—"

I fought the urge to run to her. "Come here, quickly!"

She rushed the final few feet, and I threw my arms around her neck when she reached the broken wall.

"When I heard that howling, I thought for sure it had caught you," she said. "It moved so fast, El."

"I know."

"It was awful, the way it ran, the way its eyes were shining." Sweat beaded her hairline. "It never even looked at me."

"You aren't hurt, are you? It didn't come near you?"

She shook her head. "No, I'm fine."

I drew back from her. "Finn and Osan?"

"They're coming. It didn't touch Osan or me, but Finn's a mess. Why didn't it attack you?"

"It's the path; the Haunt couldn't approach it."

She shook her head. "I don't understand."

I looked up and saw Osan supporting Finn's weight as the two of them staggered over the rise. Osan's relief was obvious when he caught sight of me, but Finn seemed scarcely conscious. He didn't even raise his head.

When I started toward them, Millie grabbed my forearm.

"I don't understand what's going on," she said, "but if Haunts can't reach you on this path, then stay here. I'll help them."

I ground my teeth together, but nodded. Millie let go of me and hurried to assist Osan. Finn's shirt was soaked in gore: his own blood and the Haunt's splattered over his skin. His steps faltered. Millie supported his other arm, and the three of them awkwardly shuffled down the hill. When they came closer to the path, Finn resisted weakly.

"What is it?" said Osan.

Finn shook his head. His breathing had a rough, wet quality, and I could see the Haunt's claw marks through the rents in his shirt.

"No further," he muttered.

I could not help myself, I stepped off the path to join them.

"Put him down," I said.

Osan lowered Finn to the ground, and I knelt beside him. When I tried to peel back his shirt, he caught my wrist. Despite his injuries, his grip was firm.

"What?" I asked.

"Don't look," he murmured.

I pulled my hand away. "Don't be stupid, Finn. I have my faults, but I'm not scared of blood."

"It's not the injury." His eyelids fluttered. "The way that it heals, it's . . . unnatural. Not pretty. I don't want you to see."

Millie touched my shoulder.

"You're hurt." My throat was tight. "And you have nothing to be ashamed of."

His chest quivered as he breathed, every inhale painful and slow.

"I'll be fine." He coughed. "I need a few minutes, that's all. Don't worry."

Don't worry! I nearly exploded. He was lying in front of me, blood seeping into the dirt and his chest cut open, and he wanted to act like nothing was wrong. Bad enough that he had gotten hurt again, bad enough that it had been my fault, but the fact that he was still trying to protect me? It was more than I could stand.

And yet I could not argue with him now. He was so broken and exhausted, and I could not do anything.

"Take as long as you need," I said dully.

CHAPTER

FORTY

By midday, Finn had fully recovered. He walked alongside the path, quiet and pale and withdrawn. We had split Cyde's provisions between us, and he carried the bulk of them, but he moved as if their weight meant nothing to him.

"You called it the path of grace?" said Osan.

I felt despondent and heartsore, stretched too thin between the horrors I had witnessed over the last few hours. We had passed through the grove and into another valley, where the path looped and twisted like the random scribbling of a child. It had rained again, and the sky remained overcast and drear.

Osan's question startled me out of my thoughts; we had been walking in silence until then.

"It's just a theory that Cyde had." I cleared my throat. "About the people who occupied Aytrium before the Ascension."

He frowned. "They made the path?"

"Possibly." I considered for a moment. The conversation was moving in a dangerous direction. "From what I understand, the Eater's people conquered the continent and drove out or killed its former inhabitants. The path is a relic of that time."

"Huh," said Osan. "That's not history I'm familiar with."

"Cyde researched it while she was Chief Archivist." I pointed south. "I believe the path should extend all the way to those mountains."

"And it repels Haunts?"

I could not help glancing at Finn. "It seems that way. When

we were descending from Aytrium, I think we might have drifted over it before the wind pushed us back."

"Which is why I . . ." Finn made a bitter gesture. "Well, why I had my episode."

"At least we know the reason now," said Millie.

He sighed.

"What's at the end of the path?" asked Osan.

I tried to keep the tension out of my voice. "I'm not certain. I think it used to serve a spiritual purpose. It might lead to a place of worship, maybe a temple of some kind. I'm not sure it matters."

Millie gave me a hard look.

"What?" I said.

"You've been hiding something," she said.

"No, I haven't."

"What did Reverend Cyde mean when she said everyone might live or die by your success? Why was she already preparing to send you to Ventris before Celane found us? I'm not stupid, El. There's more going on here than you're telling us."

They were all looking at me; Finn had stopped walking, Osan's eyes were sharp. I pressed my lips together. I knew I needed to say something, but the excuses I had prepared evaporated from my mind. My behaviour had already been unfair; I could not keep up the pretence any longer.

"I'm trying to cure Finn," I said slowly. "Reverend Cyde believed that there might be a way, and that it could lie at the end of this path."

They reacted as I had anticipated they would. Initially with incomprehension, and then Millie's face lit up with wild hope and relief. Osan was more guarded, almost mistrustful. Finn . . . Finn was angry. I held my head high.

"It's not a guarantee," I said. "But if there's a way to fix you, then maybe the other Haunts—"

"You came down here chasing a fairy tale?" Finn's eyes flashed. "That's what really drove you to Ventris?"

"I have reason to believe Cyde was right."

He swore and turned away, as if he couldn't even bear to look at me.

"My visions showed me the temple," I continued, refusing to back down. "I was meant to come here."

"No," he snarled. "You weren't 'meant' to do anything. You could have stayed on Aytrium, away from all this shit, away from these Haunts. You could have been *safe*."

"Yes, safe, with half the Order trying to eat me alive." I folded my arms. "This goes beyond us, Finn. An end to Haunts would mean a waning of the Order's dominance; Aytrium would no longer depend on Sisters for its survival. No more Renewals. No more martyrs. Isn't that what you wanted?"

"I never asked for this."

"But here we are." I wished he would look at me. "And what if it works? What if I *can* stop what's happening to you? I'm willing to fight for that."

"Is it really possible?" Millie's voice was husky with emotion. "How would it work?"

I shrugged. "I'm not sure, but I hope I'll figure it out once we get there."

"Still, there's a chance?" She laughed breathlessly. "That's something. You really think it's possible?"

"Stop it, Millie," snapped Finn.

She didn't say anything else, but her eyes shone with a new fervour. Her hope was infectious; it buoyed me up and restored my determination. Maybe I could do it. Maybe this would really fix everything. As we continued down the path, Millie's face occasionally broke into a smile, nervous and fleeting, like she was fighting to keep her expectations in check.

In contrast to his sister, Finn remained angry. He stalked ahead of us, with his shoulders raised and his muscles wound tight. I knew that he was ashamed of losing his temper, and that he needed time to think everything through. But Eater, I hated when he got like this. Finn had the slowest fuse of anyone I knew, but once he was mad, he turned stubborn beyond belief. Nothing I could say was going to make him see reason now. I could only give him space.

The landscape slowly came alive the further south we travelled. Small patches of muted green began to appear amongst the stony waste. High above, a flock of birds flew westwards, their cries drifting down on the breeze. With each step away from Aytrium, I saw more signs of animal life. A grey and yellow lizard sunned itself on a rock and watched us pass, its tongue flicking through the air. Fat locusts buzzed between straggly clumps of grass. *Emergency protein,* I thought with faint amusement. Maybe my work experience would come in handy, after all.

We followed the path until the sun sank behind Aytrium. The wind had chased the storm clouds across the sky, leaving only smeared orange streaks in the deepening blue. Pale stars appeared and grew steadily brighter as evening descended.

"We should stop," said Osan.

The path widened at the base of a sheltered bluff, dry and out of the wind. My feet had been dragging for the last hour, and the temperature had dropped sharply with the sunset. I nodded and set down my bag.

"I think it'll be another day, maybe two until we reach the mountains." Osan cracked his shoulders and stretched. "Depends where the path runs."

"And how fast we walk," I said.

He snorted. "And how fast we walk."

Finn, still grim-faced, moved off to collect tinder. Millie sighed and started unpacking her bag. When she caught my eye, she jerked her head toward her brother meaningfully. *Talk to him.* I gave a small shrug.

"There's not much to burn around here, and it's all pretty damp." Finn carried a small stack of gnarled sticks to the edge of the path. He grimaced when he tried to move closer, and shook his head. "I can try seeing what lies up ahead; maybe there will be more vegetation."

Millie took the sticks from him. "No, let me see what I can do with this first."

He gave her a strained smile. "Make a lot of smoke, I suspect."

She scoffed and crouched down beneath the overhang. I wrapped a blanket around my shoulders.

"Finn, a word?" I said.

We followed the path as it curved around the bluff. Finn had his hands buried in his pockets, and he hunched a little, like he was trying to hide his height. The remains of another stone wall—perhaps there had been a building here, long ago—stood alongside the path. He sighed and sat on top of it.

"I'm sorry," he said. "I'm being unfair, I know."

"Do you really think I made the wrong choice by coming here?" I remained standing, but even seated, he was taller than me. "You saw that the Order was after me. It was only a matter of time."

"I know. I know you're right; it's just that when I lost my grip on the Haunt, I felt . . . I don't even know." He swallowed. "You could have easily died today. And if you're here because of me, that means you would have died because of me."

I softened. "I told you: this goes beyond us."

He dropped his gaze, miserable. His hair was growing back, I noticed. Still little more than stubble, but with time it would recover. A sudden feeling of tenderness washed over me.

"How are you feeling?" I murmured.

A smile tugged at the corner of his mouth. "Hungry is a bad answer, isn't it?"

"Not the best. I can give you more space, if it might help."

"No, I'm okay now." He lifted his head again, and he did appear calmer, like some unresolved tension had been laid to rest. "Can you restore your lace again?"

My stomach clenched. "Only once more. I've tried to spread out consuming the sacraments, but I think I'm risking gorge sickness anyway."

"You're scared?"

"I'm more scared of Haunts."

It might have been the light, but I thought the colour of Finn's eyes changed. "I think they're nearby. Be careful. They can't come this close to the path, but if you stray, they'll be ready."

I shivered and pulled the blanket tighter around me. It was dead silent out here, and I suddenly felt acutely vulnerable. Too loud, too clumsy, too slow. Finn stretched his neck to one side and his mouth tightened.

"Is the transformation hurting you?" I asked. "Be honest."

He was quiet, seeming to weigh his response. I waited.

"A little," he said at last. "Mostly I'm numb. It's like I'm losing the ability to feel—I can only sense. Or experience. I can't really describe it, but there are a lot of ordinary sensations that are vanishing, while others grow much more powerful. And that's not painful, necessarily, but it's different." He rubbed his neck, frowning. "Right now, I'm very conscious of the warmth you're giving off and your smell. But I couldn't feel the rain earlier, and I can't taste anything."

I absorbed his words.

"Not good, is it?" he said.

I shook my head. "No. But you can always talk to me. I don't want you to face this alone."

The rustle of wet grass startled me, but Finn did not react. I turned and saw that Millie was walking toward us.

"The fire's burning," she said. "Osan said you should come eat."

A pot steamed over the flames, where Osan crouched and prodded the rehydrated beans with a spoon. He glanced up as we approached.

"We probably have a week's worth of food," he said.

"Enough to get to the mountains, then." I took a cup out of my bag and held it out to him. Osan gave me an odd look.

"Yes," he said. "That won't be a problem."

He scooped up beans and handed the cup back to me.

"I saw rivers while we were descending," he continued. "With luck we'll reach them before we run out of water."

I nodded and carefully set the cup on the ground sheet to cool. Millie lowered herself down next to me, absently rubbing her hands together for warmth. Finn sat beside the bags, just beyond the glow of the firelight.

"Hard to believe we're here, isn't it?" said Millie. She stared up at the stars. "None of it feels real anymore."

I offered her a corner of my blanket. She leaned against me, her head on my shoulder.

"I wonder if we'll ever see Ceyrun again," she said. "I'm thinking of Hanna and Daje. Not that I regret coming here; I just keep thinking that I should have said goodbye properly."

I threaded my fingers between hers.

"You'll see them again," I said.

She drew the blanket tighter around us.

"Do you have anyone you left behind, Osan?" she asked. "If that's not too personal?"

He smiled, and took the pot off the fire.

"I have friends, some family," he said. "No romantic involvement, if that's what you're asking."

"That's definitely what she was asking," called Finn. "My sister loves to pry. She made an occupation out of it, actually."

Millie scowled. "At least one of us needed a regular income."

I laughed.

"Don't encourage him, El," she said. "Besides, I don't *pry*. I'm just a good listener."

"A good listener with an unhealthy interest in other people's business."

"Shut up, Finn."

He was laughing now too, and even Millie was trying not to smile. I picked up the cup and started eating. For a brief moment, things didn't seem so bad. Just for a little while, I could almost forget what had happened, what still needed to happen. The fire crackled. Osan added another stick to the flames.

"Are you all right?" I asked him.

He looked at me, and again I had the sense that something was bothering him; he seemed closed-off and guarded. But he shook his head.

"I'm fine. It's been a long day, that's all," he said. "And I suppose I'm wondering what Celane's next move will be. I can't help feeling she's going to try something desperate."

"But El's out of her reach now, isn't she?" said Millie. "The Order doesn't have a way down to Ventris until Aytrium sinks."

"If Cyde could build that vehicle, then so can Celane." He stared into the fire, and the light flickered across his face. "But how quickly? She's not going to give up on the Renewer's power; it's her only hope of saving the Order. And herself."

My fleeting sense of comfort and security faded. I set down the cup half finished, my appetite gone.

"That's not to say she'll catch us," Osan added quickly. "And I'm sure the Commander will be trying her best to get in Celane's way. For all we know, that battle is already won."

I tried to smile. "Maybe. And we have a long head start."

But they'll have Cats. And far more lace. Not to mention that if Celane was desperate before, she would be frantic now.

Millie nudged me. "We'll get moving as soon as it's light. For now, I think we should rest."

I nodded, my mind still churning.

"I'll keep watch," said Finn. He rose to his feet. "It's not like I'll be sleeping anyway."

"Do you want any company?" asked Osan.

"I'll be fine. I might wander a little further, see if I can find more wood for the fire."

Millie stacked the remaining tinder, and I helped Osan clean up the food and repack the bags for tomorrow. My thoughts kept spiralling back to Reverend Cyde and Lariel, wondering what I could have done differently, wondering what had happened to them. I kept hearing Cyde say that she was relying on me.

"Hurry up, El," said Millie. "I'm getting cold."

Osan spread out a second ground sheet on the far side of the fire. I lay down beside Millie and she curled up against me.

"You're shivering," she murmured.

The stars overhead gleamed bluish and bright; the clouds had all been swept away. Aytrium was wholly dark, blocking out the sky to the north.

"I'm sorry about Lariel," I whispered.

She sighed.

"It was complicated," she said. "And it ended a long time ago."

"Still. I'm sorry."

"She wasn't always like that. She used to be wild, intense, but not—" Millie shook her head. "It's not like I could ever forgive her for what she did to Finn, but I . . . I guess I just wanted her to say sorry."

"I think she was trying to."

"Maybe she was, but not to me. Get some sleep, El."

The fire dwindled to dark red embers. Beyond, Osan lay on his side, facing the bluff. My body was tired, but my brain could not stop turning.

Make it count, Elfreda.

Was I strong enough? The mountains called to me, a faint aching, a kind of thirst. She was waiting to be made whole. I could smell flowers and feel the brush of her thoughts against mine. The closer we drew to the temple, the more she would rouse.

Finn returned and quietly restocked the pile of tinder. I watched him from under my eyelashes. He moved so carefully, trying not to disturb us. Millie's breathing had grown even and slow, each exhale stirring the hair on my arm.

When he walked away down the path, I waited a few minutes.

Then I eased away from Millie and tucked the blanket close around her. She slept on.

My heart beat faster as I padded beyond the ring of firelight. The air drew goose bumps over my skin.

Finn sat on the same wall he had occupied earlier in the evening.

"What's wrong?" he asked.

My breath created a cloud of fog in front of me.

"I love you," I said.

His eyes widened.

"I love you." My heart raced, but I did not look away. "I love you, and I never want to lose you."

He rose and I kissed him, wrapping my arms around his neck and stretching to reach his mouth. He tried to speak, but I held him tighter. The chill of his skin seeped into me; the stubble on his scalp was rough beneath my fingers. I could feel the ridges of his spine and, inside his mouth, too many teeth.

He broke away. "El, no."

"I've always wanted you," I said, short of breath. "But if you don't want—"

"Of course I do," he said. "More than anything, but that doesn't mean I'll risk hurting you."

I smiled. "To be honest, pain wasn't really what I was after."

He flushed. "El!"

"Too forward?"

He spread his hands helplessly. "I'm hardly even human anymore."

"Liar." I touched my mouth. Cold. "You're still you, and I am still yours, and you are still mine. Please, Finn. Let me have this."

"But what if I can't control . . ."

"'I know what I'm asking for.'" I grinned. With a single thread of lace, I reached for his mind. A question, an invitation. His eyes went wide.

"Oh, screw it," he breathed.

He pulled me into his arms and kissed me, swallowing my delighted laughter. I discovered that, for all that the transformation had cooled his skin, he still had a little warmth left for me.

CHAPTER

FORTY-ONE

HE WAS GONE when I woke up.

I had expected it, and I don't think that Millie or Osan were surprised either. None of us spoke about it. We didn't say much at all.

"Go ahead; I'll join you in a moment," I told Millie. "I need to restore my lace."

She and Osan continued down the path, and I opened my last jar. Breathing through my mouth, I cut the flesh into smaller pieces and tried to swallow them one at a time. As soon as the first sliver touched my tongue, I gagged. Worse. This was much worse than last time. My body recoiled from the meat's rank sourness, and sweat broke out over my skin.

I managed to force down the sacrament without throwing up. Lace swelled in my gut and entwined with my nausea. Even though we were running low on water, I drained a canteen to wash my face and hands, and to rinse the inside of my mouth. The smell persisted; with every breath, I could taste Verje's flesh again.

I hurried to catch up with the others. Without Finn, we were forced to leave behind almost a third of our provisions. It would be a long, thirsty walk to the mountains.

Millie and Osan halted their conversation as I joined them. They looked tense, and Millie's eyes were red.

"Are you all right?" asked Osan.

"Yeah, I'm fine. Is there a problem?"

He pointed. "Look."

I followed the line of his finger. Overnight, Aytrium had sunk further toward the crater. I strained my eyes. Three white dots glinted against the dark mass of the island.

"Do you think it's them?" I asked.

"Probably."

I watched the pale specks descend. They were too far away to see clearly, but I imagined Celane staring down at me from above. I felt her gaze despite the distance.

"I think that they'll stay in the air for as long as they can," I said. "That would be the fastest option. And the safest."

"But it'll burn through their lace, right?"

"They'll be able to divide the load between themselves." I chewed my lip. "They're certainly going to stay airborne longer than we did."

"I guess it's too much to hope that they'll be eaten by Haunts when they reach the ground."

I shivered. "That's a horrible thought."

"You're far more generous than I am, Just El." Osan shook his head. "After everything these women have done, I'd consider it just deserts."

"We should keep moving," said Millie, her voice heavy. "Standing around only gives them more time to catch us."

She carried on down the path, bent by the weight of her bag. I cast a glance back at the white specks, then followed.

The sun rose, throwing long shadows behind us, and the morning chill dissipated. The air tasted fresh and sharp. We stuck to the path, even as it veered eastwards and away from the mountains. Ventris kept still and quiet—this morning there were no insects, no birds, no rustling in the grass—but I remembered the howl that had driven off the last Haunt. We were not alone.

The Old Ones, Finn had called them, with unmistakeable reverence in his voice. I tried to push the thought of him out of my mind.

The first building we came across had probably been a farmhouse. The roof had collapsed on one side, littering the ground with broken clay tiles. Weeds grew up around the walls.

Although I could not immediately work out why, something about the ruins made me feel uncomfortable. When Osan moved to investigate the building's interior, understanding dawned on me.

"I remember this place," I said aloud.

Like Geise's Crown, the same sense of having two realities overlapping one another. I blinked. Millie was staring at me.

"I mean, I *have* memories of this place," I said. "Not my memories. Someone, no, many people died. The bodies were brought here. Outsiders . . ."

I knew that after the winter the corpses had been stacked up like firewood, eyes glazed and lips blue. The survivors huddled together in a vast camp, their bodies shrunken and emaciated. For each that perished, another would replace them. In my mind their faces shifted and changed, woman morphing to man morphing to child, all feverish with need.

"They had walked for weeks," I said. "They were . . . stopped. Here."

I had seen them from a distance, the smoke of their fires. What could they still have to burn, after they had swept through this land like locusts? How could there still be so many?

Osan touched my arm, and I started.

"You've never seen this place before," he said gently. "Come on."

He was right. My eyes lingered on the broken roof. There had been a red chimney there, once.

After that, Osan set a relentless pace. By midday, the mountains appeared nearer and more solid. The further we moved from Aytrium, the greener the landscape became. Copses of unfamiliar steel-grey trees sprang from the valleys, and smooth, slender grasses caressed the hillsides. For all its new lushness, Ventris remained oppressively silent. The only animals we saw were birds, specks against the blue, too distant to identify.

Memories flickered through my head, fleeting and vague. They did not frighten me, although I saw Millie and Osan exchange looks of concern more than once. Hour by hour, the truth revealed itself to me—I began to grow conscious of all the patterns underlying the world, the repetitions and echoes, the way that tree branches mirrored tree roots, the way that rivers fed the land like arteries fed the flesh. It became clear to me that each element of creation possessed a correct state of being, and that deviations from those states were both offensive and glaringly obvious.

I could also sense *her.* It felt like I might be able to reach her if I closed my eyes and stretched. I followed the curve of the path with my eyes till it disappeared over the rise of a slope.

It occurred to me, quite abruptly, that I was a deviation myself. That posed a problem. I frowned. Not an unsolvable problem, but certainly one that would require attention.

"El!"

I jumped. Millie shook me by the shoulders.

"Didn't you hear me?" she asked.

"Sorry."

"I said drink some water." She thrust the canteen toward me. "You look sick."

"Maybe we should take a break," said Osan.

"No." It came out more strident than I had intended. I tried to sound reasonable. "She wants to reach the temple."

Millie tested my forehead against her wrist. "She? Eater, El, what are you even saying? You've been raving all day, and it's scaring me. You aren't sweating."

"Maybe I'm not hot."

"You're boiling. But not sweating." She pressed her lips together. "I hate asking, but how much flesh have you consumed?"

"I was careful."

"Then what is this? How much flesh, El?"

"Three quarters of Verje's heart. And I feel fine."

"Listen to me." She held my jaw. "You aren't behaving like yourself."

This wasn't right. We should be moving, not talking. Did that mean that Millie was a deviation too? How was I supposed to set everything right when these aberrations cascaded upon one another, multiplying, gathering momentum. We were sliding, we were sliding, and I needed to do something drastic to correct matters.

"You should let go of me," I said. I imagined biting down on her fingers, the spray of blood and crack of bone. "You're upsetting the pattern."

"Kamillian," said Osan, with a note of warning.

She stepped back, releasing my jaw. I smiled. That was better. Millie looked angry. She held her hands close to her chest, and her cheeks were high with colour.

"How could I let this happen?" she muttered.

"No one is at fault here," said Osan. He scanned the path. "We should try to get her out of the sun."

Another ruined building lay a few hundred feet ahead. It was smaller than the farmhouse, and the squat shadows cast by the crumbling walls disturbed me. The sunlight swam like liquid as we approached.

"This is where they used to bring the tithes," I said, and then threw up. My vomit was bloody, and the smell of rotten meat overwhelmed me. I clutched my head.

Osan looped his arm underneath mine and pulled me to my feet. Millie helped him drag me over to the shade. I squirmed in their grasp as they sat me down against the wall.

"Easy," said Osan. "Just take a breather."

"It's not right, it's not right, it's not right!"

He held me down.

"Listen to me," he said fiercely. "You have gorge sickness. We are not trying to hurt you, we are trying to stop you from hurting yourself. Do you understand that?"

I bared my teeth at him in a snarl, but at the same time, a sensory memory tugged at me. I knew the feel of these hands on my shoulders; Osan had restrained me before. The last time I lost control. Everything was jumbled, too bright and gleaming and hazy, but that memory cut through the tangled threads of my thoughts. He had held me back during Finn's execution.

"El?" Millie peered at me anxiously.

"Can't think straight," I said. "Please help me."

"You're safe, and you're going to be fine," said Osan. "But I think you need to burn off some of your lace. Can you do that?"

I shook my head. *I need it. She wants it back.*

He kept his tone even and friendly. "Come on, just a little? Stick with me here, El. Your lace is making you sick, can't you see that?"

But she's already so angry, I wanted to argue.

Instead I nodded. With difficulty, I grasped my lace and wove a defensive net around the three of us, knitting it tight and dense. The sensation of drawing on my power was all wrong—a horrible, clotted tugging, like dragging a hook through oil and thick mud. I stopped.

"Any better?" asked Millie.

"A little." The world appeared less shiny. I straightened and rubbed my forehead. "But it's such a waste."

"No, it's necessary," said Osan. "Do it again."

I wove a second net around the first. With the fog lifting from my thoughts, I could sense how tainted and warped my lace had become. I burned off a little more.

"I'm sorry," I said quietly.

Osan let go of my shoulders. "Apology accepted. So long as I never have to hear about 'the patterns' again."

I sat up. I still felt groggy, but the sensation was no worse than a bad hangover. "I, uh . . . Was I saying all of that out loud?"

Millie offered me her canteen again. "Don't worry about it, okay? Have some water."

I drank, and wiped my mouth with the back of my hand.

"How much do we have left?" I asked.

"Three canteens," said Osan. "But the vegetation is getting greener. Hopefully we'll find fresh water before nightfall."

I shut my eyes for a few seconds, then nodded. "Let's carry on, then."

We moved slower than before. I was frustrated by my weakness, and the thin layer of delirium that still coated my brain. Millie and Osan were patient with me and relentlessly positive, but we had lost a lot of time; it was long past midday. If Celane was still pursuing us, she would be closing the distance fast.

The path meandered downhill, and the earth became softer and damp as we passed into a fecund wetland. White lilies burst from the peat, and water pooled in shallow, stagnant puddles. The rich smell of decay hovered in the air.

And yet there were no frogs, no fish, no insects. The silence seemed deeper here; it pressed up against my eardrums like I was moving underwater. The further we walked, the more the water rose, and the path began to give underfoot. In places it crumbled away entirely, leaving gaps where we were forced to wade through black silt. The broken stretches never extended more than ten feet, but my sense of vulnerability always increased as we stepped off the path. We were being watched.

Osan abruptly turned to the left, away from the curve of the path. Mud sluiced up to his knees.

"Hey," I called. "Where are you going?"

He stopped.

"Osan?"

"Sorry." He was quiet for a while, not moving. "I must have been confused."

He returned to the path, and we continued. After that incident his behaviour seemed normal, but the moment stayed with me.

Step after step, one foot in front of the other. I tied my shoes to my bag and went barefoot. The wetland seemed endless; mud sucked at my ankles hungrily, dragging me down. Time blurred into a haze of shambling exhaustion as the sun gradually slunk toward the western horizon. We could not stop here. The sky was clear; once night fell, the temperature would plummet. So we continued through the indeterminable expanse of swollen grasses and sedge, the fat reeds bobbing as we trudged past, the deceptive softness of the soil that abruptly gave way to water, sinking us knee-deep in sludge.

The idea of navigating the maze of pools in the dark scared me. It would be all too easy to lose our way. And it would only take one misstep, one error—

"Slopes upwards," said Osan.

I lifted my head. The sky over the mountains had turned orange. "What?"

"We're walking uphill. That's good; we must nearly be at the end of it."

"Thank the Eater," muttered Millie. She pulled her foot out of the mud with a scowl.

My own feet were ice-cold and aching, but the weight on my shoulders lightened. Osan was right. We had been gradually climbing for a while; I had just been too fixed on the ground in front of me to notice.

Despite our fatigue, we moved faster. The ground dried, and the reeds were replaced by scrub, then small trees. A few stars winked in the pale evening sky.

"Up there," said Millie. "There's a building."

Along the ridge of the hill, a dark square stood silhouetted against the sky. I sagged with relief. I was so tired that I could hardly stand; the idea of shelter and warmth and rest was almost enough to bring tears to my eyes.

"Go on." Osan gave me a small push. "I'll see if I can find anything to make a fire."

I hesitated.

"It's fine," he said, sensing my unease. "I won't stray again. Go."

I followed Millie up the hill. For the first time, the path split—one way led up to the house, and the other snaked away over the verge. I struggled up the final rise and gasped. A vast lake, dark and glittering, gleamed with the last rays of sunlight. Further along the water's edge lay a wide beach dotted with sunbleached trees, all long dead.

I squinted against the light. I could have sworn I saw larger ripples peeling away from the shore.

"It's not a lake." Millie gazed over the water, her expression thoughtful. "It's a reservoir."

The stone building sat beside the path, right on the waterline. Thick moss coated the walls, black and slimy where the stones met the water, fuzzy and green higher up. The roof was entirely gone, open to the air, and the entrance had collapsed.

"A boathouse?" I suggested.

"It looks ancient. I wonder when someone was last here." She turned to study the marsh stretching into the distance behind us. "It makes you wonder what all of this looked like before."

Sunlit hills, green spreading forests, soil so fertile and rich that plants overran each other, the melody of water over rocks, and a city that glowed, flowers of every shade, every colour. I said nothing. The memory hung over the present like a honeyed glaze.

"At any rate, Celane won't be able to travel any further before morning." Millie nodded to herself. "No one would dare cross that marsh at night."

I wasn't so sure. I scanned the landscape, straining my eyes as I searched for any sign of smoke or movement in the distance. I could see nothing beyond the wetlands, and yet I knew she was out there. I felt tied to the Reverend, like there was an invisible chain around my neck and she held the other end. Although she was little more than a stranger, I knew Celane, understood her, recognised the shape of her convictions and ideals—because they were the Order's convictions and ideals. She was not like Verje, self-interested and sadistic, and so I didn't fear her as a person, not exactly. Instead she stood in my mind as the Sisterhood made manifest, both in its failings and its glories. She *was* the Order, and I knew her as well as I knew myself.

In that, she terrified me in a way that nothing else could, because, in the depths of my heart, I could not quite believe that Celane was *wrong* for wanting to martyr me.

"El?"

I shook myself. I just needed to stay out of her reach a little longer. Millie was looking at me, her head tilted to one side.

"Want to check out our lodgings?" she asked.

The boathouse's interior was divided into two rooms: one leading to a stone jetty, and the other overgrown with flowering weeds and vines. We set about clearing a place to sleep.

Osan returned as we finished, carrying an armful of scrubby branches. He set them against the far wall where the light would be obscured from outside. Building a fire was much easier with the drier tinder—by the time the sky had darkened, we had a pot of water bubbling away over the flames.

I leaned against the wall, warming my hands and feet, my chin resting on my chest.

"Are you feeling okay?" asked Millie.

"Just tired."

She pushed a cup of beans and a strip of dried meat into my hands. On the other side of the room, Osan was sorting through our supplies. Planning, rationing, keeping busy. Millie sat down beside me.

"Do you think he's still nearby?" she asked.

No need to ask who. I shrugged.

"He was trying to do the right thing," I said.

She poked the fire with a stick, sending sparks scattering. "Yeah. I know. I just wish he'd given me a chance to say goodbye."

"You wouldn't have let him go."

She fell quiet. The fire crackled and the water hissed softly.

"After our parents died, I was meant to take care of him," she said, staring into the flames. "I knew that. And I failed."

"Millie—"

"I ran away. I was the only one he had left, and I abandoned him."

"You were fifteen."

"He needed me to protect him." She drew her knees closer to

her chest. "Afterwards, I promised myself that I wouldn't ever let him down again. I wanted so badly to make it up to him. And I couldn't. Couldn't save him from this either."

"But we're *going* to," I said forcefully. "I'm going to fix him, you'll see. We're so close."

Millie's downcast eyes reflected the firelight, flickering orange. In the distance, an owl hooted, and a draft of cool air blew through the entrance to the room.

"We both know I'd make a terrible counsellor," I said softly, "but trust me on this: you never needed to earn Finn's forgiveness. And when you see him again, he'll tell you that himself."

She breathed out slowly.

"Hope is a dangerous thing," she murmured. "But I want you to be right."

CHAPTER FORTY-TWO

ONCE MILLIE HAD eaten a little, she seemed to relax. Despite the missing roof, the space between the mossy old walls had grown warmer and it was almost cozy. I tended to the fire, then laid out the ground sheets and blankets. When Millie set down her cup, I pushed her to the warmest corner, furthest away from the entrance.

"I'll join you soon," I said. "I just have to help Osan finish packing for tomorrow."

She nodded. "El?"

"Yes?"

She looked down. "No matter what happens, thank you for trying."

I stooped and kissed the top of her head. "Get some sleep."

Osan was rearranging the supplies for a fourth time while pretending that he had not heard our conversation. His face was drawn and tired; he seemed older than when we had first met.

"I want to talk to you," he muttered as I joined him. "Alone."

I made a subtle questioning gesture.

"It isn't an emergency. Just want to ask you something."

I glanced over at Millie. She had curled up on her side with the blanket tight around her. Her eyes were shut.

"In a few minutes," I said.

He nodded.

I carefully filled our canteens from the pot, then collected more water from the edge of the jetty. The moon had yet to rise, and the lake beyond the boathouse was vast and dark and quiet. The water lapped against the smooth stones at the base of the house.

I returned to the fire and set the pot back over the flames. Millie's breathing had eased and her face was slack. I smiled slightly. She must have been exhausted to fall asleep so quickly. A stray lock of her hair had slid across her cheek, and her forehead was smudged with ash.

"El?" said Osan from the entrance.

Outside the boathouse, the temperature dropped sharply, and I wrapped my arms around myself, shivering. A yellow semicircle of firelight gleamed through the gap in the crumbling wall. Beyond that, the landscape was only illuminated by the stars.

"What is it?" I asked.

Osan stood, looking out at the water, his back to me.

"You still aren't telling the truth," he said.

It was not an accusation, just a statement of fact, but I noticed his fists were balled. I stayed silent. He turned to face me.

"Last night, you were only worried about our provisions lasting long enough to reach the mountains," he said. "That struck me as strange. Almost as strange as the fact you concealed the possibility of curing Finn. Why hide that?"

"Because I might be wrong."

He shook his head. "You promised Kamillian that *she* would see Ceyrun again. You haven't once mentioned your own future—because for you, it all seems to end at the mountains. So please, I'm begging you, tell me what is going on."

My throat was dry.

"El."

"A debt of blood," I said. "That's what Cyde told me. If the Renewer pays the debt of blood, it could mean the end of Haunts."

A log shifted inside the boathouse, and the firelight flickered.

"You can't be serious," he muttered.

"If this works, there will be no more martyrdoms, no more Renewals, no—"

"No more *you,*" he interrupted angrily. "You expect to die, don't you? I thought we were helping you escape the Order, not leading you to your new martyrdom."

"It isn't like that."

"Isn't it? Then tell me where I'm going wrong, because I don't see it."

"Osan, please," I whispered. "Please stop."

"How could you lie about this?" He raked his hands through his hair. "I thought we were friends."

"I didn't want to burden anybody." It was difficult to breathe. "And if I can't escape the Order, if I can't escape the Haunts, then this is all I have left. Maybe I can set things right. That's worth something."

He was silent.

"I'm sorry that I lied."

"I can't accept this. I can't just—" He broke off.

I didn't know what to do. I just stood in front of him, ashamed and weary and defeated. Osan swallowed and shook his head.

"I need space," he muttered. "Go back inside."

I wanted to tell him to stay, it was too dangerous for him to wander off into the dark alone, but his expression stopped me. I nodded.

He turned and walked away from me.

"I'm sorry," I repeated, softer.

Inside the boathouse, Millie remained soundly asleep. I adjusted the blanket to cover her legs, and she mumbled to herself. Would it be better if I told her? I felt so heavy. I trudged over to the fire and sat down.

One way or another, it would be over tomorrow. Regrets, doubts, fears: they were pointless now. Worse than useless. Distractions. The flames burned steady in front of me.

I took my mother's letter out of my pocket. The envelope was a little creased, and one corner had folded over. I smoothed it out, then slid one fingernail under the seal and opened it. Inside were two pages.

My dearest Ellie,

I stopped for a moment. I could see my mother sitting in her study with the lamp burned low, her pen scratching on the paper, and it was almost too much. I breathed deeply.

My dearest Ellie,

By the time that Shaelean Cyde gives you this letter, five years will have passed since my martyrdom. I want to believe that you are doing well. It is strange to imagine you grown-up, when in my mind you will always remain my serious little girl.

By now you will probably have found a place for yourself, and maybe some measure of happiness. In delaying the delivery of this letter, I hope to give you time to come to terms with everything. I know it won't be easy; you are too young and no one is ever truly prepared to bear the Sisterhood's burdens. And yet I also know, without a shadow of doubt, that you will be strong enough to survive what is asked of you. Because that is who you are.

I suspect you will be angry. You will probably have worked out that my early martyrdom was no accident, no coincidence. I meddled in the wrong affairs and asked the wrong questions. In truth, ever since the fire that killed Finn and Millie's parents, I have made myself a target—and with my latest efforts, I went a step too far. When Shaelean told me about the possibility of ending the Order, I lost sight of caution.

But that is not why I'm writing this letter.

Ellie, we both know that I made many mistakes in raising you. I have been cruel and temperamental and impatient. Before you came along, motherhood was only ever a source of fear. I feared my own martyrdom. I feared that you would inflict the same wounds upon me that I inflicted upon my mother. I feared that I would hate you.

And I know that I have not been the best mother, but somehow you have blossomed in spite of me. You, my Ellie, my serious, clever girl, were a gift I never deserved. Even facing the end, I know that this is true.

I love you. I am so proud of the person you have become.

The letter was unsigned. I carefully folded the pages, tucked them back into the envelope, and put it into my bag. My shoulders trembled, and I stepped out of the building to catch my breath.

The cold air cut like a knife, but I inhaled deeply anyway; I invited the chill into my lungs, I let it hurt. I had always known it would hurt. My vision was misted with tears. The moon was bright on the water, a yellow disk floating in space, and the blurred stars wreathed the sky in specks of light.

"El?"

The voice was soft, floating up from the direction of the beach. I was so disoriented that for a moment I thought I had imagined it.

"Finn?" I rubbed my cheeks with my sleeve. "Finn, is that you?"

"I'm over here."

"Where?"

"Down here."

Confused, I hurried toward the water. Pebbles rolled under my boots, loud in the silence. The old trees threw long shadows over the ground.

"I need help." The words drifted out across the lake.

"But where? I can't see you." I came to a stop at the water's edge and cast around. "Tell me what's wrong."

"I'm hurt."

My throat tightened. His voice seemed to come from the trees further up the beach, but I could not be certain. It was painfully quiet, and our voices moved strangely between the water and rocks and trees. Why couldn't I see him? I took another step down the shore and then stopped dead.

"Fuck," I whispered.

Too quiet. It was still too quiet. And I was nowhere near the path.

"Finn." My voice trembled. "I need you to tell me where you are."

"Come quickly!"

I did not move.

"What was your grandfather's name?" I asked.

"El, I need help."

I could see the page in Celane's book about Haunts, the descriptions of their abilities. *They appear able to accurately mimic human voices.*

"Finn?" I whispered.

I was met with silence. I turned around. The path and the boathouse had vanished, all I could see were miles and miles of dead trees and pebbled shore.

"Osan! Millie!" I shouted.

My heart pounded in my ears. I had made a terrible, stupid mistake.

This way.

For the first time, I felt the compulse. I severed it, but new threads slipped past my defences, pulling me in different directions.

This way.

This way.

This way.

It could use lace. My only real defence, and it could wield the same power. Fear surged through me. What kind of Haunt was this?

The Old Ones, Finn whispered in my mind, his eyes shining gold.

This way.

I forced myself to breathe. I was still within the bounds of the path's protection, or I would be dead already. If I stayed calm, I could fix this.

"El, please!" Finn screamed in agony. "Please help me!"

"Not real," I muttered, pressing my hands to my ears. Resisting the barrage of compulses made my stomach turn, and my sense of direction was rapidly dissolving. "You're not real."

I took a step toward where I thought the boathouse should be, and water splashed under my boot. I jerked backwards. How was that possible? The lake should have been *behind* me. I glanced over my shoulder and found only more trees, more beach.

"Eater," I whispered. There was a roaring in my ears, growing ever louder.

"El, what are you doing?" shouted Millie.

I whipped around. Her voice would lead me to safety; I should go that way—

With a curse, I severed the compulse again. My breathing came out ragged. At the corner of my vision lurked a presence, an abomination just out of my line of sight. It moved when I moved, melting from one shadow to the next.

I breathed out. No panic. No mistakes. Although it went against every instinct, every terrified animal impulse, I shut my eyes. *Slow down.* I focussed, blocking out everything but the faint, elusive pull in the recesses of my mind.

Even dreaming, even now, the Star yearned toward her temple. Like iron to a magnet, I felt drawn by the same invisible tie.

The temple lay behind me.

"Okay," I muttered. If I could not trust myself, I would have to trust her instead.

Once again, I turned and slid my foot forward. Water lapped up the side of my legs. I clenched my fists and took another step.

"You did this to me!" Finn accused.

The water rose to my knees, ice-cold and bitter. I kept my eyes squeezed shut.

"You said that you loved me, El." His voice was raw. "How can you leave me here?"

"Not real," I breathed.

"Look at me! Look at what you've done to me!"

I took another step, and another. The water came up to my hips. I wanted to flee back to the beach. This could not be right. The lake reached my neck.

"I hate you," he cried.

I took a final breath and let the water cover me.

The Old One howled. The sound cut through me, freezing the blood in my veins. I was choking, I was drowning, and still the howl rang out. It burrowed itself into my brain and erased everything but terror.

I took another step, clutching my head, and suddenly the water was gone. I fell to my knees, heaving. There was blood in my mouth where I had bitten my tongue.

The sound stopped.

I could do nothing. I sagged onto the hard dirt of the path, and my body trembled. My clothes were dry.

"El!"

"Not real," I whispered.

Osan dropped to the ground and wrapped his arms around me. "Hey, hey, hey. It's okay now, I've got you. You're safe."

I buried my face in his shirt. His heart was pounding.

"I'm sorry," I croaked. "I was so stupid."

He squeezed my shoulders. "It's all right now."

"I'm sorry I lied to you. I was trying to do the right thing."

"I know you were. Don't worry about that, it doesn't matter. Lean on me now, let me help you inside."

"I'm so sorry. You *are* my friend, Osan."

"Shh. Come on, I've got you."

I let him guide me back to the boathouse. The lake was placid and the air still, the night deceptively calm. Although I could not see the Haunt, I knew that it was still watching me.

CHAPTER FORTY-THREE

WHEN DAWN ARRIVED, we saw the smoke of their campfires.

"They're here," I said.

The thin grey ribbons rose from beyond the marsh. I strained my ears. In the distance, I heard the yapping of a Cat.

We had doused our own fire hours earlier to conceal our location. In the morning light, the slopes of the mountains seemed much closer, and the marsh would slow our pursuers. But with Cats . . . I laced my boots and stood. It was going to be close.

"Let's get moving," said Osan.

The path looped around the edge of the reservoir. I could see my footprints in the mud above the waterline, evidence of where I had strayed last night. No Haunts had troubled us again after the incident, but I remained uneasy. A moment of thoughtlessness, and it had nearly cost me everything. I could not afford to make the same mistake again.

The sun rose. Reflections gleamed off the water, dazzling our eyes. On my right, the land dropped sharply to a valley of dense scrub and bristling thorn trees; the vegetation growing denser toward the foothills of the mountains. The hair on my arms stood on end. There was an electricity in the air—even though the skies were clear, it felt like a storm was approaching. I knew Millie and Osan could feel it too: that tense, prickly tightness hanging over our heads. We moved without speaking, faster than yesterday.

Too fast, thought a traitorous, stifled part of me.

I wished my friends would talk. I didn't want to think about the temple.

By midmorning, we reached the far side of the lake, where a wide river drained into the reservoir. Our canteens were empty, and we drank directly from the rushing channel of water. The hills ahead were taller, scattered with huge circular boulders.

"We won't make it," said Osan abruptly. He stared across the lake in the direction we had come from.

"It's not much further." I followed his gaze. "It can't be much more than an hour. If we run—"

"Even then. They're closing the distance too quickly; we have to do something to slow them down." He glanced at Millie. "Kamillian, you're a reasonable shot with a crossbow, right?"

"I think so," she said.

"No, we can't fight them," I protested. "I don't have enough lace to hold off one Reverend, never mind a group."

"It doesn't have to be a fair fight." Osan narrowed his eyes, still watching the path behind us. He nodded to himself, as if he had reached a decision. "Give me your bag, El."

I handed him my rucksack, expecting him to open it. Instead he slung it over his own shoulder.

"Right, you'll need to run." He reached beneath his shirt and drew out his belt knife. "Don't stop. We'll buy you enough time to reach the temple."

"Have you lost your mind?"

He pushed the knife into my hands. "Like I said, I have no intention of fighting fair. We'll hide and ambush them, try to pick them off one at a time. If Kamillian and I keep our distance, their lace won't be able to reach us."

"They will just *close* that distance."

"Then we'll keep moving. Besides, with the threat of Haunts hanging over them, I think they'll want to stick to the path."

"No." I shook my head fiercely. "No, if they see you, they'll break your neck in a heartbeat."

Millie stepped forward and hugged me.

"You're wasting time," she said.

"No." I pushed her away. "I'm not leaving you. I can't lose everyone!"

She smiled, her eyes shining. "You promised to save Finn, remember? It's not goodbye. I'll be right here when it's over."

She was lying; they were both lying. I felt like I was suffocating. I had not come all this way only to abandon them now. Osan grasped my forearms.

"If you choose not to pay the debt, that's fine," he whispered. He drew me close for a second. "But you need to run, all right? For Finn, for Kamillian, for me. Run, Just El."

He let me go.

"You can do this," said Millie. "Go."

"It's not goodbye," I said, backing away. "Promise me it's not goodbye."

She nodded. "I'll be waiting."

I turned, my heart breaking, and ran down the hill. I could hear Cats, their coarse braying calls ringing out in the silence. Stones skittered over the ground around me; I almost tripped, but caught myself and stumbled on.

Make it count, Elfreda, whispered Cyde.

The path curved sharply, drawing a red slash through the narrow valley. On either side the rocks stood like an honour guard, and the dark orange soil grew powdery, rising up in clouds of dust each time my feet hit the ground. I could hear Millie and Osan's voices behind me; they had reached the valley floor.

I swallowed the lump in my throat. *Stay safe.*

The Star's consciousness flickered inside me, and the landscape stuttered as visions rippled through it. A sea of black blossoms burst open from the grass, then wilted in seconds and evaporated like smoke. With a crack, the path split in two. My foot caught on the edge of the fissure and I was sent sprawling.

From the top of the reservoir, a shout rang out. I had been spotted.

I picked myself up. *Run.* The ground trembled like an enormous creature disturbed from its sleep. Out of the cracked path, a seething mass of termites surged to the surface. Their bodies crunched under my feet, and still more kept appearing, emerging from the ground as the cracks branched and grew wider, pouring over one another in a furious river. From deep below, I heard a plaintive keening sound.

Adrenaline powered me forward, and I pushed myself to run even faster. Ahead of me, where the fissure gaped open widest, a white hand emerged from the ground.

I did not stop. The termites swarmed ankle-deep, biting, vicious, their tiny mandibles tearing at my calves. The pale hand gripped the side of the fissure and levered itself upwards. Drawing closer, I could see that it was composed entirely of buzzing locusts with chalk-coloured wings. Another hand groped through to the surface, crushing the termites in its path. Then the headless torso appeared, followed by legs and twitching feet. A grotesque parody of a body. The creature took a step forward, and its chest split open to reveal crimson ribs like teeth, stretching outwards to devour me.

I ran straight into it.

The locusts swallowed my arms, their sharp legs scratching my fingers, wrists, chest, face. Blind, I fell through the creature and out, beyond the limits of the vision. Locusts clung to me, but I slapped them off, then dropped to the ground and rolled, crushing those that remained. My legs streamed with blood from hundreds of bites.

"Deal with your own nightmares," I snarled.

I staggered to my feet and when I raised my head, I saw the temple for the first time.

The building looked like it had grown right out of the rockface—the yellow walls curved and melded to the cliff at its back, and the roof rose high and peaked. Empty rings marked where there had once been stained-glass windows. At the temple's base, the river coursed like a living creature, hissing and wild, the old bridge long since washed away. Smaller buildings clustered at the water's edge, all of them overgrown with vines and trees, their foundations obscured by sheets of long grass.

The path of grace ended a hundred feet from the river, red soil crumbling into earth and grass. My stomach sank. The distance was too far; the path's protection would not shelter me all the way. In this last stretch, I would be exposed.

With a fervent, wordless prayer, I broke into a sprint.

My world narrowed to just the temple, to just the shining, sunlit curve of the arched entrance, and my lungs emptied. I had no thoughts, no fear, no pain. I moved like light.

Declan Lars caught me.

I never heard him. He slammed into me from the side, taking us both down. With a crack, I felt one of my ribs break. I gasped and thrashed, but he was twice my size and far stronger; we tangled and he wrapped his hand around my neck. His touch was cold enough to burn me.

With a growl of victory, he sank his teeth into my shoulder.

I screamed. Lars's face contorted in ecstasy, golden eyes shining, his pupils small as pinpricks. The agony increased; my vision went white. I tried to weave a net, but my tainted power was slick and slid away as I reached for it. Blood bubbled up in my mouth.

Lars's teeth drew free from my shoulder. I struggled to rise, and he grinned, rows of unnaturally long teeth glistening. He clamped his hand down on my forehead, holding me still so that he could rip my throat out.

"Please," I choked. "Please don't."

Just as I had been taken by surprise by his attack, Lars failed to see Finn until it was too late. His teeth grazed my skin and then he was thrown off me, slamming into the ground.

Finn had changed. His spine was bent and the skin on his face had turned colourless. He jerked me to my feet and pushed me toward the temple.

"I'll deal with him," he said, his voice like sandpaper, tongue struggling to form words. "Go."

He released me and flung himself back at Lars. The two collided with shattering force.

I clutched one hand over the gushing wound on my shoulder, and lurched toward the river. The world glowed; I smelled incense and metal and decay. Visions danced through the air. Behind me, I heard Finn and Lars snarling, the crack of breaking bones. One of them screamed in agony.

I waded into the water, breathing heavily. Hot blood seeped over my arms and chest. Not much further, not much further. The current unbalanced me—I slipped on the algae-streaked rocks and went under. Cold water rushed into my mouth. I floundered back to the surface, gasping, and scrambled up the bank to the far shore.

Lace coiled around my limbs, freezing me in place.

"Elfreda," said Celane.

No!

"Don't be afraid." I heard her splashing through the river behind me. "It will be over soon."

I drew on my lace and cut through the Reverend's nets. I stumbled a few feet further, and Celane paralysed me again. She stood tall and proud, a little flushed from the chase through the valley, and the glow of victory shone in her eyes.

"Enough," she said.

She was so strong; her lace wrapped around my legs like steel bands. *No, no, no!* I felt sick. This could not end here; I had not come all this way to be martyred here. She reached the shallows, and I sliced through her nets again, crawling away on my hands and knees. She followed me.

"It's all right," she said, her voice soothing. "I know you're scared, but this is necessary. You know that, don't you, Elfreda?"

Her expression was almost tender; she looked at me with a kind of pity, like I was a child to be punished. *Look what you've done,* said her eyes. *Look at the mess you've made.* My defences buckled beneath the force of her power, and I was frozen, unable to move. She drew a scalpel from her pocket.

"No," I gasped.

"I understand." Sunlight reflected off her hair; she briefly appeared radiant, holy. "But this is too important, and your actions have already cost us too much."

I bared my teeth in a snarl. "You're one to talk."

"Generations of Sisters have given up their lives to protect our home." She advanced. "Don't spit on their sacrifices."

I threw lace at her head, but my power bounced harmlessly off her defensive net. Celane's face hardened, glittering with droplets of water from the river.

"You *know* your duty." Her lace wound tighter around me. "Think of your mother, your grandmother. Think how proud they would be."

"Shut up!"

"They gave everything for you." She shook her head. "You can't possibly be selfish enough to throw that away."

"Don't you dare"—my voice trembled with rage—"talk about my mother."

Celane's eyes bored into mine, and she recognised my hatred; the deep, bloody depths of my heart, the burning core that would never bend to her will, to the Sisterhood's will, to the will of the Eater.

"I wanted to offer you the chance to redeem yourself," she said, and for a moment she sounded sad, even though it didn't show on her face. "But so be it. I will restore the Order myself, and save Aytrium."

Not here. Not when I had come so close.

I let go of all my protective nets and wove the last of my power into a single rope. I thought of Asan at Geise's Crown, I thought of my lace catching Osan's foot in the Gardens, I thought of everyone who had ever underestimated me. One last gamble, one last chance. Celane smiled, assuming my power had run dry.

"You will save no one," I whispered.

I hooked the rope around her ankle and yanked as hard as I could. Shock crossed Celane's face; she had not thought to shield her legs. Her foot slipped on the slick river rocks, and she fell backwards. Her lace tore loose around me. Freed, I lunged after her. With the full force of my body, I drove Osan's knife through the water and into her chest.

A rush of air bubbled from her mouth, and her power knocked against me, wild cords of lace lashing my arms. I let go of the knife handle, and Celane surfaced, drawing a shuddering breath. The river ran red around her. She convulsed. Her lips turned scarlet.

"Eater," she gasped. "Eater, help . . ."

She choked, her hand closing on the handle of the knife. Then all the force seemed to drain out of her body. Her face went slack.

I did not move. At any second, I expected her to rise out of the water. Her scalpel shone in the shallows, and her hair washed across her face. Her body swayed with the movement of the river.

She was dead. I had killed her.

"I'm so sorry," I whispered.

Celane stared, glassy-eyed and silent, at the sky. I felt cold. Moments ago, she had seemed to tower over me, but now she looked small and unremarkable. She could have been anyone; just another woman, a complete stranger.

"May the Star light your dreaming," I murmured.

Too weak to stand, I crawled to the threshold of the temple. My blood dripped along the stone steps, leaving a long smear behind me. Each breath hurt. I passed below the shadow of the arch and into the cool interior.

The chamber filled with brightness. It mirrored my dream: the trees growing from the floor, the rays of sunlight pouring through the windows. Other images crowded the room, visions of this place from an older time. Hundreds of shining ghosts passed through the walls; memory and dream and reality flowed into one gleaming haze, each rewriting each other, reforming in front of my eyes.

Through the waves of light, a tall man walked toward me. I could not see his face; the world had blurred too much. He lifted me off the tiles. His hands were silver, or perhaps he wore gloves.

My thoughts moved slower. With ease and gentleness, he carried me to the front of the temple where the altar waited.

"I'm scared," I whispered.

He laid me down carefully. I saw the spikes imbedded in the altar at the level of my wrists, the channels that ran away from them.

"It will not hurt," he said. His voice incongruous, female, whistling, pure. Lights swarmed above my head, darting like birds.

"But I don't want to die." My face was wet.

He touched my cheek.

"Will you return what was stolen?" he asked.

This was how it ended.

"Yes," I said.

The light flared. I shut my eyes against the brightness. When I opened them again, he was gone. I could no longer feel the pain in my shoulder, and my wrists were only faintly warm. Metal jutted through them. I regarded the spikes without feeling, watching blood seep from my arms.

"You are here."

The Star's voice came from everywhere, and from within my own mind. I tried to speak, but my lips would not move. It did not seem to matter.

"It has been a long time," she said.

The temple dissolved in golden light. I could no longer feel my body. When the light dimmed, the spikes were gone. A woman with curling black hair leaned against the edge of the altar.

"Mom?" I croaked.

She turned to me. Her eyes were kind.

"No," she said. "Just a memory."

Thousands of candles illuminated the temple, and the windows were whole. Wreaths of flowers cascaded across the tiles, lilies and cherry blossoms and orchids. Their fragrance filled the still air. When I looked down, my wrists were smooth and unblemished, but I still felt an odd pressure just below both palms, like someone was pressing their thumbs against my veins.

"Are you the Star?" I asked.

Her liquid eyes were full and dark, flecked with sparks of gold.

"I have been given that name, yes," she replied.

I should feel afraid. I sat up. *But I'm not.*

"You aren't what I expected," I said.

"And what did you expect?"

Someone more frightening.

She smiled as if she could hear my thoughts. Her face flickered, and I caught a glimpse of something else behind my mother's features. I flinched.

"Elfreda, I won't harm you," she said, with a small hint of amusement. Her voice was calm, resonating, painfully familiar. "I only wanted to meet you. You have dreamed my dreams, and we will share this one for only a little while longer."

I could hear birdsong outside the windows, laughter in the distance. "This is a . . . dream?"

"Of a sort."

Everything seemed entirely real to me. I turned back to her. "So what happens when it ends?"

"Then I will return to the world and discover what remains for me there."

My chest tightened at the thought of Aytrium, the possibility of her revenge, my friends. The Star shook her head. She reached out and touched my shoulder.

"I am not so vengeful as you believe," she said.

Her hand was warm and unexpectedly ordinary, nails clipped short like I remembered. I swallowed. Just a memory, just a dream, but it felt so real. Around us, the candles burned steadily.

"I must go soon," she said, withdrawing her hand. "But I am glad we had this chance to speak."

"When you leave, can I . . . can I stay here?"

She shook her head, smiling sadly.

I suppose I had already known, but strangely, I still didn't feel afraid. I was only a little drowsy. I wanted to lie down and sleep, bathed in the warm light of the candles and the smell of flowers.

"I guess that's okay too." I returned her smile. "Thank you for the dream."

The Star opened her arms, and I was grateful, so grateful to have this at the end. I embraced her and the world faded.

She smelled like home.

AFTER

THE WALL OF the house had split. The crack that ran through the stonework was a foot wide, and a potted plant was wedged into the gap.

Similar damage was prevalent everywhere—when Aytrium struck Ventris, the impact had sent shockwaves rippling across the island for days. The Sisterhood had burned through all the lace they possessed to slow the fall, but it had not been quite enough. Ceyrun now sloped at a new angle, and a huge section of the city's outer wall had collapsed.

Still, many things continued as usual.

Rhyanon sat on the garden bench with her ankles crossed, eating a pastry and watching her daughter dig small holes in the soil along the side of the house. Jaylen's hands were covered in dirt, and a tuft of wispy brown hair stuck up from her forehead. Beside her, a line of daffodil bulbs waited to be planted.

"Congratulations?" said Rhyanon. "Although I'm not sure that's an appropriate response under the circumstances."

From the other side of the bench, I tipped my glass toward her. "I'll take it."

"It *was* a foregone conclusion, though. A relief to get the weight off your shoulders, I suppose."

The trial had finally ended this morning, three months after the fall of Aytrium. Judicial Affairs had been overwhelmed, not only because of the staggering number of new cases—mostly the merchant guilds trying to extract compensation from the Order—but because the High Court building itself had been badly damaged during the impact. While my case had taken precedence, the proceedings had still dragged out much longer than originally anticipated.

"Amnesty, huh?" I said. "Doesn't that set rather a dangerous precedent?"

"I think it would be difficult for anyone to replicate your exact crimes or circumstances. But I'm not a Judicial Affairs officer, what do I know?"

I leaned back on the bench. The sun filtering through the trees warmed my legs.

"I was expecting at least a slap on the wrist," I said.

"Saskia would never have stood for that. And Deselle Somme advocated pretty fiercely on your behalf too."

"Even so."

Rhyanon made an exaggerated gesture of impatience. "If the Order wants to make a big show of being generous and benevolent and forward-thinking, for Eater's sake, *let* them." She jabbed her pastry in my direction. "You're a free woman. Be happier."

"I am happy."

"Then act like it."

I rolled my eyes. "Maybe if you stopped telling me off."

Rhyanon was right, though—even now, I felt unsettled. Cyde's death continued to haunt me; until returning home, I had harboured a faint hope that the Reverend might have made it. I knew it wasn't really my fault; she had chosen to make that last stand. I just couldn't quite let go of my guilt.

Jaylen placed a bulb into the soil and buried it.

Lariel's body, on the other hand, had not been recovered. Maybe Celane had pushed her off the Edge, but I didn't believe that. A couple of weeks ago, Millie had found a single crossbow bolt driven through the wood of her front door.

"Are you sure you're all right?" asked Rhyanon. "You're quiet today."

"Just caught up inside my own head."

"Well, if you're after a distraction, I have a lot of work—"

"No," I said sternly.

As the administrative chaos of restructuring the Order mounted, Rhyanon had been dropping increasingly obvious hints about me joining her on the new Council. With so few of the original Councilwomen remaining and everyone stripped of their lace, the process had turned into a logistical nightmare. Scheming was already rife amongst the various factions—traditionalist, civilian, and, well, those following Saskia Asan.

"I thought, now that you've been cleared . . ." Rhyanon began.

"You don't need me."

She huffed. "Of course I don't *need* you. But you would certainly help."

"Sitting in a room and listening to people yell at each other for eight hours a day is just about the last thing—"

"I know." She glanced at me. "I'd love to have you around, that's all."

Jaylen moved on to the next bulb. Rhyanon's dog wandered over to her and sniffed at the turned earth.

"Consider it?" she said. "Maybe not yet, but I'll make sure a seat stays open for you. If you want it."

"You're far too kind," I murmured.

She brushed pastry crumbs off her leg. "Just building up future credit. So?"

"I'll think about it."

"Oh good, a definitive answer."

"I will. Really."

She snorted. "All right, fine; I'll wait. But what's your plan now?"

From the street beyond her garden, I heard someone singing. An orange butterfly settled on the spout of Jaylen's watering can. It unfolded its wings, soaking in the sunlight.

"I'm leaving," I said slowly. "Not permanently. It's just . . . with the trial over, it feels like the right time."

Rhyanon sighed.

"You'll miss me terribly?" I asked, amused.

"Of course not."

"But I'll miss you."

"As you should," she grumbled. "So you're going to leave me with all the difficult work, and run off to join an expedition. What about your friends?"

"Millie's coming with me. I tried to win over Osan, but—"

"What?"

"But he said he would stay in Ceyrun for now. Old loyalties die hard, apparently."

Her eyes narrowed. "And yet, he did not see fit to tell *me* any of this."

"He's good at keeping secrets."

Rhyanon gestured irritation, but she was struggling not to smile.

"When are you leaving?" she asked.

"The first of the expedition teams is departing this afternoon. The trial ended just in time."

"Then this is your goodbye."

"For a little while."

She nodded, thoughtful, and we drifted into an easy silence. In the distance, the bells rang out. Some things changed, others stayed the same. The breeze tousled my hair.

"Have you had any more visions?" asked Rhyanon. "Since . . . since then?"

I shook my head. She knew about my experience in the temple; I had told her most of what had happened. But it remained a difficult subject. I watched Jaylen carefully water her bulbs.

"Does that mean she's gone?" Rhyanon's voice dropped. "Even after all that 'debt of blood' stuff, she let you go?"

I was silent.

"Elfreda?"

"She's no longer with me," I said, relenting. "I don't know where she's gone, or if she'll return. But I think she extracted a small price."

Rhyanon made a gentle gesture of enquiry.

"I haven't menstruated since the temple."

Her face fell.

"It's not the worst thing that could have happened," I added hurriedly. "It's nothing, really, all things considered. Three months ago, I would have considered it a gift."

"Could you be pregnant?"

I felt my cheeks flush. "I mean, I did consider that too."

"And?"

"It's not . . . impossible. But unlikely."

Rhyanon wavered, then sidled across the bench and put an arm around my shoulder. The gesture surprised me, and I smiled.

"It's fine," I said. "Either way."

Her dark brown eyes stayed serious. "Are you sure?"

"Yes." I leaned into her hug. "Don't worry so much."

She went quiet for a moment. Her skin was sun-warmed against mine, and her hair smelled like lavender. I was going to miss her, I realised. I would miss this—the quiet, peaceful afternoons in the shade. As if sensing my thoughts, her grip around my arm tightened.

"When you return, you know you'll always have a home with us, right?" she whispered.

I looked down, a little embarrassed. "You might want to ask the Commander first."

She drew back, giving me a small, playful shove.

"Saskia will be fine with it." Her eyes glinted. "Besides, you've seriously misinterpreted who's in charge in our relationship."

I blinked, then her words sank in and I burst out laughing. Rhyanon smiled at me fondly.

"Make sure you're careful out there," she said. "Come back safe."

I left via the front gate. The air was cool and fresh; the recent rains had washed away seasons of dust. People moved without urgency, enjoying the sunshine. I walked slowly and tried to soak it all in: the boulevards, the streets that felt both familiar and new, this place that was both home and not. When I returned to Ceyrun again, it would be a different city. I strolled toward the graveyard. For better or worse, I suppose that it already was.

Finn waited at the gate. His hair was growing longer—although it was still not *quite* the length I preferred—and his skin had lost its terrible whiteness. Over the course of a few slow months, he had begun to transform back into his old self. His spine had straightened, and the extra teeth had fallen out. He was even returning to his original height, just a few inches taller than before.

His eyes, however, remained a stubborn shade of bright green. In twilight hours, the colour came closer to yellow.

"You're late," he said.

"I was enjoying my freedom."

He smiled. "I'm glad. Millie said she'd meet us at the South Gate. Are you ready?"

I was. We walked through the sunlit streets of Ceyrun, and no visions darkened the shadows, no voices murmured in my mind. I was happy. I was just myself.

ACKNOWLEDGEMENTS

I FIND DRAWING UP a book's acknowledgements to be a rewarding process, and this is particularly true of *Star Eater*. This novel owes much to the people who supported me along the way.

The Tordotcom Publishing team has been uniformly gracious and kind in their dealings with me. On the publicity, marketing, and social media side, thank you to Lauren Anesta, Mordicai Knode, and Amanda Melfi. From production, particular thanks to Lauren Hougen for ensuring that last-minute edits were integrated. Thanks also to interior designer Greg Collins, and digital asset designer Jess Kiley.

On the art side, I have enormous gratitude for the work of Christine Foltzer and Sam Weber. I could not imagine a more beautiful cover for this book.

Thank you to copy editor Ana Deboo for handling my chronic issue with commas. Thank you to publisher Irene Gallo, and to editorial assistant Sanaa Ali-Virani.

Ruoxi Chen: my brilliant, sharp, kind, formidable editor. Thank you for your criticism and encouragement, your patience and your insight.

I am also deeply appreciative of Jennifer Jackson. Thank you for being a calm voice of reassurance, and for championing my work. I'm so glad that you chose to represent me.

There are a host of strangers who have been unfathomably nice to me, and they include: Apophis, Sabine Cazassus, G. V. Anderson, Indrapramit Das, Aoife Nic Ardghail, Daragh

Thomas, Suzan Palumbo, and Eugenia Triantafyllou. I appreciate you all.

Thanks to Allison Senecal—your passion and enthusiasm has meant more to me than you realize.

I owe a lot to Scott H. Andrews. Thank you for tactfully keeping quiet while I neglected the *Beneath Ceaseless Skies* slush pile. You are an underappreciated force for good in the industry, and I always enjoy your emails.

My appreciation, once more, to the Mandela Rhodes Foundation and the 2016 cohort. Thank you to Imraan Coovadia for his input on this novel.

Sarah Boomgaard, thank you for being That Person from high school to get loudly excited about my books. Thank you to Ruby Parker and Kaitlin Cunningham. As always, thanks and love to Sabina Stefan.

Emma Kate Laubscher, you are brilliant and funny and passionate, and I think the world of you. Also, thank you for scheming to get your book club to read my work.

Thanks to my dad, Stephen Hall, for your support and love. I hope you enjoy this book, and are not unduly concerned about all the cannibalism and murder.

Thank you to Tessa Hall. I'm fortunate beyond measure to have a sister as exceptional as you are. Thank you for being my first reader and my most trusted friend.

And finally, thank you to Sylvia Hall. Writing this book was challenging, but you were behind me every step of the way. Thank you for believing in me. Thank you for your attention to detail, and for your encouragement. Thank you for everything. I hope, one day, to be half as brilliant as you.